THE HOUSE PARTY

MARY GRAND

Boldwood

First published in Great Britain in 2020 by Boldwood Books Ltd.

This paperback edition first published in 2021.

1

Cover Design: Nick Castle Design

Cover Photography: Shutterstock

A CIP catalogue record for this book is available from the British Library.

Paperback ISBN: 978-1-80280-357-0

Ebook ISBN: 978-1-80048-168-8

Kindle ISBN: 978-1-80048-169-5

Audio CD ISBN: 978-1-80048-175-6

Digital audio download ISBN: 978-1-80048-167-1

Large Print ISBN: 978-1-80048-170-1

Boldwood Books Ltd.

23 Bowerdean Street, London, SW6 3TN

www.boldwoodbooks.com

*To my wonderful husband and gorgeous children, Thomas and Emily.
Thank you for your constant, unending, love and support. I can never
thank you enough.*

1

Beth hurried towards the cliff edge, following the tiny solar lights that lit the path. She stopped at the fence, where Kathleen stood staring out at the sea. Beth paused, petrified of doing or saying the wrong thing.

Reaching out tentatively, she touched Kathleen's arm.

'What is it? What's wrong?' she asked.

Kathleen swung round; no familiar smile or hug, her eyes wide with fear: an animal caught in a trap.

Beth wanted to put her arms around her but, for the first time in their long friendship, she wasn't sure how Kathleen would react.

'For God's sake. I've been watching you all evening. Tell me what's wrong,' she repeated.

Kathleen ignored the question and waved up the garden towards the house. 'What do you think of it?'

Beth looked at the giant glass cubes, each room brightly lit like a designer doll's house. 'It's incredible. You and Patrick have worked so hard. I thought you'd be ecstatic now it's finally finished.'

Kathleen didn't answer, her expression the same one that had been painted on all evening: thin lips pressed together, wide-eyed, as if she hardly dared to breathe.

Beth frowned. 'Sami told me you've given in your notice at the pharmacy. He didn't understand why. You're so good there. He'll be lost without you.'

'He's just being kind. Anyway, he has his new partner now.'

Beth moved closer. 'I don't know what has been going on. We haven't spoken properly for ages – it must be last November. I've missed you at yoga and our weekly catch ups.'

'I'm sorry.'

Kathleen pulled her cashmere wrap around her shoulders and walked over to the swing seat. Beth followed her. The gentle rocking of the seat matched the sound of the sea dragging on the shingle far below. It seemed to sooth Kathleen, and she loosened the grip on her wrap.

Beth heard a soft, clucking, purring noise coming from a large hen coop. Kathleen looked over and said, 'They're settling in well. I collected a new baby yesterday. Well, a rescue.' Beth saw a whisper of a smile and heard the soft Irish cream in Kathleen's voice. 'She's in a cage within the coop. She's in such a poor state, losing feathers; bless her. It'll be good when they can come out of the run and roam, but I can't let them out until we've put in the permanent fence.'

Beth glanced at the row of flimsy plastic fence panels. 'I suppose so. Even a hen might knock those over, if the wind didn't blow them down.'

'I know, but it's handy being able to move one or two panels when I come down to do my mindfulness in the morning. I can sit on the ground and look straight out to sea.'

'At that time, I'm in old joggers and wellies feeding the guinea pigs and walking Ollie. Not quite so zen.' Beth grinned, but it didn't reach Kathleen. Instead the damp air seemed to cling to them, and Beth zipped up her fleece.

Laughter floated towards them. Beth saw that her husband, Sami, and the other adults had come outside, their teenage children choosing to stay in the comfort of the house. Beth was aware that Kathleen was now sitting very still, gazing intently at the group. Beth's gaze, however, was fixed on the way Kathleen was winding her necklace round her finger, seemingly unaware that the heavy chain was digging deeper and deeper into the flesh of her neck.

Beth took hold of Kathleen's hand until she let go of the chain. 'I've never seen you like this before. What are you so frightened of?'

Kathleen flinched. 'Not something, someone.'

'Who?'

Kathleen looked down at the patio. 'I can't tell you.'

'Why not?'

'It's somebody we both know. I don't think you'd believe me.'

'Really? Try me.'

'It's someone here at the house party.'

'You can't be scared of anyone here. We're friends, we all know each other so well.'

'I used to think that. But when I saw one of them do something, I realised I'd got them completely wrong. It's like an art expert will spot a tiny error in a forgery: a signature in the wrong place or the wrong brushstroke. They know immediately it's fake. That's how it was.'

'But you should have told someone. Didn't you tell Patrick?'

'No. I couldn't do that.' Kathleen looked away.

'But then you should have told me. Why keep it to yourself?'

Kathleen started to play with her chain again. 'You see, this person found out something I'd done. It was stupid, wrong, I was so ashamed. They said they would tell everyone if I even mentioned what I knew.'

Beth sat back stunned. She wondered how much her friend had been drinking.

'I'm not drunk,' said Kathleen, reading her mind. 'I know it sounds incredible. These things don't happen in our neat, orderly world, do they? Oh Beth, you are so lovely, but the world isn't—'

Beth pushed the swing gently with her feet. 'My life hasn't been as perfect as you might think. But you can't have done anything bad enough for someone to be able to use it against you.'

Slowly Kathleen lowered her hands, clung on to her wrap, looked down. 'I did, I made a dreadful mistake. December was such a hellish month: first Amy died, then that damn skiing weekend. I was so unhappy.'

'Oh God. Kathleen, why didn't you tell me? I knew from your text you were upset about Amy's accident, and that weekend away, but I never realised how bad things were. If I'd known, I'd have come to see you.'

'The trouble was things happened so fast. After I sent you that text I did something really stupid. It was so wrong and all my fault. Afterwards I was too ashamed to tell anyone. I tried to live like it hadn't happened even though the shame was gnawing away inside me every day.'

Beth wanted to grab Kathleen's hand, tell her she knew exactly how that felt, but instead she said, 'But it can't have been that terrible—'

'It was to me. I tried to imagine what you'd have said if I'd told you. Maybe you'd have tried to understand, but I was so frightened that I'd lose your friendship. It's not something you'd have ever done.' Kathleen started to pick at an imaginary thread on her wrap. 'I thought if I kept quiet, tried not to think about it, it would be like it never happened. That was stupid, wasn't it? The truth doesn't go away. It sits there patiently, waiting for someone to stumble across it. Unluckily for me, that's what happened.'

'I still can't believe you did anything that bad.'

'That's because you don't know me, not all of me. If I'd been a better person, I'd have owned up to what I'd done. I know that a sin is a sin and all that, but this so-called friend has done far worse things than me. I've just been so frightened of losing everyone's respect, my friends, my family, my life here.'

'Can't you at least try to tell me what you've done?'

'I don't know what to do. The other day I actually told this person that I was tired of it all, the lies, covering up, but you know what they did?'

Beth shook her head.

'They laughed at me. I saw in their eyes, utter contempt, loathing. They told me I was pathetic, useless; like one of the millions of grubby grey pebbles on the beach that people trample on. They said if I was to so much as whisper what they'd done they would pick me up and flick me into the sea. I would disappear. Nobody would know. Nobody would care.'

Beth saw tears shining in Kathleen's eyes. 'Who said this? Please, tell me.'

'I want to, but I'm so scared. Anyway, I don't want to drag you into this mess. This person, this wolf, may turn on you then. You know that thing about fear making the wolf bigger? Well, I tell you, Beth, I have found out my wolf is far greater than my fear; its teeth are sharper, it is cruel, wicked.'

Kathleen pulled her feet up on to the seat, cuddled her knees into her chest and enveloped herself in her wrap.

Beth put her arm around Kathleen's shoulders. 'You need to tell me everything. I'm so sorry you've had to battle this on your own. You can't be manipulated like this. I understand how you are feeling more than you know. Whatever you've done, I'm always on your side. I will fight for you.'

Kathleen reached out slowly, placed her hand on top of Beth's. 'If you really mean that, then maybe I will. I can't go on like this.'

Beth removed her arm from around Kathleen's shoulder and

placed it on top of her hand as if making a pact. 'I promise, but you have to tell me everything.'

Patrick's voice from the patio disturbed them, 'What are you two cooking up?'

Kathleen snatched back her hand and stood up. Patrick, Sami, and the others started walking towards them.

'You two have been down here for ages. What have you been talking about?' asked Patrick again.

The others reached them quickly. Sami slipped his arm around Beth's shoulders. He wasn't much taller than her, he was losing his hair, he desperately needed to update his glasses, and she loved him very much. Moving closer to him, she felt like a sea bird sheltering in the nook of the cliff.

'You all right?' he asked. His accent was a warm mix of Iraqi and her own Swansea Welsh.

'I think so.'

'It's beautiful down here in the mornings, isn't it, Kathleen?' said Patrick. He turned to the others. 'She's down here every day at about quarter to seven for her mindfulness if you want to join her.'

There was a muffled laugh, but no one spoke. As they walked back to the house Beth glanced at Kathleen. She was sure she saw a slight fixed smile as Kathleen walked stiffly next to Patrick, who had his arm firmly around her shoulders. Her friend seemed unable to move away.

Inside the house, Patrick grinned at Beth. 'So, you approve of the new house? I can't wait to get all my London friends here. They think the Isle of Wight is some sleepy backwater. Wait till they see this: make them think twice about their million pound one bedroom flats up there.'

Beth smiled warmly at him. Patrick probably cared too much about trying to look younger and trendier than he was, but she liked him, and he adored Kathleen. 'They'll be very jealous.'

'I'm coming over to the Castleford house this evening.' Patrick turned to Sami. 'Could I cadge a lift back with you? My car is in the garage until tomorrow.'

'I thought you'd sold the old house—'

'Not quite, complete tomorrow. I want to give it one last clean. I've left an old mattress and a sleeping bag there.'

'You're welcome to a lift, but we were going to leave soon. The kids have school tomorrow.'

'That's fine. Things are wrapping up.' He looked at Kathleen, a slight nervousness in his voice. 'You'll be all right here on your own?'

'Of course. I must get used to it. You'll be off again soon.'

'Not so much now.' Patrick turned again to Sami. 'I've requested more work in the UK. I've done my stint of work abroad. No, me and Kathleen are going to make the most of our new home now.'

Beth didn't want to leave without speaking to Kathleen again, or at least arranging to meet, but Kathleen had closed off. She didn't seem to want to look at Beth.

It wasn't until they were outside the front door that Beth finally caught Kathleen's gaze. Kathleen put her hand on Beth's and said, 'You'll keep your promise?'

Beth squeezed her hand. 'Of course.' She smiled, looking for one in return, but all she saw in Kathleen's face was fear and dread. She resolved to speak to her soon and to find out what on earth was going on.

2

Beth woke the next morning to the sound of the dawn chorus and Sami changing into his running gear. Peering at her clock she saw it was half past six.

'So, I thought I'd take some fertiliser for the tomatoes.'

'Oh, right,' Beth mumbled. 'Good idea.'

'I got a message from the Hendersons. They said they're loving Australia and their new grandchild arrived yesterday.'

'Girl or a boy?'

'Girl. They'll have a few more months out there with the baby before they come home. I love their garden but it's a lot of work. I'm not surprised they've let it go so much. Still, I've got a few bits of it back under control.'

'You're only meant to be watering the plants in the greenhouse.'

'I know, but I enjoy it and I get to run in their fields. It's bliss, no other dogs or patients.' He unzipped a small pocket of his track suit top. 'Good, got the key. Right, I'll be off.'

Beth heard him thump down the stairs with the energy of a

'morning person', closed her eyes and stretched over the extra expanse of bed.

She listened to the front door slam, the car's engine starting, and finally heard Sami drive off. Sinking back into her pillow, her mind drifted back to the previous evening. Whatever had been happening with Kathleen? She couldn't imagine anyone at the house party threatening Kathleen in the way she said. Her friends, people at the pharmacy, everyone loved Kathleen. There had been times in the past when Beth had envied her. For her to look that gorgeous, keep that stunning red gold sunset hair and petite figure with apparently so little effort, never seemed quite fair. Added to that, she was gentle and kind of naive. However, Beth also knew that Kathleen's life had been harder than most people realised, and it was sharing their problems that had brought them close. As she thought of that, Beth felt a pang of guilt: she should have been a better friend to Kathleen, tried harder to keep in touch. Well, she was determined to help Kathleen now in any way she could.

Reluctantly, Beth got out of bed. It was Monday, so at least there was no work to go to, but of course there was studying.

As she did every morning, Beth picked up her mobile, set on silent for the night. She always kept it next to her bed; now the kids were older she was often in bed before them and she liked to keep the link until she heard they were in.

Beth threw on her 'dog walking' clothes and went downstairs. Ollie, her cocker spaniel, came to her, tail wagging in anticipation of their morning routine. He was a blue roan with stunning markings, soft black ears and a white stripe down his forehead to his black nose.

Together they went out into the garden, which was Sami's pride and joy. It couldn't have been more of a contrast to Kathleen and Patrick's 'outdoor living space'. There were no large paved areas with expensive furniture. This garden was about work: intensive plants, shrubs, borders, a small cottage garden with wooden seats, a concrete bird bath, meandering paths. Sami spent hours out here, and to Beth it was a slice of heaven.

Ollie came into the shed with her to feed the guinea pigs. Beth loved the cosy smell of hay, the squeaking of the animals; on a wet morning she would stay longer than she needed. 'You'll be out in your run soon,' she assured them.

After the emotional conversation the evening before, Beth decided to take Ollie somewhere special, and so she picked a small bunch of daffodils and carefully placed them in her dog walking bag.

'Off we go then,' she said to Ollie, who was already standing beside the dresser where his lead was. Guessing what they would do next was all part of the game.

It was fully daylight when Beth parked her car in Parkhurst Woods. With Ollie, she walked purposefully through a deserted part of the pine woodland, well away from the main paths and the other dog walkers. Soon she reached a high concrete wall, the boundary between the forest and the prison grounds, and knelt. Pulling aside a tuft of grass she found the ammonite fossil she had placed there six years before. She felt a thin, deep rapier of sadness, picked the fossil up and wiped it clean. From her bag, she took the daffodils, relishing the smell of childhood, of vases of daffodils on St David's Day, and laid them next to the stone. As she knelt there, tense, alone, she closed her eyes. Inside she was aware of feelings buried deep down, pain and anger, but she knew they had to stay there wrapped in a blanket of shame. However, the doctor had been right: creating this place, this ritual, helped. Most days she had to live as if this had never happened, so at least coming here gave her a few moments to acknowledge it, tell herself that it happened but she survived. Slowly she knelt forward and blade by blade she gently wrapped the grass back around the stone until it was completely hidden. Kathleen's words seemed to reach out from the darkness in the woods, 'The truth doesn't disappear;

it sits there waiting to be found.' Beth tried to smother the words and walked quickly, but then her phone pinged a text from Kathleen.

See you at yoga tomorrow. We'll talk after. lots of love xxx.

The text had been sent at 6.40.

The message was so calm, so every day, and the fact she was coming back to yoga must be a good thing. They could talk properly, and Beth could find a way to help. 'That's a relief,' she said to Ollie.

Beth walked back into the dark, deserted patch of woodland. Ollie mooched around the dry pine needles, chasing scents from the night before, and Beth stood very still, waiting for the red squirrels who she knew were there watching her to come out of hiding.

Time slipped away. On a morning like this it was easy to start the process of editing the conversations of the night before, making them less fraught and disturbing; the text showed that Kathleen herself was calmer today.

Beth went through her own day in her mind. She needed to talk to Layla about her flute and singing exams without it turning into a battle. Adam would be in his room revising for his A levels, or on some game: he needed reminding to leave his cave occasionally to encounter daylight. He was off to Oxford University in October, and she dutifully hid the dread she felt at the thought of him going and the empty bedroom he would leave.

When she arrived home, she fed Ollie, showered, and went back down to the kitchen. She cleared the mugs and plates scattered by Adam from late-night snacking. Living with her eighteen year old son felt much like living with a benign poltergeist.

Layla came down, texting with both thumbs in the way she and all her friends did. She didn't look up, her face invisible behind a curtain of brown hair. Short and slim, she looked younger than fifteen. She had been happy in her world of music and fossils until recently.

'Hiya,' said Beth. 'Um, you know your flute and singing exams—'

'Mm—'

'They are both on Saturday morning. Your teacher suggested you go over and get some extra practice with Julie on Friday evening.'

Layla looked up. 'Can't do that. Conor's band are playing in Southampton on Friday night; Elsa and I are going over to hear them.'

Beth took a breath. It was a new tactic of Layla's to present things as decided rather than asking for permission. She was ready this time. 'I don't think so, love; you have your exams early the next morning.'

'We'll get the last ferry, so we won't be that late. I'll be with Elsa.'

'I don't know why you've started hanging around with Elsa all the time.'

'Elsa and I have been friends since we were little. We've been catching up. We always did get on.'

'But she's eighteen now. She can drink and go to places that are not appropriate for you.'

'It's a concert, not some rave, Mum. Be honest; it's not Elsa you're worried about is it? It's Conor.'

Layla was right. Conor was Kathleen's nineteen year old son, who had returned from a few years of living with his father in Ireland. He'd had a pretty wild time out there, failed his exams and come back to live on the island in the hope of retaking A levels and passing them this time. Kathleen was desperately trying to get him to settle back down, but it wasn't going well.

'He's dead talented, Mum. His band may be given a gig, you know, at the festival this year.'

'I'm glad for him, but that's beside the point. You can't go on Friday.'

'You don't understand. Conor asked me to go. I have to be there,' insisted Layla, her voice high and passionate now.

Beth felt Layla's desperation, but said, 'I'm sorry—'

'No, you're not.'

Beth rubbed her forehead; the headache didn't go. She poured her cereal, glanced at the clock: twenty to eight. 'Your Dad's late.'

'I don't care. Conor is OK. You should give him a chance.'

'None of that matters; he's too old for you.'

'We're just friends; you should trust us. Like last week when I played in the concert, he would have given me a lift home, but you insisted Dad came and picked me up.'

Beth spilled the milk she was pouring over her cereal. 'You're not going on a motorbike. I've told you that.'

'Everyone does. It's amazing.'

'Hang on. Have you been on it?'

Layla looked away.

Beth grabbed a dishcloth and started scrubbing at a spot of milk spilt on the worksurface. 'You are not to go on it. Got that? Next time Conor's band are playing on the island, maybe you could go then.'

'This is pathetic. I wish I was getting out of this prison like Adam,' said Layla as she stormed off.

Beth looked over at Ollie, who, head on the edge of his basket, was watching with interest.

'Everything's a bloody battle,' she murmured to him, then poured another coffee, and moved the oven gloves off a chair so she could sit down. Her kitchen had wooden cupboards and work-tops and an old Welsh dresser that had been her mother's. On this stood ornaments: a Welsh dragon next to a beautiful Iraqi chukar partridge.

Beth reluctantly opened her laptop. She had completed A Levels at the college and now she was taking an English degree online. She secretly found it tedious, but Sami and friends seemed to find it gratifying that she was 'making something of herself'.

Beth heard the front door, and Sami rushed in. 'Sorry, everything took longer than I thought. Right, I'll go and shower.' He raced up the stairs.

Ollie plodded over and sat on her feet. 'Life is so simple for you, isn't it?' Beth smiled down at him and stroked his ears.

A few minutes later, Sami returned, turned on the radio and ate his breakfast. Beth closed her laptop and loaded the dishwasher. It was all very quiet, all very normal, then Sami's phone rang. Beth continued cleaning up. However, she slowly became aware of the tone of his voice shifting. It became stressed and clipped. He was asking a series of questions. 'Who?' 'Where?' 'How?' 'When?' and then, 'Oh no, I am so sorry. I can't believe this.'

Beth turned to him, questioningly. He grimaced and mouthed something, but Beth couldn't read his lips.

'I don't know what to say. Anything we can do, you know, me or Beth, do ring—'

Sami slowly put down his phone. He sat staring ahead as if in a trance, then put his head in his hands. 'What is it?' asked Beth.

He turned off the radio. 'That was Patrick, it's Kathleen—'

She felt a wave of nausea, dread.

'I'm so sorry, love—'

3

Beth held her breath as Sami explained. 'Kathleen's had an accident. I'm so sorry. She didn't make it.'

Beth slumped down. It was like the air had been sucked out of the room. A long way away she could hear Sami asking, 'Beth, are you all right?'

It hurt to move her head. 'What happened?'

'She had a fall beyond the fence at the bottom of her garden; she fell down the cliff. A woman walking her dog found her on the beach.'

'Oh God.' Beth covered her face with her hands.

Sami reached over and took her hand. 'They think she died quickly.'

'When?'

'Very early. Kathleen was dressed in her leggings and top. Patrick thinks she'd gone down to do her mindfulness.'

'She sent me a text. We were going to meet up tomorrow at yoga, have a chat—' She covered her eyes with her hands again. They sat quietly, together, until she asked, 'Was she on her own?'

'Yes. Conor had gone to a mate's for the night. As we know,

Patrick was over here. The police came around to tell him what had happened and took him over to the Freshwater house.'

Beth was unaware of the warm tears that were falling down her cheeks. 'What will he do? She was his world.'

'He is in complete shock. He just kept saying he should have been there. He should have sorted out the fence.'

'I know she took part of the fence down to do her meditation, but she knew the cliff edge crumbled. She wouldn't have gone close to it.'

'The police will find out exactly what happened.'

'The police?'

'They're bound to be involved. When the woman found Kathleen on the beach and called for an ambulance the police had to be contacted as well.'

They sat, for a moment unable to look at each other, their own grief alone too much to bear.

'I can't believe this has happened,' said Sami. 'How am I going to tell them at work? Everyone loved her so much.'

'That's what I was trying to tell her. No one would have wanted to upset her. Everyone loved her.'

'Eh?' Sami looked up, bemused. 'You were quiet when we came home from the house party. You two were down the end of the garden talking for ages—'

'We had a lot to catch up on.' Beth paused. 'I'd left it too long. She was very stressed last night. You saw her every day at work. Did you notice anything?'

'She'd been distracted. I think there might have been one or two personal matters playing on her mind.'

'Like what?'

'I'm, um, not sure.' He looked away.

Beth fiddled with the edge of the table. 'She seemed so unhappy, frightened of someone.'

Sami lay his hand on hers. 'She was scared?'

Beth rubbed her bottom lip. For a moment, she wanted to push it all away, but she resisted and said, 'Kathleen told me she'd made a mistake, and someone knew about it and was using it in some way. Anyhow, she told them she was tired of all the lies. She was going to have to own up to something. This person then threatened her.'

Sami's eyes were darting left and right as he tried to compute what she'd said. 'Are you sure about this?'

'Yes, but she wouldn't tell me any names. All she said was that she'd found out this person was not what they appeared to be.' Beth held her hand to her mouth, every part of her shaking. 'She was so brave, but she was petrified of what this person was going to do to her. Oh God, Sami, she's dead now. Has this bastard attacked her or something?'

Sami put his arm around her. 'Try not to jump to conclusions. Are you sure Kathleen didn't give you any indication who she was talking about?'

Beth cringed. 'You're not going to like this, but she said it was someone who was at the house party.'

'But that's absurd. Who was there, apart from Patrick, Kathleen and Conor, that is? Of course, I was there with you and the kids and then Alex, Imogen, her daughter, Elsa, and William. I mean, that was it. All people we know very well; our friends, all very respectable, normal people.'

'But she said we had been fooled by this person; that they were acting a part.'

'But I know for certain that every one of us is qualified in what we do: me and Alex pharmacists, Imogen a head teacher, William a doctor. I don't know what she meant.'

'Nor do I, not really. My poor Kathleen.' Beth again covered her face with her hands, trying to block everything out.

Sami gently eased her hands away. 'Look, I happen to know Kathleen was in a pretty emotional state: something personal had happened. I promised not to tell anyone, but it will have affected her. I'm not saying she was making things up, but she might have not been seeing everything quite in perspective.'

'What was it? Please tell me, Sami.'

'I'm sorry. I want to keep my promise, but it's not anything that anyone else needs to know.'

'She didn't seem depressed to me: scared but not that. Sami, you're not saying she might have taken her own life, are you? Did I miss something?'

'I don't think so. As I say, something happened, but she was picking herself up, wanting to make changes in her life.'

'Yes, that's more how I saw her.'

'I know you're concerned about what Kathleen said to you. It sounds very upsetting, but try not to let it play on your mind. You know the police will be doing a thorough investigation of this accident. They'll find out exactly what happened to Kathleen. You're not to worry.'

'But I should tell them what Kathleen said to me.'

Sami shook his head. 'No, don't say anything yet. The police will have strict procedures, and if they find any reason to suspect anything other than an accident then that is the time to tell them about your conversation with Kathleen. I promise I will tell them what I know as well, but I only want to do it if it's necessary. Kathleen would have hated what she told me to be made public. As for what she told you, it was quite vague: no names, no detail, and as I said she was in a highly emotional state.' He placed his hands on hers. 'If the police find this was an accident, it won't help anyone, particularly Patrick, to have had a load of rumour and insinuation thrown about. What if the local paper got wind of it? No, don't say anything yet; let's wait.'

Beth soaked in the reassurance. It was what she wanted to hear. Leave it to someone else: not her problem, probably nothing to worry about.

Sami gave a sad smile. 'It's been a horrible shock, hasn't it, but I am here for you, to look after you.'

Sami sat down, motionless, shoulders bent, looking older and greyer.

Beth grasped his hand. 'You know, you were a really good friend to Kathleen and you're an amazing boss. You encouraged her to do that course. She appreciated that you took her seriously, that you saw potential in her.'

'I hope so.'

Beth went to the dresser to get a tissue, then sat down again with Sami.

'I wonder who is looking after Patrick and Conor today?' he asked.

'I don't know. All their family are over in Ireland.'

'That's what I was thinking. I would go to them, but I ought to be in work, a lot of the older patients are going to be so shocked, as well as the staff, of course.'

'You could close the pharmacy. People would understand.'

'I can't, love. Mondays are hectic, and people need their medication.'

'I'm not working today. Do you think I would be any help to Patrick?'

'That's a good idea. If you don't mind. You're better at this sort of thing than me, anyway. I'll ring Patrick, see what he says.'

Beth listened as Sami talked quietly to Patrick. At the end of the call he said, 'Patrick sounded very grateful. Apparently, they won't let him or Conor down on the beach to see Kathleen. They said it would be better for him to see her later.'

'Who found her?'

'It turns out the dog walker was a neighbour, someone called Jilly, I think. She keeps hens as well, so she got to know Kathleen. At least they have a definite ID.'

'Poor woman.'

'I know, ghastly.'

Sami's phone rang, he answered it. 'Ah, Alex. That's OK. I'll check that. Actually, I'm glad you phoned.'

Beth heard Sami explain the situation to his new partner, Alex. When he had finished, Sami said, 'That's good, Alex has offered to come in, though it's his day off. It will give me the time to speak to people properly.'

'Not an easy start to his first full-time week at the pharmacy.'

'No, but I'm glad he's here.'

'You're right, of course.' Beth kissed him lightly and went upstairs to change. Thinking vaguely what the most appropriate thing was to wear, realising quickly that no one was going to notice or care, she found her tidier jeans and a light baggy jumper. She brushed her curly brown hair and slapped on some moisturiser. She wanted to talk to the children before they heard the news from anyone else. She knocked gently on Layla's door, and as she waited for a reply Sami walked past her.

'I'll be off. I'll be in touch later. Good luck, and, you know, be careful – all the business last night—'

'I know. I'll be careful what I say.'

Sami kissed her gently on the cheek. 'I don't know how everyone will take the news. I can't believe Kathleen's not going to be there.'

Beth looked at him, his eyes creased in pain, and spoke gently, 'You'll be just the person they all need; see you later.'

Beth knocked again on Layla's door.

'What?' shouted Layla, still angry.

'I need to speak to you: it's about Kathleen. It's important.'

She gently pushed open the bedroom door. Layla was sat on her bed, her phone in her hand. Her bedroom was the strange mix of all fifteen year olds' rooms: cuddly toys, a Winnie the Pooh poster, the bookshelf with John Green books sat next to Jacqueline Wilson, DVDs stacked next to her laptop ranging from Disney to

The Shawshank Redemption. There was no pink, but also not the black Layla had wanted on three of the walls. One wall had a huge poster about fossils, and those they had found on the beaches around were all displayed and labelled on a table.

Beth carefully and calmly passed on the news about Kathleen and for a moment their row was forgotten. 'Oh shit. That's terrible. Are you all right, Mum?'

'I'm fine. I wanted you to know before you went to school.'

'Poor Conor. I know he rowed with Kathleen all the time, but she probably meant well. I liked her really. And she was so pretty; she could have been a model. She was a lot younger than you, wasn't she?'

'No, we were the same age actually,' said Beth, trying to ignore the sceptical look on Layla's face.

'You sure? Still, it's an awful thing to happen, and just when they'd got that amazing house.'

'It's all terribly sad. So now, you'll be OK?'

'Yes, I'm fine.'

'I am going to go out to be with Patrick and Conor. Dad has gone into the pharmacy. Are you OK for school?'

'Of course. I'm going to Elsa's after school. She's going to help me with my biology coursework.'

'OK, but, well, be careful. Phone me if you need me.'

Beth was glad to have spoken to Layla. Sometimes there was a light in their relationship, and the little girl she used to make up stories for in bed, who she made sandcastles with on the beach, was still there.

Beth knocked on Adam's door and pushed it open a little.

'I'm not going into school, study day. Mum, is it true about Kathleen?'

Beth slowly pushed open the bedroom door to go in. Through the gloom of the darkened room she could make out the light of Adam's phone in his hand. He was sitting on his bed.

'I'm afraid it is.'

Adam sat up. He had coal black hair like his father. It reminded her of photos she'd seen of Sami when he was younger, living in Iraq. He moved over to the chair.

'It's all over Instagram. A friend of the person who found Kathleen's body on the beach has written about it.'

'I'm sure they shouldn't have done that.'

'They said they've been contacted by the *Mail* already, but the police have told them not to talk.'

Beth shuddered; to have her friend's sudden death turned into social media gossip was horrible. She hoped Patrick wasn't aware of it.

'It's on Twitter as well. Someone has said they think she killed herself. Do you think that, Mum?'

Beth gasped. Why would people throw such insensitive things up on social media, things that would only be whispered in 'real life'.

'I don't know why they're saying that. There's no reason to think that.' Beth sat down. 'Look, the police will look into everything, don't put anything online.'

Adam swung back on his chair in a way that always made her heart rush. 'Kathleen helped me a hell of a lot in the pharmacy on Saturdays. The old people like her as well; she's been there for ages.'

'Nearly ten years. I remember meeting her at church, she was looking for work and I told her Dad was advertising for someone in the pharmacy. It seems a lifetime ago now. Listen, I'm thinking of going over to be with Patrick and Conor. Have you heard from Conor, by the way?'

'Nah. Me and him, we're not close. You know that, Mum. Different friends and interests.'

'I know, but I thought now that Layla seems to be hanging about with him—'

'I wish she wouldn't. He's a bit of a prat. Him and his mates in the band think they are rock stars; it's pathetic.'

'Could you say something to her?'

'No way. I'm not having her going off at me. She'll find out soon enough.'

'Fair enough. I'm off then. What will you be up to?'

'Revision, the usual.'

'Could you work downstairs, keep Ollie company and take him for a walk later?'

'OK.'

'Don't forget, will you? He needs his walk. There's pizza and things in the freezer. Make sure you take a break.'

'I'm OK, Mum.'

'All right. Well, I'll have my mobile. See you later.'

Beth left the house and climbed into her car, but then paused. She felt sick, dreading the thought of facing Patrick and Conor, the police, the house. Why had she been so ready to offer to go over when she could have stayed home, worked on her thesis, walked Ollie? Anything, in fact, other than face all this pain?

Beth pushed the key into the ignition, telling herself firmly that Kathleen had been one of her closest friends, someone she'd let down lately. Of course, she should go and look after her grieving husband and son. Like Sami said, she wasn't to worry about anything else. Her role now was to look after Patrick and Conor: that is all that mattered.

4

Beth knew the journey would take about fifteen minutes, and she drove to Patrick's house along the winding 'middle road' that cut through the farmland from Castleford to Freshwater. She turned off this road, through the village of Brook and then out on to the Military Road. The views were stunning this morning, On the left was the sea; on the right, fields; and ahead white chalk cliffs and Tennyson Down. She passed the carpark for Compton Bay, saw a few vans and people going down to surf, and finally, just before the hill down into Freshwater, on the left, she arrived at Patrick and Kathleen's house. From the front, the house looked less aggressively modern, with soft brick work and large but normal windows. As no cars could park on the road itself, she could see straight down the hill to the bay. It was quiet this morning out of season, with just a single dog walker and someone running.

The parking area in front of Kathleen and Patrick's house had on it a number of vehicles Beth didn't recognise, including a police car. She parked her little silver Golf next to it. As she got out she breathed in the fresh bright air; it didn't feel like the day of a tragedy.

A policewoman answered the door. To Beth's surprise, it was someone she knew, a woman who used to work with her at Castleford Primary.

'Goodness. It's Sue, isn't it? I've not seen you for a few years.'

Sue smiled. 'No, I keep meaning to pop in. I hear Imogen is a great head. As you can see, I joined the police. I'm a Family Liaison Officer now.'

'Congratulations,' Beth said, smiling, her voice loud. She paused. For a moment, she realised to her horror, she'd forgotten why she was there. Lowering her voice, she looked past Sue into the house. 'I've come to be with Patrick and Conor. How are they?'

'In shock. I'm glad you've come.'

Beth followed her into the house, which now felt cold and empty. It seemed a lifetime since she was last there, not just the evening before. Patrick was sitting on the plush white sofa, staring at the floor.

He looked up slowly, peered at her, his eyes full of pain. At the sight of the anguish in front of her she felt her lips tremble.

Patrick stood up, his arms falling helplessly by his side and she walked over to him, held him. She could feel his body shake, emotion rumbling deep inside him. 'I'm so sorry,' she said quietly.

They sat down, Patrick holding her hand as if to stop himself drowning.

'How is Conor?'

'He's upstairs. He insisted on driving himself over here earlier. He could have come in the police car with me. They sent a car, you know. I should have been here. That fence. It's all my fault.'

Beth glanced out into the garden, and saw a large section cordoned off with people in white suits working. It looked like a crime scene from television, but this was real life. She quickly turned away, and sat with her back to it, next to Patrick.

Sue asked quietly, 'Can I get you a drink?' Their eyes met and Sue gave her a reassuring smile. Beth was glad she was there.

Standing in her smart uniform with her fair hair in a neat bun she gave off the air that you were in safe hands: however frightening things appeared, she could handle it.

'Coffee, please.'

Sue strode efficiently toward the kitchen area. She looked too at home. It did seem odd that a stranger to this house was here making the coffee, already familiar with the kitchen, Kathleen's kitchen; but then nothing was normal now, was it? Sue put Beth's mug down and left them.

Beth noticed that Patrick kept his back to the window. 'They asked me how Kathleen was, if she seemed down. I said she had been tired, what with the move and everything but nothing else. They seemed to think she may have, you know, done something.'

'I expect they have to ask things like that. Don't let it upset you.'

'It made me feel like I'd missed something. You two were talking a lot last night. Did she say she was unhappy or depressed? I'd noticed she seemed a bit on edge but despite that I thought she was excited about the house. I wanted her to love being here.'

Beth looked at his white, grief-stricken face, and chose her words carefully. 'Patrick, I am sure she loved this house. She was so pleased to have her hens here and loved going down to do her meditation. We did talk about some other things. We had a lot to catch up on. In fact, she sent me a text this morning telling me she would see me at yoga tomorrow. We were going to have another chat then.'

'So, she was planning things? That's a good thing isn't it? You must tell the police that—' He stopped, tears again in his eyes. He waved his hand around aimlessly. 'This was all for her, you know.' Beth accepted the partial truth. 'She was going to put chandeliers everywhere, had found a firm in France that made them. There's already one upstairs, but she wanted them everywhere. They cost nearly as much as the house, but I'd have done it for her.'

'I know,' said Beth.

'They haven't let me see her yet,' he added. 'No one saw her fall. I keep wondering what she was thinking as she fell. And how long did she lie there, dying? Was she in terrible pain?'

His words conjured up terrible images. Beth hadn't realised Sue was so close by until she spoke.

'Patrick—' Sue spoke gently but firmly. She waited until he looked at her. 'It is most likely she died quickly. Remember, we told you she had a nasty cut on her head. We think she bumped it when she fell. She may well have died instantly, known nothing about it.'

Patrick looked at her, surprised, as if it was the first time he was hearing it. 'You think that?'

'Yes. We will know more soon, but you are not to let your mind go to those places.'

'And when will I be able to see her?'

'As soon as we can arrange it. Kathleen's body will be taken to hospital. They just need to do a few things first.'

He nodded. Beth's mind raced through too many things. Patrick, however, seemed to be wrapped in invisible cotton wool.

Sue returned to the kitchen and Beth heard the kettle boiling again. She sat feeling so helpless: nothing seemed the right thing to say.

Suddenly, Patrick asked, 'How is Jilly?'

Beth frowned, 'Jilly?'

'She's the neighbour who found Kathleen,' explained Sue, coming over to them. She spoke to Patrick. 'Jilly's husband is with her. She's upset but her doctor has been to see her. It was quite a shock.'

'I'm glad it was her,' said Patrick. 'She liked Kathleen. I'm glad it was someone who knew her.'

'Of course,' said Sue. Turning to Beth she said, 'Patrick's brother is on his way.'

'He's coming from Dublin?'

'He's in Essex on business; he said he'd come straight here.'

'It'll be good to see him,' said Patrick. 'He's a lawyer, you know, understands paperwork. He told me he'd contact Conor's dad. I couldn't face talking to that man. He was so dreadful to Kathleen. I couldn't bear him pretending to be sorry.'

'Sean is the best person to talk to him, I'm sure.'

Patrick turned to look out of the window. 'I've no idea how to look after them.'

Confused by the sudden change of subject, Beth looked out of the window.

'The hens,' said Patrick. 'I don't know anything about looking after them. I don't suppose you could have them?'

Beth shook her head. 'Layla would love them and so would I but, no, I'm sorry. I'd have loved to take them on, but we've not got the space in the garden.'

Sue interrupted, spoke to Patrick. 'You're not to worry. When they have finished in the garden Jilly is going to come over and look after the hens. She could even move them in with hers if you would like?'

'That might be a good idea. I blame them a little, you know—'

Beth blinked in confusion. Sue explained. 'When we came here earlier with Patrick, the hens were running around down the bottom of the garden. Patrick didn't understand why they were out.'

'It's odd. Kathleen wasn't going to let them out of the coop until the permanent fence was up.' said Beth

'That's what Patrick told us. One theory we are working on is that they escaped somehow and it was while Kathleen was trying to catch them that the accident occurred. It is possible that one of the hens went too close to the cliff edge, Kathleen chased it and tragically fell. Patrick seemed to think Kathleen would have taken that kind of risk to save one of her hens. Do you?'

'She may have done. She was besotted with her hens. I could

see her doing that, but I don't understand why they would have been out at all.'

'We don't know details yet. We'll look into it.' Sue spoke as if the matter was closed.

'I see. Were any of the hens hurt?'

Beth saw Sue's eyebrows shoot up.

'I know it sounds silly, but Kathleen loved them so much.'

Sue shook her head. 'No, I don't think so. Jilly's husband made sure they were all put away and accounted for. He and his wife had helped Kathleen move them in.'

'Good.' Beth could feel tears again. 'I'm sorry, but it matters. So, um, what time do they think everything happened with Kathleen?'

'Kathleen was in her comfy clothes, and her mat was down there. Patrick told us she'd started going down there about quarter to seven, took down some of the fence, and used an app on her phone to do mindfulness, so sometime between when she went out and when Jilly found her at twenty to eight. We'll know more soon.'

Beth nodded. Patrick stood up. 'I'm going up to see Conor,' he said, and left them. When he was out of sight Beth stood up and looked out at the garden again.

'It feels unreal,' she said. She glanced towards the stairs and then in a soft voice she asked, 'I suppose this is like routine to them. I mean, it doesn't mean anything, does it? They don't think anyone came over and attacked Kathleen, do they?' Beth tried to keep the desperation out of her voice.

'They have to consider every possibility,' replied Sue.

Beth felt a knife of fear twist inside. 'Someone might have killed her?'

Sue softened her voice, like a mother reassuring her child as they go to the dentist. 'There's nothing obvious to suggest foul play, but they have to make sure.'

Beth turned her back on the garden and picked up her mug, but didn't sip her coffee.

'Patrick said you were asking about Kathleen's state of mind.'

Sue sat forward. 'We naturally need to ask these things. You two were good friends, weren't you? Patrick said you were here last night and had a long chat with Kathleen?'

'Yes, we were down the bottom of the garden.'

'How did Kathleen seem to you?'

Beth bit her lip. 'To be honest, I've been a bit out of touch with her recently, but last night she was worried, uptight.'

'About what?'

'I don't know exactly.' Beth's mind was racing: how much should she say?

'I know it's difficult, but it helps us get a picture of how things were. Who was at the house party?'

As Beth saw Sue take out her notebook, she realised her role was a lot more than just making the tea. She panicked. Was she giving an official statement?

'There was myself and my husband, Sami, with our kids, Adam and Layla.'

'Sami Bashir?'

'That's it. He runs the pharmacy in Castleford. Also at the get-together was Alex Thompson. Alex has been based in London but has been coming weekly as a locum for Sami to cover his lecturing. This week Alex starts full time. He has moved to the island and is becoming a partner in the pharmacy. There was also Imogen from school, now Imogen Parker-Lewis, with her daughter, Elsa, and her husband, Dr William Parker-Lewis. He's been a GP for five years now in the surgery that Sami's pharmacy is attached to.'

'And that was everyone?'

'Um, and of course Patrick, Kathleen and her son, Conor. That's all.'

'Thank you,' said Sue. 'It's been so helpful having you here today. I assume it was Patrick who let you know what had happened.'

'Yes. He rang us, early. Sami had come in from his run, I'd just walked my dog.'

'Where did you go?'

'I drove to Parkhurst Woods and walked there.'

'Was it quiet there this morning?'

Beth fiddled with the cushion. 'It was where we walked. We didn't meet anyone. I went home, talked to Layla, then Sami came back. He was later than usual, didn't get in until about ten to eight.'

'Why was that?'

'At the moment our friends, the Hendersons, are away. Their house is further along the Whitcombe Road. Sami goes up there to check on things, water the plants and stuff.'

'So, does Sami run from home?'

'Usually, although today he took the car. He was taking some bags of fertiliser. He went out about half six.'

'That's early.'

'He had the house to check and then he runs in their fields. He loves the solitude.'

'So, he didn't meet lots of people?'

'I don't think so. He'd told me he liked it because it was so isolated up there.'

'Now, you say Kathleen seemed a bit tense at the house party?'

Beth crossed her arms, spoke carefully. 'I got the impression that she felt she'd upset someone who was there last night, and that they might be angry with her for some reason.'

'Any idea who or what it was all about?'

The question hung in the air with Sue's hand holding the pen, waiting to write down something. Beth remembered Sami's warning to think of Patrick, not to say anything yet.

'No, it was probably nothing,' she said. 'Kathleen could be a bit, how would you say, over-dramatic.' As she spoke, the words felt a betrayal of Kathleen. 'She sent me a text first thing this morning. She said she would see me at yoga tomorrow.'

'Can I see the text?' Beth took her phone out of her bag and handed it over.

'I see, 6.40. Well, she sounds positive in this text, and she was planning to see you. Patrick doesn't think she was on any medication for depression. Obviously, we will speak to her doctor.'

'That's Imogen's husband, William: Dr Parker-Lewis who I mentioned.'

Patrick returned. He walked slowly as if each step was an effort. 'Conor's best left.' He looked over at Sue. 'He doesn't want to come. Have you mentioned it to Beth yet?'

'As I said, Patrick will be going to see Kathleen's body at the hospital later,' said Sue. 'He was wondering if you would be willing to go with him.'

Beth tried to hide her feeling of horror. Images from TV dramas flashed through her head: bodies pulled out of freezer drawers or bags unzipped. Her stomach clenched. She put her hand to her mouth.

'Sit down a minute,' said Sue.

Beth took deep breaths. Slowly, the room stopped spinning.

'I know it sounds difficult, but maybe I can reassure you. Kathleen will be lying on a bed. Her body will be covered.'

'I will be able to touch her hands and her face—' said Patrick.

'They will make her look as peaceful as they can. Her injuries are not extensive,' replied Sue.

'Please come with me,' said Patrick. 'I need to say goodbye. I don't feel I will believe this has happened until I see her.'

Beth felt guilty. 'Of course. It would be a privilege.'

The morning passed, the police quietly searched rooms in the house. Patrick was asked questions occasionally, but he was handled gently. When Sue suggested she made sandwiches, Beth was surprised to realise that she was hungry. As Sue and Beth ate,

Sue chatted easily to Beth, while Patrick sat apart, looking stunned.

It wasn't long after lunch that Sue was told they could go to the hospital, and it was a shock to leave the safety of the house. The cars sounded too loud; the wind too harsh. Beth sat in the back of Sue's car with Patrick. She found herself doing up his seat belt for him. As they drove along, Beth watched people going about their normal lives. She wanted to be with them, not in this nightmare.

As they pulled into the hospital car park, Patrick grabbed her hand. 'It might be a mistake, mightn't it? It might not be Kathleen. She could have gone for a walk, got lost. It could be someone else.'

Beth couldn't understand the madness but squeezed his hand. They followed Sue. Beth averted her eyes from the sign announcing that they were headed for the mortuary. Inside, they were taken to a small room.

Sue went in with them. Beth nervously approached the bed, and then she saw Kathleen, lying so still, her face white, a horrible gash at the side of her head. The sheet had been pulled up to her chin; only one arm was resting on top of the sheet.

Patrick began to shake, grabbed the hand and held it. 'She's so cold; my poor Kathleen.'

Beth found her gaze fixated on Kathleen's face. Only hours ago, she'd been alive, doing her mindfulness, feeling the fresh morning breeze, listening to the sea. One minute she'd been 'greeting the dawn', and then it ended. It was chilling: that infinitesimal line between life and death. And, if Kathleen had slipped over it so easily, why couldn't she come back? Beth desperately wanted to shout, to wake her up, but in her heart she knew that however loud she shouted, Kathleen had gone. This was the end.

Beth squeezed her eyes tight. Her throat felt on fire. Shaking, she put her hand over her mouth. This had really happened.

After a time, she looked again at Kathleen and it was then the grief almost overwhelmed her. She stood, hardly breathing, holding in the emotions that charged around inside. Words started to form in her head. 'I am so sorry, my lovely friend. We were meant to see each other tomorrow and now we will never talk again. I am so sorry that you were going through all that without me. I failed you. I don't want our last night together to have been so full of stress and fear. Is it really a coincidence that you fell this morning, or did someone do something to hurt you? I don't know what to think.

'Sami doesn't think I should tell the police what you told me, not until they've found out how you died. Maybe he's right, but seeing you now, even if it was an accident, I don't think I can just forget what you told me. The fear was real and someone at that house party made you feel that way. I promised last night to help you. Well, that promise still holds. I will try to find out who frightened you, who was so cruel. I'm scared you know. These are our friends. Oh God, Kathleen, why did it have to be one of them? I wish I knew more, but that's my fault, I should have talked to you before last night. I'm so sorry. I'm going to miss you so much, I wish you'd known how much I loved you. The world is going to be colder, lonelier without you.'

Beth held her head. It was thumping. There was a boulder in her throat; her eyes burned with tears. Then she saw Patrick speaking softly over Kathleen. 'You will always be mine now.' It seemed to bring him comfort, but all the same she found the words unsettling.

Sue came close to them.

'When will we be able to have a funeral?' Patrick asked.

Beth felt shocked by the sudden return to practicalities.

'That will depend on the coroner. There will have to be investigations and then he will say when the body can be released. I've been meaning to ask if you have a reason, such as your religion, that makes timing more pressing. I'm not promising anything, but the coroner tries to be sympathetic.'

Patrick shook his head. 'No. Kathleen was brought up Catholic, but she went to a local Church of England church. We will have a simple service there.'

After they left the room Patrick held Beth's hand tight. In the adjoining room an officer came over to them. 'I wonder if I could check this with you, sir. We found it next to your wife's body. It looked like it had fallen off. Do you recognise it?'

Patrick looked at a clear plastic bag in the officer's hand. Inside was a butterfly necklace. 'Yes. It's Kathleen's. I think she bought it before Christmas. It's not valuable or anything but she wore it a lot.'

'Thank you. We'll hold on to it for now.' The officer left them, and Beth and Patrick walked back out of the hospital.

Sue drove them back to the house where Patrick slumped onto the sofa, exhausted. Beth went upstairs to the bathroom, glad of some time alone; it had been so emotional, so painfully sad. She opened the window. This side of the house looked over towards Mottistone Down which was one of Beth's favourite places to walk on the island; life somehow made more sense up there. She must go there with Ollie again soon. After washing her face with water, she left the bathroom. As she walked along the landing, she saw a closed door, and was drawn to it. It had a brass doorknob. She turned it slowly and opened the door.

5

Bedrooms intrigued Beth. They were shut off from the rest of the house, often untidier; dressing tables showed insecurities; wardrobes told stories of clothes worn and those that were not. In the drawers next to the bed were stuffed letters, test results, cards a person couldn't face throwing away but had nowhere to put. Above all, bedrooms were private, secret places.

Kathleen and Patrick's room was bright, light, feminine. Kathleen had clearly had a lot of say in the design of this room, unlike the rest of the house. From the ceiling hung the beautiful cut glass chandelier Patrick had mentioned; beautiful prints of butterflies were in light gold frames. The carpet was white; the bedding duck egg blue, with matching heavy curtains. Books about pharmacy were on a small shelf, alongside some Jackie Collins mega reads and photography books. On the dressing table expensive makeup and perfume were neatly arranged. On the bed sat a large collector's Stein bear and neatly arranged embroidered cushions.

'Why are you in Mum's room?'

Beth spun round and faced Conor, tall, good looking, red haired like his mother. He wore a tight short sleeved black t-shirt which showed off the tattoos which covered both his arms. She felt herself blushing. 'I'm sorry—'

'You shouldn't be in here.'

Beth backed away. 'I'm sorry. How are you, Conor? I am so sorry about your mum.'

Conor didn't move, his arms crossed defiantly. 'You hate me for not coming to the hospital, don't you?'

'No. Of course not.'

'I'm a coward. I don't want to see her dead. Mum was more alive than most people. I know we argued, but that's family and we worked it out in our own way. I loved her.'

'Of course, and she loved you. She understood you'd found it difficult settling back here.'

Conor kicked the skirting board with the toe of his boot. 'It's all bullshit.' He blinked tears.

'It's very hard for you.'

Conor clenched a fist, thumped the side of his leg. 'Patrick's a decent guy, whatever Dad says. He'll be broken up by this. He was always worried about her, worried about losing her. I saw him checking her phone a few times and he was always asking her where she was going and when she'd be back.'

'Did he?'

'Yeah, and I saw him in here going through the drawers. My dad said she was always after other men.'

'I don't think that was true,' said Beth quietly.

'You didn't know her properly. Lately something was up.' Conor moved closer to her. 'Last night, when everyone was here, I saw her read a text and then look up. She looked dead scared. I went over and asked her, but she said it was nothing and put her phone away.'

'She didn't tell you who the text was from?' Beth waited, holding her breath.

'No. She just was looking round the room.'

Beth watched Conor, now trying to pick the paint off the lintel. 'Have you spoken to your father in Ireland today?'

'He rang me. Uncle Sean had told him what happened, but I didn't want to talk to him.'

'Why not?'

Conor kicked the skirting board again and glared at Beth. 'I just didn't.'

Beth felt desperately sorry for him 'When you're ready, I think you should talk to someone. They can arrange it at school. You could ask your form teacher or there's the Youth Centre. Ring them. It's free.'

Conor's face looked angry. 'You think I'm mad?'

'Of course not, but you are grieving. Talking to someone can be a lot of help. Honestly. I talked to someone when I lost my Mum.'

'I don't need anyone,' he shouted, and walked away.

Beth stayed with Patrick for the afternoon until there was a knock at the door.

Sue answered it. Beth looked over to see a middle aged man in a smart suit. 'I'm Patrick's brother, Sean.'

Beth was amazed, both at the similarity and the difference between the brothers. They were the same height and build, but looked so different. Patrick had slicked back hair and tended to wear a leather jacket. They were replaced on his brother with a smart if dull barber cut and a suit: smart, conventional.

Patrick stood up and his brother came towards him. Sean held out a rectangular black box.

Patrick read the front. 'Bushmills, twenty-one year old. Oh, Sean.' He burst into tears and the men hugged.

Beth felt it was now time for family. She glanced at Sue, who seemed to understand.

'I'll be off now, Patrick.'

Sean came over to her. 'Thank you so much. I'm so grateful I was over here. I'm going to stay as long as Pat needs me.'

'That's wonderful. Look, I'll give you my mobile number,' said Beth. 'If there is anything—' Sean took out his phone and they exchanged numbers.

'Thank you for coming,' said Patrick. His voice broke and Beth felt herself well up again. The framed photographs of Kathleen on the walls caught her eye, and, as if for the first time, she realised that she would never see her friend again.

Patrick followed her glance. 'So beautiful, perfect. I never thought she'd stay with someone like me, but she did, right to the end.'

'Remember where we are. Sami will be in touch soon.'

Sue walked with her out to her car. 'Can I check one or two things?'

Beth groaned inwardly but put on a polite smile.

'You gave me the names of everyone who was here last night. Is there anyone, apart from yourself, who was particularly close to Kathleen?'

'My husband, Sami, has known and worked with her for a long time. She started working with him at the pharmacy soon after she and Patrick moved over to the island about ten years ago.'

'What was her role there?'

'She was on the counter. She was studying to be a technician. She had lectures at the South London Academy on the first Tuesday and Wednesday of every month, so she went last week.'

'Did she travel each day for this?'

'No, she stayed in London on Tuesday evenings, actually at Alex's house. You know, Sami's new partner.'

'She stayed with Alex?'

'No, at his house. He wasn't there. Kathleen originally stayed with his wife, Amy, but she died a few months ago. After that Kathleen was staying by herself. Alex was here on the island every Tuesday evening. He covered for Sami, who also goes to London on Tuesdays and Wednesdays, but he goes every week. He lectures in King's College and stays at the college on the Tuesday night.'

'Was that on Kathleen's course?'

'No, Kathleen's course was at the London Academy and that was only once a month.'

'I see. So, last week, as it was the start of the month, Kathleen went to the London Academy on Tuesday and Wednesday and stayed at Alex's house. Sami went on the same days but to King's College and he stayed there on the Tuesday night. Alex, his new partner, was down here, covering for him like he does every week.'

'Exactly.'

'So, if I'm right, Kathleen would have worked with Alex the weeks she was not on her course?'

'That's right, yes.'

'Right. It's handy to know how well people knew Kathleen.'

'Oh, I should add that Kathleen was working her notice. She'd decided to leave the pharmacy a few weeks ago, and she'd also decided to give up her course.'

'Really. Why?'

'She told me she wanted a fresh start. I guessed she meant with the new house and things.'

Sue glanced back at the house. 'And would you say Kathleen's marriage was a happy one?'

'I'm sure it was. I think she wanted to spend more time with Patrick and, of course, she has her son, Conor, here as well.'

'That's helpful. Thank you.' Sue closed her book. 'I'll give you my card. If you think of anything, this is my direct number.'

Beth took the card and put it in her bag.

It was mid afternoon when she arrived home, but it felt as if she'd been away for days.

Sami returned from work, came straight to the kitchen, and slumped into a chair. 'How are you? How did it go?'

Beth sat opposite him. 'Patrick, as you'd expect, is in pieces. His brother Sean arrived this afternoon. He was over on the mainland on business, so I guess that was lucky.'

'I remember meeting Sean a few years back; nice chap; yes, he'll be practical, supportive.'

'When I arrived at Patrick's I was met by a woman who used to work at the school and is now a police officer. Her name's Sue and she's Patrick's Police Liaison Officer. It was good for Patrick to have her there. She kept explaining things. I think she'll be a lot of support for him. It was horrible seeing all the police in the garden, in these suits, everything cordoned off.'

'Did you tell this Sue about your conversation with Kathleen?'

'Not really. I said she seemed on edge, that she was worried she might have upset someone who was at the party, but I didn't go any further.'

'Good.'

'She was there with her notebook. It made me realise how official everything was.'

'Exactly.'

'Sue asked me and Patrick about Kathleen's state of mind. I guess, like you said, they have to look at everything at this stage. I told them I didn't think Kathleen sounded like she wanted to end her life, but she wanted to make some changes to it.'

Sami took off his glasses and rubbed his red, tired eyes.

'One thing happened that I wasn't prepared for, though,' said Beth. 'Patrick asked me to go to the mortuary with him. We went this afternoon.'

'Oh goodness. Were you all right?'

'It was desperately sad. Kathleen still looked beautiful. There was a gash on her forehead where she'd fallen. I've never been to a mortuary. It was weird, tucked away in the hospital. I didn't want Kathleen to be there.' Beth covered her face with her hands, and Sami moved his chair closer to her.

'How was it at the pharmacy?' she asked.

'Awful. Even people who didn't need anything came in. No one could believe it had happened. I had to go through it so many times; it made me realise how loved Kathleen was. She always went out of her way for people, would take prescriptions round to them, give them time. Ironically, this morning was the kind of situation she'd have handled well. Alex was a big help. He's not exactly touchy feely but he quietly kept everything together.'

'Actually, I can imagine that. He's reliable but not very chatty, is he?'

'No. He's quite introverted, but for all that he cares deeply about people. You can see that, and he's very good at his job. I'm lucky he was prepared to come here permanently. He's already implemented a lot of the changes asked for when we failed the inspection last Thursday. I'm hopeful the inspectors will be satisfied when they come back.'

Beth turned to him. 'You've hardly mentioned that. You've never failed one before, have you? Will it be all right? What was wrong?'

Sami got up and put the kettle on. 'The problem appeared to be that we were unable to account for some of the controlled medication, things like methadone and morphine.'

'That sounds serious.'

'It would be if we somehow lost a large quantity of them. As it is, the numbers are small and it could be a recording issue. The inspectors like a clean audit trail and Alex has been working hard to make sure the whole system is transparent. We're also going to change some of our routines: more people will be checking at each stage. We will model ourselves on some of the best practice Alex has seen. It's a good thing really. We should have been more on our game.'

'Didn't Kathleen do all the ordering and stock control?'

He paused, and Beth saw the lines of worry deepen on his forehead.

'She did and, because she was so good, I left her to it. I shouldn't have done that. I tried to explain that to the inspectors. They gave Kathleen quite a grilling on Thursday. I didn't think that was fair.'

'So, this was her fault?'

'She may have made mistakes, but it wasn't intentional. I did my best to reassure her.'

Beth gasped. 'Could this be the horrendous mistake she said she made?'

'Not if she said the mistake was before Christmas. The errors appeared from January onwards.' Sami gave a half smile. 'Which I have to say is a relief. I would hate that to have been on her mind. She had enough to worry about.'

Beth leapt on his words. 'What do you mean, enough to worry about? What was this personal problem she had?'

He took two mugs off the mug tree. 'It doesn't matter. Anyway, I can't tell you.'

Beth knew that once Sami closed down like this there was no point in pushing him, but it was annoying, and so in retaliation she snapped, 'When Kathleen said everyone keeps secrets, I thought to myself, but not Sami. I was wrong, wasn't I?'

Slowly Sami unscrewed the lid of the jar of coffee. He seemed to measure each grain into the mugs.

Finally, he answered. 'I have no idea what she was talking about.' He poured in the boiling water, added the milk and brought the mugs to the table.

'I'll be going up to King's tomorrow as usual. The students will be expecting me. They have exams coming up.'

Beth looked over, saw a flash of pain shoot across his face, and felt a wave of compassion. 'It's been a terrible day, hasn't it?'

He looked down at his mug. 'I've been trying to look after people all day, be philosophical, tell people, "These things happen," but inside it hasn't sunk in at all.'

'I know. If someone walked in now and told me it was a mistake, that Kathleen was fine, I think I could believe them.'

'I keep thinking about Patrick,' he said. 'Yesterday he had his wife. Today she's gone. I don't know what I'd do if that was me. Me and the kids would fall apart without you. You are our safe place.'

Beth was too moved to reply, but Sami gave a weary smile and said, 'Takeaway?' He pushed himself out of his seat, went to get the menu out of the drawer. 'Kebab?'

'Great.'

'You go and turn the TV on. I'll bring you a glass of wine.'

When the kebabs arrived, the whole family sat round the TV, eating. Curled up on the sofa, Beth sat with a glass of wine in her hand, pushing away the events of the day. On TV the detective programme was doing a recap of the past few episodes: the highlights you need to remember to make sense of what was coming up. She realised that was happening in her head. Images of Kathleen talking to her, then the end of the garden cordoned off with tape, the police looking like aliens in their hooded overalls, then Kathleen's cold, dead body, and now what? What happens now?

Beth put down her glass, picked up her tapestry, a cottage on a sunny day, but held the needle in mid air. Tonight, there was no escape.

6

Down at Castleford Primary School, the headteacher, Imogen, packed her things into her briefcase. She needed to go home. It was gone ten and it had been a very long day. The news about Kathleen first thing that morning had shocked everyone. It was a small community and everyone had worn a stunned look as they went about the day. As Imogen stood up and leant forward to switch off her laptop, she felt a spasm in her back. She took a painkiller from her bag.

Most of the school had been shut down by the caretaker but he had left the light on for her. She unlocked and then relocked the one door she needed to get out of the building. It was all highly irregular. She'd been told there was no insurance covering her if anything was to happen, but she wasn't worried about that. She loved having the place to herself: no disruptive pupils being brought to her, no parents grumbling at her, no teachers breaking down under the pressure. Once they'd all gone home, she could get through admin at twice the rate she did in the day. She could phone people, find them at home, sort things out. After that, she could allow herself the luxury of making plans, dreaming dreams for her school, and she had so many. It was exhausting for her staff, but if she had no vision then where would her school go?

Imogen walked out of the front of the building. The caretaker, who had a house next to the entrance to the school, waved over at her.

'Goodnight, Mrs Parker-Lewis.'

It wasn't far to drive home but once she'd gone through the gate into the wood, she felt she'd entered another world. Her parents owned a smart detached house in Surrey with manicured lawns and despaired of what they called her wooden hut in the woods, but she loved it, living here, in the heart of the forest: her refuge.

She was pleased to see from the cars parked that William and her daughter, Elsa, were home.

The house was warm, with a comforting smell of cooking coming from the kitchen.

William came out of the living room to greet her and, as always, the fact that this rather startlingly handsome man lived in her house and, in fact, had been married to her for five years warmed her. That thick brown hair, gentle smile with neat designer stubble, the beautiful tailored suit that he wore so well, still took her breath away.

'You've come home,' he said, wrapping her in his arms.

'I'm shattered. How was your day?' she asked.

'Awful. I had patients come into me in tears over Kathleen. It's shaken the community.'

'We said prayers for Patrick and Conor at school. It was surprising how many of the kids knew her.'

'Come on, I've a casserole in the oven. Me and Elsa have eaten but there's plenty left. I'll pour you a glass of wine.'

Imogen hung up her coat and put down her briefcase, taking out her phone. The furniture was second-hand but good quality, comfy. There were a few beautifully bound books on the bookshelves, enough to give off that smell she loved.

William spooned delicious smelling casserole onto a plate, brought it over to her and spoke in a low voice. 'Elsa is strung up about what happened with Kathleen. Be careful what you say.'

'She talked to you about it?'

'Yes. It's a shock at that age, isn't it, to lose someone, even if you were not that close, and in such a traumatic way?'

Imogen patted his hand. 'You handle her so much better than me.'

At that moment Elsa came down. Eighteen years ago, Imogen, on finding herself pregnant by a partner who her parents disapproved of, had moved to the island. Her partner, as prophesied by her parents, quickly abandoned her, but she had determinedly brought up Elsa on her own while at the same time pursuing a career in teaching. Meeting William had brought her parents back into her life, and they were the ones who persuaded her to allow them to pay for Elsa to go to the local private school for her sixth form. The influence of that and a generous allowance from her grandparents had given Elsa a new air of confidence and sophistication, but Imogen felt an innocence and childhood had been left behind prematurely. This evening Elsa came down dressed in a 'preppy' way, with an expertly made-up face with large eyebrows painted on.

'How are you? Such sad news about Kathleen,' said Imogen.

Elsa stood biting her nails. 'It's awful.' Her red eyes filled up.

Despite what William had said, Imogen was shocked and rather thrown by the level of emotion her daughter was expressing: she hadn't known Kathleen that well, after all.

William stood next to Elsa. 'Come on, Elsa. I've made you some hot chocolate. Of course, it's terrible but we talked about it. Accidents happen and as awful as it is for everyone, we three have each other.'

Elsa sniffed, but her eyes brightened. 'We do, don't we?'

'How was it at school?' asked Imogen.

'OK, but over there not many people knew Kathleen. I tried to contact Conor, but he doesn't want to talk.' She looked at William.

'It is going to be hard for him to process. It's a difficult day for a lot of people,' said William.

Imogen saw him pour another large glass of red wine. She left her meal and went over to him. A man passionate about his work, she was used to seeing him stressed. Sometimes she'd hear him mumbling about a patient, trying to find words of comfort, or struggling with a diagnosis.

'It's been a difficult day, are you OK?' She smiled as he wiped his eyes. 'Not going down with a cold, are you?'

His face broke into a reassuring smile. 'Sorry. You have to hold it in, don't you? I hate seeing people so upset.'

'Your patients would never guess how much you care.'

'I hope it makes me better at my job. Oh, by the way, I'm not sure if it was me or you who left the shower running—'

'It must have been me. I showered after you. Was there steam everywhere again? Sorry.' Imogen turned back to Elsa. 'Is the supply working out all right for photography?'

'She's hopeless. Thank goodness I had Patrick to help me with my portfolio. I'll download it tomorrow and send it off to the university. The head of art said he would expect them to take me unconditionally once they've seen it.'

'Good. She told me it was outstanding, but I'd still like to see the school supporting you better. You shouldn't have needed to be so dependent on Patrick for it. Your grandparents are paying them enough. They're the ones responsible for teaching you.'

'Don't ring, Mum. It'll cause all kinds of stress. I'll talk to my form teacher.' Elsa sat down. 'Have you spoken to Patrick today?'

'I tried ringing, but he didn't answer his phone.'

'Layla told me Beth went around to see him. She's so kind.'

Imogen, ignoring the swipe, took a swig of wine and refilled her glass. 'I was at work.'

William's phone rang, and he left the kitchen.

Elsa moved closer to her mother. 'It's not all negative, is it? You know, about Kathleen?'

Imogen looked up. Her eyes widened. 'What are you talking about?'

'It will be a bit easier for us now, won't it?'

Imogen's eyes widened in horror. 'I don't know what you mean.'

'You must, Mum.'

'No. That's a terrible thing to say.'

Elsa blushed. 'OK.' She looked towards the hallway where William was talking on his phone. 'It's good having him here, isn't it? It was OK when it was only me and you but with William it's much better, isn't it?'

'Of course, and I'm delighted you get on.'

Elsa twisted the little silver ring on her finger. 'I don't ever want William to leave us.'

'He's not going anywhere.'

'Even if he had, you know, strayed a bit, you would forgive him, wouldn't you? I mean, you are out so much, I expect he gets a bit fed up with it.'

Imogen coughed. 'For goodness sake, Elsa, all that stand by your man stuff. I thought I'd brought you up better than that. A woman does not have to put up with or make excuses for a man misbehaving.'

'I know.' Elsa dismissed the words too easily in Imogen's mind. 'But it's not like we need the money now; William's got money. I know it's tied up or something, but you could ease up.'

'My career has always been very important to me, remember that. Anyway, me and William are fine.'

'But you're never here to make him meals, or even have breakfast together.'

Imogen's face hardened. 'That's enough. I know you think I'm obsessed, but to do a job like mine you have to be totally committed to it. William understands that.'

Elsa swung back on her chair. 'I'm just saying be careful. Life is so much better now – even Grandma and Grandad love him and now they love us. It's amazing looking into my account and seeing it go up. They put another five hundred in yesterday.'

'I told them at Christmas they could only do this if they kept to a hundred once a month. It's too much. I shall have a word.'

'No, Mum. Leave it.'

William came back into the room. 'Everything OK?' he asked, looking between them.

'Everything's fine. I was saying to Elsa though that Mum and Dad shouldn't be putting so much money into her account.'

'Leave them be. Like I said, they like to spoil her. She's their only grandchild. They're making up for lost time.'

Imogen didn't reply, too weary for another battle. Instead she left them and went upstairs. She shut the bedroom door firmly behind her, went to her bedside table, carefully removed a pile of underwear, and took out a makeup bag.

* * *

At his house in Freshwater, Patrick held up a cut glass tumbler of whisky, and admired the way it burned amber in the light. He breathed in deeply. The police had left. He looked down the garden. The solar lights lit the path to the end; the tape left by the police fluttered in the distance. It was over. She'd gone. They said you feel numb after losing someone, but he felt numb and in agony at the same time.

Sean came and sat opposite, leant forward and poured himself a drink. He went over to a large portrait of Kathleen and made a small gesture to it with his glass before he took a swig.

'She was a rare beauty, Pat.'

'She was.' Patrick blinked. 'You know, I can still see her that day when she came into the studio with Conor. About five I think he was, bit of a handful. She wanted me to take his picture. All I could do was look at her, but I could see she was miserable.'

Sean smiled. 'Clever move to get her to work for you.'

'I know. How I managed to pay her, I don't know. I was struggling but it was worth it.'

'You were wasted in that job. You did right to move over here. If you'd not been ill, you'd have made money quicker.'

Patrick stood up, went to look out of the window. 'There were dark days when we first came here. I thought we'd made a terrible mistake. We were scraping along. Then I got so ill, I was sure she'd leave me, go back to Ireland.'

Sean poured himself more whisky and took the bottle over to Patrick who was holding out his glass. 'You turned it around though, didn't you? Got the all clear, and then that job. Who pays people to do their social media for them? We live in a mad world.'

'If businesses want to pay me, then let them.' Patrick looked around. 'But what's the point of it all now?' Patrick sat down, and took a long swig of whisky.

Sean sat opposite him. 'It's going to be hard. I don't think I have ever seen anyone love someone the way you loved her, but you'll do it.'

'I feel completely lost. All those years I've been frightened I'd not be enough. In a way, I suppose I'll never have to worry about losing her again, will I?'

'She loved you, Pat. I know she did.'

'I hope so; you never could tell with Kathleen.'

'Of course she did. I was always telling you, and you know your family are here for you now.'

'Thank you, Sean. Having you here means the world to me.'

Sean put down his empty glass. 'I think I'll be getting to bed now. Are you coming up?'

'Soon. You go on up.'

'Not too much more of the whisky,' Sean said gently.

'Hope you sleep.'

Sean went upstairs. Patrick sat back. It had shocked him, the police going into their room. He hadn't thought of that. Still, they'd only really wanted to see her phone, and laptop. Well, they had the laptop: that was OK. Later, he'd better check the drawers; you never knew what Kathleen might have hidden away.

Sami had left early as he did every Tuesday. Sometimes Beth dropped him at the Red Jet; sometimes, like today, he took a taxi.

Beth was exhausted, but she knew that she had to go to work: the day somehow had to be got on with. Also, if she was lucky, she would see Imogen at work. It would be a start to talk to one of the people who was there on Sunday evening. She grabbed yesterday's clothes and went downstairs. She pulled on wellies and coat and went out to the shed, to be greeted by the usual squeaking of the guinea pigs.

'You don't care about anything as long as you get your food,' she said out loud to them. There was something comforting about the way they happily crunched on their fresh food.

Reluctantly, she left them and went out with Ollie. As she walked down Castleford Shute towards the ford, she passed the thatched bungalow she'd always fantasised about living in. By the back gate were the flowers she waited for all year: the peonies were finally out: a mass of white, cream, blush, pinks and red petals with a heady fragrance. Every year she and Kathleen would walk here to see them. She stood on the bridge over the stream gazing at them and her eyes filled with tears. Kathleen wouldn't see them this year, she'd never see them again. Ollie was waiting patiently by her side. She leant down and stroked him. 'Ollie, we've lost her. She was so sweet; something soft, comforting in a cold hard world.' Beth started to cry, at first gently, but then she sobbed.

'Can I help?' The voice was quiet.

She turned. It was Alex, Sami's new partner. He was a tall, thin, quiet man with a face that showed little emotion. She had met him occasionally over the past year; never talkative, he had become even more reserved since losing his wife.

'I'm sorry. These were Kathleen's favourite flowers,' explained Beth.

'It was very sudden.' Alex started to pick the leaves off the hedge. 'She'll be missed at the pharmacy and I was very grateful to her for looking after Amy.'

Beth lengthened the flexible lead to allow Ollie to walk to the ford and paddle. 'Kathleen got on well with her, didn't she?'

'She did. I mean it wasn't for long: just those Tuesdays when Kathleen did her course last year. I suppose she only stayed with Amy about three or four times, but they became fond of each other. It was a huge comfort to me to know she was with Amy when I was down here.'

'Kathleen told me Amy had been through so much, losing her Mum and then the car accident.'

She watched Alex scrunch a leaf up and throw it on the ground. 'She had. The car accident, in a way, was the result of losing her mum. Amy was devastated by the loss, went around in a dream, you know she just walked in front of the car. The injuries meant she had to give up her job; she was devastated.'

'Didn't Kathleen tell me Amy had been a dancer?'

Alex's face lit up; she could see he was grateful that Beth remembered. 'Yes, she was very talented. Her injuries meant she had to stop dancing, teaching. The whole thing destroyed her.'

'Life doesn't seem fair sometimes, does it?'

'No, it doesn't. I thought life had thrown everything at us, and then for Amy to die in a fall while I was away just added to the nightmare. My only comfort is I know Kathleen was in the house. Amy wasn't alone.'

'Kathleen was very upset by it all. She sent me a text. I should have talked to her properly about it—'

Alex looked sideways. 'At least she contacted me as soon as Amy had her fall, it meant I got back to London to be with her in time for the end.' Alex threw a pebble in the brook. 'I'm grateful that my last memory of Amy is someone finally at peace.'

'I'm so glad.' Beth brushed away tears with the back of her hand as she remembered her last meeting with Kathleen: all she had was fear and stress.

'I'm sorry to be pouring out my troubles,' said Alex. 'You have enough to deal with at the moment.'

'It's all right; it's difficult; that's all.'

'To lose your friend so suddenly must be heart breaking.'

Beth saw warmth in his eyes: compassion; he understood. 'It is. I've still got the text on my phone from her saying she'd see me at yoga tonight. We were going to talk. I was going to help her—'

'Help her?' He asked in a quiet, considered way, like a priest or a doctor. Beth longed to confide in someone but was torn, she'd agreed with Sami not to say anything.

'I can't say anything, it's better to keep things to myself.'

'But you look very distressed. It could help to talk to someone, you know it wouldn't go any further. As you know, people confide in us pharmacists all the time.'

Beth bit her lip. It was tempting. She needed to talk, and Alex had known Kathleen quite well; maybe he could even shed some light on her problems. The other thing was, of course, how was she going to find out who was threatening Kathleen if she never spoke about their conversation? Taking a deep breath, she decided to take a risk.

'On Sunday evening Kathleen told me she was very scared of someone. They'd been threatening her.'

'My goodness. Who was it?'

Beth swallowed hard. 'She didn't give me a name, but Kathleen said it was somebody who was there that night, one of our friends.'

Beth gripped the lead, waited, expecting Alex to dismiss it. However, his reaction was very different. His face seemed to turn to stone, the warmth in his eyes was replaced with – what was it? Anger... guilt... fear? She wasn't sure. Eventually he spoke.

'Kathleen was a complicated person,' he said, his words tight. 'I believe we create our own Karma, we can choose to create heaven, but we can also choose to create hell.' His face was white. The words, spoken so softly, held a kind of menace. He picked another leaf and shredded it vein by vein. Usually it felt serene down there, but it was as if a cold, thick cloud had descended. She heard a car approaching, walked off the bridge and led Ollie back on to the side to safety. By the time she returned, Alex was walking away.

'Bye then,' she called to his back, but he didn't reply,

'Blimey,' she said to Ollie. 'What was that all about? He said Kathleen was complicated but he's far from straightforward himself.' From the little she knew of Alex she'd assumed he was rather grey, dull. His reactions today showed she had been quite wrong. He hadn't shown surprise or even sympathy when she'd told him about Kathleen's fears. The one thing she had discovered now was that there was a lot more to Alex than she realised. Beth felt sure she needed to be careful of him.

When she returned home, Layla was in the kitchen and, before she had unclipped Ollie's lead, Layla spoke. 'About Friday, Mum.'

Beth groaned. 'What about it?'

'Elsa said we could get an earlier ferry.'

'Layla, I said no.'

Layla thumped down the cereal packet, sending Shreddies everywhere. Ollie was there in a flash, hoovering up any that had hit the floor.

'You are such a crap mother,' Layla said, and stormed out of the kitchen.

Beth looked down at Ollie. 'Crap mum today: great!'

She cleared the surfaces of Layla's mess, and then sat to eat her toast. Going into work wouldn't be so bad. She worked as a learning assistant in classes, sometimes supporting a child with special needs, and she loved it. The good thing about working in a school with young children was that once you were there you were in their bubble; the rest of the world ceased to exist.

Beth collected her things. She was looking forward to seeing Imogen at work, hoping they might have time to talk about Kathleen. Although quite different to her, Beth admired Imogen and had enjoyed looking after her daughter Elsa when she was little. She appreciated Imogen's pragmatic approach to life; as Adam would say, 'She cuts through the bullshit.'

As Beth walked down the road, she was aware that the world was carrying on as normal. She was later than usual and walked quickly, appreciating how fortunate she and Sami were to both be able to walk to work.

However, when she reached the community pub on the corner, she was distracted. Throwing a bowl of water down the steps was Gemma, one of a small team who ran the Hub. Wearing her usual polo shirt and jeans, Gemma, ten years younger than Beth, worked incredibly hard. She was a proper islander, with family everywhere.

'The Castleford Community Hub', as it was officially called, was originally called the Castle. It had closed and been bought by the community. The locals still called it the Castle, but everything else about it had changed. It had been a huge success, with a community room, a comfortable café-cum-eating area and a much smaller, modern 'adult only' area for alcoholic drinks.

'Hi Beth... glamorous life I lead—'

Beth approached Gemma and asked, unnecessarily she knew, 'You've heard about Kathleen?'

'Of course. I am so sorry. It was upsetting enough when she decided to move all the way to Freshwater—'

Beth nodded: the fifteen minute drive from Castleford to Freshwater would be nothing to people on the mainland, but she knew what Gemma was saying: here, it was like moving to a different country.

Beth crossed her arms. 'I went to see her new house on Sunday.'

'Ah, the new house,' said Gemma, distracted. 'Sounds amazing. A few people have been grumbling about it. Don't know how Patrick got planning permission. Still, I guess none of that matters now, does it? Do you know how Kathleen actually, you know, died? She fell off the cliff?'

'That's right. I don't think they know the details yet.'

'Poor Patrick and Conor. They must be devastated.'

Beth saw that Gemma was ready to settle down for a natter but heard the church clock chime nine. 'I'm ever so late. Sorry, I must go.'

'Are you still coming to yoga tonight?'

Beth blinked. She hadn't thought about it. 'Um, yes, OK. I suppose so. I'll see you there.'

'Good. See you later.'

The village of Castleford was large, dominated by the castle that looked down on them all. Having passed the Hub, Beth turned right and walked down the steep hill at the heart of the village. On her left was the small Norman church she went to early some Sunday mornings, and she regretted that there was no time today to go and sit in the silent, cool building. Funny, she wouldn't consider herself a particularly religious person; none of the rest of her family went, but that half hour early on a Sunday morning, sitting quietly, was her refuge. She guessed it had been the same for Kathleen.

Walking down the high street, Beth passed the hairdresser, shop and post office, all that remained now of the shops that had, when she arrived, included a butcher's and a large ironmonger's. There was a small unkempt lane leading to a disused chapel, and then the long white building that housed the surgery and pharmacy. At the end of this was a large car park, a fence and the school where Beth worked.

The staff car park was in front of the school and Imogen's red Golf was in its usual parking place.

Beth pushed open the door into the reception area. Imogen had worked her headteacher magic here. She had been determined the entrance would be neither a minimalist white gleaming hotel lobby nor a riot of primary colours with signs shouting implausible mottoes. Imogen was not one of the 'All you have to do is dream and you can do anything' school of thought. She worked incredibly hard, and her enthusiasm was infectious, both among the staff and children. The lobby was a calm space: creams and beiges, sofas, bookcase, tasteful displays of the children's work. The reception area was an arced wooden desk. Behind it sat June, quietly smiling as the phones rang and parents handed her letters. It was a space that aimed at least to make you slow your breathing. Beth could hear the noise from the hall where the staff from the early morning club were clearing up. June was smiling politely at a parent, who was saying in a loud voice, 'Is it true that I actually have to ask permission now to take my child out of school for the day?' Beth shot June a supportive smile and made her way to the reception class where she was to spend her morning.

'Sorry I'm late,' she mouthed to the teacher, Jo, who was desperately trying to tie up a conversation with an over anxious parent. Beth knew the mother better than Jo, who had only started in the school last year. She had three other children there. She was pleasant but also, Beth knew, going through another messy divorce. Beth took off her coat and went into the lobby to help children hanging up coats and backpacks, take messages from parents, and make sure book bags made it to the right drawers.

Finally, the children were all sitting on the mat for registration while Beth went to photocopy work sheets ready for literacy later.

The photocopier was in the staff room. As she went in, Beth saw Imogen going into her room, smiling professionally in a smart suit and black mules, white-blonde hair in a tidy bun. She always looked as immaculate at the end of the day as she did at the start.

They caught a glimpse of each other. Imogen grimaced: now was not the time to talk.

It was the usual hectic morning and Beth was glad of it in some way. It helped distract her from thinking about Kathleen. She was a lot more tired than usual, though, when it came to leaving at lunchtime. As she made her way through the lobby, Imogen emerged from her room, spotted Beth, and invited her in.

8

Imogen's room represented a continuation of the entrance area. There were calm creams, a large rug and comfy armchairs. Imogen's desk was to the side, with a laptop and files all neatly arranged. Imogen sat opposite Beth, upright in an armchair; legs crossed tightly.

'How are you?' Imogen's enquiry was made in a business-like tone that was surprisingly comforting.

'Numb. It's like watching myself in a film going through my day. It was such a shock, wasn't it?'

'It was. I know how you feel. By the way, William told me she was planning to leave the pharmacy. It couldn't have been because of the drive; it's only, what, fifteen minutes from here. Do you know why she was going?'

'I asked her about it on Sunday. Sami didn't understand why she'd given her notice in, but she didn't explain it to me either. Didn't she say anything to you? You two seemed pretty engrossed chatting when I arrived at the house party,' asked Beth.

Imogen re-crossed her legs and tapped her manicured nails on her knee. 'No. We only talked about the house, the lighting in the kitchen, that kind of thing.'

'Oh. It looked more intense than that.'

'Not really, although I thought Kathleen seemed a bit all over the place.'

'I agree. She said some odd things to me that evening, disturbing things.'

'Like what?'

Beth paused. She'd already broken her agreement with Sami once that morning, but it had actually been helpful in telling her things about Alex and his relationship with Kathleen. Maybe if she told Imogen she might learn something from her. 'Kathleen actually told me that someone there on Sunday had been threatening her.'

Imogen raised her eyebrows. 'Good grief. That *was* dramatic, even for Kathleen.'

Beth tried to be brave. 'I don't think she was saying it for effect.'

'But that's absurd,' said Imogen, waving her hand as if to brush the idea away, but then, almost casually, she asked, 'Did she say who?'

'No, nothing.'

'Well, I shouldn't take too much notice. Kathleen was inclined to exaggerate. I'd say she bordered on being a fantasist at times, and she was drinking a hell of a lot on Sunday.'

'I don't think she was drunk.'

Imogen sat back on her chair, but her body was rigid. 'I know you think I'm being a bit harsh, but Kathleen had become very difficult of late: rather attention-seeking, extremely needy.'

Beth frowned. 'I know Kathleen was often the centre of attention. With her looks and charm that was inevitable, but she was also warm, funny, kind. I wouldn't have called her needy.'

'Don't get me wrong. I liked Kathleen and she was a lot

brighter than most people gave her credit for. But I began to see a different side to her when we all went away last December.'

'When you went on that skiing weekend?'

'That's it. I've not said much to you about it, but it was such a disaster. It was a stupid time of year to go away but William said it would be good for me. I'd had that row with my parents. He said I needed to get away, but I regretted going.'

'Kathleen mentioned the holiday on Sunday, I don't think she enjoyed it either. She was saying what a terrible start to December she'd had. Of course, a few days before you went away, Kathleen had been with Alex's wife when she had that fall, she must have still been very stressed by that. By the way, who went away that weekend? I know it there was Kathleen and Patrick, you, William, and Elsa. Was there anyone else?'

'No, that's all.'

'I remember you didn't say much after it, and all I had was a text from Kathleen saying random things about Amy and not having a good time away. It didn't sound too good.'

'That's an understatement. It started with Kathleen in hysterics at the airport: you know Alex's wife had died when she was staying with her a few days before we went. Kathleen should have stayed at home, really. I think it was Patrick who persuaded her to come. Anyway, she calmed down a bit but then I had the fall down the steps of the restaurant a few hours after we'd arrived. I never even got out on the slopes. William, bless him, hung around and looked after me, but then Kathleen refused to go out as well, kept pouring her heart out to William. When we got back, she carried on ringing him at all hours. I don't know what had got into her, but it was driving me mad. William works so hard, and now doctors have to do these accessible hours appointments. Mondays and Fridays, surgery starts at quarter to eight, which means he gets into the office any time after six to keep on top of his paperwork so, you see, he didn't need work calls at home.'

Imogen finally paused for breath. Her face was red, her hands in tight fists.

'Did William tell you why Kathleen was phoning him all the time?'

'No, but I reckon she was just looking for attention from him. I told William it had to stop and things did improve. But I saw her differently after that. She wasn't quite as angelic as people thought.'

Beth was annoyed at this outpouring against her friend. 'I don't think you're being fair.'

Imogen raised an eyebrow. 'You're quite innocent, aren't you? You must have worried about her and Sami. Working together and then him getting her on that course so she could travel up to London once a month.'

'They travelled to London on the Tuesday and back on the Wednesday. That was all,' said Beth sharply. 'Kathleen's course at the academy was nothing to do with the one Sami was teaching on at King's. I know they were both up there overnight, but they never met up. He stayed at King's; she stayed at Alex's house.'

Imogen gave her a look, the one that bright people give when they have picked up on something. 'So you have thought about it, haven't you?' Beth could feel herself blushing as Imogen continued. 'Still, it was probably all perfectly innocent.'

Imogen stretched her legs in front of her. 'In any case, it's not right for us to sit here bitching after what's happened to poor Kathleen.'

Beth was about to point out that she hadn't been the one bitching when Imogen said, 'Elsa told me you went over to see Patrick and Conor yesterday. How was Patrick?'

'Heartbroken; in shock. You know, he asked me to go with him to identify the body up at the hospital.'

'That's grim. Well done you. I don't think I could have done that. You have a good heart, Beth.'

The phone rang on Imogen's desk and she reached over to answer it. 'They gave me their word they would deliver them by next Monday at the latest. Don't worry. I'll speak to them. I'll sort it out.' She replaced the receiver. 'Bloody contractors,' she mumbled, then put her hand on her back. She took a small packet out of her handbag. She swallowed some pills and replaced the packet in her bag.

'Your back still playing up from your fall?' asked Beth, wondering if that accounted for Imogen's touchiness.

'Yes. I told you, that skiing holiday was never meant to be.' Imogen sat back down, breathed deeply. 'Still, that's all in the past and, of course, it's nothing compared to what's happened now. Tell me about Kathleen. She fell on to the beach, didn't she? Do you know who found her?'

'It was a neighbour walking her dog.'

'Poor woman. After all those crime programmes, I swore I'd never have a dog. It's always the dog walker who finds the body. You know, when Patrick said on Sunday about her taking part of the fence down it sounded pretty reckless.'

'The police had all that end of the garden cordoned off when I went around.'

'They were bound to. Presumably they'll check no one went out there and pushed her off. There are some weird people around, you know. I'm always going on at Elsa not to wander off into the woods around us on her own. Having said that, I can't imagine they are seriously considering that for Kathleen. It must have been an accident.'

'They were asking me about her state of mind.'

'I suppose they have to check. William said the police talked to him yesterday evening. He told them he considered her vulnerable, but that she wasn't on antidepressants or anything.'

Beth noted that William was obviously a lot more relaxed

about breaking confidentiality than Sami was. Sami wouldn't tell her if someone had gone in to buy a pack of plasters.

Imogen continued. 'Personally, I would have said it was highly unlikely Kathleen took her own life. At the end of the day she had what she wanted: that house, Patrick totally besotted with her. Even her son had come back to live with her. The thing with someone like Kathleen was, she may have cried on everyone's shoulders, but she knew exactly how to get what she wanted.'

Beth grimaced. 'That's a bit tough. She'd had hard times. Her first husband treated her badly, and Patrick was so ill when they came over here. She was always there for him, and she was a good friend to me.'

Imogen rubbed her forehead. 'Of course. Sorry, I didn't mean it to sound like a criticism. What I meant was that Kathleen was a lot stronger and more determined than people gave her credit for.' She stifled a yawn. 'Sorry: not slept well since Ofsted.'

'Well done, by the way.'

'It went well, but it was exhausting, and now there's the changes to the SATs which the teachers blame on me. What with that and parents... the kids are the least of my worries. But anyway, sorry. I shouldn't have said those things about Kathleen.' She seemed to crumple back into her seat. 'I don't feel quite myself lately, don't feel quite on top of things. It's not like me to forget things, lose things.' She paused.

'Your job is enormously stressful,' said Beth, gently.

Imogen opened her mouth to speak but then pushed herself to sit more upright with her hands. 'No more stressful than a lot. I can obviously cope, but everyone gets a bit tired.'

'Of course,' said Beth. She glanced over at a few family photos on Imogen's desk.

'That's a lovely photograph of Elsa. She's getting to look more and more like you.'

'Patrick took it. He was showing Elsa different techniques for taking portraits. I loved this one, and so, surprisingly, did Elsa. She had a few prints taken.'

Beth looked at another photo. This was Imogen and William with Elsa, but also an older couple Beth had never met.

'Another one I've not seen,' she said. 'Is that your mum and dad?'

Imogen nodded briskly. 'Yes, a friend of my father's took it when we went over at Christmas. It worked out well, we patched a few things up.'

'It's good to have you all together. Layla told me they bought Elsa the car for her eighteenth last November.'

'That is what all the rows had been about. Our present had been paying for driving lessons. Anyway, my parents talked to William, said they wanted to buy Elsa a car. The first I knew about it was when William and Elsa picked one up from the garage.'

'They never told you?'

'Nope; they all kept it a secret from me, they knew I'd say no. I was so angry with them all, it was all I could do not to send the thing back. Anyway, eventually William talked me round and I let Elsa keep it. It goes against my better judgement, though.'

'I think you're quite capable of putting the brakes on when you want to.'

'Thank you,' said Imogen. 'But I've learned in five years of marriage that I need to make a few compromises. Elsa adores William, although he is inclined to spoil her. He just bought her a brand new phone and her other one was only a year old. I wonder what Kathleen's boy, Conor, will do now?'

'He either stays with Patrick and goes to college here in September or goes back to Ireland.'

Imogen shrugged. 'At least that would get him away from your Layla.'

Beth blinked. 'She's too young for him. He's had a lot more life experience than her. I don't want her hanging around with him.'

'I agree, but take it from me, don't let her know what you feel. If my parents hadn't been so dead against Elsa's father, I would never have gone off with him.' Imogen looked over at the photograph. 'They sent me to the most expensive boarding school, and I got pregnant by a chap from the local pub, a lorry driver with tattoos.'

Beth grinned. 'He couldn't be more of a contrast to William, a doctor, and weren't his parents some kind of old money? That would have impressed your parents.'

'That's right. Shame they are not still alive. Mum would have loved showing off about them. My father is hoping William will join his team sailing at Cowes this year.'

'Impressive.'

Imogen smiled, seeming more relaxed at last. 'Now, back to the present. Have you got that final unit in yet? You're going to miss the deadline for applications for teacher training this September.'

'I know, but I don't want to rush it.'

'No one can accuse you of that. You need to get on, get motivated.'

Imogen's phone rang again and she answered it. 'I think I need to speak to them. Hold on. I'll come out.'

Imogen turned back to Beth. 'Sorry.'

Beth stood up. 'It's OK.'

As they walked to the door Imogen said, 'I meant to ask you. Are you and the family free a week Sunday for lunch?'

'I think so.'

'Come around to us then. I thought it would be nice to have a get together for Alex, now he's here permanently. He must find that flat depressing after his beautiful London house.'

'Kathleen told me it was elegant. You and William stayed with him for a few nights earlier in the year, didn't you?'

'William, Elsa and I had a long weekend with him at New Year: me and Elsa shopping, William doing his social history research down in the East End. I thought Alex might enjoy some company, and we did find we had books in common, but he kept himself to himself; poor man was totally bereft. I've tried inviting him round since we came back, but he's something of an introvert, isn't he? He did invite us to his caravan over here once. He has an amazing pitch, just by the cliffs. Elsa was talking about doing some night-time photography out there and he very kindly said we were welcome to go out there when he wasn't using it, even gave us a spare key. We've never taken him up on that, but it was a kind thought.'

Beth moved to go, when Imogen touched her arm lightly.

'Beth, try to put Sunday evening out of your head. Remember the Kathleen you knew before that, eh?'

As Beth walked home, she considered how much had happened to Kathleen in December. She'd told Beth it was a terrible month. Of course, there had been the death of Alex's wife, the skiing holiday didn't sound much fun and then there was 'the big mistake'. Beth thought then about Imogen. The level of Imogen's bitterness towards Kathleen had shocked her. Was is possible William had had an affair with Kathleen? Beth dismissed it immediately: Kathleen would never do that, and no way would William be that stupid. Apart from the fact she was sure he loved Imogen; Kathleen was his patient: he could lose his job. Still, it had rattled Imogen. All that talk of Kathleen ringing William, being needy, no angel. Was that jealousy? Even if it was possible Imogen had been the person threatening Kathleen, what would Kathleen have known about Imogen? Imogen was the epitome of an upright citizen; harsh, self-righteous at times, but the last person you'd imagine having some terrible secret.

Beth remembered she'd promised to go to yoga that evening. Maybe she would get a chance to chat to Gemma. If anyone could fill her in on gossip, Gemma could.

9

That evening Beth went into the community room and tucked herself at the back of the class. She wore comfy jogging bottoms and a baggy t-shirt, nothing like the outfits of some of her friends. Kathleen was always in the latest gear but at least had never taken it too seriously. They'd both had a laugh when Gemma had added, 'and for those of you who would like to go a bit further—' She looked to the front, saw Gemma watching her, and was grateful for the knowing smile.

The session started. Beth found it good to have her mind taken up with the multitasking of yoga, remembering how to breathe as well as the positions she needed to try to do.

It was the end section that Beth and, she guessed, many others were waiting for. From the side of the room they all collected blankets. Some had even brought a pillow and a sleeping bag. Complete overkill as far as Beth was concerned, this wasn't a sleep over: it was a ten minute relaxation at the end of the class.

Beth picked up her cardigan and lay down on her mat. The rather depressing music had started. She lay back and let her mind drift to her safe place. A house stood among fields, there was a little black cat, Ollie, hens and a garden that miraculously looked after itself while she sat on her swing seat reading. It was while she was turning the page of her book that she was brought back to the present by the sound of a gently tinkling bell. Reluctantly, they all started to sit up. Gemma at the front bowed to them. 'Namaste,' she said. The class reciprocated and started to roll up their mats.

'Thanks, everyone. See you next Monday.'

Beth suddenly saw something glistening. She blinked, and then she saw her. More clearly than any person in the room, she saw Kathleen, who stood in front of Beth in that long white dress, pashmina round her shoulders. On her forehead was a gash, but her eyes told the same story of terror and dread she'd seen on Kathleen's face when she had left her the night before she died. Beth reached out, her hand shaking, but in an instant Kathleen was gone.

Beth's hands were shaking. She couldn't move her feet. Someone touched her arm.

'Are you all right?'

She blinked and saw Gemma. Her mouth trembled. 'I saw her—'

Gemma put her arm around Beth. 'Come and have a drink with me. It's quiet. They can get me if they need me.'

They went through to the small pub part of the Hub, which was as quiet as Gemma had said. Beth waited until Gemma returned with two large glasses of red wine.

'There you are,' she said. 'You thought you saw...?'

Beth picked up the glass, her hand still shaking slightly. 'Kathleen. I'm sorry. Honestly, I think I'm going insane. I've never had anything like that before, not even after Mum died. I don't believe in ghosts or anything. I know you do, but I never have.'

'But something happened. I saw your face.'

'I don't know. I don't understand.'

Gemma looked at her seriously. 'Do you think Kathleen was trying to tell you something?'

'She didn't speak but, apart from the gash on her head, she had that same look on her face that she had on Sunday.'

'And that was?'

Beth took a long sip of her wine. How to describe that look? 'Fear, terror.'

'Really? Whatever was the matter? I thought she'd have been over the moon celebrating her stunning new house.'

'She had other things on her mind. We had this heavy conversation.'

Gemma picked up her glass but before she took a sip she asked, 'Did she, um, did she mention a mistake she'd made?'

Beth grabbed the word. 'She did, but she wouldn't tell me what. Do you know what it was?'

Gemma shifted in her seat. 'Ah, I thought she'd told you.'

'No, but please tell me what it was.'

'I don't know. People talk to me here; a few pints and they tend to open up, a bit like a confessional. I don't repeat much.'

'But if it's about Kathleen I need to know. Please. I'm desperate.'

Gemma took a deep breath. 'OK.'

Beth waited.

'It must have been around New Year. Kathleen was in here with Patrick for a meal. She walked past me to the toilets; she looked pretty upset. When she didn't reappear for a while, I went in to see if she was all right. I found her in a right state, crying hysterically. She grabbed my arm and started to ramble on, about being her fault, what a mess... Well, I made an educated guess and asked her if it was a man, and it was like the flood gates opened.'

'A man?'

Gemma nodded. 'She said she'd slept with some man a few weeks before Christmas, but it was a terrible mistake.'

'Kathleen had an affair!' Beth sat back, her mouth open.

'I wouldn't call it an affair, more like a one night stand by the sound of it.'

'But all the same – are you sure she meant it? She could have just been drunk—'

'I don't think she was that drunk, to be honest. No, she was serious. She came in the next day, told me she'd been talking rubbish, but she knew what she'd said and had meant it. She'd never so much as hinted to you about it?'

'We'd not talked for a while. As you know, she'd stopped coming to yoga. I can't believe it.'

Gemma paused, then said, 'Is it really that unbelievable that someone like Kathleen had a fling? It didn't surprise me at all. I think she was pretty insecure and could have been looking for someone to reassure her.'

'But Kathleen had always told me how much she disapproved of any kind of infidelity, she called it a grave sin. I guess that was her Catholic upbringing. Anyway, why would she be insecure? Patrick adored her. Look at all those photos of her at their house: she was stunning.'

'But when I visited the old house, the pictures I saw, and there were loads and they were huge, they were all of Kathleen years ago. If I was Kathleen, I'd feel that was the me he loved, and the pressure to stay like that would be soul destroying. No, if she found someone who told her how lovely she looked now, someone who made her feel good just as she was, well, she might have liked that.'

'But she saw it as a mistake?'

'I think she was deeply ashamed of what she did. I am sure she didn't love the man, or I suppose he could have also been married?'

'Have you any idea who it was?'

'Nope. I assumed it was someone at the academy in London.'

'And do you think Patrick had any idea?'

Gemma rubbed her lips together. 'I don't think so, but he was extra attentive after that visit. But I could have imagined that. I get bored sometimes and weave these intricate stories in my head about the people in here,' said Gemma, smiling.

Beth sat twisting her wedding ring on her finger. This must be the mistake Kathleen had been talking about. Gemma's explanation of someone at the academy made sense. So, who would have known? Who used it to have a hold over her?

'You look ever so upset,' said Gemma, suddenly serious. 'Sorry, I shouldn't have told you. Don't let it spoil your memory of her. It was a mistake, that's all. She told me how much she loved Patrick. Even if he did suspect something, all he wanted was to make their marriage work. These things happen in marriages.'

Beth sipped her wine. 'It's all right. I'm glad you told me. It's like I'm trying to put together the pieces of the puzzle of what Kathleen said to me on Sunday, and I think this must be part of what was worrying her.'

She felt Gemma scrutinising her, as if she was trying to work her out. 'Did Kathleen say anything else to you?'

Beth glanced around. There was no point in holding back now. The pub was nearly empty, but she lowered her voice. 'It's complicated. Kathleen told me someone was using this mistake, presumably the affair, to kind of blackmail her. Not for money but to stop Kathleen telling people about something she knew about them.'

'My God! Who was it?'

'I don't know, she was too scared to tell me names. What Kathleen also told me on Sunday was that she'd informed this person that she wasn't going to hide things any more. She was very scared of this person but had decided she was going to expose them. Obviously, she was prepared for them to tell the world about her affair.'

'How did the person react?'

'They were very angry. Kathleen was scared witless as to what this person might do, but she was determined, with my help, to have everything out in the open.'

'She told you all this on Sunday evening?'

'That's right.'

'And the next morning she died?' said Gemma. 'Do they know yet exactly what happened that morning?'

'It's early days. It looks like Kathleen was down the garden doing her mindfulness. She'd taken a part of the fence away. For some reason the hens got out. She was trying to stop them running over the cliff and fell herself.'

'So, it looks like an accident?'

'I think so. The police were looking for signs of anyone else down there, but they said so far, they'd not found anything. Also, they've asked about her state of mind. I don't think there's an indication of her taking her own life.'

'I see. Is there anything you know of that might suggest it wasn't an accident?'

'There are one or two things, but I don't know if they really mean anything. Take the hens. Kathleen told me she would never let the hens out until a proper fence was up, so how did they get out? Then there's Kathleen's phone. The police can't find it or the headphones she used to listen to her mindfulness app on.'

'Have you told the police about what Kathleen told you?'

Beth looked down. 'I don't think I should.'

'Why ever not?'

'Sami told me to keep it to myself. He thinks as her death was most likely accidental, anything she said on Sunday evening should be kept private. He thinks it could upset people.'

'But surely the police should know if someone was threatening her?'

'The thing is, she didn't give me any names or details and Sami said she was very emotional, not everything she said could be trusted—' Beth hesitated, glanced around and lowered her voice again. 'And there is another problem. You see, Kathleen claimed that this person who was threatening her was one of the people there at the house party on Sunday. We were a small group; they're respected people, my friends. I can't go around accusing people like that to the police without any evidence, can I?'

'Who was at the party?'

'Oh, just me and the family, Patrick and Kathleen, Conor, of course, and then Imogen, William and Elsa. Oh, and Alex.'

'I see what you mean. None of them seems the sort to be going around threatening people.'

'Exactly.'

Gemma grinned. 'I know Imogen pretty well: scary kind of woman, but, no seriously, she's a good head, cares a lot about her job, and she's certainly licked that school into shape. Elsa is working here now so I am getting to know her better.'

'And how do you find her?'

'She's not bad. Flirts too much, but she's obviously bright, gets on with it. William, now, I don't know much about him, what can you tell me?'

Beth smiled as she saw Gemma sit forward.

Beth spoke again. 'Well, you know about five years ago, he met Imogen and they got married quickly. I'd never imagined Imogen marrying but I guess when you are older you know your own mind better.'

'He's very good looking and a great doctor according to everyone who talks to me. He picked up on my uncle's problems and got him in to see a consultant within two weeks. That must be a miracle, in anyone's book. William lived in London before, didn't he?' asked Gemma.

'Yes, Imogen told me he was married up there to what she described as a "Made in Chelsea" kind of girl. According to Imogen, this woman thought it would be romantic to be married to a doctor, but it turned out not to be. William was very unhappy, let her have everything when they divorced, just wanted to get away.'

'Blimey. Stupid girl, throwing someone like him overboard.'

'I know, but still I think Imogen is a perfect match for him and actually her background is pretty similar to his.' Beth paused, having got lost in the story. 'Anyway, William and Imogen were at Kathleen's on Sunday, but I can't imagine a more upright pair, can you?'

'No, and Alex seems nice. He's been in a few times to eat. I feel sorry for him; not very talkative, but very polite.'

'Of course, they are all good people; they are my friends, and yet—'

'Yes?'

'I believe Kathleen.'

'But you don't you have any idea who it could be?'

'No. Kathleen said they were hiding this side of themselves, playing a part—'

'She didn't give you much to go on, did she?' said Gemma.

'She was too scared to tell me their name.'

'You could see if you can find out a bit more and then go to the police if you have anything definite to tell them.'

'I agree, and, despite what Sami said, I've started to tell people what Kathleen told me, see how they react, see if they can tell me anything, but I have to be careful. I don't want to offend my friends —' Beth sipped her wine. 'I know what it's like to be isolated, to be rejected by friends. It's the worst feeling.'

'No one is going to fall out with you. I think you'll be the politest inquisitor ever.' The smile melted into something more sober. 'I think you need to do this, but you will be careful, won't you? If you're right, you do realise what this person could have done and it's more than a few threatening words.'

Beth shuddered, sat forward, crossed her arms tight. 'I've been too scared to think too much about that, but it has to be possible that this person drove over to Kathleen's on Monday morning and decided to silence her once and for all. The thing is, for Kathleen's sake I ought to try and find out what happened, I owe her that. But I'm scared, Gemma, and have no idea how I am going to do it.'

Gemma leant forward and tapped her knee. 'Kathleen has faith in you; that's why she came to you. You can do this but be careful now. Be very careful.'

10

Beth lay in bed alone that night wishing Sami was home. Normally it didn't worry her when he was in London, but tonight when she returned from yoga she was on edge. She'd even found herself double-checking the back door and windows, and had felt uneasy when she went out to shut the shed up for the night. Maybe it was drinking too much red wine, but she knew that wasn't really what was unnerving her. It was saying those words, admitting that a friend may have killed Kathleen. Kathleen said they hid in the shadows. Beth felt that tonight: they were here, listening to her, watching her.

She shivered, got out of bed, and went downstairs. Ollie wagged his tail at the sight of company, and she gave him a treat. After finding her book, they went and curled up on the sofa unit. Together, they fell asleep.

Over the following days, whenever Beth tried to think about Kathleen's fears or her death, she felt only despair. She got nowhere, just frustrated and confused. In the end she decided the only thing to do was to try to step away from it for a day or two. And so Beth went automatically about her routines and her work.

Layla mooched about, not speaking to her, but she silently conformed. Each morning she slammed the front door. Beth was glad she didn't have to teach her.

On Friday evening Sami had arranged for them to go out for a meal at the Hub with Alex. Beth was glad of an evening away from the house. It would be good to have a normal evening with Alex and get to know him better. Of course, he had been there at the house party, and it was possible he was the one who Kathleen had been talking about, but it didn't seem likely. He had had little to do with Kathleen and he didn't seem the sort to be hiding any dark secrets.

Beth made an extra effort getting ready. When she'd married Sami, his mother had given her the traditional gift of gold in the form of a necklace and earrings. Beth kept the deep yellow twenty-two carat gold for special occasions, and tonight felt a good time to wear it. She added a smattering of makeup. As she looked in the mirror, she decided her face was probably ageing slightly better than the rest of her. If she smiled right and had just brushed her hair she looked quite pretty; the rest of her body had slipped a few sizes up, but she had given up worrying. She had done the slimming club thing, followed the new shiny diet for a week or two, lost a few pounds, but quickly got bored. It then became a game of simply starving herself the day before she went to be weighed, and the day she realised all she was doing was paying someone to weigh her, she quit.

As they walked to the pub, Beth guessed that most people would be with family or in a couple; it couldn't be easy for Alex. It was the position Patrick was in now; maybe they would become friends. She quickly dismissed that idea. Patrick was fighting middle age. Alex looked like a man who'd been waiting for it from his teens. His hair was cut in an old-fashioned way and the jumper was a size up to be comfortable.

When they arrived, Alex was sitting with a bottle of red wine.

He gave a thin smile as he saw them. When they sat down, he said, 'I ordered a bottle. I know you don't drink, Sami, but I think Beth does?' He looked at her nervously. Sami gave Beth a quick sideways look. Having been brought up as a Muslim in a family that never touched alcohol, he still found her drinking difficult.

'That's perfect, thank you,' she said.

The restaurant area was decorated in lemon and white, wooden bookcases stacked with books for all ages and games. It was homely and relaxing in the daytime. For the evening, the games were hidden away, and subdued lighting and candles gave a more 'bistro' feel.

Sami, looking down the menu said, 'How about a shared Mezze? That's tonight's special.'

'Fine with me,' said Alex.

'And me,' said Beth.

Beth saw Imogen's daughter, Elsa, approach them. 'Gemma told me you were working here.'

Elsa grinned. 'Mum thinks it's good for me.'

They ordered, then Beth asked Alex, 'How are you settling into the flat?'

'I shall start house hunting soon, but it's not easy.'

'I can imagine. Had Amy ever been to the island?'

He smiled. 'She came once. I bought a caravan over here, hoped she'd come down more often, but she wasn't well enough. The time we came we went to a silversmith and I bought her a pendant. She loved jewellery.'

'Kathleen told me. Of course, Amy gave her the butterfly necklace; very pretty.'

'Yes. It was very valuable, but I saw Kathleen wore it every day.'

'The butterfly necklace was real diamonds? Good grief. I'd assumed it was dress jewellery. I know Patrick did. They, er, they asked him at the mortuary.'

She saw Alex flinch, and immediately regretted mentioning the mortuary. Alex fiddled with the single bud flower in the vase but must have pinched it too hard as the bud fell off in his hand. She saw the hurt in his eyes, pain still raw.

'How did you find the police yesterday?' Sami asked, with a swift change of subject.

'It was OK. They were with you much longer.'

'They mainly asked me about Kathleen's work, how she got on with people, that kind of thing. Mind you, they did ask me a few questions about where I'd been the morning she died. Silly, but I found it unnerving.'

'You didn't say the police went to talk to you, Sami,' said Beth.

'It was nothing. I told them I was out running up at the Hendersons'.' He looked back at Alex. 'Did they ask you that kind of thing?'

Alex put his head to one side. 'Yes, it seemed odd. I asked them why they wanted to know.'

Beth's mind was running on; the police were asking questions. No one was simply taking Kathleen's death as accidental.

'Did they give a reason?' asked Beth.

'Said it was just procedure.'

'So, where were you?'

'At the caravan I mentioned. I went off early cycling.'

'It's odd, isn't it, them asking that,' said Beth.

'I expect they were ruling us out of their enquiries,' said Sami, laughing, trying to lighten the mood. Beth noticed Alex was refilling his glass. He held the bottle up questioningly and she held out her glass.

'I didn't know whether to mention about Kathleen being ill last Tuesday,' Alex said to Sami.

'It was nothing,' he mumbled.

'But she was in hospital,' said Alex.

'I didn't realise you knew,' said Sami. Beth tried to read the silent messages Sami was sending Alex.

'She sent me a text on the Wednesday, just letting me know she hadn't stayed at my house the night before. I was concerned, relieved when she told me you were missing lectures to travel back with her, and you stayed the night before with her. That was very kind.'

Beth's eyes darted between the two men, then her gaze settled on Sami. 'I didn't know Kathleen had been ill, or that you'd been with her.'

'I forgot. It was nothing. She just asked me to go around and be with her at the hospital.'

'So, you didn't stay at Kings College on the Tuesday night?'

'No, um, not that night.'

'What was the matter with her?'

'It was precautionary. She'd had a panic attack, but her heart was racing. They wanted to keep an eye on her. I went over. They were just being careful: let her out the next morning.'

'You said you were back early because your students had exams. You never told me about Kathleen,' said Beth.

'No. She asked me not to say anything.'

This was followed inevitably by an awkward silence, which Sami chose to break.

'I hope you won't miss London too much. It's pretty quiet down here,' he said to Alex.

'I'm trying to settle, so I haven't been back yet.'

Their food arrived; a huge variety of dishes: baba ghanoush; hummus; stuffed grape leaves; olives; goat's cheese; brined roasted peppers and tzatziki, but Beth wasn't hungry. Always one to avoid a scene, she didn't feel she could ask Sami for an explanation in Alex's company. It felt like trying to discuss the weather when a hand grenade has been thrown into the room.

'This looks good,' said Alex, apparently oblivious to the tension at the table.

Beth felt sorry for him. They had invited him here; he was their guest. 'It does,' she said. 'So, I hear you enjoy cycling? Didn't Sami say you sometimes do charity rides? Which charity do you support?'

'One for people with mental trauma after a car accident like Amy. It's small but very effective.'

'You raise money for them with your online business as well, don't you?' said Sami. 'Selling coins, collectables; you were saying you can make a lot of money online—'

'How interesting,' said Beth.

'Not everyone says that,' he said, a gentle smile on his lips showing a hidden sense of humour. 'I'm afraid it's in the blood. It was my father's life.'

At that moment Gemma came in. To Beth's surprise, Gemma leant down and gave Alex a hug. He blushed, but didn't seem to mind.

'This man is the reason for our rise in profits,' said Gemma, smiling.

Alex grinned, and the lines of pain for a moment seemed to drop away. 'My secret is out.'

'We enjoy a catch up now, don't we?' said Gemma, smiling at him. 'We are so lucky to have you and Sami at the pharmacy. It's going to be the go-to place on the island.'

Beth pointed with her fork to her barely touched food. 'This is fantastic.'

'I'll tell the chef. We've had him a few months. He's great. I need to keep him a secret from the rest of the island restaurants, don't want him getting poached.' Gemma grinned at Beth and looked around. 'This has all been so much more successful than we expected. I think we're going to need to take on another person to take care of the community room side of things. It's not being used anything like as much as it should be.' Looking back at Alex she said, 'Now, you persuade this chap to find a house in Castleford. I don't want to be losing one of my best customers.'

Sami looked over his glasses at Alex. 'You be careful what you tell Gemma. She's more effective than the *County Press* at spreading the news.' If Sami had smiled it would have helped, but he went back to eating his meal.

Beth laughed, but she was annoyed with Sami. Why spoil the one moment when Alex seemed to relax? However, Gemma ignored him. 'By the way, do you still want your table here tomorrow evening for St Patrick's night? I didn't know, given the circumstances, if you wanted to cancel. Please don't worry about it.'

'Oh, sorry,' said Beth. 'I'd forgotten but, thinking about it, I think we should keep the table. I'll let people know and it's up to them then if they want to come. I don't expect Patrick will, of course, but I think it's a way of remembering Kathleen. She loved it.'

'That's fine with us,' said Gemma.

'Alex, if you fancy coming here two days running, we'll be here about half seven,' said Sami.

'Thank you. No cooking two nights running: suits me.'

'I'll leave you to eat. See you all tomorrow, then,' said Gemma, and left.

Sami leant forward. 'I am very grateful for the work you put in on Saturday. Is everything OK?' he asked Alex quietly.

Beth sensed work talk coming on and concentrated on choosing from the dishes and then looked around. The restaurant was comfortably full. She was pleased for Gemma: they needed numbers like this.

'Has Sami told you about all our plans?' Alex asked Beth.

'He was telling me about your plan to expand the online side of the business.'

'We want our pharmacies to grow.'

'Pharmacies?'

Alex nodded earnestly. 'Well, one step at a time.' Beth saw the light burning in Alex's eyes, and Sami joined in.

'When Alex moves out of his flat, we are going to redesign the space up there for consulting rooms.'

'Will the doctors feel you are stealing their jobs?'

'Not at all. It lightens their load, improves the provision for their patients.'

They continued eating. Sami talked about the pharmacy until Alex turned to Beth and asked, 'Didn't Sami mention you are doing a degree?'

'Yes, online. I'm doing it in modules. It means I can go at my own pace.'

'That's interesting,' said Alex.

'She could do with some pressure, get that final assignment in. Beth's going to be a teacher one day. I'm so proud of her.' Sami turned, and patted her hand, adding, 'and her dad would have been as well.' Sami smiled at Beth. 'She doesn't talk about her father much, but he was a very clever man, an English lecturer in an American university.'

Beth gave him a glare, but Sami said, 'It's good to remember him, love. I know it was wrong of him to leave you, but he sounded such an interesting man and I'm sure he'd have been so proud of you.'

'Do you have to do a thesis?' asked Alex.

'They call it an extended essay, but yes. I'm doing it on literary connections to the island. People have no idea how many writers have links here. Obviously, there is Tennyson, then Lewis Carroll, Edward Lear, Charles Kingsley. Queen Victoria kept a diary here. Enid Blyton stayed here. It goes on. In fact, I think I've made it too broad. I might start again and concentrate on Tennyson.'

Alex sat forward and surprised her by saying, 'I would love to read it when you finish it. It sounds fascinating. I love poetry, all kind of reading actually. Imogen and I swap novels, usually crime.'

'Imogen said you discovered you both loved to read.'

'Yes. Her and William came to stay with me after Christmas.

They wanted to see some of London. I needed company. I was in a very dark place then, having only just lost Amy. Imogen and I discovered we both liked reading and she helped me get back into books. It was a real help, an escape I guess.'

'I can understand that. Sami, on the other hand, only reads medical books. So, what are you reading now?'

Beth wasn't sure if it was the wine, but Alex seemed genuinely interested and they carried on chatting about books. Sami, she noticed, was very quiet.

They ordered pudding and then left the pub as soon as they had finished.

As they walked up the street Beth was burning with questions. To think Sami had lied to her was so shocking: he never lied. But then he'd explained it all, hadn't he? Was she over-reacting? She had to say something, but she and Sami didn't do rows. She'd joked they could easily ignore a whole room full of elephants if necessary.

When they got in, Sami and Beth started to go through the usual night-time routines, both knowing their roles but also knowing they were avoiding talking. Sami let Ollie out in the back garden. Beth tidied the kitchen. Ollie came back in and sat on his bed waiting for his treat before he was left for the night.

Sami was pouring himself a large glass of water, and Beth knew they could easily go to bed with nothing sorted, but she'd never be able to sleep. So she coughed, and started awkwardly. 'I think you should have told me about Kathleen being in hospital. When you said she was emotional, was it something to do with that?'

'Kathleen went in for observations after a panic attack. That's all. Her heart had been racing most of the day. They wanted to monitor it.'

'But why didn't you tell me?'

'Kathleen didn't want anyone to know she'd stayed in hospital. You know how people over-react.'

'So, I am just "people", am I?'

'Of course not, but she asked me not to say anything to anyone, not even Patrick, so please don't mention it to him.'

Sami opened the cake tin and nibbled at a Welsh cake.

Beth pursed her lips. 'I've asked you where you were last Tuesday evening. You let me believe you'd stayed at King's, and now I find out you were at the hospital with Kathleen. You lied to me. You told me you came back early because the students had an exam.'

'Look, I admit I didn't tell you the truth, but I was protecting Kathleen. If you like it was a lie for the greater good, a white lie.'

Beth understood his reasoning more than he realised. It was how she often justified keeping her own secret to herself, telling the lies she did to Sami. But deep down she knew it was not all about others: it was to protect herself, to avoid being looked down on, rejected, even by Sami.

Beth looked at her husband. The problem was working out if he had been lying purely to protect Kathleen or if there was some other, darker reason. That was what was really tearing at her, but she didn't have the courage to go there. Instead she took a different path.

'I can just about accept you were trying to protect Kathleen, but in the light of what's happened, I think you should have told me. I mean, why did she have this massive panic attack?'

'It was just one of those things, the move and everything getting on top of her. It was nothing to do with her death; it was personal. She had her reasons for wanting things kept private and I respected that.'

'But for God's sake, Sami, she's dead now and none of us know why she died.'

'The police will find out what happened. It was most likely an accident.'

'_ _ those things she told me on Sunday, I can't just click my fingers and magic them away. I don't want to. I've already started to find out things about Kathleen I never knew. They may not be important as to why she died, but I've a feeling they may be. Gemma understood why I've been asking questions; she doesn't think I should stop.'

Sami's eyes widened in alarm. 'What have you been saying to Gemma?'

'I only told her what Kathleen had said to me on Sunday evening.'

'For goodness sake, of all the people to tell it to! It'll be all over the island by tomorrow.'

'No. You underestimate Gemma. She has a lot of insight, and I needed to talk to someone who wasn't going to dismiss everything I say like you and Imogen do.'

'You talked to Imogen about it as well?'

'Well—'

'For goodness sake, Beth!'

Beth stood upright, crossed her arms. 'I only said what had happened. That is all. And you know – I'm not sorry. I know it involves our friends, but I am trying to be brave and face it.'

Sami came close to her. 'You can't go around casting aspersions about our friends. The police pick up on these things. Look at them questioning me and Alex about what we'd been doing on Monday morning. They probably did that because you said Kathleen thought she'd upset one of us. It's dangerous to go spreading gossip. You have to be careful when police are involved.'

'I was very careful, but I have a right to talk to my friends about what I'm worried about, and I am still very anxious about Kathleen.'

'This is not about what you think you need. It's about not offending our friends and, even more importantly, Patrick and Conor. They need protecting from rumours and speculation that will hurt them.'

Beth clenched her fists in frustration. 'You talk as if I am enjoying all this, but I hate the whole thing. I want to ignore it all, but how can I? I believe Kathleen was being intimidated by one of our friends. I don't want that to be the case, but it is. Gemma made me realise nothing is as simple as I want it to be.'

'What did she say?'

Beth swallowed hard. 'She told me that Kathleen had an affair.'

Sami coughed, as if choking on his biscuit, grabbed his glass of water and sipped it, before asking, 'Where the hell did she get that idea?'

'Gemma told me she'd found Kathleen crying in the toilet one evening. Kathleen was going on about some man and how it had all been a terrible mistake.'

'A combination of Kathleen drunk and Gemma's gossip: that's a very reliable basis for a story!'

'Gemma was sure Kathleen was serious.'

'That's ridiculous. I don't know where she got that from. You mustn't go around saying this to anyone.'

Beth held her fist in the air. She never thumped or hit things, but she was desperate to do so. 'You keep telling me what to do, what not to do. If you would trust me, talk to me, it would stop my mind running away with me.'

Sami shook his head. 'You need to control yourself, stop playing games. I need to go to bed. My head is thumping.'

He stormed off and Beth stood very still, staring at the table. Why was Sami so angry with her? Why wouldn't he talk to her?

She went over to the window, and she allowed the dark thoughts out into the light. People joked about it; she had laughed it off, but it never went away. Sami and Kathleen. No, Kathleen's affair had been with someone on her course. But the thought boomeranged back. Gemma had only been guessing. It could be someone much closer to home. 'Innocent', Imogen called her. What if Kathleen had never been in hospital, and they'd been in some fancy hotel room? Beth felt her throat constrict; her heart was pounding. It couldn't be, could it? Sami wasn't the type. She stopped. How many women had thought that before they'd found out their husband was being unfaithful?

* * *

Alex had returned to his flat. Coming back after a night with people was always the time he felt most alone. He had taken his key out of the old filing cabinet drawer on the landing and let himself in. The flat was very tidy. He had hung up pictures, but still it felt cold and lonely. Alex went into the kitchen and poured himself a glass of whisky: one more drink wouldn't hurt.

Slumping into his armchair, he thought about Beth. He could see Kathleen's death was playing on her mind. When he'd met her that day at the ford and again tonight, he'd seen the intensity with which she talked about Kathleen. What exactly had Kathleen been saying the night before she died?

Alex picked up his wedding photograph that always stood on the table next to his chair. That had been an incredible day, one that made him fully realise the new world he had entered. He'd not grown up in a wealthy family. Concepts like 'money is no object', and 'only the best will do', were foreign to him. And it wasn't just money: it was taste. Fortunately, when it came to the wedding, all he'd had to do was turn up, wear the clothes picked out for him, read the speech that had been gone through by Amy and the family. He'd wondered if it was like that for royalty when they attended something as a guest of honour. The one thing he had done was buy that butterfly necklace and earrings for Amy. He had used his savings, had had to sell some of the most valuable coins his father had left, to afford them. He had been shocked when Amy gave the necklace away. He tried to tell himself it was

Amy's way of thanking Kathleen, but at the very least it had been an uncharacteristically insensitive thing to do.

Kathleen had come into both their lives as something warm, something soft in a hard world during a hard, dark time. Amy had been slowly, physically and mentally, crumbling. She became more and more dependent, and he had been exhausted, never able to relax. When he went to work, despite having carers in for Amy, he felt he should be home. Giving up his practice had been devastating, but he had made his reputation and had made sure he was doing locum work in the right places. However, he couldn't go on courses, attend lectures, be seen in the right places. Wherever he was, he was always waiting, watching, checking his phone. There were all the near misses, the accidents, forgetting to turn off taps, ovens, to lock doors. He'd tried everything to make Amy's life accident proof: he organised her clothes, her medication, everything. His escape each week had been coming here to the island to cover for Sami, his Tuesday night here in the flat an oasis. His one night off when someone else cared for Amy, once a month, that person being Kathleen. He'd been so grateful, but it was more than that. He knew he looked forward to the times Kathleen worked with him too much.

However, like he had said to Beth, Kathleen was complicated. There had been a side to her he could never have imagined. He saw it too late. He felt the anger bubble up inside him, burning his stomach, his throat. He stumbled to the kitchen, and refilled his glass.

11

Beth was woken by Sami, already dressed in running gear.

'I'm off.' He paused, then sat on the edge of the bed. 'Look, I'm sorry about last night. I shouldn't have snapped at you. Everything has got on top of me lately.'

'You're out early?' she said, not smiling.

'Lots to do. Adam is coming into work today, by the way. If he was awake, I'd have taken him up to the Hendersons'. The grass is so long, I need to mow it.'

It was a relief when Sami left. Beth opened the curtains, let the light in, but it didn't let anything even close to happiness in with it. She had slept badly, throwing around the questions about Sami. She would allow anger and despair to take turns as she allowed for the possibility of her husband having an affair with her best friend, but before she could go over that edge a voice would hold her back. What if she was wrong? Then she felt guilty for even contemplating such a thing.

Some women she knew would have already confronted their husband, demanded the truth, but that wasn't Beth's way. In any case, even to question someone's fidelity was a massive step. Even if they could prove they'd done nothing, surely your relationship would never be quite the same again?

Beth was greeted as always downstairs by Ollie wagging his tail and asking for fuss. Leaning down she stroked him, trying to catch his enthusiasm for a new day. 'At least you're pleased to see me,' she said, and smiled at him.

She checked her phone. There was a message from Patrick.

Would you be able to come over some time to help sort out some of Kathleen's clothes?

She groaned. Not today. Of all the things to do. Then she stopped: that wasn't fair. Patrick was suffering heartbreak. If this is what he needed help with today, what right had she to say no? She replied that she was free later that day, and it was arranged that she would go in the afternoon.

Layla came into the kitchen.

'We'll leave about half eight?' said Beth.

Layla didn't answer. They were back into the row about Layla not being allowed out the night before to see Conor's band. Elsa had probably been texting Layla about it, winding her up.

'I could make pancakes or something.'

'Don't bother,' said Layla as she stormed out.

Beth knew some people thought you could let these rebuffs float past you, that you could rationalise that 'this is the way teenagers are', but just because she didn't shout back didn't mean she didn't feel angry and hurt.

Beth went out and fed the guinea pigs, mumbling, 'Remember the day you came home, Layla said "Mum, I promise you, you will never ever have to clean or feed them." Great, eh? It's a good job I never believed her. Maybe even a crap mother has her uses.'

Beth could see Ollie waiting for his walk. 'You have a treat this morning. We'll take Layla to her exam and then me and you will go up Mottistone Down.'

She had breakfast and showered, then knocked on Adam's bedroom door.

'I'm taking Layla to her exams soon. Have a good day at the pharmacy. Don't forget it's the St Patrick's meal tonight.'

'That again?'

'You don't have to come, but—'

'It's all right. I'll probably come.'

They were about to leave when Sami returned. He'd bought a copy of the local paper but put it on the table still folded. They both ignored it.

'I'm taking Layla in a minute. Patrick has asked me to go and help sort out Kathleen's things.'

'OK. Good luck with that.'

Sami disappeared upstairs. Anxiously, Beth looked at the time. Layla stomped down the stairs.

They drove in silence to Freshwater and reached the end of the road where Layla's flute teacher lived and where the flute and singing exams would take place.

'Drop me here,' said Layla.

Beth pulled in and Layla got out. 'Good luck,' she called, but Layla turned and said, 'Don't wait. I'll get the bus back,' and walked away.

Beth gripped the steering wheel in irritation. Fine, Layla could get the bus. There was only one every hour or so, so she would have to wait.

'Come on, Ollie. Let's go. Hopefully, she will be in a better mood later.'

Beth took Ollie up on to Mottistone Down. She hadn't been up there for a while. The fresh air and wonderful views welcomed her like a warm blanket. It was a bright spring day. In the distance the sea was dark blue, the sky clear above it. Opposite, she could see the woods, and even from here she could hear the woodpeckers, the pheasants. There was no one else up there and so she let Ollie off the lead. Nose down, he dashed around, gathering the smells. Beth stopped and watched a kestrel, hovering, wondering how it stayed so still in the winds, then saw it dive, arrow shaped, into the long grass.

Up here she could breathe. Her mother's house had been on the outskirts of Swansea, well inland from the sea, but at the same time it never felt as if the sea was far away. The house had originally been the farmhouse of her mother's parents. Beth's early years had been idyllic. As she walked, she realised it was a time of her life she often forgot. It was hard to get past things that happened in her teens, but up here on the downs she sometimes felt in touch with it again.

However, today nothing could push away her anxieties about Sami. He was such a straightforward person. In a world of nuance and greys he had always been her rock. Or so she had thought.

Was sleeping with Sami Kathleen's 'big mistake'? Had Sami loved Kathleen? Had he slept with her because she was prettier, thinner, more seductive, than Beth? But Kathleen said she'd regretted the fling: that would mean she hadn't wanted to leave Patrick. Sami may have loved her, but he'd have discovered that she didn't feel the same.

Now, of course, if Kathleen had said she was going to confess all to Patrick, if Sami's infidelity had been made public, that confession could mean the end of her marriage, of Sami's reputation in the village, his parents' approval. He would lose everything and not even have Kathleen. How far would he go to prevent Kathleen ruining his life? Had Sami been playing the part of a happily married man all these years?

The brash bleating of lambs in a distant field temporarily distracted Beth, and as her mind was dragged back to her thoughts about Sami, she frantically tried to find a sense of perspective. She had to remind herself of the Sami she knew. He was not a violent, cruel man. Surely, whatever Kathleen said, it was impossible to live with someone for eighteen years and have them completely wrong?

Beth looked around for Ollie. 'Come on. Enough of this. Let's get on.' She attached his lead, returned to the car and then took Ollie home. The house was still: no sign of Layla. Beth tried ringing her but there was no answer, so she sent a text.

Hope the exams went well. I am going over to help Patrick this afternoon. See you later. Mum x

As she sent it, she thought again of the effect of Sami having had an affair on the children, her home. She swallowed the lump of emotion in her throat. No. She couldn't go there: not again, not now.

The rest of the morning flittered away, questions still rushing around in her head, each shouting for attention.

Later that day Beth drove over to Patrick's. She rang the bell but no one answered. Beth didn't know what to do. It was very isolated out there, and different to the rural quiet Beth had grown up in. In the daytime there had been the sounds of farm animals, tractors; somewhere someone could be seen in the distance, working, walking their dog; but this was different. There was no one, and the only sounds were a few small birds high in the trees.

There was a double garage, the door open. Beth could see a motor bike and Patrick's car, back from the garage. He must be here somewhere: she rang the doorbell again; still no answer.

Beth walked along the front of the house. She couldn't see anyone through the windows. Either side of the house there were enormous locked gates. There was no way she could get around the back.

She called out for Patrick, and finally someone shouted, 'Hold on. I'll unlock the gate.' Sean opened it and let her in.

'Sorry. I rang the doorbell. Patrick asked me to come round.'

'He's probably got his headphones on. Come on through into the garden while I find him.'

Sean locked the gate while she walked ahead. There was no one in the garden and she felt rather self-conscious walking on her own. She started to feel like she was intruding. The temporary fence was still there. She walked down towards it; was it really less than a week since Kathleen had died?

Beth looked out to sea and then realised something was missing from the scene. A sound. She looked to her left: the hens, they had gone, and not only the hens but the coop, the run, everything. There were holes in the grass, and some grain but nothing else remained. Beth found it heart breaking. Kathleen would have hated it. However, her mind returned to the morning Kathleen died. It was odd about the hens. Kathleen would never have let them out, so how did they come to be running around the garden?

'I've tracked him down,' said Sean and she followed him back towards the house.

'How is he?'

'He doesn't say much. He is on his computer a lot, looking at photos.'

Beth looked back to sea. 'The last time I stood there was with Kathleen, in the dark. I feel somehow like I'm stuck there. Nothing makes sense any more.'

'I've been speaking to Kathleen's mother. She's devastated, of course.'

Beth blinked. 'I'd not even thought about her family over there; only how it was affecting me. That's awful, isn't it? She has a sister, hasn't she?'

'Yes. Roisin. A few years older than her.'

'Do you know her family? Sorry, I tend to assume that because you are from Dublin as well you are bound to know her, like people think everyone here on the Isle of Wight knows each other.'

'I do know them a bit. I first met them at Pat and Kathleen's wedding. My wife had been to school with Roisin.'

'Your wife must be missing you. How long are you staying?'

'I'm not sure. I'm concerned about Pat. I can't leave him yet. He worshipped her, you know, from the first time he saw her. You know, he wouldn't let me meet her for months.'

'Why ever not?'

'He was paranoid, scared she'd prefer me. Crazy. I was happily married, but he had this thing that I was in a steady job, she'd prefer that and, of course, if she made a play for me, I wouldn't be able to resist. Pat never trusted anyone with Kathleen.'

Beth looked down. 'And their marriage stayed strong, did it?'

Sean screwed up his face. 'Of course. Why are you asking?'

'It's a bit confusing.' Beth looked at the badge of a shamrock pinned to Sean's jumper. 'Erm, happy St Patrick's Day. Sorry, I'm not sure if it's the right thing to say.'

'It's fine. Kathleen loved it.'

'I haven't cancelled the get-together at the pub tonight. You could mention it to Patrick. You are both welcome, but obviously I'm not expecting him to come.'

'I'll tell him.'

'It's one of those things we have done for years. On St David's Day Kathleen always brought me a bunch of daffs, and we'd go up the pub, just the two of us. This year was the first time we missed that.' Beth paused, remembering the text:

Sorry, I can't make today. Life's hectic, but Happy St David's Day.

Beth felt a pang of guilt as she remembered she'd been offended by Kathleen cancelling, and had been off hand in her reply. Why on earth hadn't she realised then that something was very wrong?

'The Family Liaison Officer, Sue, has been round a few times,' Sean said.

'Oh, good. I wondered if they were keeping you up to date.'

'She seems competent, reassuring. Tells Pat just what he needs to know.'

Beth tried to keep her voice level, calm. 'On the morning that Kathleen died, when they were all down here, do you know if they found anything unusual?'

'I don't think so. I've had a few chats with them. Sue said they didn't find any footprints, no physical objects that had been left, no scraps of material or hairs: nothing. She said they also check things like broken branches or for signs of a struggle. No, there was nothing.'

'So they don't think anyone had come down here? There wasn't a hint that someone could have come and attacked Kathleen?'

Sean looked puzzled by her intensity. 'That's been troubling you? I have to admit it seemed highly unlikely to me.'

'Sami and Alex were saying they were asked about what they were doing on Monday morning. Obviously, I don't think they were suspected of anything, but I did wonder if they were doing routine checks because they had suspicions of foul play as they call it.'

'I'm surprised they were asked questions like that, but in my conversations with the police, no one suggested anything had been amiss.' Sean gave a slight smile. 'Having said that, Patrick did tell me they'd checked he'd not taken out some massive life insurance on her, but of course he hadn't.'

They started to walk back to the house.

'Patrick told me you were coming to go through some of Kathleen's things. That's kind of you. By the way, if you find Kathleen's phone and headphones could you let us know? We can't find them anywhere and they should have been down there. She usually used them for her mindfulness, and anyway, she always had her phone with her.'

'It's odd. Weren't the police concerned about that?'

'They said they had noted it, like the hens.'

'Ah. Did they manage to find out how they escaped?'

'Funny. They did look into it. There were never padlocks on but the hen coop door and the gate to the run were secured with substantial sliding bolts. Both had been slid back. It must have been something Kathleen did by mistake.'

'I can't think why she would do that.'

'I think it will be written off as one of those things.'

Beth couldn't feel as relaxed about it as Sean: things didn't add up.

'It's great you are helping with the clothes. Pat has no idea what to do with them, and I'm no help with that kind of thing. It seems a shame to dump them.' Sean sighed. 'Sorry, it's not a particularly pleasant thing to have to do.'

'I don't mind. Anything I can do to help. You more than most of us know how much practical stuff needs doing when someone dies. I hadn't been at all prepared for it when my mother died. I'm an only child. I was so glad of a solicitor who was joint executor. I'd have been lost without him.'

'I've been working through things. I've already sorted out her car, so he doesn't need to worry about that.'

'And what about Conor? How is he doing?'

Sean bit his lip, raised his eyebrows. 'Conor's a complicated lad, isn't he? Him and Pat get on well. He might stay, although he had been talking about going travelling after his exams. I'm not sure what he'll do now.'

They walked through large patio doors into the open living space. At one end Beth could see Patrick with his back to her, engrossed on his computer. She walked towards him and then stopped. On the screen she could see a picture of Kathleen. Patrick seemed to be using a programme to enhance the photo, making the eyes a bit bluer, a bit wider. Beth watched, feeling uneasy, remembering what Gemma said about Patrick's obsession with Kathleen, remembering his words, 'You are mine for ever now.' Was it possible that Patrick's obsession was deeper, darker than anyone had ever realised and Kathleen was secretly desperate to get away? Patrick might have been fighting to keep her, threatening even to kill her if she tried to leave him and so she'd kept quiet. If Beth was right about that, then Kathleen's plan had been to reveal all the next day, but death had intervened, silenced her.

Beth steadied herself, some of that was possible, but the final step was not. Patrick had conveniently ensured he was not here. He appeared at least to have no way of getting here that morning.

Beth heard Sean shout, 'Pat.'

Patrick turned, slowly blinked as if surprised to see them, and then quickly closed the programme. 'Beth. Hi. Sorry, I didn't hear you come in.'

'Sean let me in the garden. I see it's all back to normal out there.'

'Thank God. They've taken down that awful tape.'

'The hens have gone?'

'Jilly next door has taken them on. Honest to God, I had no idea what to do with them. I feel guilty. Kathleen loved them so much, but they are better off with Jilly.'

'That's a good idea. Kathleen would have wanted the best for them.'

'Jilly's made up with them. Strange isn't it?' Patrick stood up. 'Let me get you a drink. Have you had lunch?'

'Yes, thanks. A cup of tea would be lovely, though.'

Although Patrick had stood up, Sean went to make her drink.

They went upstairs together, Beth carefully carrying her mug of tea. Patrick pushed open the door to Kathleen's room, but Beth noticed he stayed at the entrance.

'Sean has put boxes there. If you could put in things for the clothing bank, things for charity. If you want anything—' He paused.

Beth smiled. 'Kathleen was a few sizes smaller than me, so, no thank you. Don't worry. I'll sort things out.'

'Her books as well?'

'Of course.' Beth was aware Patrick was looking straight at her, averting his eyes from the rest of the room. 'Are you sure you want me to do this today? You don't have to rush this, you know.'

'No, please. I'd like you to do it.' Beth saw the flash of pain, real grief.

'OK, fine. You can leave me to it if you want.'

Patrick walked quickly away. Beth felt awkward: this was Kathleen's private space.

She found a coaster and put her mug on the bedside table, Then she went over and nervously opened a large fitted wardrobe, full of beautiful clothes that looked like and smelt of Kathleen. It was a shock, more upsetting than she anticipated.

At the bottom she saw a small wooden box, which she opened. Inside were some scarves which Beth took out and put on the bed. Inside, at the bottom, was a small jeweller's box which she opened. Inside was a pair of stunning earrings, which Beth recognised straight away as matching the necklace Amy had given Kathleen. She held them up. The light shone in a thousand tiny beams of light. What surprised her was the name on the box: De Beer, the diamond company. So, they were real. Her hand shook. These were very expensive earrings and they matched the necklace Amy had given Kathleen. But why were the earrings shut in a box down here?

She picked them up and went to Kathleen's dressing table, opened the drawer. In there was a large, leather jewellery box. She put the earrings inside it, alongside the other bracelets and earrings: very good quality but nothing as special as these. Beth noticed a small clear bag containing a thin square box and was curious. She opened it, and found a large silver coin with a heart and butterfly engraved on it. It was very Kathleen. Beth smiled, put it back and returned to sorting clothes.

Taking a deep breath, she realised most were immaculate and, she reckoned, could be folded carefully and put in the box for the charity shop.

Beth decided to start with coats and jackets. Put the heavy things at the bottom of the box. Starting with a beautiful camel jacket, she checked pockets before folding them. She realised that if someone did this with her coats, they would be pulling out handfuls of tissues, a roll of dog poo bags, the odd cough sweet, but Kathleen was obviously far more meticulous than her. It wasn't until she got to a thick wool coat that she found anything, and that was a tiny scrunched up piece of paper, pushed deep inside the pocket.

Beth pulled it out and was about to throw it in the small wastepaper bin when out of curiosity she started to unfold it. It was a receipt from a supermarket in London: not many items. What caught Beth's attention was one item: a pregnancy test. It had been purchased in the January of that year.

Beth stared at the piece of paper. Was it possible that Kathleen had been pregnant? Had she been pregnant when she died? Beth sat on the edge of the bed. It would come out in the post-mortem. No one had mentioned it yet. Had Patrick known he was about to be a father? What if the father had been the person Kathleen had the affair with? Beth felt a wave of nausea. She thought of Sami. Oh God, no.

The idea of Sami being unfaithful broke her heart. The idea of him fathering a child with Kathleen smashed that broken heart into a million pieces. A one night fling she might have eventually forgiven, but to have fathered a child... No, she didn't think she would ever get over that. Sami would have known that. He knew his whole way of life would have been lost for ever, and if any part of him had wanted to preserve that, the pressure to silence Kathleen would have been immense. Beth stared at the receipt: a tiny, scruffy bit of paper, but one that might be the touch paper that destroyed her entire life.

12

Beth returned home numb, exhausted. On the kitchen table she saw the copy of the local paper Sami had brought in that morning. She picked it up, expecting to read about one of the usual rows about whether to build a fixed link to the island or how to fulfil the latest quota of new houses. She was not prepared for what faced her. Smiling at her on the front page was Kathleen, a copy of one of Patrick's photos taken in the garden of their old home, the hens in the background. 'Much loved local woman dies in tragic cliff death'. The whole page was given over to Kathleen's life and death.

Shaking, Beth sat down and read the article. It was so strange: she had to keep reminding herself this was her friend they were writing about. There were warm words from people Kathleen had worked with, a few from Patrick. The detective inspector overseeing the case spoke briefly, saying that Kathleen's death was being treated as 'an unexplained death, but at present it appeared to be a tragic accident'.

It was the next part that was news to Beth. 'Early on the morning the victim died, close to the house, a silver car was seen parked between 6.50 and 7 a.m. The car was parked off road, in the entrance to a house opposite. If you have any information, please contact us on this number—'

Beth reread the sentence: a car parked by Kathleen and Patrick's house at the time she died? Her heart beat faster. A car, why would they be asking about a car? Did anyone who had been there on Sunday evening have a silver car? Of course, her car was silver but neither Sami, William, Imogen or Alex had a silver car, and Patrick's had been in the garage.

Obviously a different car could have parked close by in all manner of places but this showed that the police were still asking questions. The matters of the phone, the hens, and now the car all stacked up. Despite Sean's reassurances, the police believed that there were at least some reasons to suspect someone had been involved in Kathleen's death. Beth had a moment wondering if she should be sharing what she knew with the police but dismissed it immediately. She had to know more about Sami and Kathleen before she did anything.

Ollie, as always, seemed to sense she was unhappy and came and sat next to her. 'I think I'd better at least pretend to do some weeding. I'll go mad just sitting in here,' she said to him. He followed her outside. Ollie rolled around on the grass, wonderfully at peace with his existence.

When Sami arrived home from work, he looked exhausted. He stood, half turned back to the back door.

'Hi. So, how did Layla get on with her exams? How did you get on with Patrick?' he asked.

'I have no idea how Layla got on. As for Patrick's—' she paused, wiped the mud off her hands. Sami was clearly impatient to go up and change out of his 'work clothes' and so she said, 'It went OK.' Sami headed upstairs.

Beth started to empty the dishwasher but decided no, she had to talk to Sami. They couldn't go out this evening acting as if nothing was wrong. She couldn't face asking him about his relationship with Kathleen, but there was something she could ask him. How he answered may well give her the answers she needed. Before she could change her mind, Beth ran upstairs, went into their bedroom, and closed the door behind her.

'Sami, I need to ask you something,' she blurted out. 'Was Kathleen pregnant?'

Sami did a long hard blink, and sat on the edge of the bed loosening his tie. 'Why do you ask that?'

Beth told him about the receipt.

'That doesn't mean anything.'

'Kathleen bought a pregnancy testing kit. She thought she was pregnant. I think that matters. Has this anything to do with her being in hospital?'

'Beth, stop pushing me about all this. It doesn't matter any more.'

'It does. Why are you keeping secrets from me?'

'Beth, what has got into you? I made a promise not to tell anyone certain things. You have to respect that.'

'But—'

'No, enough.' He stood up. 'Now, can we have a decent night out at this St Patrick's meal without you endlessly speculating about Kathleen?'

He opened the bedroom door, anxious to get away, but she said, 'Did you see all that stuff about a silver car seen by Kathleen's house the time she died?'

He turned. 'It doesn't mean anything. I don't want to talk about it.'

'You don't want to talk to me about a lot of things, do you?' she said quietly.

Sami turned to face her. They stood, like High Noon, waiting to see who would be the first to draw their gun.

Beth was breathing fast, close to tears. From the corner of her eye she saw Layla come out of her room. Sami took the opportunity to escape downstairs.

'I didn't realise you were back. How did it go?' Beth asked Layla.

Layla shrugged, looked at the floor.

'It's the St Patrick's day meal this evening.'

'Oh crap.' Layla responded by going back into her room, and slammed the door.

'Don't be so rude,' Beth shouted at the door. 'I wish someone in this house would talk to me like I'm a human being.'

There was, of course, no answer. Beth went back into her room, changed into the new dress she'd been saving in her wardrobe, brushed her hair, applied some makeup, and added her favourite earrings.

Sami came in, and glanced at her. 'You're not going to be warm enough in that,' was his only comment. Beth scowled, grabbed a cardigan and dragged it on.

They walked down the street in silence, Adam and Layla lagging behind.

For the second night running Beth walked into the restaurant. Gemma had done well, having decorated the room with green bunting and shamrocks and put on a special menu that was obviously proving popular.

Only Alex was there when they arrived, with a glass of red wine in front of him. Beth went to sit next to him, realising that Gemma had given them the same circular table as the year before. Alex hadn't been there, of course. In fact, he was sitting where Kathleen had. Tonight, the evening sun shone a reddish beam on to the table, the colour of Kathleen's hair, and it felt, in a way, that Kathleen was there with them. Sami said he'd go and get drinks. Adam and Layla sat as far away from their parents as they could.

'You already know Adam—' said Beth.

'Of course. He's a great help at the pharmacy.'

Beth grinned. 'Good, and this is my daughter, Layla.'

'I hear you're very musical,' said Alex.

'I do like other things as well,' said Layla pointedly. 'How are you finding living on the island? Must be so boring after London.'

'No. I enjoy cycling, and going to the beach.'

'You should go to some of the West Wight beaches, look for fossils,' said Layla. 'Me and Mum used to do it all the time.'

Beth was relieved to see her daughter chatting pleasantly. She noticed a book on the table next to Alex. 'Brought some light reading with you?'

He smiled. 'Imogen and I are swapping books again. I went to the library after work today and borrowed some Tennyson poems.'

'Good. It's a great library. I took the kids a lot when they were little.'

Sami returned with a tray of drinks, and put them down without speaking. Beth wasn't sure if Alex noticed the tension but, if he did, he politely ignored it.

Imogen, William and Elsa finally arrived, with the rushed air of busy people. Beth was surprised to see Conor come in as well. He made a beeline for Layla. As it was a set menu, they all settled down to eat their steak and Guinness pie, and Irish apple cake. Beth chatted to Alex and found it calming to talk books and walks. Sami stayed quiet, only occasionally talking to Imogen or William.

At the end of the meal William went to the bar and returned with a bottle of Irish whisky, and small glasses. He poured everyone except Sami a glass, including the teens.

'Let us raise our glasses in memory of our beloved friend, work colleague, and mother, Kathleen.'

Beth raised her glass and then sipped the drink. She wasn't used to spirits, but her Gran had been a whisky lover and she knew she liked the taste.

'Have another,' said William leaning in front of Sami. 'You look like you need it tonight.'

She ignored the scowl from Sami and held out her glass. It went down easily and, on top of the glasses of wine she'd already had, she began to feel light-headed, numb. Beth didn't care: it was a relief to be free of the nagging pain and unhappiness she had been feeling.

There was a lull in the conversation when Conor said, 'Anyone see in the paper about the silver car then?' There were awkward murmurs, but everyone occupied themselves with their drinks or food. 'It means the police think someone could have been out there with Mum, could have killed her. You can't all ignore that. You all say how much you loved Mum, so if some bastard went out and killed her, you must care about it.' His voice was hard, menacing. He turned to Beth. 'Layla said you told Sami you were worried. Did you?'

'Conor, leave this,' said William.

'But you did say that?' Conor repeated to Beth.

Everyone turned to her. Beth could feel her face burning. She could deny it all, side with her friends rather than this volatile young man, and maybe a few weeks ago she would have done. But things had changed. Beth looked at Conor, and for the first time she realised he had his mother's eyes, the same deep grey pools, and behind the bluster she saw just how unhappy he was. She also knew that, for all the mixed emotion she felt towards Kathleen at that moment, she had to speak out.

'Conor's right to ask questions,' she said, her voice shaking. 'The police are. It's not just the car. They don't know where her mobile is or the headphones; they should have been with her. Also, why were the hens out? They know that's not right. We all know how much Kathleen loved them. She'd never have let them out when the fence was down. The police are clearly not certain Kathleen's death was an accident.'

'Of course they are,' said William. 'This is just covering the bases. I spoke to them. They think it was an accident.'

'That is what they say to us, but I don't think it's what they really think. This car proves it.'

'This is police business. It's nothing to do with us,' said Sami, firmly reaching out and tugging gently on Beth's arm.

'Get off me,' she shouted. 'Stop telling me what to do. What are you covering up?'

William coughed. 'I think, Beth, it would be better to leave all this now.'

Beth looked at their faces, one by one, met their eyes. What she saw shocked her. It wasn't simply that they wanted her to shut up. She saw hostility and fear, and her heart ached. Part of her desperately wanted to appease them all, apologise, back track. But that beam of light, now dispersed into a gentler glow over the table, reminded her of Kathleen, and she couldn't deny her.

'Why do you all want me to be quiet? What are you frightened of? Is it because Kathleen was speaking the truth when she said one of you was threatening to ruin her?'

'What do you mean, threatening her?' shouted Conor. 'What did Mum say to you? Who was it?'

The restaurant fell silent, as people stopped talking out of embarrassment and curiosity. Only the noise of crockery, and the distant laughter from the bar filled the vacuum.

Beth steadied herself, but suddenly felt cold, sober. 'I'm sorry, Conor, but your mother told me she'd made a mistake, that someone was using it to stop her from exposing what they'd done.'

'What they'd done?' Conor demanded.

'Your mother knew something this person had done, something terrible.'

'But who was it?' shouted Conor.

Beth looked around the table. Everyone was looking at her now. 'Kathleen said it was someone who was there that night. She also said she was going to own up to everything, expose this person. She was very scared. They were desperate for her to keep quiet. The next day she died.'

Conor slammed down his glass. 'You're saying someone here killed my Mum?'

Sami intervened. 'No one is saying that.'

Beth suddenly felt dizzy and sick. She couldn't speak. Imogen turned to Conor, and spoke in measured 'teacher' tones. 'Your mother was a special person, but she was prone to be a bit dramatic. She exaggerated things; that was all.' Imogen then looked over at her. 'Beth, it's been hard for us all. You two were close, but you need to stop going over and over things. Leave things be now.'

Beth looked over, bleary eyed, at Imogen. 'I wish I could. I'm so tired. I don't want you all to hate me, but I have to fight for her. I owe it to her. I can't give up.' Beth covered her face with her hands and started to sob helplessly.

Sami stood up. 'Time to call it a night, I think. This evening's meal is on me.' There were shouts of protest, but he held his hand up. 'No, seriously. I want to do this.'

There were mumbled thanks but everyone seemed eager to leave. Sami went to the bar and then the four of them walked back up the road.

'Dad, you'd better hold onto Mum,' said Layla. 'She's pretty pissed. I've never seen her like this.'

When they went to bed, Beth lay on her back, her head spinning.

'Beth, this has to stop. You actually said one of our friends had been threatening Kathleen. Good God, you practically accused them of murder. I say "our friends" but as I was one of the people there on the Sunday maybe you even include me. Remember, Beth, relationships that have taken years to build can be destroyed overnight. You need to be very careful.'

Sami switched off the light and Beth turned over. Tears ran

onto her pillow. What he said frightened her: he was right. She knew that once a group of people all look back at you, united with the same contempt, you are well on your way to being an outsider. Beth cuddled her pillow. What was she going to do? She'd known it would be hard, but she had never thought this fight would be a choice between Kathleen and the life she knew.

13

At three in the morning, hot, her head thick, but no longer dizzy, Beth went downstairs, poured a large glass of water and sat sipping it. Ollie came running over to her.

'At least I've still got you, Ollie,' she said, 'but the others, what am I going to do? All that stuff last night was awful but the worst thing of all is all the stress about Sami. Was he having a having a fling, an affair? I don't bloody well care what anyone calls it, but I need to know if he chose someone else over me, even if it was only once. I need to know if he slept with Kathleen.'

On the work surface in the kitchen she saw Sami's phone charging. Picking it up, she saw one saved voicemail, dated the Tuesday night before Kathleen died, the night Sami looked after her in hospital. Beth looked around. She felt a pang of guilt, then thought, sod it, she would be one of those women who checked her husband's phone. She held the phone to her ear, and listened to the message. It was Kathleen, her beautiful Irish voice. Beth blinked. She'd started to forget what Kathleen's voice sounded like already but now it was as if she was in the room with her. She was giving Sami an address.

Beth replayed the message. The address was strange: not a hospital she'd ever heard of. In fact, it sounded more like a private address. Her instinct was to turn off the phone, pretend she knew nothing. But, of course, she couldn't. Feeling very sober now, she turned on her laptop, started to type the address into Google and immediately a map highlighting the address came up.

She clicked on the red marker and the map zoomed in, with a picture of the building at that address on the right-hand side. Beth felt very sick: that wasn't a hotel, or a house. Beth copied and pasted the name and Googled it, went to their website.

The place Beth was looking at was a private clinic which offered several gynaecological services, but primarily it was a clinic which offered abortions. This was the kind of clinic you booked to go to in advance. If Kathleen had been miscarrying, she would have been taken to the local NHS hospital, not to some private clinic. No, if she'd gone here, she'd have booked in and the only thing Beth could see that she would have gone for was for an abortion.

Beth's hand started to shake. She checked the address: this was definitely the place.

She sat down, stunned. Kathleen had never seemed far from her Catholic roots. It would have been an incredibly difficult decision for her. Had Sami made her do it?

Beth didn't dare move out of her chair in the kitchen. She had no idea how long she sat there, staring at the phone, until Sami came in.

'I wondered where you were,' he said, his eyes scanning her face all the time, looking for clues as to what was wrong.

Beth picked up his phone, her hand shaking, switched it to speakerphone and played him the voicemail. Kathleen's presence filled the kitchen.

When it finished Beth tried to steady her voice. 'I looked up the address. Kathleen wasn't in a local hospital for a panic attack. She'd booked this clinic, and I know why.'

Sami held the back of the chair, manoeuvred himself round to sit down, put his head in his hands.

'Kathleen had an abortion, didn't she? It was planned, and she asked you to be with her.' Beth was taking deep breaths. She was close to throwing up.

'It's a clinic for all kinds of gynae problems.' Sami's voice was shaking, weak.

'Are you telling me Kathleen did not have an abortion?'

Sami took off his glasses and rubbed his eyes. 'Yes.'

'Why was she there then? And don't you dare say you can't tell me.'

He reached over to touch her hand, but she pulled away. 'Get off. Tell me what happened.'

He gnawed at his lip. Beth waited. 'I am breaking my word, but I will tell you. You can't tell anyone this.'

Sami looked at her questioningly, but her face stayed frozen.

He took a deep breath. 'Kathleen rang me at King's College, early Tuesday evening. She was crying, hysterical. She told me she was at a clinic and frightened of what was happening to her. She pleaded with me to go and, of course, I went there. When I got there she was in bed, and then she told me she had been pregnant.'

'Had been?'

'That day at the academy she had been unwell. She was bleeding very badly. She had been to this clinic before with Patrick and she rang them. The consultant she'd seen before agreed to admit her and operate.'

'Why didn't she go to a normal hospital?'

'She knew the consultant there, trusted him. She knew she could trust them not to contact Patrick.'

'Why was she so worried about Patrick knowing?'

Sami scratched his forehead, but she didn't reach out to stop him. 'The thing is, the baby couldn't have been Patrick's.'

Beth clutched her arms around her body; the room was swimming. Sami kept talking, but voices kept shouting at her not to listen, to make it all go away. If she didn't hear it, it couldn't be true. The cold touch of Sami's hand, however, forced her to focus.

'Listen to me, Beth. The chances of Patrick fathering children after the chemotherapy a few years ago were remote.'

'Kathleen never told me anything about this—'

'Patrick was ashamed. It was silly, but that was the way he felt. I was one of the few people who knew. He trusted me not to tell anyone, but he wouldn't use our pharmacy or have a doctor at our practice. I did know that last year they went to the clinic that Kathleen was admitted to, talking to the consultant about fertility issues.'

'Kathleen got pregnant, didn't want an abortion, was she hoping Patrick would stick by her or was she planning to leave him?' Beth looked at Sami through half shut eyes.

'Kathleen was not planning to leave Patrick. She planned to tell him that it was a miracle, that they had beaten the impossible odds.'

'She really thought he would believe that?'

'There was a one in a hundred million chance or something. She thought he'd want it to be true so badly that he would believe her.'

'But in fact, she had an affair – and you knew.'

Sami rubbed his lip with his finger.

Beth held her breath and then took the plunge. 'Who was the father?'

She waited; there was no explosion. Instead in a calm, measured voice, Sami said, 'I'm not sure. I assumed it was someone on her course, although she didn't tell me. All she said was that she'd slept with someone once before Christmas, done a pregnancy test in January and found she was pregnant.'

'Did she tell the father she was pregnant?'

'I don't know. She didn't say much about him at all. Before she lost the baby, she had been planning to let Patrick believe it had been a miracle. And then, of course, that Tuesday she had the miscarriage. By the time I got to her at the hospital she was distraught. Despite all the problems she'd really wanted the baby. She was grieving and consumed by guilt at the same time.'

'Poor Kathleen.' Beth hesitated. 'You say she was distraught? You told me she was emotional when she was talking to me, and yet you dismissed the idea that she could have taken her own life. Surely this makes that at least a possibility. I knew Kathleen; she'd have been heartbroken.'

Sami shook his head. 'No. If I'd thought that was likely, I'd have felt obliged to talk to the police about it. No. She was upset but she admitted to me that it made the decisions she was making simpler. I think she felt a bit guilty because of that sense of relief. Remember, I worked with her on the Thursday and Friday. I checked up on her, but she told me that apart from feeling very tired and sore, she was OK. Of course, then we had the whole inspection thing. We were all on edge, but no one was suicidal. All Kathleen said to me was that she'd been confused but she could see a way forward now.'

'By that I assume she meant that she was going to tell Patrick the truth.'

'I urged her to. I felt it was important she did.'

'You wanted her to tell Patrick everything – even who she'd slept with?'

'Yes. Patrick would want to know. I was sure it was a one night fling with someone from her course, like I said. In fact, I wondered if that was why she was leaving her course. It was her way of breaking all ties. The relationship was not a threat to her marriage any more. I was sure, in time, Patrick would forgive her.'

'What about the father of the baby? How was he feeling about it all?'

'I have no idea. As I said, she didn't tell me anything about him.'

Beth went over to the sink, poured herself another glass of water, sat back down, straight backed.

'You must realise how all this has looked to me? You've no idea how confused and hurt I've felt, where my mind has been.'

He scratched his forehead. 'You didn't think there was anything between me and Kathleen, did you?'

Beth fiddled with her wedding ring. 'I've been thinking that, yes. I've been thinking all sorts.'

'Like what?'

The clock on the dresser ticked.

'Like, would you threaten Kathleen to keep her quiet?'

'Good God, Beth. Do you know me at all?'

'I thought I did, but you've been lying to me and you left all these questions unanswered. I've had to answer them as best I could.'

'I was simply trying to keep to a promise, to let Kathleen sort things out with Patrick, and then she died. I didn't know how to tell you.' He looked up. 'I can't believe you thought I was capable of treating anyone like that.'

'My mind has been all over the place. Once the idea that you'd slept with Kathleen got into my head, that you might have fathered a child with her, everything went crazy.'

'I don't know what to say, but I promise you I never slept with Kathleen. I've never loved her in that way. You're the person I love, have my children with, want to grow old with. I thought you knew that.'

'If you'd been less secretive, told me what was going on, I'd have understood.'

'I'm so sorry. Look: there are the texts I sent to Kathleen when we got back from London on Wednesday evening.'

Putting his glasses back on, he read them out. '"Tell Patrick. It's the best way. He loves you. He will forgive you." Kathleen didn't answer me, but then we had the inspection and failed. That evening I wrote again, "Try not to worry about work. Concentrate on sorting things with Patrick." Kathleen replied to that. "I'm sorry about the mistakes at work. I will try and talk to Patrick soon. There are other things, though, I have to sort out first." I had no idea what these things were that Kathleen was talking about, but on Saturday evening she wrote to me, "Thank you for your help. You and Beth are such good friends. I am going to try and put things right soon."'

Beth read them herself: it was all so sane and normal.

'From the bottom of my heart, I can tell you, there was nothing between me and Kathleen,' said Sami. 'I love you. I never loved her. You do believe me, don't you?'

Beth read the words. Her eyes blurred with tears. She sat back in her chair. She sipped water to sooth the burning in her throat. 'I want to—'

Sami grabbed her hand. 'If you'd let your mind go to me threatening Kathleen, did you let it go further? Please tell me you never thought I would have done anything to harm Kathleen.'

She stood. The sound of her breathing seemed to fill the kitchen. He was waiting. Would she speak the truth? She'd already accused him of infidelity, of fathering another woman's child. How would he cope with her saying she'd considered him capable of murder?

'No, of course not. I know you better than that.'

'Thank God. I'm so sorry for what I've put you through. I'm

sorry for making you so anxious. You look exhausted. Have I reas-
sured you? Do you believe me?'

'I will try. It's been a terrible time. All the anxiety about Kathleen, and the secrets—'

'I know. Listen, I can see now I've made it all a million times
worse, but please try and let some of this stuff with Kathleen go.'

Beth shook her head. 'If someone we know was threatening to
ruin Kathleen over an affair, her pregnancy, I want to know. It's a
terrible thing to do, and when you think about it, they must have
been desperate to cover up whatever they were doing. Actually,
you don't have any evidence that the affair was with someone on
her course, do you?'

'Well, no.'

'So, it could have been someone here on the island—'

'I'm sure it wasn't.'

'But you don't know. Don't you see, there is so much I need to
know about Kathleen: who she had the affair with, who was threatening her, what they were covering up.'

'But it probably has nothing to do with her death. You can't
make that link. It's bad enough accusing friends of threats, but
murder?'

'Look, one step at a time. I owe it to Kathleen to find out who
was threatening her. If I can, I'd like to know who she had the
affair with; it might help.'

'Beth, you are not a confrontational sort of person. You need
friends, the security of being part of a group. You need it more than
me. I saw it last night. You could lose all that and achieve nothing.
Please, I can't bear to see you as ill as you were six years ago. Please
don't go there again.'

She saw the pain in his eyes. 'I'm not in that place, I promise
you. You're not to worry.'

'But, as I've no idea what caused your breakdown last time, I'm
bound to worry, aren't I? All I know is you went off to your aunt's

funeral, came back, and everything fell apart. You wouldn't talk to me. I didn't know what was going on.'

Beth could hear the unspoken pain, resentment, confusion. It tore her apart, but still the fear held her back from telling Sami what had happened. It reminded her of when she was twelve, she had been with a friend to the Olympic pool in Cardiff. When the guard wasn't looking, she'd gone to the top board, as a dare. Clinging onto the bar she walked right to the edge of the board. It had been like standing on top of a skyscraper looking down at a blue world. She could see the pinpoints of her friends, waving, egging her on. She was desperate to dive. She'd been for lessons, knew the techniques, but fear paralysed her, and it was all she could do to creep backwards and come back down the steps.

That memory never left her, and whenever she came close to telling Sami about her secret it was as if she was back there, stood on the edge, peering down and, each time, like today, she crawled away.

'I don't know what to say,' said Sami. 'I can't stop you, can I? But please, be careful.'

Sami came round to her and pulled her to stand next to him, held her and kissed her hair. She stood there in his arms, relieved to feel close to him, but in her head, she was still there, standing on that board, shaking.

14

Beth hadn't been to church for a few weeks, but early the next morning, after only few hours' sleep, she decided to go. She'd gone to Sunday School in the local chapel when she was young but by the time she met Sami, as she had not been for years and he had stopped going to the mosque, religion was something they had put behind them. However, when she moved to the island, Beth had been pregnant, lonely, disorientated. One morning on her way to the shops she had gone to look inside the church and had felt a peace and stability in there. It was a simple Norman church, untouched by Victorians: plain benches, old worn stone slabbed floor, and only one stained glass window. She'd sat alone on the wooden bench, and felt the cold coming off the walls but the sense of calm provided a refuge. Beth hadn't wanted to get involved, but occasionally she went to the early service on a Sunday morning which only a few elderly people attended. No one expected anything; they said good morning and left. The vicar would smile but was wonderfully unobtrusive. She had been going for a few years before one morning Kathleen had arrived, and it was like

stumbling across a tiny, perfect wildflower in an old piece of scrub-
land. Kathleen had come up to her, started chatting and that had
been the opening line of their story.

Today, as Beth sat in the front pew waiting for the service to
start, she felt the loss of Kathleen more poignantly than ever. This
was the place special to them; they had had their own rituals, sat in
the same place. She had felt the warmth of Kathleen's arm next to
her as they knelt for communion. They were both strangers here,
which brought them closer. Although she'd learned new things
about Kathleen, today she felt at peace with her again and missed
her. Beth breathed heavily, willing herself not to cry.

The vicar went through the liturgy, and the familiar words
coated the pain. As she returned to her seat after communion, she
noticed William, sitting with his head bent. He didn't come often
and, as usual, he didn't go up for communion.

As they walked out of the cold stone building, Beth wondered
what type of reception she would get from William.

'How are you this morning?' asked William, half a smile but
not the usual grin.

'That whisky was lethal.'

'It leads people to act out of character sometimes, to say things
they don't mean.'

Beth wasn't in the mood to be either patronised or
reprimanded.

'I didn't mean to offend anyone, but I only spoke the truth.
Kathleen said those things.'

'Even if she did, you can't go around accusing friends.'

Despite feeling more resolute, Beth cringed. Her default reaction to criticism would be to apologise and plaster over any cracks
as quickly as possible, particularly with William. She respected
him and he was usually kinder, more forgiving, than a lot.

He sat down on the bench, the gravestones silently watching.

Beth, sitting next to him, thought how tired and weary he appeared. 'You look exhausted.'

'Occupational hazard,' he said, but she thought it was more than that. Beth bent down and picked a few daisies from the bank next to them. She started to make tiny splits in a stem, and carefully threaded through a daisy.

William continued. 'Seriously, Beth, you can't really believe what you said last night. Think about the people you are accusing. Me, Imogen, Alex, Patrick, even Sami, you must see how absurd and hurtful that is.'

'I could have said more.'

'Like what? You should tell me, I was Kathleen's doctor. I would hate to think I missed something important.'

Like all good doctors, he had a way of getting you to talk. 'Kathleen told someone at the pub that she'd had an affair. I believe that is the big mistake she felt she'd made.'

William leant forward, scrutinising her face. 'You believe this?'

The one thing missing from the tone of his voice was surprise. Was that him reacting instinctively as a doctor, hiding emotion, or had he already known?

'I do. Didn't Kathleen tell you anything about it?' she asked.

'Of course not. I knew nothing.'

She screwed up her eyes. 'But I know Kathleen had been talking to you a lot when you went on the skiing holiday and afterwards.'

'That's nonsense.'

'But Imogen told me Kathleen was constantly phoning you before Christmas. I think she got quite jealous, actually.' She was watching his face. All she saw was a slight twitch of his cheek.

'Imogen can be a bit insecure, but she knows I love her very much. Any affair Kathleen had was nothing to do with me. Kathleen was my patient. It would be completely unethical for me to have any kind of relationship with her and, in any case, Imogen,

Elsa, my work, mean everything to me.' He stood up. 'I'd better be off now; enjoy your day.' Beth watched him walk briskly away.

Beth was shocked by how defensive William was being: she'd obviously upset him more than she realised. However, she didn't regret it. It had taught her a few things. Firstly, she felt sure that he knew about Kathleen's affair. So, it hadn't just been Gemma and Sami. If William knew, did it mean Imogen did as well? The more people who knew, the more likely it was that Patrick knew. Anyone who knew could have used the knowledge to threaten Kathleen. And so, what if that person had been William? William could have slept with Kathleen, but listening to him just then there was no way Beth could see it as more than a fling on his part. He loved his work and his family. He'd want an affair kept secret. Beth paused. The secret Kathleen described seemed more than that. Maybe he had been seducing her over a period of time, tried to make her end the pregnancy? Initially, maybe Kathleen might have been happy to keep the affair under wraps, but what if she'd changed her mind, wanted it all out in the open? William would have had so much more to lose, nothing to gain. How far would he go to protect himself?

As Beth walked down the steps, she saw Alex standing by the bus stop. She wondered how he would greet her.

'Where are you off to?' she asked.

He turned and she was relieved to see a smile. 'Southampton, shopping for a few things for the flat from IKEA.'

'Not cycling anywhere today then?'

'Later, I hope.'

'I could give you a lift to the Red Jet if you like.'

'Oh, no thanks.'

'Honestly. I could walk Ollie down the front there. Sami has gone into work. I might as well. Why don't you walk up to the house with me to pick up the car?'

They walked up the road. Alex didn't chat like most people, but this morning she appreciated it. She picked up Ollie and they drove off.

'I should work on my essay today,' Beth said, thinking it was time to make conversation. 'I could do with a walk up Tennyson Down, get some inspiration.'

'I'd love to go again sometime—'

Beth sensed his shyness. 'Would you like to go with me one day? I told you, Sami's not interested in walking. Funny, he loves his morning run but not walking, and there are so many gorgeous places over here.'

As they stopped at the traffic lights Alex coughed. 'I hope you feel better after last night—'

'I know I drank too much. William just had a go at me about what I said, but I had to stand up for Conor even though I know everyone wanted me to shut up.'

'But they are a very respectable, friendly group of people.'

'I'm sorry if there was any awkwardness on Friday as well,' said Beth. 'I knew nothing about Kathleen being ill. Sami should have told me. Still, we've talked now. It's all sorted.'

She saw him fiddling with a thread on the seat. She hoped he wasn't going to pull it any longer.

Aware that she had Alex captive in the car, she realised it was an opportunity to ask him a few questions. But after the frosty reception from William she was rather nervous.

'I saw you've become friendly with Gemma. She told me something that quite shocked me—'

She waited. Even Alex must want to know what it was. Eventually he said, 'What was that?'

'Gemma said Kathleen had an affair.'

'Gemma thinks Kathleen had an affair?' Beth could hear his voice shaking.

'Oh yes, and I know it's true now. I wondered if you'd picked up anything about it. Maybe she'd told Amy something about who it might have been with.'

'Um, no. Nothing. I never heard anything.' Beth had a feeling that if he could Alex would have jumped out of the car, but she persisted.

'The reason I'd really like to know who it was is that it would help me understand things with Kathleen. What did you really think of her?'

Beth stopped the car at the crossing, waited.

'Kathleen was excellent at her job,' said Alex. 'She was kind to Amy when she stayed with her.'

'And the "but" is?'

'It's complicated. Look, I can't talk about this and it might be better if you left all this alone. Don't go getting obsessed with it.'

The words had been said lightly, but Beth felt uncomfortable. Was it possible he was threatening her?

Beth turned on to the dual carriageway, past the hospital and then the prison on her left. Trying to ease the atmosphere, she remarked, 'Our silent neighbours.'

'It's odd, isn't it?' said Alex. 'A whole community shut away, forgotten.'

'But they're not forgotten by everyone, are they? They are people with parents and families.'

They paused, as Beth waited. The driver in front had stopped, without pulling in, to talk to a woman at the bus stop. He appeared to be offering her a lift, but she was telling him a long story about why she would rather take the bus.

'Honestly,' said Beth. 'He's creating havoc.'

'It wouldn't happen in London.'

'No. Sami and I moved here from Cardiff. It wouldn't happen there, either.'

'You've both been here a long time?'

Beth appreciated the effort he was making to get past the

earlier awkwardness. 'Eighteen years. I was pregnant when we came. We'd only just got married.'

'You were a teacher back there?'

'Oh no. I messed up school. I was working in a shop in Cardiff when Sami came in. He was a pharmacy student then. We got married quickly, really because I was pregnant. For Sami there was no question of not doing, as he would say, "the right thing". His family were shocked, though. I wasn't the kind of wife for Sami they had in mind at all. They are all bright. His father's an engineer, mother a GP. They had come from Iraq and they expected their children to marry people in those kinds of professions, not someone working in a shop.'

'It's to Sami's credit he saw past all that.'

'Mm, yes. His parents moved out to New Zealand to live with his brother and his family. His brother and his wife are both consultants in hospitals out there, earning pots of money. Their life is very different to ours.'

'I'm sure they are proud of you and your family.'

Beth smiled. 'As long as they are proud of Sami, that's all that matters to me.'

She pulled into the stopping bay outside the Red Jet, turned and grinned at Alex. 'Sorry, spilling out my life story to you. You are easy to talk to.'

He blinked. 'Part of my job.'

Beth looked up at the entrance of the terminal. 'You'd better get a move on. It's twenty to ten. You've got five minutes. Have you got your ticket?'

'I have a book of tickets for regular travellers.'

'That reminds me. I need to ask about times.'

Beth walked into the terminal with Alex, and with Ollie on the lead. As she asked for the information, she saw Alex looking in his pockets.

'My phone must have fallen out of my pocket in your car—'

Beth could see the people coming off the Red Jet, the people waiting starting to board.

'You keep walking. I'll go and get it,' she said.

Ollie entered into the excitement, running next to her as she rushed back to the car, picked up Alex's phone and ran back.

'Thank you,' he said, and Beth watched him disappear down the tunnel.

'Phew, that was close,' she said to Ollie. Together they returned to the car.

Beth drove along the coast, parked at Gurnard and went down on the beach with Ollie. It was mainly shingle and Ollie kept away from the sea, preferring to sniff the seaweed and pebbles.

When the children had been young Beth had taken them to the beach a lot, but she realised this was her first time this year. She and Sami had only been a handful of times last year. In fact, now she thought about it, they did a lot less together than they used to. They worked, ran the kids to things, went for a meal with friends, stayed in. As she threw pebbles into the sea, she realised that she and Sami had never been on a proper holiday on their own. It was rather daunting: how would they get on, just the two of them, day after day? Maybe soon they should summon up the courage to find out.

Beth carried on walking, watched a mother with her toddler collecting shells, both totally engrossed in their task. She could remember collecting fossils with Layla and smiled; they were good days.

She breathed out and was starting to feel more relaxed than she had for days when her phone rang.

Beth looked down, expecting to see a call from one of the kids. However, it was a number she didn't recognise. She answered her phone. It was silent.

'Hi,' she said, waiting to see if someone was going to speak... and then they did.

'Stop obsessing about Kathleen. She had to die. You are like a grubby grey pebble that people trample over. I could throw you into the sea. No one would notice, or care, and you would disappear forever. I know your secret. You are living a lie. I can end your marriage and your life here.'

15

As suddenly as the call started it ended. Beth stared at her phone, the voice echoing in her head: an unnaturally deep man's voice, dragging out the words. The voice had not been human. Like a clown, the disguise was sinister, and crept under her skin.

Her lips started to tremble; nausea gripped her stomach. As Beth stared at her phone it seemed to have become the enemy. Who was that? Her eyes darted around the beach: were they there, watching her?

Terrified, she called Ollie, staggered up the beach to the low concrete wall, and sat down. Gradually she started to steady herself. Ollie was sniffing the pebbles at her feet; his normality helping to ground her.

That voice, think about it: of course, they must have used one of those voice app things. The kids had shown her them, found them hysterical.

What had they said? From her bag she took a pen and an old appointment card and scribbled down what she'd heard as best as she could remember it.

*Stop obsessing about Kathleen. She had to die. I know your
secret. I can end your marriage, your life here. You are pathetic,
a grubby grey pebble that people trample over. I could throw
you in the sea, no one would notice, or care and you would
disappear forever.*

Beth reread the words: this wasn't a prank; this was serious.

'She had to die.' They said that about Kathleen. Why would
they say that?

The bit about knowing her secret scared her. How could they
possibly know that? No one did; please God they were bluffing
about that. Beth felt the nausea return; she was so hot. Stumbling
back down the beach, she dabbled her fingers in the cold water,
and then patted her cheeks. Ollie started to bark, waiting for her to
throw pebbles in the water. She threw a few mindlessly but, as she
did, she suddenly remembered that last line: like a grubby grey
pebble people trampled over. Beth clutched a pebble; those were
the same words as Kathleen heard. Tentacles of fear wrapped
themselves around her, crushed her; she couldn't breathe. This
was no coincidence. Beth tried to remember if she'd told anyone
else about this, but no, she didn't think she had. There was only
one explanation: the person who had been threatening Kathleen
was now close to her, was using the same words to try to instil fear
in her. That meant the caller was someone who'd been at the
house party. Oh God, Kathleen had been right, because the people
she knew didn't make calls like that, and so someone really was
acting a part, but who?

Beth looked around the beach again. The woman and child
had gone, taking innocence with them. Clouds covered the sun,
the sky now grey, the air cold. She felt very alone.

Ollie came close to her. He was soaking wet, but she collapsed
on to the pebbles and cuddled him, crying. What was she going to
do? All this time she had been hoping and fearing that she would

turn over a stone and find out something that proved what Kathleen had said was true. But now there was no escape.

Slowly Beth got up and wiped her face. She had to get home.

She put Ollie on the lead and hurried back to the car. When she arrived home, she took Ollie through the back door, and was sitting on the floor trying to dry him when Sami came in.

'Hi. I came home. I was too tired to work. Have a good walk?'

Beth looked up at him. She was still shaking. She couldn't speak. Sami rushed over to her. 'What's happened? You're soaking wet.' He helped her up. Ollie, glad to be released from being dried down, went over to his bowl and noisily drank his water.

'Let's get you dry.' Sami was speaking to her as if she was a child. Beth followed him upstairs, shivering. Sami handed her dry trousers and a top. She changed as he put the wet clothes on top of the washing basket. He handed her a small throw, soft and comforting, and wrapped it around her shoulders.

'Tell me what happened.'

Beth started to cry. The words came out in small chunks. 'I had a phone call, anonymous, not a number I knew,' she sniffed, and Sami handed her a tissue. 'It was awful, the things they said—' She started to cry again, and Sami put his arms around her.

'What did they say? Tell me. It's only words, Beth.'

'They told me to stop obsessing about Kathleen; they said she had to die.' She stopped: she couldn't tell Sami about the mention of a secret. 'They said I was pathetic, that they could end my marriage and my life here.'

'Did you recognise the voice? Was it a man or a woman?'

'I don't know. They used a voice thing. It was so scary.'

'Hang on. Is your phone downstairs?' Sami ran down and brought it back up. He looked through her calls.

'Was it the last call?'

'Yes. That's it. I don't know the number.'

'Did you phone them back?'

'No. Of course not.'

'Well, I'm going to.'

Sami tried the number. He let it ring. It went through to voice mail and he left a message. 'I don't know who you are but if this call is repeated, I shall refer this number to the police.'

'I don't think they will ring again,' he said.

Beth sat very still and then spoke, 'Look Sami: there's more.' She repeated the lines about the pebble.

'Seems a bit melodramatic.'

Her mouth was very dry; it seemed like a menacing presence was in the room, but Beth made herself speak. 'Those were the same words the person who threatened Kathleen used to her, word for word.'

Sami scratched his forehead. 'Are you sure?'

'Yes, and I never repeated those words to anyone else. I am certain the person who phoned me is the same person who Kathleen said was threatening her; and she said that it was one of the people there on that Sunday night.'

'So, you think one of our friends made a threatening, anonymous call to you today?'

'Yes, it must be. But don't you see? In the call they revealed so much about themselves. Underneath this disguised voice I could detect the sort of person they really are. This isn't someone who makes idle threats; this is serious. One of our friends is playing us along. They've fooled us all. They are wicked, like Kathleen said.'

Sami put his arms around her. 'Hey, slow down. You're in shock. That was a very nasty call, but don't jump to conclusions. If this is seriously someone trying to warn you off, they could have all kinds of reasons. They could be scared you're going to dig up something embarrassing. It doesn't even have to be anything major. If you did my job, you'd see people get defensive and feel ashamed about all kind of things we might think are quite trivial.'

'This isn't trivial. This person had something major to hide, and I'm convinced more than ever that they were involved in Kathleen's death. I heard it in their voice: they would do it as easily as throw a grubby grey pebble in the sea.' Beth watched Sami, waiting for him, hoping in some way, he would say it was all nonsense.

However, his face was grave. 'This is getting more serious, isn't it? I don't think one of our friends would kill, but maybe deep down one of them is disturbed. They would have to be to make this call, wouldn't they? Of course, they might be able to justify it to themselves, but all I know is I don't want them anywhere near you. I meant it last night when I said I didn't want you getting ill again. I don't care who made this call; this is not acceptable. You must report this to the police.'

Beth panicked. She realised that she had been telling Sami because she thought he would talk her out of action, water down what had happened. 'I don't know. Involve the police?' She pulled the throw around her shoulders in the same way as Kathleen had wrapped her pashmina around herself.

Sami threw his hands up. 'You've been saying you'll track down the person who terrorised Kathleen, and now maybe you have a chance to find them. If the police can trace this call, you might find out who it was.'

Beth could feel her chest pounding. 'I don't know. You didn't hear them: I'm scared. What if the police don't do anything, don't catch the person? If I'm right, and they killed Kathleen, I'm not safe, am I?'

'If the police can trace this person, I am pretty sure you will find out they had nothing to do with Kathleen's death, and that will be a good thing. Come on. We need to follow this through.'

Beth saw the determination on his face. 'OK. We can call the police, but I should make the call. But Sami, I am going to tell them everything. Everything Kathleen said to me, about her fear of one of our friends, the affair and the pregnancy. They should know everything now. If I give them everything I have then maybe I could finally let them take over.'

Sami rubbed his mouth with his fingers. 'Yes, I think you're right. I hope they will be discreet though. I do worry about Patrick and Conor. But I can't have you being upset like this. You can tell them to come and talk to me about the pregnancy side of things. I was the one with Kathleen. I can tell them what they need to know.'

'I could ring that officer, Sue. I've got her number in my bag.'

'Good. Give her a ring in the morning. Now, you and I deserve an afternoon off. How about we go out for lunch somewhere and then have a walk with Ollie?'

'A walk?'

'Yes. I ought to get out more with you.'

Beth smiled. 'I think that would be good. I'll tell the kids to sort out their own lunch.'

They drove out to a dog friendly pub near the coast, ate a comforting meal of fish and chips, while Ollie munched on his treats under the table. Beth found it reassuring to be among people carrying on their normal lives; the fear that had gripped her started to loosen it's grasp. When they'd finished eating Sami said. 'How about we go down Shepherd's Chine? We've not been there for a long time.'

They clambered down on to the beach, using the few steps that had not crumbled away. Beth started, as she always did, to look for fossils.

'I'll take this one home to Layla,' she said. 'It's a good specimen. I know she's grown out of it all now, but she might like to see it. So, what do you think of her and Conor?'

'I think she's more interested than him, and I think it will end in tears.'

'The sooner it ends the better. I feel sorry for him. I know I stood up for him the other night, but I don't want him and Layla seeing too much of each other.'

'I agree. Kathleen told me about his temper. She reckoned he got that from his father. I think it might be more to do with frustration and confusion. His dad messed him up. Whatever, I'd rather he did his growing up away from Layla.'

They walked to the end of the beach. Then, as they made their way home Sami said, 'Can we pop into the Hendersons'? I've a few things to do.'

'Have you got the keys?'

He grinned. 'I don't need to go into the bungalow, so we'll be fine.'

'It's ages since I've been up there, be good to see it again.'

Sami drove them along the Whitcombe Road until they reached the bungalow, which was surrounded by a variety of scruffy outbuildings.

'Wow. It's even more run down than I remembered.'

'I know. One day, I reckon they will move out to Australia. Their heart isn't in this place any more, but it's a fabulous situation, and quite a bit of land.'

'I could see myself with a smallholding here. Just think, I could keep hens, grow vegetables.'

'I can't see you growing vegetables. You never do anything back at ours.'

'That's because the garden is yours. Every space is allocated to plants and flowers. I'm not complaining. I have my own little slice of paradise to sit in.'

'I'm glad you enjoy it,' Sami said, smiling. 'Now, let's get down to work. We'll go around the back of the house. I'll come with you to the greenhouse and show you where everything is. I need to get my tools from there.'

Sami quickly found the key for the greenhouse under the watering can. 'There are keys dotted all over the place here,' he said, laughing. He gave Beth meticulous instructions and then left her. It was hot and stuffy inside, with that strong smell of tomatoes, but she was quite content watering the plants.

After a while Sami returned. 'This is so much better with two. Could you hold the steps while I trim the top of the buddleia? It's leaning onto the greenhouse out there.'

As she held the steps and Sami pruned, Beth looked over at the fields.

'Not a bad place to run.'

'I love it. It's so quiet. I shall miss it when they come back.'

Beth stood soaking in the quiet evening sounds as he clipped away. When Sami came down, he started to gather up the clippings.

As they were leaving Beth looked over at the garage, 'Didn't you say the Hendersons bought a new Peugeot before they went away?'

'Yes,' he grinned, 'and it's the one you've been hinting about. Actually, it's the three door version you fancy. Honestly, it would drive you mad. Look, come and see what I mean. I think the key is under a stone. I've not been in there.'

Sami found the key, and opened the garage door.

Beth saw a small black Peugeot. 'It looks good, doesn't it? I wouldn't want it in black, though.'

'I don't think they have taken it further than Sainsbury's. It's like new. Hang on, you can look inside. They said the key is in the drawer.'

Once Sami had opened the car he said, 'You can peep inside, but we're too muddy to get in.'

Beth relished that new leather smell. 'No dogs have been in here,' she joked.

'You see what I mean, though, about the doors. I know neither of our kids are that tall, but it'd be a squash getting in the back. Also, this driver's door is heavy for you to open and close.'

Beth shrugged. 'Maybe. I'll have to test drive one sometime.'

Sami grinned. 'You'll agree with me in the end.'

Back home, after tea, feeling refreshed, Beth took out her sewing. Sami was back in the garden. It had been good to get out, but normal life had not resumed. The thought of making the call to the police frightened Beth more than Sami could understand. He didn't think this person had anything to do with Kathleen's death, but he hadn't heard their voice. That voice, those words had found a way to burrow deep inside her. Beth put down her sewing. Her hands were shaking. Should she just do what that person said? Why not leave it alone? What good was she doing? Why not stop stirring things up, keep her friends, stop fighting?

16

Next morning, Beth sat cradling her mug of coffee.

Sami arrived back from his run and on seeing her his face wrinkled with concern. 'I'm glad this is your day off,' he said. 'You must rest today. Do you need to get an appointment with the doctor?'

'No, really. I'll be OK.'

'Why don't you let me ring the police about this call?'

'No. I'll do it later.' Beth forced a smile. 'I'll be all right, you know. Don't worry.'

'You must ring me at the pharmacy if you need me.'

After Sami had left, Beth made coffee. She was still completely torn about this call. Sometimes, when she was like this, baking helped, so she went into the kitchen and started to make some Welsh cakes. As she rubbed together the fat and the flour, she imagined herself on the little step stool in her mother's kitchen. 'Perfect, good girl,' her mother was saying. The griddle Beth used had been her mother's, made for her by the ironmonger, and as Beth placed the cakes on it, she relished the comforting smell as they cooked. She knew exactly when it was the right time to turn them over and then when to place them on the cooling rack.

Beth made another drink, and sat eating the first Welsh cake, smothered in butter. The call was still on her mind and, as she sat sipping her tea, she realised that Sami was right. She had to do it: for her sake, for Kathleen's.

Wiping the crumbs off her fingers, she picked up her phone and rang Sue's number. Fortunately, Sue answered straight away. Although Beth had planned what she was going to say, she just blurted out that she had had an anonymous call. Sue seemed to catch the level of anxiety in her voice, and said she'd be round that afternoon.

It seemed a long wait, full of misgivings. Fear of the caller was slowly being replaced with fear of what Sue would say when she found out how much Beth had held back.

When Sue finally came, Beth already had the mugs and Welsh cakes on a tray. All she had to do was pour in the boiling water and take them out into the garden.

'Wow. It's fabulous out here. Who's the gardener?'

'It's all Sami's work.'

'You're lucky,' said Sue, as she sipped her tea. 'Now, tell me about this phone call. When did the call come? What exactly did they say?'

'The call came yesterday morning. I guess it was about ten, I'd dropped Alex at the Red Jet, gone for a walk at Gurnard. I think the caller used a voice distortion thing. I don't know if the person talking was a man or woman, old or young.'

'There are so many ways they can do it now with these apps. We get calls at the station; some idiots think it's funny.'

'This wasn't—' Beth heard her voice crack.

'I know. It's all right. Tell me about it. What did they say?'

'That I must stop obsessing about Kathleen, that she deserved to die.'

'They said that?'

'It was horrible. The thing that alarmed me most was that some of the things they said convinced me that this was the person who had been threatening Kathleen.'

Sue held her tea mid air. 'Threatening Kathleen? What do you mean?'

'I'm sorry. I know I told you Kathleen thought she had upset someone, but it was worse than that. She told me she was very scared of someone.'

'In what way? Did she think they might physically hurt her?'

'I think that she did.'

Sue carefully put her mug on the ground beside her. 'This is serious. Why didn't you tell me before?'

Beth felt very small. 'I'm sorry. It involves my friends. I didn't know what to do.'

Sue took a deep breath. 'You'd better tell me everything now.'

So that is what Beth did, starting with her conversation with Kathleen, finding out about the affair, and the pregnancy.

'And so, you see, I think someone who was at the house party had been using the affair to silence Kathleen because she knew something about them.'

'And the person who threatened Kathleen was someone there at the party?'

'That's it.'

'OK. I've got that clear. Have you talked to any of the people who were there about this?'

'I've asked questions, and last Saturday I did have a bit of a meltdown with them all. I told them I thought one of them was the person who Kathleen was terrified of, hinted they could have had something to do with her death.'

Sue's eyes widened. 'You think one of them killed Kathleen?'

Beth cringed. The words said out loud by Sue suddenly sounded so extreme. 'I don't know. Maybe.'

'You had this meltdown, as you call it, two days ago and then yesterday you had the phone call?'

'That's exactly it.' Beth sat back. Telling Sue was a kind of cathartic experience. She was exhausted, but had a feeling of resignation. It was like going to a doctor, telling her all the things that you had been secretly worrying about.

'OK. Well, that's a lot to take in,' said Sue, who had been quietly taking notes the whole time. She flipped back some pages. 'Let me make sure I've got this right: the person being accused was someone at the house party and that was, let me see, yourself and Sami, your children, Patrick, Kathleen and Conor, Imogen from school, her husband William, and Elsa.'

'That's right. And Alex.'

'I had a feeling you were underplaying things when you said Kathleen was worried about upsetting someone. I certainly didn't realise the extent of Kathleen's stress, but I did mention what I knew to the detective in charge. He decided that when everyone was questioned about Kathleen's state of mind on the Sunday evening they should also be asked about their relationship with Kathleen and their movements that morning.'

'Ah. Sami and Alex said you'd asked them. I wondered why.'

'We probably pick up on and check out a lot more things than you realise. We try to do it discreetly, but we know more than you think. We didn't know, however, that Kathleen claimed to have been threatened by someone.'

'I'm so sorry,' Beth said, crossing her arms tightly. 'Can you imagine thinking one of your close friends was capable of such a dreadful thing?'

Sue shook her head. 'I think in my job there's not much left to surprise me. Sometimes I miss the innocence of working at school. Now, maybe I can reassure you a bit. Although we didn't do a thorough investigation of everyone at the party, we did look into their relationships with Kathleen. To be honest, they all seem respectable, and there was no motive for any of them to have wished her harm. In fact, they all seemed genuinely very upset by her death and to have been very fond of her.'

Beth realised that Sue was holding back on a lot, which was frustrating, so she decided to try and push her a little.

'You said you checked what everyone was doing the morning Kathleen died. Can you at least give me a hint, you know, so I can stop worrying about it all?'

Sue bit her lip. 'I don't know.' She looked at Beth. 'Well, I suppose it can't do any harm. I can see it would be hard for you to ask your friends, but it's all pretty normal stuff.'

Beth waited.

Sue flipped over her notebook.

'Firstly, I must stress that the scene where Kathleen died has been thoroughly examined. There is no evidence that anyone was there, no physical signs, and on Kathleen herself no evidence of a struggle. So, you can see why, to date, we have been veering towards thinking Kathleen's death was an accident. Now, we were able to ascertain the approximate time Kathleen died. Her body was found at 7.40. Her yoga mat was put out at about 6.45. We also know she sent you a text at 6.40. The pathologist would like an early time, say between 6.45 and 7 a.m. but it could be as late as 7.15.'

'I'll start with you,' said Sue, giving her a grin. 'Now, at the time we think Kathleen died, you told us you were walking Ollie. We don't have any witnesses, but a neighbour saw you return, and we could check your phone location as you replied to Kathleen.' Sue took a breath. 'Now, your Sami says he was running on his own at the house he is looking after.'

'Yes, the Hendersons'.'

'A few people saw his car. He is well known. It never moved so that covers him.' Sue smiled. 'It's great living on a small island, isn't it? Sami's partner, Alex, was off cycling. He was seen at the caravan site a few times between half six and quarter to seven. That is only a five minute ride to Kathleen's house, and he doesn't have any sort of alibi, but then he also had no motive that we can find, and their relationship was not that close. Added to this, of course, is the fact there is no evidence of anyone being at the scene of the accident.

'William and Imogen were both in work ridiculously early. William's car was seen, he arrives at 6.30. He started surgery at 7.45. His car never left the car park. Imogen was at school. Her car was seen by the caretaker at 6.30 and it never moved. Imogen went for a walk for about half an hour after she arrived, but was back in school sometime after seven.'

'I didn't know she went out walking.'

'She told us that she often does to clear her head: up round the cemetery at Mountjoy. She said she doesn't meet people up there.'

'I see. William, Imogen and Sami's cars were all here the whole time, and Patrick didn't have a car, so none of them could have gone over.'

'No. The only adults who had the means to go over were you and Alex.' Sue grinned. 'Seriously, Beth, Kathleen was much loved, adored by her husband and the people she worked with. Of course, things are never completely straightforward, but we think it was most likely a tragic accident.'

'What about the silver car?'

Sue groaned. 'That was reported by an elderly lady who lives opposite Patrick's house. She swears she saw someone stopped in her driveway. The lady had got up to have a shower and the radio said it was 6.50. She was annoyed as she has one of those "no turning" signs in her driveway, and is obsessive about it. Anyway, she showered, and when she got out, she said it was gone. She heard the news headlines so guessed it was seven. She has no idea of the make of the car or the driver.'

'So, it's not a lot of help?'

'No, but we'll keep asking. It was early, and a bit odd that the car stopped. It could have been a tourist taking a call, looking at a map or something. But as I say, we've not found anything yet.'

Beth nodded. 'Yes, thank you. I can see that, but now you know about the affair; this person using it against her, well, you must view things a bit differently.'

'A lot of what you say is just Kathleen's words. She gave you no names, few details. She could have misjudged something, been exaggerating—'

'I don't believe she was, and the affair, the pregnancy—'

'I can't discuss those, but just to say we probably know more than you realise. You say Sami was with Kathleen the night of her miscarriage?'

'He was, and he said he'd be happy to talk to you about that.'

'It would have been useful if he'd mentioned it before.' Sue said this with a heavy note of sarcasm. 'But I will go and see him. Is he in the pharmacy today?'

'Yes. He's working.'

'The phone call still worries me,' said Beth. 'Could you trace who owns a phone from the number?'

'Possibly, but the call could have been made on a burner phone.'

'What's that?'

'People buy them so you can't track who it is calling. They got a reputation from people selling drugs, but all kinds of people use them. I will ask if they can trace the call, but it probably doesn't mean anything. I am sorry to say but after incidents of this kind there are sick people who get kicks out of making calls or posting things on social media. It's hard to believe, but I've seen this kind of thing before. Still, I'm not just dismissing this out of hand, I will make sure it's looked into.'

'By the way, did you find Kathleen's phone and earphones?'

'No. We did have a good search of the house and the area. We know she used it to text you. She must have sent it from the house and then not taken the phone out with her.'

'And the hens. Did you work out why they were out?'

'We have to assume Kathleen made a mistake. It's odd, but then there are always a few things you can't explain. You have to balance things up and go with what's the most probable solution.'

They heard squeaking from the guinea pigs in the shed as the door was propped open, allowing the sunshine in.

'Listen, Beth. Sudden death like this is hard for everyone to deal with. Be careful what you say to people. From what I've seen, your friends are good people, but no one likes to be accused of things they didn't do. Maybe this call is like a warning that you have overstepped the mark. Leave all this to us now. Are you sure you've told me everything?'

'I think so, yes.'

Sue stood up; her cup of tea stood cold and untouched. 'Sometimes we have to accept that accidents happen.'

Beth walked with her to the front door. 'Thank you for coming.'

'You take care.'

Beth watched her walk away. Sue had been respectful, had listened to her, but she had the impression Sue was more annoyed with her for withholding information than excited at a new line of enquiry. The point was that they knew everything now; she could hand it over. She'd tried to fight for Kathleen, but this was too much for her. Leave it to someone else now; back to normal life.

The following evening, Beth went again to yoga. She lay during the meditation trying to get to her safe place, her cottage, but as soon as she closed her eyes, she started to drift off. The bell startled her, and as she put her things together Gemma approached her.

'Fancy a drink?'

They went into the bar, where Beth bought them both a glass of red wine.

'How are you then? Did you sort out things with Sami?'

'I did. If he'd talked to me it would have made life a lot easier. So much has happened since we last talked, but yesterday I had a long chat with the Sue, the Family Liaison Officer.'

'Oh Sue, she's married to my cousin. He's a pain, but I like her.'

'She's been very good, actually. I have finally told her everything. I feel a bit stupid. I assumed they'd just accepted it was an accident but, of course, they'd looked into it a lot more. Sami had said to leave it to them, and I should have listened to him.'

'But you'd had that conversation with Kathleen; you were very worried. I think talking to the people who'd been at the party made sense.'

'I'm not sure I did anything more than wind people up. I had this anonymous call, basically telling me to keep out of things.'

'No! But surely that means you were onto something?'

'It could be, or maybe it's someone messing about.'

'Is that what you think?'

Beth shrugged. 'I don't know, but anyway it frightened the life out of me.'

'What happened?'

Beth told her about the call.

'That's awful. I hope they catch the bastard.'

'Sue didn't reckon they would be able to trace the caller.'

'You're kidding! They have to take this seriously.'

'The problem is, she said something about it might be a burner phones or something and you can't trace them.'

'Oh, yeah. A friend of mine found her partner had one. He used it to contact this woman he was having an affair with, the rat. Anyway, I hope they don't simply write this off and put some effort into tracing it.' Gemma took a sip of her drink. 'By the way, is your Layla still hanging around with that Conor, Kathleen's lad?'

'She still talks about him. Why?'

'Just that he was in here the other night talking to Elsa. He was drinking a lot. Now, I'm sorry for him and all that, but when I told him to ease off, he got very nasty. I turfed him out in the end. Just thought I'd let you know.'

Beth closed her eyes, rubbed her aching forehead. Before Kathleen's death she'd had a normal parent's concern over her daughter's teenage crush on an older, more experienced, boy. However, Beth was slowly realising Conor was a far more volatile, angry person than she'd realised. Who knew what he was capable of? She didn't want Layla anywhere near him and yet she knew the harder she tried to keep her away, the more she would fight against her. What on earth was she going to do?

17

The following Sunday started with a gentle, warm morning. The first day of April: the bluebells were out, bees and butterflies busy in the garden. Beth had worked hard all week at putting Kathleen's death out of her mind. She had immersed herself in her work, kept busy. Sue had rung one day to tell her that the call could not be traced. She wished this was a sign she should stop digging, move on, but she knew in her heart it was no such thing.

As they drove to Imogen's for Sunday lunch Beth looked out at the beautiful spring day, and she realised how much she had missed of her favourite season.

'It's a shame you have to go to London this evening,' Beth said to Sami.

'It's a pretty intensive day of revision classes, but then I won't be teaching the rest of the week. Alex has said that cover tomorrow is no problem, and—' Sami looked in the driver's mirror, grinned at Adam, 'he has extra help.'

Beth looked round at Adam. 'No school tomorrow?'

'It's only revision classes now. It'll be good to earn a bit of extra cash. I like working with Alex: he teaches me stuff all the time.'

'I hope your sister will get down to some work. I'm not happy with her going over to Gunwharf today, but maybe she needs a break.'

'I'll drop you off home after this and go straight to the Red Jet,' said Sami.

Imogen's house (as Beth still thought of it) was an isolated house tucked away in the woods. The roadway approaching it was barred by a gate which had been opened ready for them, but it gave a feeling of privilege to drive up there.

It was a perfect day, woods full of bird song and the hammering of woodpeckers. They parked in the large space in front of the house, next to Elsa's silver car.

Beth looked at the car. 'Isn't that the Peugeot I want?'

'Yes. This one has five doors. See: it looks fine.'

Beth lowered her voice. 'But the Hendersons' car looked nicer.'

'But I'm right about the problems with the back seat. Elsa was like you; she wanted a three door when she was choosing a car for her birthday until William took her to see the Hendersons' car. She agreed with him then.'

Beth was still not convinced, but dropped the subject and they walked over to join the others. She was surprised to see Patrick there. He appeared isolated and alone, although he was standing next to Alex. William was preparing a barbeque.

William greeted them. 'I know it's on the early side but I couldn't wait to have our first.'

Beth poured herself a glass of wine, then noticed the sound of the gentle fall of fir cones from the trees. She went to see if she could spot a red squirrel. Knowing you had to be patient to see these shy creatures, she stood very still until she saw one run further up the trunk of a tree on to the fine branches above. How they never fell or missed she couldn't understand.

It was while she stood being charmed by the squirrel that

Imogen came over. 'I hope you are in a better frame of mind than the other night—'

'Eh?' said Beth, shocked at the abrasive greeting.

'You were extremely rude, Beth. It wasn't like you.'

'I don't think I was rude; possibly a bit blunt.'

'It wasn't appropriate. You upset everyone. It wasn't a good way to behave.'

Beth swallowed, cross with herself for feeling tearful. 'I didn't mean to upset anyone.' Her voice was shaking now.

'Well, it's time to stop obsessing about it all. Patrick's here and he needs a break. He's heard the results of the post-mortem, so handle him with care.'

Beth had to ask, 'What did they say?'

'Patrick chose to share the results with us because he knows he can trust us not to go shouting our mouths off about it. If he wants to tell you, that's his decision, but I shall respect his privacy.'

With that Imogen strutted off. Beth felt herself blush, humiliated and angry. She never used to be so aggressive. Glancing over, she noticed Imogen was now having a go at William, telling him off for not lighting the barbeque earlier. Beth felt sorry for him, slightly vindicated that clearly Imogen was out of sorts with everyone today.

'How about a short walk in the woods? You could go to the squirrel hide while the barbeque heats up,' said William. 'You can leave me here. I'll be fine.'

Recognising his need for space, everyone agreed. Beth put down her glass and left with the others. Elsa walked ahead with Patrick. Imogen talked to Adam and Alex. Sami walked some way behind with Beth.

'What's got into Imogen?' he asked.

'I don't know. She had a go at me as soon as we arrived.'

'I know she can be a bit overbearing, but she's not usually downright rude. Poor William.'

'She's getting worse. She's like it in school as well.'

'You said she was winding up some of the staff?'

'None of the teachers want to approach her now. The deputy head has become a kind of mediator between Imogen and the rest. Two teachers are leaving. It's sad. The school was on the brink of huge success, but it's going to fall apart if Imogen carries on undermining the staff in the way she's doing.'

'I wonder what the matter is?'

'No idea, but she's no right to take it out on me.'

They caught up with the others. Sami joined Imogen. Adam fell back to walk with Beth.

'It's good to see you out in the fresh air,' she said.

'I like it, having a break from the pressure.'

'You shouldn't feel too much pressure. You're well set for your grades. It's exciting, isn't it?' she said, trying desperately to add the yeast of joy to her words.

'I don't know. Going to university is a big thing.'

'You'll love it. How is that piece of coursework you've been working on? Something to do with thermo something? You must be nearly there by now.'

Adam was soon chatting about thermodynamics as if it was the most thrilling subject in the universe which, of course, to him it was. Beth loved listening to the passion he spoke with. She did occasionally make sure he didn't trip over logs or walk into trees, but that was all that was needed of her. As he talked, she managed to calm down from her conversation with Imogen.

They sat for a while in the squirrel hide. Beth had never seen a squirrel from in here and she often wondered if they had quietly gone to live somewhere else, but it never stopped her waiting and hoping. She was so engrossed that she didn't notice the others leave. Realising she was alone, she turned to go back, but stopped when she heard two people arguing. She recognised the voices of Elsa and Patrick.

She heard Elsa say, 'How can you say you loved her when it's obvious what she did?'

Patrick's words were indistinguishable, but whatever he said sent Elsa running in her direction, and then past her. Beth felt uneasy. The tone of the conversation seemed intense, intimate even.

Patrick appeared.

'Is everything OK?' she asked.

'Something needed clearing up; that's all.'

'So, has Sean gone back to Ireland?'

'Not yet. His family are over here, so he's gone to the mainland to meet up with them, but he said he would stay with me a bit longer.'

'That's good of him.'

'I know, he's talked to them at work and they are happy for him to have prolonged leave but, of course, he will have to go back eventually. I shall miss him when he does.'

'Any idea what Conor will do?'

'Not yet. I told him I'm happy for him to stay with me. We get on and he's independent. He's off today somewhere with his mates.'

They were catching up with everyone else, but Patrick took hold of Beth's arm and held her back.

'I wanted to talk to you. That police officer, Sue, came to see me. They've had the results of the post-mortem.'

'Was everything as you expected?'

'Well, as they thought it was the bang to her head on the cliff-side as she fell that caused her death. So that's a relief. She'd not have known much of what was happening, and not suffered long. However, something new did come up. They found that very recently Kathleen had miscarried. It had been early on in her pregnancy.'

'I am so sorry. Um, did you know?'

Patrick nodded. 'Of course, but I was sorry it showed up in the post-mortem. I'd worked so hard checking her room, you know, for pregnancy tests or anything. I didn't want the police to know.'

'Why?' Beth watched him carefully.

'Because I know how people think. I was told after the chemotherapy that there was little chance of fathering a child. I told no one, but I know people work things out for themselves. I could just see the rumours spreading around that Kathleen had had an affair. I couldn't bear that. Because I knew I was the father.'

'I see.' Beth saw the fire in his eyes. She wasn't going to argue with that, and in any case, if that was his way of handling things, who was she to add to the pain?

'I know it's not trendy, but I believe in miracles. The baby was mine. I know it. When I heard Kathleen being sick in the mornings, I didn't say anything, but I was so excited: our miracle. I waited for her to tell me, but then a few days before she died, I saw some of those pads in the bathroom. She looked so pale and was so exhausted, I guessed then that she'd lost the baby. It was so sad. I respected her space and never said anything, but it gave me hope. We could have tried again.' Patrick was picking bits of bark off a tree.

Beth watched him. Kathleen had told Sami that Patrick would have been prepared to believe it, but then Gemma had said she thought Patrick knew about Kathleen's affair. Did he seriously believe that it had been a miracle, or was he simply acting a part?

'I am so sorry.'

Patrick seemed to relax. 'They're saying Kathleen's body will be released soon so that I can organise the funeral. I'll be pleased to do that. It's been awful, all this waiting.'

'Have the police stopped looking for the silver car?'

'Nothing's come up. That was always a long shot. No, it was an accident. They are sure of that, thank God. I thought we had to wait for the inquest before we could hold the funeral, but Sue said that could take weeks, even months.'

'I see. Well, the funeral will be hard, but a good thing to do.'

'I'm trying to see it as the end of one chapter, the start of another.'

They returned to the garden where everyone stood around chatting. Beth nibbled on a burger. Imogen was asking Alex how he was settling in, and about the changes they were planning, before turning to Sami.

'So, will you continue lecturing in London next year?'

'They've asked me to carry on next year, so, yes, for the time being. I'll be glad to get this lot through their exams. I've a day of revision classes planned tomorrow, so I'm going up there tonight.'

'They're lucky to have you,' said Imogen. Beth watched her, smiling pleasantly. She found it annoying that she could turn the charm on when she felt like it.

'I have to say I don't feel so happy leaving Beth now,' said Sami. His words set a different tone; people became more alert. Beth wondered what he was going to say. 'You see, Beth had an anonymous phone call last Sunday.' Sami blurted the words out without warning.

Beth stared at him. What had possessed him to bring that up now? She hoped he saw the horror in her eyes and would stop, but instead he continued. 'Yes. It was awful. The person used a voice distorter, the coward.'

Beth looked around; their friends were looking anywhere other than at Sami. The atmosphere was like an elastic band pulled to breaking point.

William scowled. 'It must have been some kids messing about.'

'Of course,' said Imogen. 'These things are best ignored.'

'I didn't think so,' said Sami. 'Beth has reported it to the police. The person said some pretty nasty things. They can't be allowed to get away with that.' He looked round the group. 'Even if it was someone we know, I want them caught. The police agreed, and are tracing the call.'

'It sounds dreadful,' said William.

'It was. I hope nothing like this happens again,' said Sami, and he went back to eating his chicken.

Imogen glared at him. 'I'm sorry about that, but we are here for a break from unpleasantness. Now, I think it's time I brought out the puddings. I've got your favourite macaroons, Patrick.' She walked off briskly to the house, and William started to talk about a friend who had recently returned from an around-the-world sailing trip. It was easy. Everyone seemed to relax, but Beth was watching Sami; it was so unlike him to stir things up like that.

After dessert was eaten, Beth went inside to use the bathroom.

To the left of the hallway, she peeped into a room which she knew was William's study. There was a cabinet with his medals and awards for sport, and on the wall the certificate for his first-class degree. It seemed a bit over the top, but it made her realise how proud Adam would be when he'd achieved his degree. Yes: it was good that he was going. Next to the certificate she noticed a small home safe, and thought that maybe living in such an isolated place you needed to think a bit more about security. Beth went upstairs to the bathroom.

On her way back, she heard noises from Imogen's bedroom and peeked in. Imogen stood sideways on, pressing pills out of a foil container into the palm of her hand. Beth watched, struck by the intensity of Imogen's actions and saw the whole of Imogen's body relax as she swallowed them. Maybe her back was giving her a lot more pain than she was letting on: that could, in part anyway, explain how uptight she seemed lately.

Beth tried to creep past. She didn't want another confrontation but Imogen, seeming to sense her presence, turned and, to Beth's relief, smiled. 'Oh, hi. Just taking something. I didn't want to say too much in front of Patrick, but I'm sorry about that call you had. Are you OK?'

'I think so—'

Imogen interrupted her. 'Good. I saw you and Patrick talking. Did he tell you about the post-mortem?'

Beth stood on the threshold of the bedroom, and glanced around. The room spoke far more of Imogen than William, with piles of files, a desk with a laptop, prints she knew Imogen had put up when she moved. 'Yes, we talked on the way back from the hide.'

Beth felt Imogen watching her, and could tell that, as in a game of strategy, Imogen was trying to work out what she knew.

'So, did he tell you everything they found out about Kathleen?'

Beth nodded. 'He told me she'd been pregnant, had lost a baby.'

Imogen breathed out. 'I was so shocked. Of course, I'd known she was pregnant.'

'You'd known?' Beth had wondered, but was still shocked.

Imogen looked out of the window. 'I overheard a conversation William had with her on the phone a few weeks before she died.'

'Did you talk to William about it?'

'No. I wasn't meant to know, was I? I did wonder about it, though. You know, with Patrick having been so ill—' She looked at Beth.

'Patrick's treatment meant it was unlikely that he could father children, didn't it?' said Beth.

'Yes, exactly,' replied Imogen. 'And so we know what that means—'

'Patrick insists the baby was his and it was a miracle.'

Imogen waved her hand impatiently. 'Yes, yes, but we know that's rubbish.'

Beth moved closer to her. 'So, you've suspected Kathleen of

having an affair for a while? Did you have any idea who the affair was with?'

Imogen went red. 'No, of course not.'

'But you didn't know she'd lost the baby?'

Imogen shook her head. To Beth's surprise her eyes filled with tears. 'No. I wish to God I had.'

'It must have been a terrible thing to go through on her own,' said Beth.

Imogen sniffed. 'I guess it was.'

Unspoken words hung in the air until Imogen said, 'Well, it's all in the past now. I guess we all want to move on.' She paused, then asked, 'But what about you?'

'I'm trying to.'

'Patrick tells me he can organise the funeral now. I really think, Beth, that will be a good thing, and will put an end to all this.'

Imogen walked past her, and Beth, realising the conversation had come to an end, followed her back outside. They walked past a montage of old, small photographs of Imogen and Elsa, hanging in the hallway.

'They were taken the day we moved in,' said Imogen. 'I was so proud: my first home, all paid for by me.'

'I remember. I brought you up Welsh cakes.'

'You did, and we sat outside. Elsa and Adam were five then. It was a sunny day and I felt I'd landed in paradise. I'd hate to leave here.'

Hearing the sadness in Imogen's voice, Beth asked, 'You've no reason to, have you?'

'William's happy here, even though it's not anything like as smart as he's used to. Then my parents found details of some huge house in Cowes advertised by one of the London property agents and have been persuading him that it would be a good move for us. It's their kind of house: modern, stunning views over the Solent; neat, tidy lawns, posh neighbourhood and all that.'

'It sounds expensive, but William has money, doesn't he?'

'Yes, but Mum and Dad say they would come in with us, a kind of investment for them as well. Still, I'm holding out. I have to put my foot down sometimes, like I did last year. I know they don't like it, but William doesn't understand. They'll take over our lives completely if I don't. No, this is my home.'

They went outside and Imogen left her. Beth found a quiet spot in the garden and closed her eyes. So Imogen had known about Kathleen being pregnant, and had known that she'd had an affair with someone. Imogen had been so bitter when Kathleen died, which would be no wonder if she'd suspected Kathleen had been pregnant by William. Having wondered that about Sami, Beth knew how much that hurt. Why did Imogen seem to wish she'd known about Kathleen losing the baby? Did she wish she could have supported Kathleen, or was there another reason? Did she regret something she'd said or done to Kathleen? Beth stopped herself: she had moved on from this. It was the job of the police now.

Soon it was time to leave. Adam had already left, using work as an excuse, and had walked back. As Sami drove her home, Beth asked, 'Why did you bring up the anonymous phone call?'

'If it was one of them, I didn't think it would hurt to know we'd been to the police.'

'It's not like you to confront people like that. You didn't mention that the police can't trace the call.'

He grinned. 'No. Let them sweat! My aim really was to frighten this person so at least they don't do it again.'

'I hope it works. Thank you. By the way, Imogen told me she knew about Kathleen's pregnancy. She overheard William on the phone.'

'They both knew. Did they know about Patrick's infertility?'

'I think William did, and I think Imogen had worked it out. I wondered if she'd been worried about William and Kathleen having an affair.'

'No way. William would never take that risk, even if he was tempted. He's only been here five years. He loves Imogen, I'm sure, and there is no way he'd be so stupid as to have an affair with a patient. No, he wouldn't do that.'

'I'm not sure Imogen is so convinced. I talked with Patrick when we went for the walk. He knew about the pregnancy as well, he says it was a miracle.'

'Yes. He said that to me.'

'Do you believe him? Does he genuinely think that?'

'I think some people are more than capable of lying to themselves if they don't like the truth. I see it when people discuss their illness or that of someone they love.' Sami patted her knee. 'Anyway, you don't need to worry about any of that now, do you?'

She forced a smile. 'No, of course not.'

They arrived at the house. 'OK, then. I've got all my stuff. I'll see you tomorrow evening. I'll give you a ring when I get on the Red Jet.'

Ollie came running to greet Beth.

'Come on, you need a good walk.' They went down Castleford Shute and up around the farms where Beth used to take Layla and Adam to see the horses. While she was there, she sent a text to Layla, asking her what time she would be in. The unhelpful reply said:

Don't know.

After having tea with Adam, Beth spent the evening sewing, watching TV but really waiting for Layla to come home. When she did finally come in, Beth tried to sound relaxed as she said. 'You're late. Have a good day with your friends?'

Layla shrugged. She looked miserable.

'Something up?'

'I'm going to bed.'

Beth watched her stomp up the stairs. Tomorrow she hoped they would talk.

That night Beth tried not to think too much about the day. She had promised herself not to dwell on Kathleen any more, but still she felt uneasy. Outside she heard rain starting to pat the windows: they'd been lucky today. In the distance she heard thunder, which was building up. The lightning started. The storm felt like it was overhead and she was surprised to see Ollie had come to find her, as he was usually fine with storms.

'It's nothing to worry about,' she said calmly. 'But listen. Dad's away. You can sleep on the rug here. Don't tell him.'

Ollie quickly settled next to her bed, and soon they were both asleep.

18

The next morning, looking out of the window everything looked fine. When Beth opened the window, the air felt fresh and clean. Ollie looked up lazily. 'Come on,' Beth said, 'We've work to do.'

The stream was full and muddy as they walked down the shute, and Beth stood on the bridge watching it rush beneath her feet. Her phone rang, and without looking at who the caller was, she answered.

'Going to the police was a mistake, Beth. I'm watching you. I know your secret. Keep your mouth shut.'

Beth's hands shook. The sickness, the panic she felt were deeper than before. It was the same voice, the same number. It had to be someone who was there yesterday, didn't it? Sami's words certainly hadn't scared them off. And then it dawned on her that of course, however much she might want to think this was all closed down, the person was still there and presumably thinking they'd got away with it. And now they were trying to control her. If she kept quiet, stopped digging, they'd won, hadn't they? Beth stared at her phone. What should she do? The police had told her they couldn't trace the call, and Sami, even though he had been supportive, didn't really think this person was dangerous. Who knew what he'd do? She'd been shocked when he'd told everyone about the last call at Imogen's. It wasn't how she would have handled it. No. For now she would keep it to herself.

Instead Beth decided to occupy herself with more practical matters, and so headed upstairs to see Layla.

Beth found Layla still in bed, saying she was taking a day off.

'What's up? You look pale.'

'Must have been something I ate. I've not been sick, just tummy ache.'

Beth put her head to one side. 'OK. Well, have today off then.'

Adam left for the pharmacy and Layla stayed in bed, while Beth tried to settle to work in the kitchen with Ollie sitting close by.

Beth was disturbed by Elsa arriving. She didn't look her usual together self either. She was wearing little makeup, and her hair was pulled back into a ponytail.

'Hi, Elsa. Come on in. Is everything all right?'

'I came to see Layla. She sent me a text, said she's off today.'

'She's not feeling too good—' Before Beth could finish, a voice behind her said, 'It's OK, Mum. Me and Elsa can go in the living room.' Layla, still pale, was wrapped in her dressing gown. Beth left them to it and went back to the kitchen. As she sat trying to work, she realised she could hear the girls talking.

'... and then yesterday we had this row,' Elsa was saying.

'What happened?'

'Patrick was so annoying; I'm really pissed off with him.'

'He's bound to be a bit out of it now. It's awful about Kathleen. I liked her.'

'I don't know why.'

'She was so sweet, one of Mum's best friends. Mum has been really cut up about it; she's been weird. Not like her to get plastered on that Saturday. Parents shouldn't do that, should they? Dad was well fed up with her. I don't blame him. It was dead embarrassing.'

Beth cringed.

'I know your mother was friends with her,' said Elsa, 'but she was manipulative. I told you she hated Patrick helping me with my photography. She interfered, nagged him he was doing too much. She was just jealous. And she was always after men. She was good looking for her age and knew it. Only a few weeks ago, I warned Mum that Kathleen was after William, told her to be careful, work a bit harder at her marriage.'

Beth listened more carefully.

'You said that?' said Layla.

'I did. Mum is such a workaholic. She's never at home.'

'Your mum has a right to a career.'

'But she was losing him. I'm sure of that.'

'You're assuming that Kathleen was looking for someone else. Patrick worshipped her: look at that house they've got.'

'He's always been blind to her faults.'

Beth stood up, and moved closer to the door. So, Elsa had been worried about William and Kathleen as well. What worried her more, though, was the way Elsa was talking about Patrick. She felt, as she had the day before, that the relationship was too close, and was surer now than ever that Elsa had some kind of feelings for Patrick.

'What do you mean?' Layla was asking.

'I heard Mum and William saying the post-mortem showed Kathleen had been pregnant at some time, and that Patrick couldn't have been the father. I always knew she played around. I said to Patrick yesterday he could move on now, forget her.'

'What did he say?'

'Not a lot. I thought it might show him what she was like, but he seemed to shrug it off. I should have realised then that he was never going to see the real her. I was stupid, got it all wrong.'

'What do you mean?'

'It doesn't matter. I don't want to think about it. How was your day with Conor? Go well?'

'Not really. Something happened,' said Layla, and at that point Beth heard Layla get up, and she shut the door firmly.

Beth, momentarily distracted from what Elsa had been saying, allowed a wave of anger to wash over her at Layla's lies. How dare she say she'd been with friends when she'd been with Conor?

Soon after Beth heard the front door shutting. Layla had gone back to her bedroom. Summoning up the energy for a confrontation about Conor, Beth marched up the stairs. There was no reply when she knocked and pushed open the bedroom door. 'We need to talk about—' she started, but then was shocked to see Layla crying on her bed.

'Whatever's the matter?'

'Everything, Mum.'

Beth went over and put her hand on her shoulder.

'What do you mean?'

'Life is shit.'

'Did something happen yesterday? Were you just with your friends?'

Layla looked around.

'Tell me. Tell me what happened.'

'I didn't go with my friends. Don't go crazy, but I went with Conor.'

'Layla, you shouldn't have lied to me.'

'But you'd never have let me go. Anyway, now I wish I'd not bothered.'

'Why? What happened?'

'You'll go mad.'

Panic gripped Beth. Various scenarios rushed through her head. Was Layla taking drugs, being attacked by Conor, shoplifting...

'Tell me.'

'You're not to tell anyone, though. Don't be mad with Conor or anyone—'

'What's happened?'

'Promise, Mum.'

'Oh OK. Tell me.'

Layla lifted the top of her pyjamas. Her belly button was a mess: a red weeping sore.

Beth stared in horror. How could Layla do this? Of all the times to do something so stupid? 'What the hell?'

Layla sniffed. 'It hurts so much.'

Beth's heart melted. 'What's happened?'

'It was a belly button piercing.'

'Where did you have that done?'

'It was somewhere in Portsmouth.'

'But it's illegal at your age.'

'It's not, Mum. It's up to the place.'

'That's awful. It should be illegal.'

'I knew what I was doing.'

'Was it dirty in there?'

'No, ever so clean.'

'Why did you have it done?'

'We were talking, and, um, Conor—'

'Conor?'

'You said you wouldn't say anything.'

'OK. So what did he say?'

'He was saying about his piercings. Elsa has one as well. You know, her nose one. Well then, Conor said why don't you get one done. I thought I'd have my belly button—'

'So I wouldn't see it?'

'I suppose so. Anyway, I had it done.'

'And did it hurt?'

'Quite a bit. So, I came home, and then I panicked. I never

wanted it, not really. I tore out the ring and it started to bleed everywhere. I washed it with soap and put a plaster on it. Now it's weeping and there is a huge red lump here. It really hurts, Mum.'

She started to cry again and, speaking though the sobs, said, 'I looked it up online. It said if you take the thing out you can get an abscess because there's nowhere for it to drain. I think that might be what's happening now.'

Beth looked at the red, sore area. 'It looks infected. You need to see the doctor.'

'You're not to have a go at Conor. I decided to have it done.'

'He should have known better, but let's get you sorted out.'

'You don't sound mad. I thought you'd go apeshit.'

Beth put her arms around Layla. 'Life's hard. I do understand. I did some pretty stupid things at your age, you know.'

'I can't imagine that.'

'We're human. We make mistakes.'

'Dad doesn't.'

Beth smiled. 'He's different.'

'Like Adam.'

'I guess. They bury themselves in their work, but it doesn't mean they don't have their own worries. Right, I'll go and see if I can get an emergency appointment. Not easy on a Monday, but you never know.'

'Will you come with me?'

'Of course. I'll go and phone, and then I'll make you pancakes for a late breakfast.'

Beth rang the surgery. Once she'd explained what the matter was, she was given an emergency appointment for later that morning. After she'd made the pancakes, she took them up to Layla.

'I hope it's not Elsa's stepdad. It would be so embarrassing,' said Layla.

'It doesn't matter who you see. I was glad to get an appointment. William will be fine. He's seen everything.'

When they were leaving the house, Layla groaned as Beth suggested they walk.

'Come on. Fresh air will be good for you. It's literally down two roads.'

Layla was unhappy throughout the walk and, by the time they arrived at the surgery, Beth secretly regretted not taking the car.

They went in the main entrance, were hit by the familiar doctors' smell, and the rows of worrying leaflets about all the symptoms you needed to see your doctor about. The pharmacy entrance was on the right. Beth peeped in, saw Adam working, and felt a rush of pride.

They walked down to reception, and sat in what was, for a doctors' waiting room, a very pleasant space. It had recently been redecorated in pastel colours. Cheerful prints decorated the walls, and current magazines, rather than ones that were years out of date, were on the table.

Beth knew they would have a wait. They were early, and William never ran to time. She always told the children, it was good, that it meant he was giving patients the time they needed but, for all that, it was frustrating. She noticed that the doctors all seemed to have dropped calling for patients over the tannoy but came out to collect them. Beth had seen most of them at different times. There was the new one who looked no older than Adam, earnest and stressed, and an older woman who was slightly scary, and lacked any bedside manner, but always knew when something was serious and was quick to sort it out. Finally, there was a much older man. He was calling his patient now with the unhurried air of a man who had been doing his job well, seen most things, but missed the days of a slower pace when he had time to talk, to get to know families and be part of the community. Beth knew he was now working three days a week and was counting the days to retirement in the summer. She also knew they were having huge difficulty replacing him because of a shortage of doctors on the island.

Eventually William came into the waiting room. He carried himself with the quiet air of a confident man who cared deeply about his work. Beth and Layla followed him to his room, which was at the end of a long corridor.

He held the door open for them. There was only one seat positioned at the end of William's desk, so Beth gestured to Layla to sit down. It all seemed much more intimate than the surgery visits she experienced as a child when the patient sat across an enormous leather desk with the doctor peering over. Of course, now there was also a laptop and printer sitting squarely on the desk next to a few regularly used instruments for looking down ears and throats. Above his desk, William had a line drawing of Christ Church and, framed on his desk, a photo of him in full sailing gear, standing with some friends in front of a yacht.

The room itself was lighter and brighter than the dark corridor had prepared her for. A pleasant breeze came in from the large open window. Outside there was a small boundary of grass and a low wall which separated them from what had been an overgrown driveway. Beth could see the roof of the old chapel that was as dilapidated as she'd imagined, but the tall grasses had gone.

'Right, Layla,' said William, 'you are my last appointment here. On to home visits then, so I can give you as much time as you need. What's the problem?'

Layla looked nervously at Beth, who felt like the mother of a nine year old again.

Beth explained what had happened and William, with that wonderful ability doctors have of never looking surprised, nodded and said, 'Mm, looks very painful. Good job you came when you did. Do you have any sterile dressings at home?'

'We do.'

'Good. Well, I'll give you antibiotics and I want you to put a dressing on it. Come back in two days to see the nurse. OK?'

He printed a prescription and handed it to Layla. 'I think they're busy in the pharmacy. Hope it doesn't take too long.'

Layla stood up but twinged with pain.

'Look, my first home visit is up your way. I could drop you off home. Let me take this script through to Alex.'

Beth looked out of the window. 'They've been tidying the old driveway. Do you think they're planning on doing anything with that old chapel?'

'Not as far as I know. I asked them to cut the grass. I need to open the window. It gets so stuffy in here and it's not good for me and my asthmatic patients: gets us all sneezing.'

As William opened the door, Beth pointed at the enormous hooded coat hanging on the back of his door. 'At least you don't need that today.'

He laughed. 'That's for home visits in the winter.'

In the pharmacy, the prescription was ready as William had got it made up for them and Beth tried to avoid the glares of the patients waiting as they went to leave. William looked out into the car park and said, 'You know, we'd be better taking the pharmacy car if it's free. Even if I can get out now, someone will have taken my space by the time I come back.'

He checked with Alex, and he signed a sheet to say he had the car.

They walked out of the surgery, through the car park, up a small slope and there, on its own, sat a small silver car.

'This is so kind,' said Beth.

'It's no problem. We are so lucky to have this car. It never gets blocked. Well done, Sami, getting it for the pharmacy and the surgery. Well, strictly speaking it's just for the pharmacy,' he said, grinning.

'I'd forgotten about it. I know he said it meant that most of the staff who are local, like him and Kathleen, can walk in to work. If there's an emergency and a prescription needs delivering, they can then use the car.'

'Exactly, and now with Alex not owning a car himself it's available for him as well. As a special concession Sami's allowed me to use it at times if it's convenient. He even allowed Imogen to go on the insurance and have keys. We went through this patch when I was doing a lot of on call and her car kept going wrong. Of course, she could only use it overnight, but it was great.'

William drove them home, and Layla got out of the car.

As Beth undid her seatbelt, William said, 'I was sorry about that phone call. You must have found it very unsettling. I hope the police will take it seriously.'

Beth was grateful that William was back to being his usual friendly self. 'Thank you. I'd better let you get on with your work. Thank you so much for dropping us off. Teenagers, eh! You never know what they're going to do next.'

William gave an empathetic smile and drove off.

However, as Beth stood watching the car disappear, something dawned on her. She had just been in a silver car, available to practically everyone she knew, including Imogen.

Inside the house, she kept thinking about the pharmacy car, remembered Sue and her warnings about keeping information back, so sent her a text mentioning it and the further phone call.

Afterwards she sat in the garden. She needed to think through the implications of the pharmacy car. Anyone could have used it: Imogen, William, Alex, even maybe Patrick or Sami. Any of them could have taken the car. Her heart raced at the enormity of this discovery. Now she knew that anyone at the house party had the means by which to drive over and silence Kathleen the morning of her death: the pharmacy car. Any of them could have used it. But which one? What secret were they so desperate to hide?

19

That evening Beth told Sami about Layla and the piercing, but didn't mention the phone call.

Sami was up early the next morning. His students had exams and so he wasn't going to London for the next two days

'What are you going to do with yourself?' asked Beth.

'I'll go for a run, then probably spend most of the day at the pharmacy.'

'You're there so much. You've not been spending as much time in the garden, and that's not good for you. Be careful.'

He kissed her on the forehead. 'Love you.'

While Beth was in the shed attending to the guinea pigs, she heard the house phone, and rushed back inside. To her surprise, it was Layla's music teacher with a new date for Layla's exams.

'But she did them a couple of weeks ago—'

'She didn't come. She sent me a text. Said she was ill.'

'Oh my goodness, I don't believe she did that.'

'I'm sorry. I did tell her that you wouldn't get a refund with such short notice.'

'I'm angry about the money, but even more about her lying to me. Thank you for the date, but I think I need to see what she is up to before we go paying out for more.'

'Of course. Let me know in the next week.'

Beth charged up the stairs and straight into Layla's bedroom.

'How could you lie to me about your exams?'

'Eh?'

'You know, your music exams. How dare you cancel them? Do you know how much they cost?'

'I told you I didn't want to do them.'

'We paid nearly two hundred pounds for you to do those exams and you couldn't even be bothered to go to them.'

'I told you I hate exams.' Layla turned over in her bed.

'Don't ignore me. You always say that, but then you always do well.'

'Just because I do well doesn't mean I enjoy it.'

'You've come so far. Grade seven in both. You'll have them all your life. They'll go on your personal statement for university. You are so lucky.'

'So you keep telling me.'

'Where were you when you should have been doing your exam?'

Layla turned over to look at her. 'I went to Shepherd's Chine with Conor. I told him about fossils. He was actually interested.'

'You went on his motorbike?'

Layla grabbed hold of the top of her duvet cover with tight fists. 'You never listen to the important stuff, do you?'

'You're not allowed on that bike, and you should be concentrating on your work, not wandering around a beach.'

Layla sat up in the bed.

'Listen to this, Mum. I hate the bloody flute and singing exams. I'm leaving school as soon as I can. I'm going to travel.'

'Well, I'm afraid to say, you're wrong. You have to stay in school or do some kind of training until you're eighteen, so you'd better just get on with it. You are so lucky. You have the chance to make something of your life. You don't want to end up like—'

'Like you? Do you hate your life so much? Having me and Adam. Is that why you're doing this degree?'

'No. Dad wanted me to.' It had slipped out so easily.

Layla stared at her. 'What?'

'I didn't mean that.'

'For God's sake, Mum. Don't you ever think for yourself?'

'Look: this conversation is not about me. It's about you, and you lying. It's about me not being able to trust anyone, any more.'

At that moment Sami returned from his run, and he came to see what was going on.

'I heard voices. What's wrong?'

Beth told Sami about Layla missing her exam.

'Do you know how much that exam cost?' said Sami.

Beth, frightened by the volcano of emotion building, and feeling calmer now herself, stepped in to mediate. 'Leave it. Layla will take her exams when she is ready.'

Layla glared. 'I'm sorry I'm such a disappointment to you. I'm sorry I'm not Adam.'

Sami raised an eyebrow. 'At least he does some work. I've not seen you exactly breaking your back recently. Your music teacher came into the pharmacy about something the other day. Told you were late with your assignment.'

'Thank you, Mr Croft,' said Layla. 'He is such a creep.'

Beth grimaced at Sami, gestured with her head and they left the bedroom. She shut the door and said to Sami, 'Why did you wind her up by mentioning the assignment?'

'It makes no difference what I say. She always gets upset. Some things have to be said, Beth. I know you hate rows, but she has to realise what she has done.'

'I blame it on this infatuation with Conor,' said Beth.

'But he's never been round here. It's all in her head.'

'She spent that other Sunday with him and before that she missed her exams to see him.'

'He should find it embarrassing: a girl her age after him.'

'Or flattering. He's pretty insecure. She's so vulnerable. I hate to see her so desperate. I should have raised a daughter with more self-esteem. All these right-on books I read to her: *Princess Smarty Pants*. I bought her a garage. "You can be anything," I said, when I kissed her goodnight.'

'But at the end of the day she has to work it out for herself. Right, I think I'll shower and go down to the pharmacy. It will seem easy after this.'

Beth found Ollie, waiting patiently for his walk. They went out down Castleford Shute again. She stood on the bridge staring at the water. How could Layla do that? It was a lot of money, and she had lied. She'd achieved so little herself. After all, Beth had enough insight to know that for her the children were her main achievement in life. However, what particularly upset her was the lying, the betrayal. It damaged the picture of family life she'd worked desperately hard to construct, of the home life she'd never had herself.

When they were first married, Beth had taught herself some of Sami's favourite Iraqi meals and endeavoured to have a family meal once a week. It was less frequent now, but today she decided it was something she desperately needed to do. She roasted lamb, cooked rice with cardamom and saffron, and made dolma, stuffed vegetables that Adam loved. As a nod to her own heritage, she made a fresh batch of Welsh cakes for dessert.

That evening they sat down together. Layla was quiet. Adam looked pale.

'You need to get out of your room, love,' she said to Adam.

'Um, yes. Look, while we're all here, I've been meaning to say something.'

Beth looked up alarmed. 'What's the matter?'

'I was thinking of taking a year out.'

'Cool. You're going travelling?' said Layla.

'Hang on. What's the matter?' asked Beth.

'I'd like to spend a year at the pharmacy, see if it's what I want to do. What do you think, Dad?'

Sami grimaced. 'I don't know. You're all set for Oxford.'

Beth watched her son: red, flustered. Although part of her longed for Adam to stay at home, she knew it was her duty as his mother to dig deeper. 'Be honest, Adam. Aren't you just avoiding facing going away to uni?'

Adam pushed back his chair and Beth heard him run upstairs. They waited, wondering if he would come back, and after a lot of thumping about, he did.

'This came in the post today.' He held out black scarf with bright yellow stripes and the crest of Brasenose College on it.

Sami blushed. 'I thought it would be a surprise.'

'It nearly killed me, Dad,' said Adam. 'Have you any idea how much pressure this puts on me?'

'I'm sorry. I thought it would motivate you, inspire you.'

'And you think I need that?' To Beth's horror, Adam burst into tears. She'd had no idea he was this stressed.

'I know going to university is daunting. It's more than I ever did, but you can do it.'

'Mum, don't make him do something he doesn't want to,' interrupted Layla.

Beth tried to focus on Adam. 'I had no idea it was all getting to you. How long have you been feeling like this?'

'A while now.'

Sami put his hand out. 'Look, I'm sorry about the scarf. It was stupid. We'll put it away. You don't need to decide this now. Keep working for your A levels: see how that goes.'

'But everyone is expecting me to get the grades, to go to Oxford.

What if I fail? Or what if I get there, and everyone is so much cleverer than me?'

'I understand,' said Sami. 'You know, I had done well at school but when I went to university, I found all these kids who'd done as well if not better than me. The ones who'd been to public schools were so confident and I felt miserable.'

Beth bit her lip. Sami had never talked about this before. She'd known he found things hard socially, but she always assumed he'd been more than confident about his academic ability.

'The thing was, soon it all settled down. I was doing something I loved, like you with your chemistry. You love it, Adam, you have a real gift for it, and you'll be with other students who love the subject as well. They wouldn't have offered you a place if they didn't think you could cope with the work.'

'But the rest, Dad, the gowns, the exams. Even the names for the terms. Nothing is like my friends' universities.'

'You'll cope with it all. Why don't you talk to William? He studied at Oxford.'

'That was years ago,' said Adam.

'What about the new doctor at the practice?' said Sami. 'I think she might have gone there. If you want to check before you talk to her you could always check the GMC register online. Every doctor is there. It's simple, and it will tell you where and when she graduated. If she did, I'm sure she'd be happy to talk to you. She's very friendly.'

Adam shrugged. 'I might.'

'But all that shit, the gowns and things don't matter,' said Layla. 'You're dead clever. You should go. You have to go, anyway, because I've told all my friends now and they're dead impressed.' Layla stood up and put her arm around her brother. 'Bro, you are so clever. But still, you know, as they say: you do you.'

Beth saw Adam put his hand on his sister's hand, was relieved that early bond between them was still there. She gave a grateful smile to Layla. And, for once, calm settled on the house.

Layla and Adam went to watch a film on Netflix together. Sami found a bottle of wine and poured two glasses.

At that moment Sami's phone rang. He put down his glass, reached over, placed one hand on Beth's, and picked up his phone with the other.

Beth watched the lines of stress crease on his forehead and felt his hand squeeze hers.

'Oh God. Oh, no.'

20

Beth stared through the windscreen as she drove through the dark streets. The lights were on in the pub, cars were already in the car park. They passed the shop where teenagers were hanging about outside, a young woman clutching a pizza in a box. Beth's emotions were ricocheting off each other like steel balls in a pinball machine. 'An overdose of pain killers', that's what William had said. Beth's mind couldn't help linking it to Kathleen. Had Imogen tried to commit suicide because she was guilty of Kathleen's murder?

As Beth parked next to Sami, she remembered that the last time she came here was to visit the morgue, and shuddered.

Sami paid and put the tickets in both their cars. 'I've put enough on for either of us to stay the night, but this way one of us can get away if we need to.'

They walked past weary looking relatives, into the brightly lit hospital.

Sami received a text and said, 'William is coming down to meet us.'

Beth had been to a large hospital on the mainland to visit a friend and it had been like entering an airport, but there were fewer shops here. Tonight you could hear footsteps echoing on the tiles. The little shop run by the friends of the hospital was closed; there was no one on reception. Beth used the hand cleanser more as something to do than anything. Then she saw William coming towards them. He walked as if he was at home, briskly. 'Thank you for coming. I didn't know who to call. Elsa is up with her.'

They sat down on some uncomfortable plastic chairs. 'So, what happened?' asked Sami.

William crossed his arms. 'It's not as bad as I feared, but Imogen has got into an awful mess with her painkillers. She has been taking over-the-counter painkillers as well as those that have been prescribed.'

'Overdosed?' Beth asked quietly.

'Not intentionally. I blame myself. I should have realised what was going on.'

Beth gave a silent sigh of relief: it didn't sound like it had anything to do with Kathleen.

'What has she taken?' asked Sami.

William reeled off a list that meant nothing to Beth, but Sami looked grim faced.

'I knew she was taking pain killers for her back after the fall on your skiing holiday,' said Beth.

'That's right. It was a nasty fall. She was prescribed opioids when we came back. I think after a few weeks, though, she was exaggerating her symptoms because she's been on them longer than I would have recommended. I know she saw a few different doctors. She told me she saw whoever was available but, looking back, I think she was playing the system.'

'What do you mean?'

'Her own doctor wouldn't have let her carry on so long. It's called doctor shopping.'

'But her doctor should have been helping her with the pain—'

Beth saw a knowing look between William and Sami.

'I think she slipped quickly from taking the painkillers for her back to using them to self-medicate for anxiety and stress.'

'Stress from school?' asked Beth.

William nodded. 'I'm sure it was. It's a hard job and Imogen puts huge pressure on herself. Everything has to be perfect which, of course, is impossible.'

Beth had to admit that what he said made sense.

'Anyway,' continued William, 'the problem was she was becoming addicted without even realising it, supplementing what the doctor prescribed with powerful over-the-counter painkillers. I can see now she must have been going around different pharmacies all over the island.'

'Imogen was addicted?' Beth asked in horror. An addict in her mind was some poor person, sitting in a squalid flat, emaciated, bruised: not a professional career woman.

As if reading her mind William said, 'Addiction can happen to anyone, and with these medications it can happen in just a few weeks.' He looked over at Sami. 'I remember back in January you mentioned something about Kathleen being worried about the number of pills she'd seen Imogen with. I did check when I went home, but Imogen must have hidden them away. Still, I should have checked more often. The trouble was I had no idea how dependent she'd become.'

Beth looked at Sami. 'Wouldn't the pharmacists have realised, refused to sell them to her?'

'It sounds like she spread out that risk. Also, some are less scrupulous about these things than others.' said Sami.

'So, what happened with Imogen today?' Beth asked William.

'Imogen had come home from work early. They're doing some work in her office. She must have taken something: a mixture. We're not sure exactly what. It was lucky I came home from work early too though. I knew she was in because her car was there, but I couldn't find her. I went upstairs, and found her on the bed.'

'Where was Elsa?'

'At a friend's house. Anyway, I dealt with Imogen, rang for an ambulance, and here we are.'

Beth shook her head. 'It's so awful. I can't believe it.'

William stood up. 'The main reason I called was to see if you can persuade Elsa to come back with you. I don't want her alone in that house.'

'Of course. We'll come up.'

A group of people walked past: porters coming on duty, joking with each other. Beth's initial reaction was to be annoyed: they should show more respect, talk quietly like they would in a library or a church but, of course, this was their place of work.

They went up a floor, and Beth and Sami waited in the corridor. Elsa came out of the ward on her own, suddenly looking much more like the little girl who would come crying to Beth when she'd fallen over. Beth hugged her. 'I'm sorry.'

'I never knew,' said Elsa.

'None of us did,' said Beth. 'Listen. We'd love you to come home with us. Your mum is in safe hands here.'

'I don't want to go. I want to stay with her.'

Beth could hear the desperation in Elsa's voice. 'I understand. Well, how about I take you for a coffee in the café here. William can get us if he needs us.'

Sami stayed in the corridor. In the café, there were a few staff sitting on one side, eating as if they had no idea what was going into their mouths. Some were texting.

The coffee was weak and milky. Beth and Elsa sipped it, trying to ignore the taste.

Elsa looked up. 'She will be all right, won't she?'

'I'm sure she will. Your mum is strong.'

'I hate my life,' said Elsa. She started to cry, dabbing under her eye with the back of her hand to stop her mascara running. Layla would have let the tears fall. Elsa was still aware of appearances, of being on show.

'I blame Kathleen,' she continued. 'You might have all been taken in, but I knew she was a bitch. I found out she'd started nagging William about my portfolio, said Patrick had given me too much help. How dare she? She knew nothing. I told him it was all my own work. She was just poisoning him against me—' Elsa stopped, sipped her coffee and grimaced. 'She was one of those pretty women who are used to getting their own way. She manipulated everyone. Patrick just couldn't see it.'

Elsa spat the words out. Beth realised now she had been too quick to dismiss Elsa's hatred of Kathleen and her attraction to Patrick as youthful passion. As she sat opposite now, seeing Elsa's arms crossed and red nails digging into her arms, she saw something deeper, more determined.

'Patrick and Kathleen had been happily married for a long time,' Beth said quietly. 'Every marriage has its problems, but usually, when two people love each other, they work it out.'

'But they didn't,' said Elsa. 'I don't care what Patrick said. Kathleen never loved him. He just couldn't see it.'

'He talked to you about Kathleen?'

'When we went on that skiing holiday, I could see he was fed up with her. She never made any effort to come out.'

'She was still grieving over the death of a friend.'

Elsa waved her hand. 'She didn't know that woman well. No, she didn't come out because she wanted to stay and flirt with William. It was obvious when she didn't come out skiing with us but stayed back with Mum and William. It was pathetic. Patrick and I had a great time, though.' She took out her phone, scrolled though the photos and then showed Beth one of Patrick with her on the ski slopes.

'See. He was happy, wasn't he?'

'It looks wonderful,' said Beth quietly.

Elsa put her phone away. 'I was right. I didn't imagine things.'

'I don't suppose you ever talked to your mum about any of this?'

'God, no. She'd have been hysterical. William did talk to me a bit after the skiing holiday. I think he guessed a bit of what was going on. He asked me if I'd enjoyed the holiday, and then he said that I had to be careful. He told me Kathleen had problems, that life wasn't easy for Patrick at that moment, but he was sure they would work it out given time. He told me that Patrick had told him how lovely I looked in the photographs and he enjoyed talking to me. I was pleased about that, but William looked all worried and said I was not to take any of this seriously, that Patrick was a married man and I was still young.' She looked up, her eyes pleading with Beth. 'Do you think when someone dies, people pretend they liked them more than they did?'

Beth sipped her coffee. 'Sometimes. It's natural to want to look back on the good things someone did. But,' she paused, trying to find the right words, 'with Patrick, I'm sure he really loved Kathleen.'

Elsa was fiddling with the handle on her mug. She didn't look up. 'That's what I was frightened of.'

Beth saw the passion, the heartache. Then, it was like a light switched on and she could see something she hadn't seen before. 'Elsa, is there something you need to talk about?'

Elsa looked up. 'I always came to you when I was little, didn't I? But this is not just falling out with a friend in school: it's so much bigger.'

'Is it something to do with the morning Kathleen died?'

Elsa was breathing deeply. Beth half expected her to run away, but she said. 'I can't talk to you, not here.'

'I understand, and I can understand you not wanting to leave now, but look. Have you got my number? You can text me any time.'

Elsa nodded, took her phone out of her pocket. 'Tell me the number. I've a new phone. I'll send you mine as well.' They exchanged numbers. 'Thanks,' said Elsa quietly. 'Now, I want to go back and see Mum.'

They returned and Elsa went straight into the ward.

Beth sat down next to Sami, who told her, 'William said Imogen is conscious now.'

'Thank God.' She sank back into her chair. 'What is happening to our safe little world, Sami?'

'I think the real world has just come crashing in. Elsa looked dreadful. It's been a shock for her.'

'I think she has more than just her mother on her mind.'

Sami didn't seem to be listening.

'What are you thinking about?' asked Beth.

'I was thinking about what William said earlier, about Kathleen being worried about Imogen. I should have taken her more seriously. It must have been January, the time of the snow, because Kathleen was telling me how she and Patrick had had to walk to Imogen's. While she was there, she saw Imogen taking pills, glanced in her drawer and saw how many pills she had. She came in worrying about it the next day.'

'But you told William—'

'I know, but I assumed he knew and had it under control. He's a doctor. I didn't want to offend him. He did come back to me the next day, said he couldn't find that many, but that he had been through it with Imogen again. I think she must have hidden stuff after Kathleen mentioned it to her.'

Beth saw Sami scratching his forehead, took his hand and said. 'You did what you could. They'll sort Imogen out now. Look, why don't you go?' She smiled. 'See: you were right about bringing both cars.'

'But you must be done in as well.'

'I don't mind staying. I'll hang around for Elsa. I can't see her wanting to come away. Go on: they'll understand me taking the morning off work.'

'Are you sure?'

Beth pulled her Kindle from her bag, and gave a tired smile. 'I came prepared. Go on. I'll see you later.'

Sami kissed her. 'Thanks.'

Beth sat alone, opened her Kindle and scrolled down, looking for a light read. She found a book of funny stories about dogs and their owners and started to read, but her mind kept going back to Elsa: all that anger; hatred. Was it possible she had had anything to do with Kathleen's death? Beth's mind went to the last visit to Imogen's. She saw Elsa's car sitting there: the silver car. Desperately, she tried to push the thought away: no, not Elsa. Please not her.

After some time, William came out, and slumped in a seat next to her.

'She's sleeping. Thanks for staying, but Elsa's not going to come. She wants to stay with her mum.'

'Of course. So, how is Imogen?'

'She'll be fine, but we will need to get a grip on things when she comes home.'

'Um, I was talking to Elsa earlier in the café. She was very, um, resentful of Kathleen, wasn't she?'

William groaned. 'It's awful. She picked up all this nonsense from Imogen. The problem with these teenagers is their emotions are so strong, just way out of proportion at times. We might dislike; they hate.'

'Yes, I see that.'

'So she developed almost a paranoia about Kathleen. It wasn't fair. I tried to reason with her, but I didn't get far. It worried me, you know. She would say things like, "I wish Kathleen was dead," which we know is nonsense, but it's not a good way to talk.' He put his hands on his knees and gave a weary smile. 'Now, you must be exhausted. We'll be fine. Thank you so much for all you've done. Don't worry about coming in again today.'

'Are you sure?'

'Of course. She'll be in until the end of the week.'

'Fine. I'll come in after work tomorrow.'

Beth went home, and fell into bed. She couldn't sleep immediately. In fact, once she was in bed she felt wide awake. She still couldn't take it in that Imogen had become addicted to drugs. Imogen had always seemed so together: forthright, independent. It was the kind of behaviour she'd have had no time for in someone else. But then understanding addiction was hard for most people. Maybe some people were more susceptible but, at the end of the day, it could happen to anyone, and today she'd seen it had happened to Imogen.

21

Eventually Beth fell asleep, and at eight o clock, when she woke, Sami had showered.

'You're up?'

'Yes, and been for my run.'

'Are you mad?'

'I had to do something to wake me up. I want to go into work early, catch up.'

'Sami, slow down. You've had about four hours sleep.'

'I know. I'll catch up tonight.' He smiled, but looked pale and tired. 'Anything else happen last night?'

'No. William said not to go in today, so I'll visit tomorrow.'

'Fine. Right, I'll be off. Make sure you rest today.' He kissed her forehead, and left.

Beth rang the school and said she wouldn't be in, and was about to go back to sleep when Layla came into her room.

'Mum, Elsa told me that Imogen took an overdose of painkillers, that she's addicted. Is that true?'

Beth sat up. 'She mixed her pills. Be careful what you say in school. You know how these things spread.'

'We had this talk about addiction, about not buying drugs online because you never know what you will be getting. Is that what Imogen did?'

'She didn't get anything online.'

'That's good. I heard that people order them on the dark net with bitcoins and things, and then they are delivered to your house in brown envelopes, just like something off Amazon.'

'Good grief. You were told this in school?

'Oh no. One of the boys was saying it.'

'Don't ever do anything like that, will you, Layla?' said Beth, panicking.

'Of course not. I don't do drugs. I'm not that stupid. Are you going back up to the hospital?'

Beth sighed. 'I'll go tomorrow.'

Layla left her. Beth was horrified that once again her children seemed to know so much more about the world than she did. She got out of bed and went downstairs. Ollie looked up, and wagged his tail expectantly.

'You need your walk, don't you? Just look at you: like a living embodiment of optimism. Your default is that something good and exciting is going to happen. It's a good way to live, but then your world is much simpler than mine. Come on, let's do the guinea pigs and then I'd better take you out. God knows, I feel like death.' She thought to herself that his was how she often felt when the kids were little and she had been up all night dealing a tummy bug. She had forgotten how awful it was.

It was a grey sort of day. Beth was too tired to think straight, and was glad to get home after the walk and rest.

She went to school the next day. It was quiet without Imogen, and Beth could sense a feeling of relief from the staff. However, it was like a force had been taken away: more relaxing, but it wouldn't be good for the school for any length of time. Even the children seemed less motivated. She had never realised how much energy came from Imogen.

As Beth looked at the board in the entrance showing photographs of all the staff, at Imogen's measured 'in control' smile, that was the Imogen she recognised, the woman she knew. Whatever else had happened, this part had really been Imogen.

After lunch, Beth returned to the hospital. Imogen was on the main ward of six beds nearest the windows. She was sitting up, a drip in one arm, her head resting against the pillow, staring out of the window.

Beth sat next to the bed. Imogen reached out a hand and squeezed Beth's. 'I'm sorry.' Tears rolled onto the pillow.

'We all just want you to get better,' said Beth.

'I shouldn't have done it,' Imogen said, her voice weak. 'I don't remember how I got so many pills. William said there were loads in my drawer. I did buy the strongest over-the-counter drugs a few times, even travelled around the island for them. I'm not saying I didn't have a problem, but the things he found: I didn't realise I'd accumulated so many.'

'I suppose going to so many doctors—'

'I only saw one or two different ones. I wanted another opinion, that's all. I felt so unwell.'

Imogen pushed herself up with her hands. 'I told William my parents are not to be told anything about this. I know he thinks it's strange, but they will never understand. They think I have my life on track now, I don't want to see that look of disappointment again.' She gazed around the room. 'Takes me back to sick bay at boarding school.'

Beth was intrigued. Imogen always seemed reluctant to talk about her childhood or school. 'Boarding schools are something I know nothing about. How old were you when you went?'

'Seven.'

'Gosh. I hadn't realised you went so young. Did you enjoy it?'

'I hated it. I never really got over that feeling of being totally abandoned as I watched my parents drive away on my first day. They never wrote to me, they didn't visit for weeks. Mum thought it would unsettle me.'

'That's awful. You were so young.' Beth tried to hide the horror she felt, thinking again how little she really knew Imogen.

'I pretended to enjoy it and I did OK, but I never excelled at anything; never got any cups, which disappointed them. Not like William: he loved boarding school, thrived on the whole thing; loved sports and all that. He talks to my parents, and I can see that is exactly how they wanted me to be about it.' Her face creased into lines of seriousness. 'I'm so lucky he came into my life. But the problem is that by being afraid to upset things between us I've allowed something to get way out of perspective.'

Beth sat up.

'I don't know how much you realised, but I was getting pretty frantic about Kathleen and William. I think it started on the skiing holiday when they seemed to be off talking in corners all the time.'

'She was disturbed, wasn't she, about Amy's death?'

'So she said, but I heard her talking about work at one point. I think she was pretending she needed help with her coursework. It was annoying. William wanted to look after me. He'd been talking to some other guest behind me when I fell. I think he felt guilty he wasn't holding my hand and I think that's why he stayed behind, but then Kathleen kept demanding attention. Anyway, when we got back from the holiday she became even more of a pain. She was phoning all the time. You know, when they came around for a meal, I found her in my room looking through my drawers: the cheek of it. For me, the real panic set in when I overheard her telling William about being pregnant and I knew that meant she'd had an affair. After that my brain went crazy. I think I was taking the pills to try and calm it all down but, of course, I was just making myself worse.'

Beth watched Imogen, saw her hands gripping the top of the blankets, her knuckles white.

'You never spoke to William?'

'No. I was so scared of what he might say.'

'Did you speak to Kathleen?'

Imogen gazed again out of the window. Her words shot out. 'No. never.'

She turned back. 'Anyway, I decided yesterday I needed to talk to William. If I am to get better, I need to be straight with him. I tried to approach it carefully, said I was sure I was wrong, but I'd been worried about him and Kathleen. I confessed I'd heard him talking to Kathleen about her pregnancy and I knew Patrick could not have been the father.'

'What did William say?'

'He was so good about it: very calm. He said I should have told him before, that Kathleen had just been his patient. He'd actually found her difficult and of course in any case he would never be so unprofessional as to have an affair, let alone with a patient.'

'Did he say who he thought Kathleen had had an affair with?'

'He seemed pretty sure it was someone on her course in London. When he explained everything, I couldn't believe I'd ever suspected him. I wish I had talked to him about it weeks ago.' Imogen lay back on to her pillow, her shoulders relaxed, a slight smile on her lips. 'So it's all worked out well in the end.'

Beth felt uneasy. Things hadn't worked out for Kathleen, but that didn't seem to bother Imogen. All she could think of, all she cared about, was her relationship with William. There was a cold satisfaction which was unsettling.

Imogen patted her hand. 'It's good, isn't it. I've decided about the house: we should move. The house in the woods will always be my house and we need somewhere that belongs to both of us.'

'Gosh. Are you sure?'

'I am. William and I will go and look at this house in Cowes when I get out, talk to my parents and put in an offer. Now, tell me, have you any news about school? They won't let me have my phone and there were people coming today to discuss the new library. It's frustrating. I should be able to go home tomorrow and then I need to get back.'

'You should take some time off.'

'William said that, but I'd go mad. I need to get back.'

At that moment, Elsa arrived. She avoided looking at Beth. 'William will be along soon.'

'OK. Well, I'll leave you to talk,' said Beth.

Imogen smiled. 'Thanks for everything you've done, Beth. I'm very grateful.'

In the car park, Beth met William as he arrived.

'How is she?' he asked anxiously, his face white.

'She seemed pretty good. You, on the other hand, look done in. Have you had any sleep the past few days?'

'I learned to do without that years ago.'

'Imogen is worried about her parents, doesn't want them to know about this.'

'It's absurd, but then her relationship with them is totally messed up. It seems wrong not phoning them, but if that's what she wants—'

'I think it is. I hear you are going to be moving.'

'Imogen seems determined to do it now. I hope it's the right thing, though.'

'I got the impression you were all for the move.'

'I'm happy to go there. It would be great to get back into sailing, but I'm not going to let Imogen's parents push her into this. Anyway, I'm sure you'd like to get home. Thank you. You're a real friend, Beth.'

Later that evening, Beth sat in the garden with Sami and told him about her conversation with Imogen.

'So, William said Kathleen had slept with someone on her course? It's what I assumed too,' said Sami.

'I don't know, Sami. I didn't like the way she smiled and said everything had worked out so well. You know, I think she is pleased Kathleen is dead.'

'Oh no, surely not.'

'I think she could be. She's been worried about Kathleen and William. Even though he's told her they never had an affair, well, she's only his word for it, hasn't she?'

'I've told you, I don't think William would ever have slept with Kathleen.'

'I know, but I'm not sure Imogen was so convinced. I think you underestimate how much William means, not just to her, but to Elsa too. He has brought this approval from her parents that she is desperate for.'

Sami scratched his cheek. 'I suppose I'd never have thought of Imogen as someone who was so stressed and vulnerable that she would turn to abusing medication. I got that wrong, so maybe she did threaten Kathleen. She can be pretty scary when she wants to be: a few words from her with that look is enough to make anyone do what they're told.'

'But what if she went beyond words?' asked Beth.

Sami held up his hand. 'Hey, no. We know Kathleen's death was an accident. The police say so, and we know Imogen was at school that morning.'

'But there are still things unanswered about Kathleen's death. We know that her life was very complicated. There's the affair, losing the baby. There are motives there, and now with Imogen we have found a secret that, surely, she would have been desperate to hide. Now, I know Imogen's car was seen at school but I've discovered a way Imogen could have gone over to Freshwater that morning.'

'How?'

'She could have used the pharmacy car. It's silver, like the car seen by that woman. Lots of people have keys for it. Imogen could have got William's easily, even had a copy made.'

'So what are you saying Imogen did?'

She drove over to Kathleen's, went around the back of the house—'

'But there are those huge gates, aren't there, by the side?'

Beth waved her hand. 'Oh, she'd have got over that somehow. Maybe Kathleen let her in. Yes. It's possible they walked down the garden together. Then Imogen let the hens out, Kathleen chased them, and Imogen pushed her over the cliff.'

Beth bit her lip: was that all really possible?

Sami shook his head. 'No, I can't see it. I can go as far as Imogen intimidating Kathleen, but not murder. No.' He looked at her quizzically. 'I thought you'd dropped all this investigating lark.'

She shrugged and smiled, but he frowned. 'Don't go getting dragged back into this. Please, leave it to the police.'

Beth watched him go back into the house. To be fair, she had no actual proof to present to Sami; so maybe he was right to be sceptical.

Of course, there was Kathleen's phone and headphones to be found. They were still missing, and then there was the burner phone someone was using. Maybe she could find a way to look for them at Imogen's. Also, she still didn't know for certain who Kathleen had the affair with. It was important that she knew. If only there was a way of talking to people on her course, maybe they would know.

22

Beth looked at the family calendar on the wall. 'Look, I was think-ing. Next week is the school holiday. How about we get away for a few days?'

Sami was astonished. 'Go away?'

'Yes. I could do with a break and you're desperate for a holiday.'

'I don't know. What about the kids?'

'They're old enough to be left for a few days. We could go up to London: see a show.'

'But Ollie?'

'He could stay here. When we're not around the kids are surprisingly good with him.'

Sami frowned. 'I'd better check with Alex, though, first.'

Beth groaned.

'No, seriously. I'm not making excuses. Where will we stay?'

'We could find a cheap hotel, or an Airbnb?'

'We could.' Beth could see Sami warming to the idea. 'I suppose if it was cheap and Alex is happy, we could go for a few days. I will still have to do my lectures. Would you mind that?'

'No,' she grinned. 'I'd find something to occupy myself with.'

'Good.'

The following day Beth received a text from William. Imogen had been let out earlier than he'd expected, so he was asking if she could pop round to sit with her for a short time in the afternoon. Beth agreed; she had an idea how she could use the visit.

When she arrived, Imogen was sitting downstairs, pale but dressed.

'How are you feeling?'

'Not so bad. A bit battered. It's so wonderful to be home. Hospitals are so noisy, aren't they?'

Beth was easing herself into a leather sofa when William came in.

'I'll make some coffee. I'm working in the kitchen. OK?'

'Thanks,' said Imogen, smiling. When he left, she said, 'He's been so kind, taking good care of me.'

'Of course.'

They chatted a bit about school. William brought in the drinks. 'Now don't go giving her the itch to go back; she needs a few weeks off.'

Imogen smiled. William raised his eyebrows before he left the room, showing that they both knew that was never going to happen.

Beth glanced at the Steinway piano in the corner. On top were scattered several brand new copies of classical pieces. Without thinking she lifted the lid and started to play a scale. However, she cringed at the sound. 'This needs tuning.'

'I would have no idea,' said Imogen. 'My parents bought that for us a few years back. You know me: I can't play a note, but William loves music.'

'I'm surprised he can live with a piano like this. It would drive me mad. I've never heard him play—'

'He doesn't like to play in front of people; it's such a waste.'

Beth sat down again. Everything seemed cosy, normal, and the idea of either of these people being involved in a death seemed madness. Had she got things all wrong? She looked over at the books. She had never noticed what a wide range of novels Imogen had before.

'Are they yours or William's?'

'Oh, both. All the Booker prize winners on the shelf are William's, but he never seems to have time to actually read them now. For his birthday last year my parents bought him a first edition of Orwell's *Nineteen Eighty-Four*. He keeps it on his desk in his study. Apart from enjoying showing off his posh book he keeps it there to remind him of the key to the house safe. Clever, eh: 1984. It means me and Elsa can use it as well.'

'Sounds a good idea. It's so hard nowadays, so many numbers to remember. I still don't know my mobile number, and then there's online passwords, credit card pins. It goes on.'

'Exactly.'

They finished their coffee and Imogen sat up and said, 'Do you fancy a walk around the garden? It's a splendid morning. Leave your stuff here.'

Beth rather expected Imogen to tell her to walk out in single file without talking.

For the first time since she'd had her concerns about Patrick and Elsa, Beth felt it was the right time to bring up the subject with Imogen. It had been on her mind. She didn't want to betray Elsa but, on the other hand, if it had been Layla she'd have wanted to know. Elsa looked so much older than her years. It would be easy to miss how vulnerable she was.

'How do you think Elsa has coped with all this?'

'She's pretty strong, but it shook her. It's quite unnerving; she keeps doing housework and things.'

'She was ever so worried about you; I think she's been under a lot of stress recently.'

Imogen looked Beth straight in the eyes, intense. 'Why, what's the matter with her?'

'Look, I don't know anything for definite, and please don't go running to her with this, but I was worried about her. It was something she said when we went for coffee in the hospital.'

'OK. Just tell me.'

'I don't know an easy way to put this, but I got the impression she had some feelings for Patrick.'

'Ah, Patrick,' Imogen didn't look surprised. 'I know about that. When we went on that skiing weekend, I sensed a bit of hero worship. Patrick was good at skiing and what with that and the photography, he could do no wrong in her eyes. When we returned William told me he was worried about Elsa's 'crush' as he called it. I did have a word with Patrick, told him to be careful. You know what he's like. I think he was enjoying a bit of attention from a pretty young girl, but I told him straight that I expected him to act his age.'

'And he did?'

'I'm sure he did. It didn't stop Elsa badgering him a bit, and he was helpful with her coursework. I did mention it a few times. William worried about it more than me. But I'm sure Patrick was sensible.' Imogen put her head to one side. 'Elsa was still talking about it this week? I thought it had all gone away: shows you never can tell how deep these things go with young people. Thank you for telling me. I shan't mention it, but I'll keep an eye.'

When they returned to the house Beth went to the bathroom. She could hear Imogen talking on her phone and knew this was her best chance. She crept into Imogen's bedroom as quietly as she could in a creaky old house, and went over to Imogen's bedside cabinet. She slid the drawers open. Unlike her own, they were very neat: no ancient, nearly finished, bottle of perfume, no cheap broken jewellery. There was a single bottle of pills, some letters, a notebook. Beth flicked through the notebook. All that was written in it were some lists of numbers ticked off on one page and a list of random words, including 'shower', 'cooker', 'keys'. Beth shrugged and looked though the other drawers: nothing. She checked the wardrobe, and was just opening the second drawer of the chest of drawers when someone said, 'Are you OK?'

Beth turned and saw William. She felt herself blushing.

'I was, um, looking for something.'

'Can I help?' he asked, smiling.

Her mind was rushing for something sensible to say. 'Imogen asked me to get her a cardigan. She was feeling cold.' It was weak and wouldn't stand up to scrutiny, but William appeared to accept it and picked a black woollen cardigan from the wardrobe.

'Thanks so much for coming round,' he said. 'I've been bringing as much paperwork as I can home.'

Imogen was at the bottom of the stairs.

'I showed Beth where your cardigan was.'

Understandably, Imogen looked confused.

'You asked Beth to get you one because you were cold—'

Beth expected a complete repudiation of this, but instead Imogen said, 'Oh, yes. Thank you,' suggesting a vulnerability and lack of self-confidence, new to Imogen but understandable with her illness.

Later, when she arrived home, Beth realised that she'd been wildly optimistic in her search for the phone: no one would just shove such a thing in a drawer. In fact, why hold on to any of them? The logical thing to do would be to get shot of them. Of course, the other reason why she'd found nothing could be because Imogen was completely innocent.

That evening Ollie needed to have a bath after rolling in something disgusting. Beth was hot and possibly wetter than the dog when she heard the doorbell ring and mumbled voices downstairs. Fortunately, she'd finished the bath, had lifted Ollie out, and was drying him down. She stood up and pushed her hair back, as Ollie gave himself a good shake, obviously deciding he could do a better job than her. She found the fitted fleece for drying Ollie that she'd been hiding and slipped it on him. In disgust, Ollie raced out of the bathroom and down the stairs. As Beth descended after him she was surprised to see Sean in the hallway talking to Sami.

'Hi, you're still on the island. Lovely to see you. Excuse the mess. I've been bathing our dog.'

'Sean has some bad news,' interrupted Sami.

'Patrick has been taken in for questioning about Kathleen's death,' explained Sean.

They moved into the living room, and Sean explained what had happened.

'Someone called the police. An anonymous call. The caller said they had seen Pat's car parked on the street by his Castleford house the morning Kathleen died. Apparently, the mechanic had run it up to his house on the Sunday evening. Pat came home from the house party to find it there—'

'We didn't see it,' interrupted Beth.

'We dropped Patrick off just before his house,' said Sami. Turning back to Sean, he said, 'Sorry, carry on.'

'Pat parked it out on the street so that when the new people came with their removal van, they would have plenty of room. When the police came to tell him about Kathleen, they assumed he had a car but said it would be better for him not to drive. He told them that his car was at the garage. Obviously he wasn't thinking straight.'

'He was in shock,' said Sami.

'Exactly. The police never asked him again and he'd forgotten about it. The phone caller said he lied to the police so that they would assume he had no way of getting to Freshwater earlier that morning. The phone caller also said that Patrick was lying when he said that he thought the pregnancy was a miracle, that he'd known she was having an affair and had a clear motive for murder.'

'Oh no,' said Sami.

Sean let out a heavy sigh. 'I know it looks so bad. With anyone other than Pat I'd have found that level of naivety unbelievable.'

'So, Patrick is at the police station?'

'Yes, I've got a solicitor going to him. I can't do it unfortunately. Poor Pat. I wish I could be in there with him.'

'You're sure he's telling the truth?' asked Beth.

Sami glared at her. 'Beth—'

'It's all right,' said Sean. 'I know how it looks but, yes, I believe him.'

'I wonder who phoned the police?' said Beth.

'No idea, but it's someone who has it in for Patrick. How did they know about the car? Patrick didn't know until he went home that evening.'

'Could it be a neighbour who saw it?' asked Sami.

'They never had what you'd call proper neighbours. There's a Priory now used as healing retreat on the one side and a Catholic retreat place on the other, but you know that, don't you? All very quiet, and they never spoke much, apart from one of the nuns who was very friendly and used to bring round veg from their allotment. She was hardly the kind of person to be making this kind of call.'

'They can't trace it?'

'It was made from a pay as you go.'

Beth looked over at Sami. 'Like my phone calls. I wonder if it was the same phone?'

'I wish he hadn't made that mistake about the car; it looks bad,' said Sean, his face creased in annoyance. 'It's absurd. We all know how much Pat loved Kathleen and she loved him. I know she did. She had a fling, but it didn't mean anything.' He heaved himself out of the chair. 'I'd better go back.'

'Is Conor OK?'

'He's gone around to a friend. Won't talk, poor lad. It's all too much for him.'

When Sean had left, Sami looked at Beth. 'You can't believe this of Patrick, can you?'

Beth said, 'I honestly don't know. I'd been imagining all kinds of things with Imogen, but now we hear all this about Patrick. I suppose I'd heard a few things that had worried me, but I'd kind of pushed them away.'

Sami looked at her questioningly.

'The first was the day Kathleen died. At the mortuary he said, "You'll always be mine now" and, I don't know, it's the way he said it. It was a bit creepy. Then Gemma seemed pretty sure that Patrick knew Kathleen had had an affair. But the thing that had really worried me lately was hearing Elsa talking to Layla about Patrick the day after I heard Elsa arguing in the woods with him. They are certainly a lot closer than I knew. He'd been telling her about his marriage, and she was talking about all the things she'd done for him.'

'Elsa and Patrick: no way. That's not right. He's, what, over forty, whatever he says, and she's eighteen. He's known her since she was a child.'

'She's not a child now. From the way she has spoken about him and her hatred for Kathleen, well, I'd say she'd had some pretty strong feelings for him. I like Patrick, but he's pretty vain, likes to think of himself as cooler, younger than he is. He would be flattered.'

'But he'd have more sense—'

'I'm not so sure. I don't want Patrick to have had a relationship with Elsa, or to have killed his wife; of course not. But if he did, then I'd rather know,' said Beth.

'Would you?'

'Yes. Living with not knowing what happened to Kathleen has been awful. I need to know.'

Sami's eyebrows shot up. 'You've changed. I've been worried all along about you getting ill again but, in a way, you seem stronger now, less innocent, less vulnerable, but yes, stronger.'

23

The next day Beth was in work at the school. At lunchtime she was shocked to see Imogen at reception.

'Fancy a chat?' asked Imogen.

Beth followed her into her office.

They sat opposite each other. Imogen looked very pale; her hands were never still, she played with her hair, tapped her knees, kept moving around on her chair. She had a glass of water that she kept taking sips from.

'Are you well enough to be back?' asked Beth.

'I'm much better. I thought Friday would be a good day to come in. I can take things home for the weekend.'

'But are you well enough? A few days ago, you were in hospital, and you need time to come off the pills.'

'I don't need to be off work to do that, and Beth, please don't say anything to anyone here. As far as the staff are concerned, I had a bad reaction to some medication.'

Beth was surprised that Imogen assumed that this story had been so readily accepted.

'So, um... what do you think about Patrick?' Beth asked.

Imogen looked straight at her. 'I'm astounded the police have taken him in. He's obviously not guilty of anything. That morning, he'd just been told his wife had died, for crying out loud. As for the pregnancy, I think it's to his credit he believed he was the father of Kathleen's baby; people are so cynical nowadays. I know you and I can talk quite easily about Kathleen's affair with this person on her course, but I think it's laudable that Patrick never even considered such a thing. Oh no. He's innocent.'

'But you said yourself it was crazy Patrick thinking the baby was his—'

'I've had time to think about it, and I can understand his position better now. That's what you do with friends, isn't it? Think the best of them. I think it's important to be loyal to our friends.'

The look and the tone of her voice left Beth in no doubt where the conversation was going. 'I believe in loyalty as well, but that doesn't mean I have to accept lies.'

Imogen leant over the coffee table. 'Did you make that call to the police?'

'Good heavens, no. Why would I do that?'

'You've been so insistent that one of us was getting at Kathleen, even hinted that one of us might have been linked to her death. Maybe you got frustrated with the police always assuming it was an accident?' Imogen took a long drink from her glass; it was nearly empty now.

Beth felt her cheeks burning. 'I didn't make that call, but if it turns out Patrick has lied and had anything to do with Kathleen's death, I would be pleased someone did.'

Imogen pursed her lips. 'You've changed. You used to be all kind and mumsy, and now you come out with things like that. It's like you are willing to think the worst of any of us. I'm lucky. I was here the whole time that morning or you'd be accusing me too.' Imogen picked up her glass and held it close to her lips.

Beth felt the full force of the challenge, the intimidation, in

Imogen's words. She dug deep, and found the courage to say, 'Your car may have been here, but you went out for a long walk, didn't you? From half six until, what, about ten past seven? If you could have found a car—'

As if in slow motion Imogen's hand let go of the glass and it fell into her lap. She grabbed some tissues and mopped up.

'What did you say?'

'I said, you weren't at school during that time.'

'I often go for a walk to clear my head. I don't go around stealing cars, by the way. Really, Beth, you need to get a grip on this. You should know your limitations.'

Imogen stood up, signalling it was time to leave.

Beth took her cue but was upset. 'Know your limitations.' How dare she?

'I'll leave you now,' Beth said, her voice shaking, 'but I've no intention of giving in. I am determined to find out what happened to Kathleen.' With more confidence than she felt, Beth strode out of the room.

After lunch, to Beth's surprise, Sean and Conor called round. The look of relief on Sean's face told the whole story. She invited them into the living room. Sean chose a comfy armchair. Conor sat on the edge of a desk chair.

'Hope you don't mind us calling in.'

'Of course not. Would you like a drink?'

'We're not stopping. I was giving Conor a lift to collect his bike from the garage, but I wanted to tell you the good news. Pat has been released. He hasn't been charged.'

'That was quick. He's free?'

'Yes, thank God. They don't want to charge him. The police, of course, won't tell me much, but I had a phone call from that nun, the one I told you about who was so friendly. She heard about Patrick's arrest and contacted the police. Apparently, she'd seen Patrick's car parked that morning at about seven when she went to prayer. It shows he couldn't have gone over to Freshwater.'

'What about the motive?'

'From what Patrick tells me I assume the police have decided that he really did believe Kathleen's pregnancy to be a miracle.'

'I'm surprised.'

'I know, but there are a few things Pat had never told me that he told them. One was about some article he'd printed off the internet talking about miracle babies born to people in his position. It was in his drawer at home. He told the police about similar articles he'd read online. He also told them to talk to his priest in Ireland. He'd emailed him when he realised Kathleen was pregnant and asked him to pray for the safe delivery of his miracle baby.'

Beth stared. 'I never realised—'

'No. He was embarrassed, I think, to talk about it, but it seems he really did believe it was possible. You know how people sometimes look for anything that might bolster up a faint hope? It's what he did.'

'But he never even said anything to Kathleen when he found out?'

'He wanted her to tell him, a kind of superstition I think.' Sean stood up. 'OK, then. We'd better make a move.'

'Thank you for letting me know,' said Beth.

'Yes, we can organise the funeral now, all try to rebuild our lives,' said Sean.

That evening Beth told Sami about Patrick, and he responded, 'That's good news. As incredible as it seems, I can believe that.'

Beth could see he was willing to accept it all; so maybe she was being too cynical? In any case, Sami moved on quickly, 'I've some good news about our time away.'

'What's that?'

'Alex has offered his house for us to stay in.'

'That's fantastic. Which days then?'

'We could go on Monday. I will lecture on the Tuesday and Wednesday, but I'll make sure I finish early so all the rest of the time and the evenings will be free.'

'It's not much of a holiday for you.'

'It'll be fun. I never see anything of London. We'll go out for nice meals and things as well. Come on, we never go to the theatre or museums.'

Beth could see he was excited, and why not?

'Great. But we don't know if we can get tickets for anything—'

'I bet we can, and it's cheaper last minute and in the week. I'll have a look and see what's going.'

Beth returned to her laptop and grinned, feeling like some amateur sleuth. It was all quite exciting.

That night she slept better than she had for a while. It would be good to get away, just her and Sami, and who knew what she might find out?

She went out early the next morning with Ollie and was busy watching him chasing a pheasant when her phone rang. Without thinking, she answered it.

'I told you to stop obsessing about Kathleen. I'm not playing games. I know everything you do and say. Go to the police again and I will ruin you. I know your secret.'

It was the same number, the same voice, but for all the threat Beth wondered why, if they knew her secret, they didn't at least hint at it. If they really knew anything, why not say? They were dead set on trying to scare her, which must mean she was getting closer; she could feel it. She wasn't going to tell anyone about this call. The caller was right: it wasn't a game. She was serious. She would keep digging until she found out the truth.

24

On Monday Sami and Beth travelled to London. There had been, as usual, more last-minute things to do than expected.

Beth arranged her lists on the kitchen table about the care of Ollie and the guinea pigs; food that was prepared or needed to be taken out of the freezer; remembering to lock the house when they left; shut windows when they went to bed; not to forget their keys, and so on. She also wrote down the address and phone number of Alex's house, knowing they would be ignored, and they would just use their mobiles.

After Ollie's shorter than usual walk, Beth found Layla eating breakfast.

'We're off, you won't forget Ollie or the guinea pigs, will you?'

'Of course not. You know I'll do them any time.'

Beth grinned but didn't pick her up on it. 'Thanks. Text me if there is anything.' She turned to Sami. 'Is anyone covering you up at the Hendersons'?'

'Yes. I asked Alex. He said he would enjoy the cycle up there.' He turned to Layla, 'No wild parties while we are away, OK?'

'Oh no, and I've posted the party me and Adam are having

tomorrow on Facebook. I'll try to cancel it. Have to hope no one turns up, won't we?'

'Not funny,' said Sami, scowling.

Layla laughed. 'Just go.'

Beth went up to see Adam. 'We're off, Layla's going to look after the animals, but can you check everything is locked up? Oh, and make sure you put the bins out tomorrow, and bring them back in. There are lists on the kitchen table.'

'Oh, you off somewhere?'

'I've told you loads of times. Me and Dad are going to London.'

'Oh, yes. Right.' Beth didn't find that particularly reassuring, but Sami was calling her. 'Come on. The taxi is here, quick.' And so, with many misgivings, Beth left the house.

On the Red Jet she sent a text to Layla to make sure she also locked up when she left the house, and not to forget to make sure there was always water down for Ollie.

* * *

At Waterloo, she started to feel she was getting away. Getting off the train in London was, as always, a shock. Beth didn't come up often, and was not used to the crowds, the noise, the smells of the city. She felt a county bumpkin when she looked at the sophisticated women who even in casual wear looked a lot smarter than her. However, she also noticed the homeless people begging, young kids sleeping rough, things she hardly ever saw on the island. The poverty on the island tended to be more hidden away. Coming here was a reminder not to forget it was still there.

They walked from the tube to Alex's house in Canonbury: a tall, white Victorian house in a crescent with a small green area in front of it. It was pleasant, but to get in they had to go through a complicated alarm system, including private cameras, which Sami navigated.

The inside was very smart: antique furniture and classic prints. There were also photographs of a dancer, who Beth assumed was Amy. She had that way of standing, like a thoroughbred racehorse, every sinew tight, highly charged. In the living room she saw a large glass cabinet full of cups and trophies. It made her realise for the first time just how talented Amy must have been.

'It's more elegant than I expected. I can see why Imogen said the flat must be a come down for Alex.'

'I think the house originally belonged to Amy's parents. Remember, Alex said they were well off. By the way, Alex asked us to use the spare bedroom.'

Beth found it quite thrilling to be away, just the two of them in this beautiful house. She realised how much she and Sami had needed a break from the island and all the stress they'd had.

In the evening they walked to one of the Middle Eastern restaurants Sami had researched. The food was wonderful. Although Sami had moved to Wales as a child, his Iraqi roots were strong, and food was a very important part of that. His mother was an amazing cook. Beth, when she visited, was never so much as offered a packet of biscuits: everything was beautifully, and to Beth exotically, home-made. As if reading her mind, Sami said, 'We should try to get out to my parents one day. It's been a few years since they saw the children.'

'I don't forget about visiting them. One day—'

'I'm not trying to make you feel guilty. They could come to us: they know that. They could afford it. But still, I'd like to see them. We'll have to see what we can plan.'

Beth didn't answer. It wasn't something that she would look forward to, but he was right: the children should see their grand-parents.

They walked back to the house. Beth was surprised at the relief she felt that they could still enjoy being away like this. Maybe life when the children both left home wouldn't be so bad.

At first, when Sami left the next morning, Beth wandered around, not sure what to do with herself. It was odd to be in someone else's house, looking out of the windows, so different to the island. Every horizon here was littered with buildings, and there was a constant hum of traffic.

Beth looked at the beautiful paintings and ornaments, the antique furniture. This place didn't shout, but whispered politely of class and money. Alex, she guessed, must have inherited a lot of money when Amy died. For the first time she wondered just why he was leaving all this behind, escaping to the island. He said he tried not to come back. Of course, the painful memories must be in the DNA of this house now, but what exactly was he running away from?

Beth walked around the tiled hallway, looked up the stairs, the ones Amy had fallen down: the floor was hard, unforgiving. It must have been awful for Kathleen. Did she hear the fall before she came out and found Amy? And Alex had not been here. Beth sat in a beautiful velvet seat in the hallway looking up at the stairs. Alex was an enigma. One of those people who shared himself piece by piece, but you never saw the whole picture. Of course, he'd been there on the Sunday evening: it had to be possible that he was the person Kathleen had been talking about.

It was so hard to imagine him threatening anyone. But then she didn't really know him and, given the right circumstances, maybe it was possible. Kathleen said she had known something horrendous about this person. If it had been Alex, what could he have done? Looking at the stairs, the obvious thing would be that she knew something suspicious about Amy's death, but how could that be possible? Alex hadn't even been here. Also, Alex claimed not to have known about Kathleen's affair, although, of course, he could be lying. He had no alibi for the Monday morning, but no one had bothered because he had no motive. Well, maybe now she'd at least found the hint of one.

Beth thought of Kathleen's phone. Alex said he had not been here recently, but he could have lied, come back, and hidden it here. It was the perfect time to look. She went through the house, room by room. Everything was neat so it didn't take too long. Finally, she came to Amy's room. She knew in her heart she shouldn't be going in there, but she couldn't resist it. It might be exactly the place Alex might hide something in.

Beth let herself into the bedroom. Like the rest of the house, it was a lovely room. There was a large photograph of Alex and Amy on their wedding day. She noticed the butterfly necklace, the earrings. She went over to the window, looked down on the gardens below and was amazed to see a fox sunning itself under the trees.

Methodically, she examined the wardrobes, bedside cabinet and finally the dressing table drawers. She slid open a long drawer. What she saw made her gasp: the drawer was full of jewellery in beautiful boxes and cases and these weren't cardboard like the boxes she had. These were made of leather and wood. As she opened them she noticed fine hinges, and she stared at a stunning array of jewellery. One box contained emerald earrings and a pendant on a gold chain. Beth picked up an opal ring. It would only fit on her little finger: Amy must have been slight. She moved her hand, watching the opals that shone a thousand colours. In another box was a creamy pearl necklace, which she held up. Each pearl was slightly different: heavy, cool, bright, and they shone individually when the light hit them. The diamond clasp was beautifully fashioned. It was exquisite. In a reddish brown Cartier box, she found a watch. This looked like a vintage piece: rectangular, with tiny diamonds and blue hands. Sami had said he wanted to get her jewellery for her birthday. She lay the watch with the pearls and took a photo. She didn't expect anything as extravagant, but maybe a small pearl necklace, a watch of a similar shape? She carefully put all the jewellery away, wondering why Alex didn't at least keep it in a household safe. Beth had found nothing of interest after all. She checked her watch: it was time to go.

She put on comfy shoes and left the house nervously, trying to remember all the security instructions she'd been given. It was such a contrast to making sure the children locked the back door and pulled the front door shut. As, with relief, she pulled the front door closed, she was aware of an older woman next door, lifting a key to her lock: obviously just returning home.

'Good morning,' the woman said. 'I've just managed to catch the post.'

'Hi,' said Beth, impressed to be greeted, and then wondering if she should explain who she was. 'Me and my husband are staying for a few nights. Alex works with my husband at a pharmacy on the Isle of Wight.'

'That's a long way. It's good to have someone in the house. Alex told me he would be away a lot more, but he's not been back for some time now. He phones me to check everything is all right, but it's not the same as having people living there. Still, I'll be sad if he sells it. I'd hate to see it broken up into flats, and they've been good neighbours. So sad what happened to his wife, isn't it? Tragic.'

Beth felt she was back in Wales; the lady was obviously looking to chat.

'Amy sounded like a lovely lady.'

'She was. I knew her mother well. She came from a distinguished family. They had the house here, and one down in Kent. Amy's father was something high up in the civil service, and such a gentleman. Amy was his pride and joy. He died abroad, an infection it was. As for Amy's mother, of course, well she died suddenly only a few years back. She was in her nineties. Amy had been extremely close to her. I don't think she ever recovered from that. Tragedy seems to follow some families, doesn't it?'

'My friend Kathleen stayed here a few times before Christmas. She was here the night Amy died.'

'I remember her: the woman who was studying to be a pharmacist?'

'That's right.'

'Amy mentioned her. She was fond of her. She was so upset that morning. Well, we all were. But in the months before her death I saw Amy going downhill. Alex became worried stiff to leave her. I came and sat with her a lot. I even stayed the night when Alex was on the island if that friend of yours wasn't up here.'

'Alex must have been very grateful.'

'Oh, he was. She was so vulnerable. Not just in the way she forgot things, but she became more and more, well, you could call it generous. She kept giving things away. She gave me a print she knew I liked. I checked it with Alex, who was happy for me to keep it, but I turned down a lot. I always felt that if the wrong person came along, well, they could have had half the stuff in that house.'

'That must have been a worry—'

'Alex worried about it, I know. He joked that that she'd bankrupt him one day.'

'Did he really?'

'Of course, he was only joking.'

Beth knew this woman would like to chat for the rest of the day. She saw the words, 'Would you like a cup of tea?' poised on the woman's lips.

'Right. I think I'd better be off. I'm hopeless in London. I get on the wrong tubes, get lost all the time.'

'Look, take this card. It's got my phone number on it. Ring me if you get lost. Everyone is in such a rush; you never know who to ask.'

'Thank you,' said Beth, pushing the card into her bag. 'That's kind.'

'Have a good day. Don't spend all your money.'

Beth managed the travelling better than she'd anticipated. She caught the tube to Covent Garden. Alighting there she was greeted with the music of buskers, colourful posters for plays and films, and people, lots of people. The atmosphere, however, was more relaxed and less frenetic than she'd feared.

Later, she phoned home and was relieved that everything seemed to be going smoothly, apart from Adam dropping a four pint bottle of milk, and Layla saying the conditioner had run out. That evening she and Sami went to see the musical *Wicked*. As always, Beth was stunned by the whole experience of a West End show and even Sami, who was there for her really, enjoyed it. They tried another Middle Eastern restaurant. The evening was a success.

As they walked back to Alex's house, Beth thought about telling Sami what she was planning to do the next day when he was in lectures but, as she was pretty sure he wouldn't want her to go, she decided not to.

Next day, Beth retrieved the map she had printed and set off for the academy Kathleen had been attending. Beth had done her research online, found out who taught Kathleen, where the lectures were held, even the group timetable. It appeared they were having extra lectures in preparation for exams, so most of them would be around when she was in London. The most useful thing she'd done was track down a girl on Kathleen's course on social media. Beth had introduced herself, explained her connection with Kathleen, and the girl appeared to have known Kathleen quite well. Beth asked if they could meet to chat. The girl had seemed happy to meet up for coffee at the academy. The best time was at 11.30 after a lecture.

Beth found the interior of the academy daunting, and she went straight to reception. She felt surrounded by people much younger and more confident than herself. This was the kind of crowd Adam would be mixing with in October, she realised. She felt overwhelmed for him.

Beth was directed to the lecture room, and she sent a message to Angela. She waited outside. Aware of how different and how much older she was than everybody else, Beth reckoned Angela would find her easily enough. When a group of students emerged from the lecture room, it wasn't as large as she had anticipated. A young girl enquired, 'Are you Beth?'

'Yes. Angela?'

'That's right. I feel I know you quite well. Kathleen talked about you and, of course, your husband Sami, her boss. I was so sorry to hear about Kathleen. We were all shocked. We're quite a small group, so we all knew each other. Even though there was a big age gap between us we got on well. But I can't think how I can help you: you must have known her a lot better than me.'

They went into the cavernous entrance hall. There were outlets for several chain fast food restaurants. Beth offered to buy the coffee.

The noise was incredible; they had to raise their voices to be heard.

Angela spoke. 'I told Kathleen about my father who had cancer, and she was saying her husband had been through that. She said how hard it was, and that she'd had a friend, you, who had always been there for her, how you'd made all the difference. She said that you were like that: always kind, always saw the best in people.'

Beth smiled. 'Well, I'm glad I asked you. What a lovely thing to say. Kathleen wasn't a difficult person to stand by.'

'I can imagine. So, what is it you need to know?'

'It's rather delicate.' Angela sat up.

'I know it sounds like I'm just being nosey, but I promise you I have good reasons for asking. What I need to know is if Kathleen had a relationship with anyone up here in London on her course.'

Angela's eyebrows shot up.

'My last conversation with Kathleen was disturbing,' explained Beth. 'She was very uptight. Although we were close, she wouldn't tell me what was wrong. I think she thought I would judge her. One explanation I thought of for her being so stressed was that she'd had an affair, and the obvious thing would have been someone up here. I don't want to tell anyone, or hunt this person down, but if I know that I would understand why she was like she was.'

Beth was aware she was babbling, but there seemed no easy excuse for wanting this information. She waited to see if Angela wrote her off as some nutty woman but was relieved to see her giving the matter serious thought.

'I think I can understand that,' said Angela and she tapped her fingertips on the table. As if making the decision to speak, she took a breath and said, 'OK. I can assure you Kathleen was not seeing anyone up here.'

'You're certain?'

'Absolutely. There are only three boys on our course. One got married last summer and spends all his time on the phone to his wife. One started dating a girl on the course after the first session and is totally besotted, and then there's Jeff, who is gay, and just got engaged to his partner.'

'I see, so no students. Any lecturers she might have been interested in?'

'None. Two are women, and the only man is about to retire, insists on us all calling him by his surname, and permanently scowls. Still, he knows his stuff.'

'No chance of anything between him and Kathleen?'

Angela laughed. 'No way. Kathleen got short changed when she tried out that flirty smile of hers on him. No. There was no one up here but—'

Beth looked quizzically at Angela, who was looking worried.

'Well, in a way I'm not surprised. I guessed soon after I met Kathleen last September that she was worried about her marriage.'

'What did she say?'

'Well, I didn't know her that well, but I was showing her some holiday pictures. Kathleen told me her husband was a photographer. I joked that I was sure he'd have taken a lot of her. I mean, even at her age, she was still very pretty. Kathleen went all serious and said not so many now, which I thought was rather sad. Then she said he'd found a new model, someone very pretty. The girl was young, and Kathleen said she was infatuated with her husband.'

Beth felt sick, knowing that this must be Elsa.

'And did she think he felt the same?'

'Kathleen tried to laugh it off, said she knew he had more sense, but she did say he'd helped this girl too much with some project she was doing. It sounded like he had more or less done it for her and yet this girl was going to get into uni on the strength of it. I said that wasn't fair and Kathleen agreed. She said at times she'd been tempted to contact the school and tell them.'

Beth's eyes widened. 'She was going to do that?'

'Oh yes. I think she would have, but she said there were other things to bear in mind, that there were things stopping her. Anyway, she didn't say that much about her after that, but we did chat a lot. I liked her. She was kind, listened well.'

'Did she ever tell you about meeting anyone else?'

'I sort of guessed—'

'What is it? Please—' said Beth.

'It was February. When Kathleen came to lectures, she didn't look well. I caught her throwing up, took her for a coffee. She told me she thought she was pregnant. I congratulated her but she didn't look happy. She said she'd made a mistake and it was hard to live with. I sort of put two and two together, and guessed that there must be another man.'

'Did she say who it was?'

'No, but she seemed scared. I wondered if she was frightened of this man or her husband. I told her she could get help, but she said she had to sort this out on her own. Her husband wasn't abusive, or anything, was he?'

'No. Nothing like that.'

'Good. I wouldn't have wanted that. I did worry about her. We'd had a long chat when she came back after Christmas in January. Firstly, I wanted to know why she'd not done the second day of the course in December. All we got was some message that a family member was ill. She told me about the woman, Amy, was it? Yes, she said she had a fall; it was fatal. It sounded awful. I said she still looked very upset by it and she said it was all made so much worse by some skiing weekend she went on.'

'I think it was rather soon after Amy's death.'

'Yes. She said she couldn't forget the accident, said something about medication.'

'She was worried about Amy's medication?'

'She got pretty upset, so I changed the subject. I thought she was getting worked up.' Angela shrugged an apology. 'I'm so sorry about everything. Kathleen was sweet and kind. She'd bring up biscuits she'd made, and she gave me a beautiful cashmere cardigan she said didn't suit her any more. She remembered, you see, my favourite colour was green. She was thoughtful. She brought me some DVDs for Dad as well. It's tragic, the way she died.'

'Yes. It was a terrible shock.'

Beth saw Angela wave to some friends, indicating to them to wait for her.

'You've got to go,' said Beth. 'That's fine. Thank you so much for talking to me. Considering how little you saw Kathleen she seems to have trusted you and talked to you a lot.'

'I think me being up here, I was away from everyone. Who was I going to tell her secrets to?'

Beth left with a lot to think about, most of all Elsa. Elsa could have known about Kathleen's affair. She could easily have overheard William in the same way as Imogen had. Now, if Kathleen had threatened to tell the school about her portfolio, Elsa could have threatened in return to tell Patrick about the affair. If Kathleen had been going to reveal all, including the truth about Elsa's portfolio, that would have been disastrous for Elsa. It would have been more than embarrassing: she'd have been shown up as a fraud to her family and friends, the school, the university. In Elsa's eyes it could have ruined her life. How far would she go to stop Kathleen speaking out?

Beth sighed. This wasn't what she wanted to learn, and she tried to push it out of her head. One other thing she had learned was that Kathleen almost certainly hadn't had an affair with someone up in London. It confirmed what she'd felt deep down all along: the affair had been much closer to home.

25

When they arrived home, Sami received a text from Patrick. The police had said he could arrange the funeral: it would be in two weeks' time.

Beth phoned Patrick and asked if there was anything he would like her to do for the funeral. He asked if she could do a reading and maybe put together some pictures that would remind people of Kathleen.

Beth enjoyed searching through her old albums, and once more promised she would print off the latest ones on the computer. There was something special about flicking through an album. She had photographs of Kathleen and her having meals out, going over to Southampton to a show, some of Kathleen with the staff from the pharmacy at the Christmas dos. Some of her favourite ones were of Kathleen in her old garden with the hens and her showing Adam and Layla how to hold them and collect the eggs. There were also trips to the zoo, the beach, the woods. So many good times she'd forgotten, and they warmed her. However, she then found some of everybody at various St Patrick's Day meals and they were less comfortable: all the usual group, sat around laughing. It hurt to look at those, hard to imagine a time of such innocence. Beth didn't include them in the montage she made for Patrick.

The day of the funeral came, grey and overcast. The funeral was to be held at the church in the village that Beth sometimes went to on a Sunday. The coffin would be taken straight from the undertakers to the church.

As Beth walked into the church with the family, gentle Irish folk music played. The church was filled with white Easter lilies. It was crowded with people from the village and relatives from Ireland. At the front was Patrick, white and tense, and Conor, looking red and angry. Behind them was a man and two women who Beth, judging by their likeness to Kathleen, guessed were Kathleen's mother and sister.

The service began with someone from the church choir singing 'Do not be afraid'. Beth sat waiting to do her reading. She felt more nervous than she had expected to and, as she walked down the aisle, which seemed to have doubled in length, all she could hear was her heels clipping loudly on the stone floor.

From the lectern, she began her reading from a Catholic Bible.

'The Lord is my Shepherd; I shall not want. He makes me lie down in green pastures. He leads me beside still waters. He restores my soul. He leads me in right paths for His Name's sake. Even though I walk through the darkest valley, I fear no evil.'

The words made Beth pause. Her voice began to shake, and tears started to fall down her cheeks. Her friend had been in a dark valley, but there had been no comfort. Nothing had made sense, she'd said to Angela. Who had made her so desperately unhappy and afraid? Who down there was acting a part? Beth looked up from the Bible. Through eyes blurred with tears, she scanned the congregation. Patrick, William, Imogen, Alex, Sami, all looking back at her, waiting for her. They looked at her anxiously. What did they think she was going to say? She felt ashamed of her tears but, no, why weren't they crying?

The vicar coughed. Beth looked over. Startled back to her task, she continued the reading. When she had finished, Beth returned to her seat. She felt as if the church sighed with relief. Feeling hot and flustered, she took off her jacket.

Patrick took her place at the lectern. He spoke movingly about the time he met Kathleen, how he loved her, how he never understood why someone so beautiful fell for him. His voice broke, but he continued. She shouldn't have died: it was too soon, she had so much left to give.

Kathleen's mother talked about her daughter in a gentle, wistful way. Kathleen's sister, Roisin, was very different. Her voice was similar to Kathleen's but there was a sharper edge to it. There was also none of the fragility of Kathleen about her. Roisin was a broad, solid framed woman, her hair red but cut in a short, rather severe bob. For all that, however, each carefully chosen word was full of pain and loss. 'I remember the day my mother brought Kathleen home, holding her tiny hand. Our closest moments were in the dark, after my parents put the lights out. We could tell from the sound of the other's breath how they were feeling. If one of us was sad, without speaking, we would reach out and hold hands. We were sisters,' Roisin looked up, tears on her cheeks, 'and now she's gone. When I reach out, her hand won't be there. I will never hold her hand again.'

Beth felt her heart tighten with emotion, watched as Roisin walked slowly back to her seat.

At the end of the service a haunting Irish song was sung, 'I'll take you home again, Kathleen', after which there was an eerie silence, followed by a collective sigh of relief.

Kathleen's body was to be buried in the church graveyard and the congregation followed the coffin outside. It was the first time Beth had attended a burial. As she was walking out of the church,

Alex approached, holding out her jacket. As she took it from him, she noticed his eyes were red and his hands shaking. 'I'm going back to the pharmacy now. You read well, Beth.'

'Thank you for covering,' said Sami.

'It's OK. Don't worry about anything.'

The burial felt to Beth like she was taking part in an ancient tradition, pagan almost. As the vicar scattered earth on the coffin, Patrick read the lines, 'So, go and run free with the angels; dance around the golden clouds.'

A subdued group of people drove to Patrick's new house for the wake. The table was laden with food; there were flowers: lilies again. Patrick stood shaking hands with people, but looking lost in his own home.

'It was a beautiful service,' Beth said to Sean.

'Patrick planned it. He's needed this: an end.'

Beth looked around the room. The sun was streaming in through the windows.

'Is there somewhere I could leave my jacket?'

'Kathleen's room,' said Sean and paused. 'I suppose we should stop calling it that.'

'Not yet. It's how I think of it.'

Beth went upstairs, and laid her jacket on the bed. She peeped in the drawers: nothing had been sorted out since she was last here.

Downstairs, she saw Imogen standing alone, looking ashen, wearing a black suit, holding a plate with an untouched piece of cake. Beth wasn't sure what to do. Should she speak to her after the previous row? But before she could decide, Imogen came to her. 'It's the end now, Beth. Let's be friends again.'

'How are you?' Beth asked gently.

Imogen replied briskly, 'I'm fine, thank you.'

Beth noticed that Imogen was pressing small crumbs of cake

on her plate together with her fingers, and her eyes occasionally darted around the room.

Beth was concerned. 'Maybe you should have taken more time off?'

'I've had the school holiday. William tells me you went to Alex's house. It's a fantastic place to stay, isn't it?'

'Yes. It was good to get away from everything for a few days. We ate in some really good Middle Eastern restaurants and went to a musical.'

'Sounds good. I'll have to see if I can get William away for a weekend again before Alex sells the house.'

'Patrick did well with the service. There are more people here than I thought. I didn't expect so many family to come from Ireland, especially the ex.'

'Ah. Is that who that man is?'

'I don't know why he's turned up.'

'He's Conor's father.'

After Imogen left her Beth went out into the garden. There was, as always, a breeze, but there was more warmth in the sun: summer was closer. Beth walked down the garden. She stopped at the new sturdy wooden picket fence. You could still see the sea. She couldn't see a gate, which was sad, as she knew Kathleen had wanted one. Looking down, she saw marks on the grass where the hen coop had been, and heard Kathleen talking about Henrietta settling in well, enjoying the sea air. Her hands started to shake; tears poured down her face. She looked beyond the fence. To think of Kathleen falling here was so painful. What had gone through her mind as she fell? Looking back at where the hens had been it seemed as inconceivable as ever to Beth that Kathleen could have let them out herself. Why would she do such a thing? She remembered talking to Kathleen, sitting out here with a glass of wine. Losing her had been so hard, but trying to live with all the things they could no longer do together seemed unbearable today.

'Are you Beth?' Her heart missed a beat at the voice. She turned.

'I'm Kathleen's older sister, Roisin.'

Beth smiled, her lips trembling. 'You startled me. You sound so like her.'

'We have the same voice but not the same looks. She was always the pretty one.'

Beth smiled in sympathy. For a woman who must be in her mid forties to still think of herself as 'the not so pretty sister' was rather sad. Roisin seemed to read her thoughts. 'You don't need to feel sorry for me. I never wanted to be Kathleen.'

Beth was slightly taken aback. Roisin was a lot more forthright than Kathleen had ever been.

Roisin walked towards the fence. 'I still can't believe it's happened. It was down here, wasn't it, she fell? Patrick brought me down here last evening to pay my respects. I laid some flowers the other side of this fence.'

Beth frowned. 'You had to walk all along the cliff path, then?'

'Oh no. You don't know about this new fence? There's a gate hidden away. I'll show you.' Roisin took her close to the end and slid three of the slats along. 'Clever, isn't it?' she said, and slotted them back. 'Just enough room for one person to get through. People walking past wouldn't know there was a way in.'

They stood, quietly, listening to the sea, the hum of voices from other guests in the garden.

'I was down here talking to Kathleen the night before she died. The hens, of course, were over there. It was a very posh new run she'd put the coop in. Seems odd looking at an empty plot now.'

'She was dotty about those hens, wasn't she? I don't really understand how she came to be chasing them around the place. She'd said to me she wasn't letting them out until the permanent fence was put up.'

Beth nodded. 'I know. I was thinking that, but as there was not meant to be anyone else here, Kathleen had to be the person who let them out.'

'It doesn't add up to me. I know my sister might have been preoccupied, but I can't see her doing that. Kathleen usually stayed pretty level headed through most things. She may have looked all airy fairy, but she had a strong inner core of common sense. Mind you, she made some pretty rubbish choices when she was younger. They usually involved men—' Roisin tossed her head towards a man slouched against the wall, smoking. 'Like him.'

'She never talked much about her ex-husband.'

'I'm not surprised. He treated her rotten. He hit her sometimes, you know; real nasty. She refused to go to the police about him. She'd come around our house with Conor as a baby, crying her eyes out.'

'But why did she marry someone like him? She was so gorgeous. She could have chosen anyone.'

'That was the problem. Being so pretty meant most decent boys were too nervous to ask her out, and if she did go out with someone, they spent their time worrying about losing her. I saw it over and over again.'

'That doesn't explain her ex's behaviour.'

'Ah. Well, instead of flattering her, telling her all the time how much he loved her, he chose to demean her, run her down so she wouldn't think anyone else would want her.'

'That's horribly manipulative.'

'I know. I told her what was happening, but she really believed that she was married for life. Fortunately, even Kathleen had to admit her marriage was over when he started going off with other women. Thank God Patrick came along. He took on Conor as well. Patrick has been a much better father for Conor.'

'And yet Conor insisted on going back to his dad in Ireland after his GCSEs.'

'The problem was that Conor had been allowed to idolise his

dad, and the separation had made that worse. Kathleen pretended birthday and Christmas presents were from his Dad. She couldn't bear him looking upset. She covered up a lot of the truth about Conor's dad. I'm not saying she should have laid it on thick but a few home truths about him to Conor wouldn't have gone amiss.'

'I was surprised Conor agreed to come back.'

'His dad told him Kathleen could help him financially, but the truth is his dad couldn't wait to get rid of him. Conor was way out of control, and he's got his dad's temper.'

Beth screwed up her eyes. 'I know I shouldn't ask, but did Kathleen make a will, make any provision for him?'

'Oh yes. She told me that if anything was to happen to her, he would have a lump sum. She and Patrick had agreed it.'

'That's good.' They moved, and sat on the swing seat.

'I wonder, did Kathleen confide in you much lately?' asked Roisin.

'I'm afraid we'd lost touch a bit. She sent me a text after Alex's wife, Amy, died. She was very upset about that.'

'Yes, she was. I told her not to go away skiing that weekend, but of course, she insisted on going.' Roisin paused; a seagull screeched overhead.

'So, did she speak to you much after that? It's about then we lost touch.'

'We did. She rang me when she got back from skiing. She seemed all over the place, kept going on about the accident. I told her Amy's death wasn't her fault, but she said I didn't understand. She told me she'd been looking up some medication information: something was wrong. And then, of course, she'd got it into her head that Patrick was getting tired of her. She said that she was losing her looks, not as young as she was. I didn't have much time for that. We all have to get older.'

Beth interrupted. 'What did you make of Patrick's arrest, by the way?'

'I was shocked. We'd been told it was an accident and then we heard that they had arrested Patrick, suspected him of murder. Well, it's a big leap, isn't it? Still, then they released him; no more said. Do you think the police have investigated things properly? There are some strange people around, and this place is the back of beyond. I wouldn't be wanting to stay here alone.'

'From what I know they have been thorough. They had a forensic team working down here, looking for clues. They found nothing. No one appears to have a motive to have been out here.'

Roisin looked at Beth intently, again reminding Beth so much of Kathleen. 'I'm so sorry this has happened. Kathleen had been making a good life over here.'

'You must have missed her when she moved here.'

'I did. They say sisters have one of the strongest bonds: shared upbringing, shared secrets. Like I said in the service, we were very close. Different, though. She was a lot more girly than me, loved clothes and jewellery. My dad once got her a shiny brooch and she'd lie in bed staring at it. It was only paste and beads. You'd have thought it was the crown jewels.'

Beth laughed. 'I love diamonds as well. I used to joke we should rob a bank some day.'

Roisin laughed, but said more seriously, 'You'd never have got Kathleen to do that. She'd never so much as pinch a paperclip from work. Never underestimate the fear a Catholic upbringing can instil in you. She felt guilty about liking material things. She was for ever going to confession about it. She had such a conscience on her. Sensitive, you know, and then she was so pretty. Plenty of temptation came her way.'

'I think it did.'

They eyed each other. Roisin said, 'I knew she'd, um, wandered, in her marriage.'

'She told you about the affair?'

'Ah, you knew. I'm not excusing her, but I don't think it was an affair as such; more of a one night fling, don't you think?'

'Kathleen never told me. I heard about it after she died.'

'She was pretty ashamed of it. She regretted it.'

'Did she tell you anything about the person she had this fling with?' asked Beth.

'No. Just that it was someone to do with work.'

'Definitely work?'

'Oh, yes. She said it was awkward seeing him. I didn't know about the pregnancy. It must have been devastating for Kathleen to lose a baby. Have you any idea who the father could have been?' Roisin bit her lip. 'I'm sorry. I don't believe in Patrick's miracle.'

'There aren't many men at work. Obviously, there's my husband, Sami—'

Roisin interrupted, smiling. 'When she told me it was someone at work, the first person who popped into my head was your husband. They got on very well, didn't they?'

Beth could feel herself blushing. 'They did, but it wasn't him. We did, um, talk about it.'

Beth heard a breath of a sigh from Roisin, showing her that Roisin's throwaway line had been more of a question than she realised.

'There's also Alex, Sami's new partner.'

'That's the husband of the woman who died when Kathleen was staying with her, isn't it? What about him? He might have been looking for some comfort.'

'I don't think so. He loved his wife so much. He's still grieving for her. But then the only other person I can think of is her GP, William. He works at the practice attached to the pharmacy.'

'I remember Kathleen talking about him when he first came. She said it was exciting to finally have someone good looking at work.' Roisin looked apologetically at Beth. 'Sorry—'

Beth smiled. 'It's OK.'

'I think she said the other doctors were all women or older men. No, she liked William. He was a good GP and friend, although she never hinted it was more than that. She said he hadn't been married long. Do you think it could have been him?'

'I don't know. It would have been a huge risk on his part.'

'Men take them, though, don't they? My money would be on him.'

'One of the things that has been worrying me has been her talking the night before she died about feeling threatened by someone. Did she say anything to you about that?'

'Not really, but she was definitely hyped up when we spoke on the Friday before she died. She said something about sorting her life out, that she wasn't going to be messed around any more.' Roisin looked over at the cliff. 'When you say she was being threatened, do you mean someone could have come out here, pushed her over there? The police arrested Patrick. Do you think he really did it?'

'I'm not saying that, but there are a few things that don't quite add up.'

'But no one really had a motive, did they? The affair thing was over; she lost the baby; she just wanted a quiet life here with Patrick.'

'Did Kathleen tell you about anyone she might have been worried about?'

'She mentioned that teacher, Imogen. Said she had tried to warn her about her pills or something. Kathleen also mentioned her daughter.'

'Elsa?'

'That's it. Kathleen kind of joked about her fancying Patrick, but I think she was quite worried about her. Kathleen said she was very pretty, looked gorgeous in photographs. Do you think there was anything between her and Patrick?'

'I think Elsa may have had a kind of crush on Patrick. She's only young, I know Elsa very well, looked after her a fair bit when she was a child. Actually, I find the idea of her having any kind of relationship with Patrick very upsetting. It wouldn't be right. Did Kathleen really think there was anything going on?'

'She wouldn't tell me. She could be quite secretive, my sister.' Roisin picked a leaf off one of the neat box plants. 'It doesn't seem right talking like this after Kathleen's funeral. It should be a day to remember her life, the good things she did, the people who loved her and appreciated her.'

'I know. I suppose the way she died was so traumatic. It's hard to see past that.'

'Yes. She was my only sister. No warning. One minute she was there and then she'd disappeared.' Roisin spotted a tiny blue butterfly. 'Did you know, in Ireland the butterfly represents a person's soul? Its wings allow the soul to cross to the other world. That's what I wish for Kathleen, to be free to go, but somehow, I feel she's still here. I can't let Kathleen go yet. I don't feel I know what happened, how she was the day she died.'

Beth nodded, tears in her eyes. 'That's how I feel. That's exactly it. Nobody else understands. They tell me to move on, to forget it all, but I can't.'

'I know it's easy for me to say things as I'm off on a flight back to Ireland tomorrow but, if you can keep looking, I'd be grateful. Something's not right. If I didn't have work commitments, I'd stay myself, but then no one is going to talk to me, are they? At least if we could find out who the father of this baby was, who had threatened her – it might not be anything to do with the way she died, but we ought to try for Kathleen's sake, oughtn't we? I mean, the truth matters, doesn't it?'

Beth nodded. 'Yes. I believe it does.'

26

Beth and Roisin walked up towards the house. As they approached the patio, Beth could hear raised voices. She saw Conor shouting at his father.

Roisin looked at her sideways. 'That flipping temper, those two. Conor is a bundle of frustration. The problem with youngsters you watch grow up is that you can miss them slipping from childhood into adulthood. They hit eighteen and we're still thinking of them as that kid whose knee we bandaged up, but they're not, are they? They've grown up; they are capable of more than we realise.'

Beth looked at Roisin, sure she was trying to tell her something, but before she could ask, the shouting on the patio got louder.

'Oh, God,' said Roisin and she raced over to them. 'Hey, this isn't the time or the place.'

Conor turned to Roisin. 'I believed him, and now I know it was all fecking lies.'

'Hey, calm down. What's happened?'

A silence fell as people watched the unfolding drama.

Conor turned to Roisin. 'You know, he just told me that I have to give him any money Mum left me. It's the only reason he's here, money. Uncle Sean had warned me about him, but I never listened. Even Nan told me that he never really remembered my birthday: it was all Mum.'

Conor swung round to face his father. 'I hate you for what you made me do. I shall never forgive you.'

Conor's father stood, his eyes bleary with drink. He opened his mouth. No words came out.

Roisin stepped forward. 'Conor, leave it now.'

His father looked away. Hot angry tears flowed down Conor's face. Suddenly he rushed at his father, grabbed the top of his tie, and raised his fist.

'You bastard.' Before anyone could intervene, he had knocked his father to the ground. He would have carried on if Patrick hadn't pulled him off.

'Enough, Conor,' he said firmly.

Conor shook him off. 'You have no idea, no idea—' He ran off.

Conor's father slowly got up, wiping blood from his mouth.

He pointed at Patrick. 'Don't you look at me like that. They all think you killed Kathleen, not me.'

'Shut it. Enough with your lies,' shouted Roisin. 'You should never have come today.'

'She was my wife. I have every right to see if the bitch left me anything. It's my right.'

'Get out,' said Patrick. The words burned with anger.

Roisin grabbed the man's arm. 'Come on. I'll take you, you heap of shite. These people don't need you here.'

She pulled him away; he staggered as he walked with her.

They heard the roar of a motorbike as Conor rode away.

Beth felt sick. The scene, the anger, the violence, had shocked her. What did Conor mean, 'I hate you for what you made me do'? What had Conor done? Beth realised that when looking at people who had a motive to kill Kathleen, just as she'd forgotten Elsa, she'd also forgotten Conor. Gemma had talked about how an affair didn't just affect two people: there were their families, their children. Conor was so angry with his mother, mainly because of the lies his father had fed him. If he'd found out about the affair, it might have confirmed all the things his father said. How far would that anger have taken him?

Patrick stood stunned, alone. He looked suddenly old. The absence of sunglasses revealed creased, weary eyes.

Beth went over to him. 'Are you all right, Patrick?' she enquired.

'I wanted it to be a day of healing, to remember my Kathleen.' Patrick's eyes looked sore with un-spilt tears.

'The service was lovely. Don't let that scene spoil the day for you.'

'But a service doesn't wipe it all away, does it? Will I always be the man who might have killed his wife? I know how gossip works in a place like this.'

'The police let you go. They believe you.'

He glared at her. 'But you don't, do you? Not in your heart. Conor told me about your outburst at the pub. Someone threatened Kathleen, someone there that Sunday, someone with a dark secret? That was the gist, wasn't it? God, no wonder the police have kept digging. Me and Conor should have been allowed to grieve. Instead people like you have made our lives hell. I bet you made that call to the station.'

'Of course I didn't,' Beth said, tears falling down her cheeks. 'I just want to know the truth. I am really sorry for what you are living with. I don't want any of this to have happened, but it did. Kathleen said the truth doesn't go away.'

Patrick shook his head. 'I just want all this to end,' he said, and walked away.

Sami, oblivious to what had happened, came over to her. 'I think we'd better make a move soon. Layla was pretty upset over that business with Conor.'

'Let's go now,' said Beth, desperate to get away.

As they went back into the house Beth saw Imogen talking intently to Roisin, and wondered what they were talking about. She went upstairs to get her jacket and sat on the bed for a few moments: what was she doing? If Patrick was innocent, she couldn't have said anything worse than she just did. She implied that she suspected him of killing his wife. And to have said it at the funeral: what was happening to her?

Her thoughts were interrupted by William, who came into the room. 'Beth, I wanted to catch you—'

'Sorry. I think the kids want to go—' she said, about to push past him.

'It's OK. Not now. I need to talk to you on your own, in private.'

She turned to him. 'OK, but when?'

'You work tomorrow morning, don't you? What time do you get out?'

'Soon after twelve.'

'Good. Could you come into the surgery when you finish? I should be free then. I'll tell them at reception I'm seeing you.'

'Is something wrong?'

'No. It would be good to chat. That's all.'

As she left the bedroom with William, Imogen came towards them. 'Ah. There you are, William. I've been looking for you, didn't realise you were hiding away up here with Beth.'

'No one's hiding,' said William. 'Are you ready to go?'

'I think so, yes. I'll see you tomorrow in school, Beth.'

Beth hurried on. It was stupid. Why was Imogen making her feel so guilty?

That evening, Sami worked in the garden while Beth tried to read her book, but she couldn't concentrate. Clips of the day kept haunting her: Conor's outburst. All that anger: what had he done? And Elsa, who had been manipulating her? Was it Patrick? Roisin had confirmed Kathleen's affair was with someone at work. It was such a small circle of people. Really it came down to Sami, Alex, and William, and Beth had to agree that William seemed the most likely candidate. Maybe Imogen's fears hadn't all been imaginary? Maybe William had been the father of Kathleen's child. If that was the case, then it must point to Imogen or William as the most likely people to have threatened and killed Kathleen. However, there were others in the mix. Kathleen could have known any number of things about Conor that he wanted kept quiet. He had anger and passion enough to silence her, but would he really kill his own mother? And then there was Elsa. She may have thought it would be better to have Kathleen out of the way. She even had her own car she could have driven over there. Her dark secret? And then Beth remembered Angela, the portfolio, Elsa. When Rosin mentioned about a child moving into adulthood, what they were capable of, was she hinting about Elsa?

Beth sat back. Today had been Kathleen's funeral, but everything that had happened had left her with little time to think about the person she had come to mourn. She knew there was something she needed to do, so she went into the garden, and picked a single pink rose that had started to bloom.

'I'm going for a quick walk,' she said to Sami.

Before he could ask where she was going, she left. The night was creeping in. She went down her street and crossed over to the church. She found Kathleen's grave, the flowers from the funeral still on the mound of earth. She knelt down.

'It's been a long day, Kathleen, and I wanted to come and say goodnight. I haven't thought enough about you today, not in a good way. I miss you, my lovely friend. Thank you for all the joy and comfort you gave me.' She lay her rose, and then noticed a rough bunch of peonies, nothing like the florist arrangements with formal white cards. This was tied with pink ribbon and there was a small piece of paper that read, 'I forgive you. May you find peace now. xxx.' No name, no explanation. Beth looked around: there was no one about. Who had left it? Of course, it might be someone who'd had a minor upset with Kathleen, making peace with her now she'd died. However, looking at the flowers, the carefully typed message, she was convinced this was something significant. She stood up and closed her eyes. 'Goodnight, sweet lady,' she said, and left.

She started to walk home. She put her hands into the pocket of her jacket, the one she'd worn to the funeral. She could feel paper in the pocket, and assumed it was an old receipt. When she arrived home, she took the piece of paper to throw it away, but could see it wasn't a receipt. She opened it, and read, 'I am watching you. I know your secret.' Beth scrunched up the note: how did that get in her pocket? They had typed on this piece of paper, put their hand in her pocket. Had she been wearing it at the time, had she felt their breath, the warmth of their hand? One thing she knew was that slowly they were getting closer.

27

Beth lay in bed that night. Sami was asleep, but she lay with her eyes open, thinking about the note. It must have been put in her jacket sometime that day. She'd only got it back from the dry cleaner's a week ago and had been keeping it tidy for the funeral. It had been in the bedroom the whole time at the wake. Anyone could have put it in her pocket. If only she could work out who'd put it there? William? Imogen? Alex? Patrick? Elsa? Conor? Who did it?

Her mind flashed to herself standing at the lectern, looking around at the congregation. It had been one of them, but she had no idea who.

She tucked the note in the unused journal she kept in her drawer.

Beth went to work the next morning, feeling tired and flat. She was glad when the morning came to an end and wished she hadn't arranged to go and see William. She just wanted to go home.

As she was leaving the school, Imogen caught her in reception.

'Off for your date with my husband?'

'Oh yes, champagne and dinner,' Beth joked, too tired to smile. However, as she looked at Imogen, she saw she was deadly serious.

'I saw the two of you coming out of the bedroom,' Imogen said.

Beth stared. 'You are joking, aren't you?'

'Why would I be joking? Why are you arranging this secret one to one?'

'It's clearly not secret, and I didn't arrange it. William asked to see me.' Beth cringed, that was probably completely the wrong thing to say.

Imogen raised her eyebrows in disbelief and came closer to her. 'Just because things are going badly with your marriage doesn't mean you can come running after William.'

Beth was horrified. 'There is nothing wrong with my marriage. This is stupid. Yesterday, you said you wanted us to be friends again.'

'That was before you made a date with my husband.'

Beth glared. 'This is madness. What the hell has got into you lately? At this rate you will lose all your friends and the support of your staff.'

Beth saw a flash of anger in Imogen's eyes. To criticise her work would always be a step too far. 'Are you insinuating I am not up to my job?'

Beth stepped back, but she wasn't giving in. 'Of course not, but you are so irritable, snapping at everyone. The staff were happy to try and meet your demanding standards when they thought you were being fair, but they are fed up with your rudeness.'

'How dare you speak to me like this? You're not even on the teaching staff. You're getting above yourself. Now, I suggest you go home and when you come back tomorrow, I expect a marked change in your attitude or I shall be going to the governors about you,' shouted Imogen.

Humiliated and angry, Beth was suddenly aware of the silence in the reception area. The staff were staring at her, open mouthed, but no one was coming to her rescue.

Afraid now of bursting into tears, Beth walked quickly to the door and out of the building. She stood still outside, breathed deeply, swallowed back the tears. Creating a scene like that was so unlike her, but then Imogen had never spoken to her like that before. What the hell had got into Imogen?

Beth walked the short distance to the surgery and told the receptionist, who went through to William and then told her to make her way to his room.

'Sorry I'm late,' she said breathlessly as she sat down.

'It's OK. I had an emergency to pop out to. Thanks for coming. Hang on—'

William got up and opened the door, to slip a sign across saying, 'Do Not Disturb'.

'There we are. They know better than to interrupt us now.'

Beth sat in the patient's chair, with all the nervousness of a patient waiting to list her problems in the allotted time.

William was quite relaxed. 'This must all seem a bit odd but there are a few things I wanted to talk to you about.' He stopped. 'Are you OK?'

'I've come from a row with your wife. She seemed to think I'd arranged this meeting and she was really jealous about it. What is going on?'

William groaned. 'I'm sorry. I hope it's not starting all over again. She got like this with Kathleen. I know Imogen is insecure. I suppose I just to have to keep reassuring her and telling her how much I love her. What worries me is that it could indicate she's not coming off the medications she should. They can make her paranoid.'

'Do you think she is going around doctors again?'

William clicked the pen in his hand repeatedly. 'It should be virtually impossible now. Everyone has been warned and I make no secret now about keeping tabs on her. I drop her off at school in the morning, pick her up when I can. If not, I ring and check where she is, and I've got Elsa on the case as well. She goes to a physio for her back once a week, but the physio is a friend of mine. He rings me when she arrives and leaves. I'm watching her all the time.'

'It sounds exhausting.'

'I want her to get better. I found a new box of pills in her drawer. She said they were left over from before, but I had been through everything. It's a nightmare.'

'At the funeral she seemed better. We'd had a bit of a falling out, but she seemed much calmer, and then today she was all over the place again.'

'Imogen told me about the conversation you two had. You must realise how upsetting it was for her to be accused of having anything to do with Kathleen's death.'

Beth felt pushed on to the defensive again. 'I know Imogen felt I should not be suspecting our friends, but everything points to one of us being the person who Kathleen was so terrified of, and that person may possibly have had something to do with her death. I'm still not convinced Patrick is as innocent as he says. I don't know what to think.'

William continued to fiddle with the pen on his desk. 'This pregnancy clearly indicates Kathleen had an affair—'

'Of course. I think Kathleen wanted to keep her marriage and it's possible that Patrick was prepared to accept this pregnancy as a miracle, but no one else seriously believes that.'

'As you now know, Kathleen told me about the pregnancy. I was convinced it was someone on her course in London. More of a one night fling than an affair. I believe Sami agrees with me.'

'He did, but I now know that's not the case.'

'How on earth could you be sure of that?

'When Sami and I went to London, I went to Kathleen's academy to see if anyone could tell me anything.'

'Really?'

'Yes, I'd contacted one of the students on Facebook.'

'Good grief. I'd never have believed you'd have the nerve to do something like that.'

'Well I did. I had a long chat with someone called Angela who had become good friends with Kathleen. It was clearly no one up there, and,' she hesitated, 'Kathleen told her sister that she'd slept with someone who she knew from work.'

'Sounds unlikely.'

'But I think it's true, and there are only a few men here.'

William screwed up his eyes, but to her relief he smiled. 'It wasn't me.'

The response 'Of course not' danced around on the tip of her tongue, but something inside her gave her the courage to say, 'But Imogen said Kathleen was always on the phone to you, and Elsa told me she thought Kathleen was breaking up your marriage.'

William's face went grey. Beth saw him tighten his fist, and thump down on the desk. 'This is all nonsense. Imogen became obsessed with me and Kathleen, and she passed on that neurosis to Elsa.'

Like wild animals challenging each other, they held the other's gaze.

'But it had to be someone,' she said, her voice shaking now.

William leant towards her. Beth was suddenly aware how close she was to him. She moved back, her heart beating fast. 'You believe I had an affair with Kathleen? To stop her telling anyone, for the sake of my marriage and my job, you think I drove over to Freshwater and killed her?'

'I don't know—'

'You're serious, aren't you?' He pointed at the door. 'You do know that my car was outside there all that morning?'

Her mouth was very dry. 'There's the pharmacy car—'

William sat back, put down the pen with one hand; the fingers of his other tapped his knee. There was a flash of anger in his eyes. 'You have hidden depths, Beth. You look so sweet and innocent. No one knows what goes on inside your head, do they?'

Steeling herself, Beth made herself maintain eye contact. 'Kathleen told me there was someone at the house party with a dark side.' From the open window came the sound of a blackbird's frantic warning song. Beth ground her teeth together.

'I will tell you what actually happened,' said William firmly. 'The morning Kathleen died, I drove here at about half six, did paperwork, sent emails. I was the only doctor doing early appointments on a Monday. We try to share them out. Everyone else was starting at 8.30. At quarter to eight I saw my first patient. I never left the building. Just inside the front door, we now have CCTV. I told the police about it. It shows no one came in or left the building between 6.30 and 7.30.'

Beth fiddled with the edge of her bag.

'I know you want everything tied up neatly, but that's not always possible in life. From what I hear Alex was cycling around the island, and I think you were alone in the woods. None of that matters of course, because the police, who have been very thorough, are sure Kathleen's death was an accident.' He paused, then added, 'But you are still wondering who the father of Kathleen's baby was, aren't you?'

William looked out of the window as if he was daydreaming, but when he looked back his face was resolute. Unable to hold his gaze, Beth stared out of the open window, and for a moment was distracted by a goldfinch sat on the roof of the old chapel. The sun shone on its bright red face and yellow wing patch. She could hear the fluid twittering song.

'I am going to tell you something that no one else knows. Before I came to the island, I had a vasectomy. I was in an unhappy marriage and had no wish to have children with the woman I was with. I've not told anyone. I haven't even told Imogen.'

'Why ever not?'

He blushed. 'It's not the kind of thing a man wants to go on about. If Imogen had wanted children, I would have considered having it reversed, but she was sure she didn't. She was committed to her career, which suited me.'

'But why not tell her?'

William gave a sheepish grin. 'I know. It's silly. I always tell my patients to tell their partners. I tell them they are making a responsible choice and all that and that you are no less of a man for having one, but for all that,' he lifted his hands in despair, 'what can I say? It was my pride.'

'I think you should tell Imogen; you know.'

'I've been thinking of it for a while, keep putting it off. The point of me telling you this is to make you realise that there is no way I could be the father of Kathleen's baby. If you want proof, I could bring up my medical records, or you could ask Alex. He may remember I bought some pain relief from him afterwards, when we were in London. I'm not good with pain and I knew Alex would be discreet.'

'I'm sorry. It never crossed my mind.'

William's shoulders relaxed. He sat back, and his face melted into a reassuring smile. 'Why should it? Look, things have got a bit intense. Let's step back. I'm sorry I got upset, but you must realise how offensive it is to be accused of being unfaithful to Imogen, to have done so with a patient, and then to even suggest I might have been involved in murder.'

'I'm sorry but—'

'My concerns for Kathleen were purely professional. I never felt any kind of attraction to her. I can promise you that. I found her rather needy in fact, but she was a patient and a friend of Imogen's. I had been concerned about her for a while, which is why, as I tried to explain to Imogen, I allowed Kathleen to ring me at home.'

'Why were you so worried about her?'

'Kathleen, of course, had been through the terrible ordeal of Alex's wife's accident, and at the same time she was going through a difficult patch in her marriage. She was concerned Patrick was getting bored with her. I didn't think she had any grounds for this, but I think she was a woman who looked for constant reassurance. I thought she was fortunate to have someone like Patrick; he was extremely patient with her.' He paused. 'After Christmas, she rang me, told me she was pregnant. I knew, as you do now, that the father could not have been Patrick. She wouldn't tell me who it was. Now, I told Imogen I thought it was someone on Kathleen's course, but actually I had someone else in mind, someone who Kathleen worked with, but I don't think you are going to like it.'

Beth grabbed the side of her chair. 'Who was that?' she asked.

'Hang on, Beth. You didn't have any worries about Sami, did you?'

'It's gone through my mind. He kept secrets from me, you know.'

'Everyone has secrets. He had his reasons, I'm sure. He's a good man, your husband. I'm sure he would never be disloyal. No, I wasn't thinking of him.'

'But who, then?'

'I was thinking of Alex.'

'Alex?'

William picked up his pen, and started clicking again. 'He's a funny one, Alex. Keeps himself to himself. You know, I knew him in London.'

'I didn't, no.'

'He ran the pharmacy attached to the practice I was in, so we got to know each other professionally. Very talented, high flying.

He was innovating all kinds of things. His pharmacy was used as a beacon of good practice.'

'I hadn't realised.'

'After I'd left, I heard his wife had severe mental health issues following a car crash. I was surprised to hear he'd left the practice to become a locum. I understand it was to have the flexibility to care for her, but it was a huge sacrifice, and for a man like him, pretty frustrating I should think. The constant need for care and supervision can go on for years. It can grind the carer down.'

'But then she died, of course.'

'Yes. A tragic accident. I know Alex feels guilty for being away the night of her accident, but it sounds like it could have happened any time.'

'Kathleen was so upset,' said Beth. 'Her sister said she'd tried to reassure her it wasn't anyone's fault.'

'Exactly. Although I know Alex feels he bears some responsibility.'

'But how could he? He wasn't even there.'

'Confidentially speaking, I heard that there had been some confusion over Amy's medication. I think it was mentioned at the inquest. I heard all this second-hand from a colleague I worked with. Of course, there was no suggestion of anything of a criminal nature, just an unfortunate error. It might well account for his wife's added confusion. Of course, we will never know but, for Alex, it all adds to the sense of guilt. It was devastating for Kathleen as well, of course.'

'That must be hard for Alex to live with. But I don't understand why you think Alex had an affair with Kathleen. I'd picked up mixed messages about Alex's feelings towards Kathleen. Frankly, I get the impression he didn't like her much.'

'The reason I suspected something was going on was because I saw Kathleen coming down from his flat. It must have been nigh on Christmas, and I was working late. She looked flustered, made some excuse, but she did look guilty—'

'But Kathleen was married, Alex only recently widowed.'

'As I said, Kathleen told me she was unhappy. Alex had been lonely. Kathleen was pretty, kind. He told me a few times how attractive she was. Yes, it seems quite likely.'

Beth sat quietly. 'Do you think Alex knew about the pregnancy?'

'I don't know. Kathleen told me that she was going to pretend the baby was Patrick's. I didn't think that was advisable, but she was sure that was what she wanted to do.'

'Kathleen told Roisin that the affair was a mistake. It doesn't sound like she was in love with Alex if it was him.'

'I don't think they loved each other. My guess would be that it was a one night stand, probably one they both regretted after. Kathleen had guilt, and I wonder if she had concerns after the inquest about Alex's part in Amy's death. She said something to me about Amy's medication. I think Alex developed his own concerns about Kathleen.'

'What do you mean?'

'Between you and me, he came to see me after Christmas. Kathleen had shown him some earrings that had belonged to Amy. She said she didn't know how they'd got in her bag. Alex was upset. He asked me if she'd ever had problems like this before: stealing and then not knowing what she'd done.'

Beth was shocked. 'I don't think Kathleen would have stolen anything. In fact, her sister was saying how aware she was of her weakness for jewellery and felt a lot of guilt about it.'

'It's sounds possible that she gave into temptation. My theory was that she'd taken the earrings and then felt so guilty she'd made up this highly suspect story.'

Beth shook her head. 'I can't believe that of Kathleen.'

'No. Alex didn't want to believe it either, but it would explain his change of attitude to her.'

'Yes, I can see that. He's been odd when he's talked about Kathleen and the necklace Amy gave her. It would make sense. I just don't like to think about it.'

'I was concerned at how angry Alex was about it. I tried to calm him down, say it was a mistake, that kind of thing, but I didn't really believe it.'

Beth looked at William carefully. 'You seem to have some grave misgivings about Alex. He doesn't sound a suitable partner for Sami.'

'I'm not saying that for a minute. He's a first-rate pharmacist. No one is suggesting he intentionally made a mistake over Amy's medication. And as for Kathleen, he may have had a one night stand with her, but that is hardly a crime, more a moment of weakness.'

'But you said you didn't know quite what to make of him.'

'We are different kinds of people, that's all. I am content staying as a GP, working hard to do the best for my patients. Alex is ambitious. It's something I have never understood, but good luck to him. We need people like him for professions to develop and improve.'

Beth could see William's eyes glancing at his laptop: it was the end of their appointment.

'You need to get back to work.'

'Thank you for coming in. It's good to get things out in the open. By the way, I'm taking Imogen up to London for the night this weekend, get her away from everything. We're taking Elsa as well: go to a show, a bit of family time.'

'We were up there before the funeral. We stayed at Alex's house. It's in a great location, but of course you know all that. You stayed earlier in the year, didn't you?'

'The three of us went in the new year. Elsa wanted to do the sales, heaven knows why. They're all year round now, aren't they? And anyway, she does most of her shopping online. Still, she and Imogen had a good time.'

'Imogen said you escaped to the East End on the bus.'

'I did. When I was a GP in London, I had a patient who'd grown up there who would tell me all about how it had changed. I was curious to see for myself.'

'I was listening to the radio. They were talking about property prices and how the East End is unrecognisable: an unaffordable place for most working people to buy a home.'

'They're right, but sometimes people romanticise places like that. Those high-rise flats with the stink of urine on the concrete steps were hard places to grow up, and very few people were able to get out of that cycle of poverty. I think it looks a lot better now. I'm glad those flats have gone.'

'I'm sure you're right.'

'We're lucky to have Alex's house, aren't we? We all need him to keep that house on for a bit longer.'

'Yes. Well, have a good time.'

Beth was glad to get out of the surgery and into the fresh air. It had been intense: that look on William's face when she had challenged him had scared her. She'd always thought of him as charming, soft, but that's not what she saw today. She had learned a lot; one of the main things being that, if William was telling the truth, he did not have an affair with Kathleen and that meant he had no motive to be threatening her. It was a great pity William had not told Imogen the whole truth before. However, who knows how far she'd gone to stop Kathleen taking William away from her?

And then there was Alex. Could he really have had this affair or fling with Kathleen? He seemed so devoted to Amy, and it was hard to imagine wild passion beneath that rather cold exterior. It was odd, though, what William said about Amy's medication getting muddled up. Alex hadn't mentioned that, but then, why would he? And there was this talk about Kathleen stealing the earrings. Beth found it really hard to imagine her friend doing such a thing but, if Kathleen had, she could understand why Alex was so angry: it would be a terrible thing to do. She could only hope that there was some kind of mistake. She desperately wanted to give Kathleen the benefit of the doubt, but she was struggling. Beth was starting to wonder if one of the people at the house party she knew the least about was Kathleen herself.

28

The following Monday evening, Beth and Sami were both at home when Beth received a call from Patrick.

'It's Conor,' he blurted out. 'He didn't come back last night. I can't find him. There's no messages from him. He's hardly spoken since the funeral. I've told the police. It's not been twenty-four hours yet, but I know something is wrong. I know he was distressed at the funeral, but then he was bound to be: the poor boy has lost his mother.'

Beth felt fear grip her heart. She could hear Conor's desperate voice shouting at his father. Had her speculation about Conor being involved in Kathleen's death been right? Where was he now? Had guilt sent him to take his own life?

'I'll talk to Layla. She might know where he is,' she said, trying to remain calm.

'Thank you. Yes, that's great. I know he's nineteen, I shouldn't be worrying like this but after all that has happened...'

'I'll go and ask Layla now, and get back to you right away.'

'It's Conor, he's missing,' Beth explained, as she rushed past Sami and up the stairs. Layla looked up from her bed.

'Something else has cropped up. It's Conor. He seems to have disappeared. Have you any idea where he is? Patrick is worried.'

Layla shook her head. 'He's not been in touch with me. Hang on. I'll message Elsa.'

Beth waited.

'No. She said she didn't even know he'd gone missing.'

'OK. Thanks. Let me know if you hear anything.'

Beth hurried back down, picked up her phone and rang Patrick back.

'Thanks for that. I'll keep ringing around.' He sounded more relaxed, but she said, 'Me and Sami will come over.'

'Are you sure?'

'Definitely.'

Beth turned to Sami. 'Come on: we need to go to Patrick's.'

An idea came to Beth as they drove over. As soon as Patrick opened the door, she asked, 'Have you been down the garden to the gate?'

Patrick looked mystified, but Beth ran down. The light was fading, but she could see the fence was intact. She pushed open the gate and looked out; there was no sign of anyone. She called Conor's name but there was no response.

As Beth returned to the garden, Patrick and Sami were waiting for her.

'I'm sorry, I didn't mean to alarm you, but I had wondered if Conor had come out here, maybe to sit where Kathleen died.'

Patrick shook his head. 'His bike has gone.'

'I should have asked. Still, it might be worth going down on to the beach. He could be there. I don't suppose you've looked down there, have you?'

Patrick shook his head. 'I've not been there since the accident. I dread it.'

'It's OK, me and Sami will go,' said Beth.

They took a torch and walked down the hill to Freshwater Bay and back along the beach.

'You seem in an awful panic,' said Sami. 'He's probably at a friend's house.'

'But he might not be. We need to go and look.'

The beach was pebbly, not easy to walk on in the dark, but the tide was well out. They shouted Conor's name, without any reply, until they arrived at the place where Kathleen had fallen. Beth looked up at the rugged cliff. There were no flowers: nothing to indicate this was where it had been. It was as if it never happened. Beth tried calling Conor's name again, but her voice was lost in the sound of the sea.

After a few minutes, Sami said, 'Come on, love. He's not here.'

They staggered their way back along the beach, up the hill, to Patrick. Beth started to wonder if she had over-reacted.

'I think he must be at a mate's,' said Patrick. 'Thank you so much for bothering, but it's probably best you go.'

'Will you be all right?'

'Of course, I'll phone if there's news and I'll phone the police again in the morning if I haven't heard from him.'

Beth didn't want to leave. She still felt uneasy but, as Sami seemed to agree with Patrick, she was persuaded to go home.

As they parked the car, Beth could see a light on in Adam's room but not in Layla's.

Inside, she looked around, and slowly it dawned on her that Layla was nowhere to be seen. She burst into Adam's room, and he lazily removed his headphones.

'Where's your sister?'

'In her room?'

'No. Of course not. Where's she gone?'

'No idea.'

'You do know Conor has run off, don't you?'

'Has he?'

Beth groaned. 'You're in a world of your own. Everyone is worried sick. Conor went off, and now Layla's disappeared.'

Adam sat up, interested now. 'Oh heck. Hang on, I've got the numbers of some of her friends and Elsa. I'll send round a message. She could have gone to see one of them. It doesn't have to be anything to do with Conor.'

Back downstairs, Sami had been texting and phoning Layla.

'No reply,' he said.

'Where is she?' asked Beth in despair.

Adam came downstairs. 'No one has any idea where she is.'

'Oh my God,' said Beth, in tears now. 'It's Conor, I know it is. I don't want her to be with him.'

Adam's phone pinged a message and, as he read it, he started to scratch red ruts in his forehead, his father's gesture.

'What the matter?'

'It's from Layla. She said, "Tell Mum and Dad not to worry. Conor came to get me. I'm fine."'

Beth grabbed the stair rail, feeling sick and giddy. 'Oh God,' she groaned.

Sami looked up, 'Hey, come on. I don't think Conor would hurt her.'

She shook her head, shaking off the reassurance, 'I saw him with his father. We have no idea what he did to Kathleen. He's very angry, unstable—'

As her words hit home, Sami's face set in icy determination. He picked up his phone and called the police.

29

A uniformed officer arrived at midnight. He took down details of what had happened and left.

They were all sat up, checking their phones, when Adam suddenly looked up. 'Remember the day Layla missed her music exams? She went out with Conor then. Where did they go?'

Beth tried to unmuddle her brain. 'It was Shepherd's Chine. Yes, I remember.'

'Could they be there?'

Beth paused. 'It's possible, not an easy place to get to in the dark, but we have to try. Adam, can you stay here in case she comes home or phones?'

Sami drove them to the tiny car park hidden off the military road. It was pitch black, but they both had torches.

'Look,' said Sami, shining his torch over to the corner. It was Conor's motorbike. Sami sent Patrick a text.

They walked, one after the other, through the bushes and then slowly made the awkward climb down the broken steps. Just along the beach they saw a small bonfire and next to it were Conor and Layla. A wave of relief flooded Beth.

'Hi, Mum,' said Layla, waving.

The panic and relief melted away, and annoyance set in. 'What do you mean "Hi"?' shouted Beth. 'We've been worried sick.'

'Didn't you see the note?'

'What note?'

'I put it on your dressing table.'

'No. I didn't see it. We wouldn't have a clue if you hadn't sent a text to Adam – and Conor, Patrick has been frantic. Why did neither of you answer your phones?'

'I sent Adam a text, and then switched my phone off. It's nice to listen to the waves.' Layla saw Beth's face. 'Don't be mad. Conor's had a rotten time.'

'But he's worried everyone to death. What's going on, Conor?'

'I had to get away. The funeral and everything was the pits. I didn't know what to do.'

'We all need to get home. We can talk tomorrow. Come on,' said Sami.

Beth had questions for Conor but, at half past one in the morning, with work the next day, it didn't seem the time to ask them. Sami was right: it was time to go home.

They drenched the fire, and all made their way back to the car as Patrick was pulling into the parking area.

'Thank God,' he said to Conor.

'You were worried?'

'Of course.'

'I didn't think you would be.'

'Well, I was. I told the police. Shall we go back now? We can talk or just go to bed. Thank you so much, Sami.'

'It's OK. Let's all get home.'

They drove home in silence, all exhausted. At home Sami updated the police.

'Are you hungry?' Beth asked Layla.

'I'll take some cake up to bed.'

Beth found a scruffy note on her dressing table. 'Gone with Conor. Don't worry.' It wouldn't have been reassuring.

Beth left Layla to sleep in the next morning, while she and Sami got themselves into work.

When she returned, she found Layla still in bed.

'What was all that about?'

Layla looked over the top of her duvet cover. 'He rang, said he was lonely. I told him to pick me up. Don't go mad about the bike. He sounded so down. He asked me not to tell anyone where he was. He had wanted to be alone and, anyway, he didn't think anyone cared about him.'

'Well they do, and we care a lot about you.'

'To be honest, it seemed exciting at first, but I was starting to think I'd ring you. I was glad when you came. Conor was so moody, and it was cold.'

'Were you frightened? Did he hurt you, do anything?'

'God, no. He just sat there. It was boring.' Layla gave her a smile. 'The only person I was frightened of was you: I knew you'd go apeshit.'

'Did Conor tell you anything about why he had run away?'

'No. He didn't talk much. Mum, I'm worried about my new trainers. They got muddy. I hope it comes off.'

'Honestly, Layla. You need to apologise for all this. Dad's having to work a whole day on a few hours' sleep; you wasted police time.'

'You called the police?'

'I was worried when I knew you were with Conor. Whatever you think of him, I have seen how he is when he's angry and the way he attacked his dad. I know he can be violent.'

'I was never worried.'

'Well, I was. Don't ever do that to me again.'

30

The next day, as Beth looked over the bridge at the bottom of Castleford Shute into the clear water, her phone sounded. It was a text from Conor. He asked her if she could go over and see him at Patrick's house. It seemed odd, but she replied that she could be there in about an hour. She walked on, up to the farm, round the top of the fields and back home.

As she approached Patrick's house, she could see Conor's motorbike in the otherwise empty garage. He seemed to be watching for her out of the window, because he answered the door without her knocking.

'I'm sorry to drag you out here. I wasn't sure what to do, but I needed to talk to you.'

Beth followed him into the living room.

'I'm sorry about the other night,' said Conor.

'We were all worried sick. Layla's only fifteen.'

'I know. She seems older. She's a good listener. There's nothing going on between us, you know. I don't feel like that about her.'

'You must have realised that she has feelings for you. You shouldn't have taken her off like that.'

'Yeah, OK. I'll lay off for a bit. Since the funeral my head has been in such a mess. Seeing Dad and everything. I saw what he was like. I wished I'd never listened to him.'

'What was it he told you to do?' Beth asked gently, wanting to hold her breath.

Conor combed his fingers through his fringe. He sat down. 'I've been such a crap son.'

'What happened?'

Conor suddenly stood up and started to leave the room, saying, 'Hang on. I need to get something.'

Beth sat waiting, wondering if he was coming back. She could hear him crashing around upstairs, but eventually he reappeared, holding a couple of large photographs which he handed to her.

'This all happened before Christmas, before I was asking Mum for money. I found them, told Dad, and he said to pretend I'd found them hidden in Patrick's room. Give Mum a bit of a scare: make her think that Patrick was in love with Elsa; make her know what it felt like. And so, that's what I did.'

'And what did she say?'

'I thought she'd laugh it off, but Mum burst into tears. She said she'd been worried for a while, knew it would happen. Dad told her Patrick only loved her for her looks, and when they'd gone, he'd move on to someone younger.'

'What a cruel thing to say.'

'I couldn't believe Dad would have said anything like that to Mum,' continued Conor, 'so I rang him. He said it was all lies, and she was putting on an act.' Conor stopped. 'It wasn't until the funeral I realised how I'd got it all wrong. He never looked sad once. I told him I thought I'd stay here, and he said it was a good idea. He's met someone else. But he said I owed him money from when I'd stayed with him. He said to give him any money that was left to me by Mum. It was like this mask fell off and I knew who he was. I realised at that moment how much Mum had loved me. I wish to God it wasn't too late to tell her that I really loved her.' Conor started to cry.

Beth touched his arm gently. 'Your mum knew; mothers always do.'

'It was weird, you know,' he said, wiping his face roughly with his arm. 'The night before she died, when I was going off to see my friend, she came out to me as I was getting on my bike. She told me she loved me, to always remember that. It was like she knew. I remembered then how frightened she'd looked earlier when that call came, and I checked if she wanted me to stay. See, I did care about her deep down. She told me to go and enjoy myself, and so I left her. I wish to God now I hadn't.'

'What are you doing with these?'

Beth hadn't heard Patrick's car, nor seen him enter the room. He sounded curious rather than angry.

'I'm so, so sorry,' said Conor.

Patrick looked confused. 'Why? These are Elsa's, aren't they?'

Conor slowly explained about the photos. 'I'm so sorry, Patrick. I know now how much I upset Mum.'

Patrick looked at the photos. 'You showed these to your mother before Christmas?'

Conor nodded and burst into violent sobs. He curled up in a ball on the sofa. Patrick sat down by him. 'Hey. It's OK,' said Patrick. 'I made mistakes as well. She asked me about these photos, you know, when we went skiing, and you know what I said? I said, "They're good aren't they? Elsa reminds me of you when you were young." I laughed and wandered off. It was cruel: I realise that now. I should have talked to her properly.'

'You know when I left her on that Sunday night, I knew something was wrong with her. I nearly came over. I got up at half six, knew she'd be doing her meditation thing. But instead I went to McDonald's. Stayed in there for ages. When you phoned me, I was still there, messing around on my phone, drinking Diet Coke.'

'Look, Conor,' said Patrick, 'it wasn't your fault. I know you've made mistakes; we both have, but you know you've a home here.'

'I don't know why you are doing this,' said Conor.

'We get on OK, and it's what Kathleen would have wanted.'

Conor's phone sounded. 'You answer that,' said Patrick. Conor left the room and Beth heard him arranging to meet some friends.

'That was kind,' Beth said to Patrick.

'He's not like his father. He has a lot more of Kathleen in him than he realises. He'll be all right.' Patrick held out a photograph. 'I've been a fool, you know. When I saw that Kathleen was jealous of Elsa, a bit of me wanted to make her experience what it had been like for me, always worrying about losing her. I could have downplayed it more than I did. It means I am partly culpable in what she went on to do, doesn't it?'

Beth blinked. 'You mean—?'

'Yes. I'm sure she slept with someone else. It was after the skiing holiday. I'd been stupid, flirted too much. At Christmas she said something like she hoped that whatever either of us did, we would always stay together. She wouldn't explain, but I wondered, thought I'd pushed her too far. Once or twice I caught her making phone calls secretly. I checked her phone, but she always wiped the call log, which was suspicious in itself.'

'Who do you think it was?'

'I thought it must be someone on her course.'

'But weren't you angry with her?'

'No. It was my fault.'

'And then you realised she was pregnant?'

'Yes, and now, you're not going to believe this. I did think it was a miracle. I still believe the baby was mine. I shall always think that. I felt it was a gift from God to mend our marriage. I felt I'd treated her badly. I'd been cruel about the photographs.'

Beth blinked: he really seemed to believe it.

'Do you know what I was doing the morning the police came to tell me about Kathleen?' asked Patrick. 'I wasn't cleaning the house. I was up at five, choosing some recent photos of Kathleen. I found some on Facebook and there were the ones I'd taken in the garden here. I was working on them, and was going to hang them here. I wanted her to know I loved her as she is now.'

'Did you tell the police you'd been doing that?'

'No. Why?'

'If you'd been online, they could track it, couldn't they? It was your alibi, wasn't it?'

Patrick blinked. 'I never thought of that. Gosh, Sean would be mad if I told him—'

Beth smiled. 'Well, it looks like you are OK anyway.'

'I still wonder, though, who phoned the police. It's not nice to think of someone wishing you ill like that. I'm sorry I accused you. It's been getting to me, that's all.'

'And what about Elsa? You've treated her badly, using her like that.'

'I didn't think it was serious.'

'I think you underestimated her. About her portfolio, how much of that did you do?'

Patrick groaned. 'Kathleen was obsessed with the idea that I'd done too much but, honestly, she was just jealous. It would go against so much that I believe in to have helped Elsa cheat. In any case, the school would never have believed it was her work if they didn't have other things comparable. And she'd have completely failed at university if her work wasn't up to a previous standard. No: that was all her own work. She could go far, that girl.'

Patrick looked around and then back at Beth, his face serious. 'Beth, I promise you there was nothing but flirting between me and Elsa. I was stupid, but there was nothing physical, nothing at all. I loved Kathleen so much. I would have done anything for her. Every time I breathe I miss her. I'm sorry I argued with you at the funeral, but the idea that anyone could think I would have killed Kathleen is unbearable.'

Beth saw the pain in Patrick's eyes. That was real, and she was sure his love and grief for Kathleen were as well. She was glad he had that alibi now. For the first time she was convinced he'd had nothing to do with Kathleen's death. 'I'm so sorry, Patrick,' she said. 'I'll go now.'

She left him standing lost, alone. As she got into the car, she knew she couldn't go straight home.

Instead Beth drove up to the Downs, and went for a walk, away from everyone. She walked down the bottom path. Although it was close to the small road that wound its way through the Downs, it was usually deserted. None of the cyclists, horse riders or even dog walkers, usually ventured that way. Sometimes with Ollie she would see a fox or a hare. There were huge bushes that you could walk into: caves made of leaves, with birds singing above you. Beth sat on a soft patch of grass, closed her eyes and tried to just breathe and as she felt the release of emotion warm, angry tears burned her cheeks. She found herself weeping for the time before Kathleen died, a time that felt more innocent. But, of course, that had been an illusion. So much had been happening then and she had been unaware of it. All the hate and passion had been there, simmering away under the surface.

It seemed her list of people who may have been threatening Kathleen was diminishing. William didn't have an affair with Kathleen. That seemed to let him off the hook, along with Patrick, Conor and Sami. Who was left? Imogen, Elsa, Alex—

'I nearly didn't see you in there.' The voice startled her.

'Oh, Alex. You surprised me. Is it your day off?'

'It is. I cycled over.'

'I'm glad you found the Downs. Stunning, aren't they? I come here when I need to clear my head, and down here is my secret place.'

'You look a bit, um, sad.'

'You keep finding me like this, don't you?'

'I'll leave you if you want to be alone.'

'No, it's OK. I was thinking about Kathleen. I've just come from Patrick's.' Alex sat down next to her in her cave of branches.

'That house is so big. I rattled around the house in London when Amy died. I still have so much to sort out. About the only thing I did was take away her medicines; that must be my training, I guess.'

Beth suddenly remembered something William had said. 'I guess she was on a lot of medication. Not easy for her.'

Alex blinked, surprised. 'She wasn't on much, actually, but I made sure it was well organised for her.'

'But she could still have got in a muddle. It wasn't your fault.'

'Her medication was straightforward and carefully managed. There were no mistakes.' She felt his whole body tighten, saw the white of knuckles on clenched fists.

'Sorry. I thought William said she took something by mistake, the night she died. Not that it was anyone's fault.'

'If anyone thinks that they should look at the report from the inquest.'

Alex glared at her. Beth saw the anger in his eyes and was shocked: she'd never seen him like this. She felt very alone.

'I'm sorry,' she mumbled, 'really sorry.'

His hands relaxed. 'It's OK. The guilt of not being there that night is still pretty raw. Why was William talking about it?'

'He was saying how he knew you before, in London.' Beth wanted to ask him to verify William's vasectomy, but it seemed an impossible thing to slip naturally into a conversation. Instead she said, 'I apologise for being tactless.'

'Time to get back, I think,' he said.

As they made their way Beth, desperate to lighten the mood, asked, 'Have you started looking for a house?'

Alex seemed to relax. 'I've seen a few. I might stay around Castleford. It would be stupid to give myself a long cycle in, particularly once we get into winter again.'

'It wouldn't be too far from around here; you could come up here after a hard day's work.'

'It's a thought.' He pointed over to the hills opposite. 'I went up there the other day, to the Longstone. Did you see that house all on its own? Now, there would be a dream.'

'Not for sale, though?'

'Unfortunately not.' he replied grinning.

'You mentioned going up Tennyson Down. Do you still fancy going?'

He nodded. 'Yes, I'd like that. The forecast next week is good. I have Thursday off.'

'The afternoon would be good for me. I finish work at twelve. I'll call after. We can pick up Ollie and I'll drive us there.'

'Perfect.'

They had arrived back at the car park. Alex started to unlock his bike.

'See you for the walk, then,' said Beth. She tried to make her voice sound light, but the words came out hard and taut. The discovery of that latent anger in Alex had been deeply disturbing and, rather than Alex setting her mind at rest about Amy and the medication, she felt increasingly anxious. Why be so angry about it if there was nothing to hide? If he could get that angry about that, how would he have been when he heard about the earrings?'

She was nervous now about this walk next week. Did she really want to go up Tennyson Down, up by the cliffs with someone she suspected of murder? She shook herself: this was silly. It would be broad daylight, lots of people around. However, as much as she tried to reassure herself, her mind flashed back to Alex's face when she'd asked him about the mix-up of the medication. She'd seen a fire there she hadn't seen before, and it frightened her.

31

Sami was up in London when the police rang Beth on the following Tuesday evening.

'Can we speak to Sami Bashir please?'

'I'm sorry. He's away. Can I help?' said Beth, her heart beating fast.

'Someone phoned to tell us that they had seen kids messing about in the pharmacy car park. We went to check it out and found things that need following up on. We were wondering if we could have a look at the CCTV?'

'I don't think they have any for the car park. I think it's only inside the front door.'

'According to our records the practice had a camera fitted in the car park last year.'

'Oh, sorry. Well, you need to speak to Sami. I can give you his mobile number. You should be able to get him or, of course, his partner Alex is living in the flat above the pharmacy. He may well know about it.'

When they had rung off, Beth realised she had never thought of there being CCTV for the car park. All that time she'd been wondering about the pharmacy car being used by someone: it would surely have shown up on the CCTV if it had been taken. She could ask Sami, but then he would start worrying about her getting obsessive. Of course, she could ask Alex. She hesitated. She would have to give Alex a reason, and that would mean telling him she was still worried about Kathleen's death. However, as he was staying at the caravan and cycling that morning, he wouldn't be thinking she had any suspicions about him. So, no; it was all right to ask him. In fact, it would be interesting to see his reaction.

On Thursday Beth called for Alex after work to go for their walk on Tennyson Down. As she stood waiting for Alex to answer the door, she looked around the car park for signs of graffiti or anything the police might have been looking out for, but it all looked pretty normal. She rang the doorbell. There was no response, but then she heard Alex calling. She turned to see him driving the pharmacy car in. 'Sorry, offered to take a delivery. I'll be there now.'

He parked the car and came running over to her. 'Sorry, Sami is so rushed and there was a large package for one of the nursing homes. I offered to take it. Anyway, I'm here now.'

'I forget you can drive,' said Beth.

'I got out of the habit up in London.'

'I was just looking around for the graffiti. I hear the police were down here on Tuesday. Did they speak to you or just ring Sami?' asked Beth.

'No, they came here.'

'What was it all about? I can't see any graffiti.'

'No. The kids had been drinking, but they left some empty wallets. The police want to see if they can identify them.'

'They asked me if you have CCTV here. I didn't think so.'

'Oh, yes. Sami had it put in. The police downloaded the video from Tuesday night. Come on up, it's quite tidy. I can't say the same for the hallway. You need Google maps to find the front door.'

Although Alex had a separate front door, the hallway led to the pharmacy and round to the surgery. Beth followed him up a steep flight of stairs.

Alex had been right about the pile of clutter outside his flat door. There were old filing cabinets, computers, some chairs stacked up and some old storage boxes. She saw him take his front door key out of the cabinet.

'That's not very secure, is it?'

He shrugged. 'I've a small home safe. Anything valuable is kept in there, but it is a bit of a contrast to my security system in London.'

Beth looked around. 'Blimey. Sami ought to do something about this.'

The flat had a living room and what she assumed were a bedroom and bathroom leading off. It was small but organised, tidy and tastefully decorated. Alex had made it a home with his books and pictures. The white bookcase had carefully arranged books in alphabetical order. On one shelf there was also a neat pile of new brown envelopes, some small reels of pink ribbon with tiny white stars on, and some small plastic wallets with coins in as well as reference books, and a small box with cotton gloves and a magnifying glass.

'Your online business?'

'Yes. I've just purchased a Beatrix Potter fifty pence coins uncirculated coloured set.'

'Oh, they're so sweet. I assumed you would be selling old coins.'

'Sometimes. They're kept in that.' He pointed to large metal safe.

'Are they very valuable then?'

'They're worth looking after, and the safe provides the perfect environment.'

'That matters?'

'Oh, yes. Most coins are made of silver or copper, chemically reactive metals, so you have to protect them from water vapour in the air, extremes of heat and cold. That is a good place to keep then.'

'Gosh. I'd never realised it was all so serious.'

'This is nothing to what my father did. He'd have laughed at the sort of thing I'm selling most of the time, said it was an insult to numismatists – coin dealers and collectors. He was a bit of a snob about it all, but then I guess it was his livelihood. I know enough to usually tell the real thing from a fake.'

Beth picked up a thin square box and opened it to find a silver coin engraved with a fox.

'That's so sweet.'

'Don't touch it,' Alex snapped, then, 'Sorry, it's quite valuable.'

'The box is the same as one that I saw in Kathleen's room. It had a coin with a butterfly in a heart on it. Did she get the coin from you?'

Alex blushed, cringed. 'I gave it to her around Christmas time. It's quite rare.'

'I'm sure she treasured it.'

His face clouded over. 'Possibly.'

'But you never wanted to follow on from your father, carry on the business?'

'No. He left me his collection, but I sold the whole lot at auction.'

On the mantelpiece was a picture of Alex and Amy on their wedding day. The woman he was marrying had short blonde hair, pretty, quiet features, and smiled shyly at the camera. She looked very different to the poised dancer she'd seen photographs of at the London house.

'Amy?'

'Oh, yes. She looked radiant that day. We never had children, which is sad. If we had, I might have caught a glimpse of her smile, her laugh, in them, but it wasn't to be.'

They walked up the road to Beth's house, where they were greeted by Ollie.

'Are you OK with dogs?'

Alex replied by bending down and stroking Ollie. He looked out of the front window. 'Great view of the castle. Better than the view from my London house.'

'I don't know. I saw a fox from Amy's bedroom window—' Beth paused, felt herself blush.

Alex scowled, his face hard and cold. 'You went into Amy's bedroom?'

'I'm so sorry. I just went in and out. I know you asked us not to.'

His face relaxed. 'It doesn't matter.'

Beth swiftly tried to move on, establishing that Alex had not had lunch, and suggested she take something with them. Beth departed to the kitchen, cringing: what an idiot to let that slip. She grabbed a few items from the fridge, put them in her bag, and put the lead on Ollie.

As they approached Freshwater, Alex pointed out a camping site. 'My caravan's in there,' he said.

'I'd not realised how close you were to Patrick's,' replied Beth. 'It's an amazing location. Gemma was telling me they had some objections when they applied for planning permission. They were lucky. It's quite unique.'

They parked at the foot of Tennyson Down and Beth had a pang of regret as she puffed her way up. However, the grass was soft, the tiny wildflowers peeped up at her, the air was fresh and, as they climbed higher, the views were wonderful. The chalky cliffs swept down to meet the vast expanse of twinkling blue sea. They didn't talk.

At the top, by the huge granite Tennyson monument, Beth sat next to Alex on the bench, and took out the picnic.

She asked, 'Do you feel you are settling down here?'

'Slowly. It's a big change, mind you, after you've lived on the mainland.' He grinned. 'See: I'm calling it that already.'

'You and Sami have a lot of plans, don't you?'

'I know Sami is a bit daunted by some of it, but we must change. I'm battling to save the high street pharmacy. I feel remarkably fortunate to be doing it with Sami. He's a very good pharmacist and much better with people than me. It's rare to have that combination of empathy and skill.'

They left the bench and walked towards the cliff edge. The view across the sea, to the white chalk cliffs was stunning.

'If you're lucky you can see dolphins or seals.'

'Not a bad place to live,' said Alex, breathing in the air.

'No, I love it here. William was saying he likes the gentler pace down here as well.'

'I was wondering again why he was talking to you about Amy?'

Beth looked away into the distance: she had to be brave.

'We'd been talking about Kathleen. It seems pretty clear she had an affair or some sort of fling with someone.'

'What has that to do with Amy?'

Beth cringed again. 'William suggested that maybe you were lonely after Amy died, and he knew Kathleen was unhappy when they went away—'

Alex went deep red. 'He assumed that meant I slept with Kathleen?'

'Um, yes. I suppose he did.'

'But I only lost my wife a few months ago. That's an awful thing to say.'

'I'm sorry, but it's hard to think who it could have been. You see, I know now it was someone she saw at work.'

'It doesn't mean that William can pull my name out of a hat. I have to say I find it extremely offensive. I suppose he thinks he's in the clear.'

'Is it right he had a vasectomy? He told me I could ask you to confirm it.'

Alex nodded. 'I wouldn't have said anything, obviously, but yes, he did. But it doesn't give him the right to go around pointing the finger at others.'

They put the picnic away in silence and started to walk back.

'How did you find working with William in London?' Beth asked, hoping to reach out, and thankfully Alex responded.

'He was a lot less sociable up there. We didn't talk much. I know he went through a messy divorce. I think he was glad to move away.'

'Did his wife leave him?'

'I think so. I think she met someone else. She had a wealthy family, but she seemed to get a lot: the house, most of the money, I heard, but then I also heard he had family money behind him so, I guess it worked out fairly in the end.'

Beth stopped to take a small piece of bracken away from Ollie's leg and they started to make their way back down the hill.

Alex asked, 'So, how are you feeling now about Kathleen's death? Do you feel at peace with it yet?'

'No. Not at all. There are quite a few things not answered.'

'Such as?'

'Well, I still haven't worked out the person who was there at the house party who might have threatened to expose her over the affair—'

'Do you still think this person could be linked to her death?'

Beth looked at Alex, but he appeared quite relaxed. There was no urgency in his voice. 'I do. The fact I had an unpleasant anonymous phone call makes me even more sure I'm on the right track. Someone doesn't want me digging around—' Beth paused.

'The police are sure it was an accident, aren't they?'

'But I'm not.' She hesitated before asking, 'Is it right that Kathleen stole some of Amy's earrings?'

Alex paused; his eyes screwed up tight. 'How did you know about that?'

'William mentioned it.'

'I did go to him. I considered it to be a confidential matter. I don't want to discuss it.' Alex frowned.

There was a silence, but Beth suddenly thought about the missing drugs at the pharmacy.

'Sorry to go back to it, but do you think it's possible she stole the pills they found missing at the inspection?'

'No, definitely not. Kathleen was meticulous at work with drugs and I don't think she would have done that.'

He'd closed the subject: that was obvious, so as they walked on a bit further, Beth said, 'I wonder if you could help me with something?'

'What's that?' Alex sounded weary.

'You told me there's CCTV at the car park. What does it cover?'

'Quite a lot; the entrance to the car park, the entrances to the main building, including my flat. There's only one way in and out, as you know, so a record is kept of everyone that enters or leaves. Why do you want to know?'

'I need to know if someone used the pharmacy car to go over to Kathleen's. The pharmacy staff and the doctors all have keys. A silver car was seen near Kathleen's. Well, it could be this one.'

'I suppose it could; seems a long shot. Still, it's all on the computer. I'm not sure which dates we've deleted. It might still be on there.'

'Would you show it to me?'

Alex nodded. 'If it sets your mind at rest, you can come and see it any time, although Sami could show you.'

Beth smiled back. 'I'd rather not ask him. He thinks I'm obsessive enough as it is. Could I come tonight?'

'Yes. Just ring the bell. I'm in all evening.'

'Thank you. I feel I owe it to Kathleen. I know I've found out new things about her, but it hasn't changed my view that she was an angel. Really, she was such a lovely person.'

'That's a good memory. Don't let anything spoil that for you. But for all that, be careful, Beth. All this digging about. You've already uncovered a lot of things. It's like the metal detectorists who send me coins to sell. They scan whole fields, never knowing what they might find. Sometimes it's a bottle top, sometimes treasure, but then, one day, if they are in the wrong place at the wrong time, who knows, they may find an unexploded bomb, so be careful.'

Beth shuddered. She wasn't sure if this was one friend advising caution to another, or something darker, a threat.

32

That evening Beth made everyone tea, and at about eight said she was going for a walk but that she wouldn't take Ollie.

'But why not?' asked Sami.

'I just need to be on my own.'

'Shall I come with you?' asked Sami.

Beth gritted her teeth. He never offered to go out walking with her. 'No. I'm fine.'

Beth went down the Castleford Shute, but not up to the castle. Instead she walked along the lane, and then back over another ford. She stood for a moment on the bridge over the ford watching one of her favourite birds, a little white egret, brilliant white, feathers once more valuable than gold. The clock on the church struck eight. She made her way into the village, past the shop.

She was about to cross the road to the pharmacy when she saw someone else knocking on the door to Alex's flat. She froze as she realised it was Imogen. She was waiting for Alex to answer but she was glancing around, trying to get as close to the door as she could. Beth saw Alex open the door, and Imogen go inside.

The whole thing had a furtive look. Feeling greatly unsettled,

Beth turned and walked home.

Next day when she went into school, Imogen's car was not in the car park. The receptionist told her that Imogen hadn't come into work but had not sent in any messages.

'I've been trying to get her on her mobile. I hope she's all right. She's never done this before.'

'Have you tried her husband? I have his mobile. Shall I ring him?'

Beth rang William. 'Hi. They're a bit worried at school. Imogen hasn't come in. They can't get an answer from her mobile.'

Beth listened as William told her he would follow it up and get back to them. Beth explained it to the receptionist, adding, 'I guess I'd better get to my class. Let me know, won't you, if she's not well. I can pop in after work.'

At break Beth enquired at reception.

'Imogen's husband rang back. She's not well. He said he'd call you soon. He did say not to expect her in for a few days.'

Beth was anxious now. She sent a text to Sami and returned to work.

As she was leaving at lunchtime, she received a message from Sami to call in at the pharmacy. Beth was growing increasingly nervous. Sami never asked her to visit him at work. What was going on?

At the pharmacy, Beth saw the queues of people so waited in the corridor. She overheard a patient being told that Dr Parker-Lewis was not in today.

Sami called her into the consultation room. 'Imogen is in hospital again.'

Her heart sank but, in a way, she wasn't surprised. 'Oh no. It's not the pain killers again, is it?'

'I'm afraid so, but this time is a lot more serious. William thinks it's an overdose of strong opioids. He went home after you phoned him. She was unconscious, the empty packet lying next to her.'

'I thought she was coming off them. Her doctor would have had to prescribe them, wouldn't he?'

'These were not from her GP. Going by the packaging, William is pretty sure she bought them illegally, probably online.'

'Like the dark web thing Layla told me about?'

'It could be. He has no idea what she has taken all together, but she is critical, in intensive care.'

'Oh no. Oh, Sami.' Beth burst into tears. 'You don't think she did this on purpose, do you?'

'Why do you think that?'

'Guilt over Kathleen?'

'Oh no—'

Beth's mind, however, was still racing on. 'Last night I saw Imogen go into Alex's—'

'He mentioned that to me this morning. Apparently, Imogen went around because she'd found some loose pills, asked him if he could identify them. Alex was able to identify them by the codes on them. They were strong opioids. He took them away and destroyed them.'

Beth collected her car and drove to the hospital. William came to meet her at reception. He looked completely different to last time she saw him: grey and older.

'It's all my fault,' he said.

'No. William, you were trying to look after her.'

'I should have made her take leave, get help, but she was so determined to keep working. I've been watching her, you know. I never thought to check her laptop. The police have searched the house, found pills in brown envelopes hidden away, places I'd never have thought to look. Now, of course, this means she was illegally in possession of controlled drugs. Even if Imogen pulls through, I don't know what they will charge her with.'

'I can't imagine Imogen being so desperate. How would she

know how to contact these people? I knew nothing about it until Layla told me.'

'When we stayed with Alex, I remember him talking about it. Imogen was full of questions, but I had no idea then the level of her problem. She must have taken note and used that information to find her way online. They would have been arriving in innocent brown envelopes, but I should have checked her post. Of course, it's illegal for these things to be sent through the post, but these people don't care, do they? It's all about money. That's all.'

'How is Elsa?'

'She's in with Imogen. It's too much for her, but she won't come out.'

Beth suddenly pictured the neat pile of brown envelopes in Alex's room. A crazy thought flashed through her mind: what if that coin business was a cover for something much darker? William had said some pharmacists were involved in it. It was all frighteningly possible. And yet Alex seemed such a reliable, trust-worthy person. Sami was no fool, and he trusted Alex completely.

William's face was ashen. 'I can't bear to lose her. I love her. She's the best thing that happened to me. She and Elsa were my new start. When my first wife left me, my life fell apart. They saved me.' William hit his fist against the seat. 'How could anyone do this? Destroy lives: how could they?'

'I don't know,' said Beth.

William looked at her and his face melted. 'I'm sorry. You don't need me sounding off at you. I just keep thinking of all the things I should have done.'

'You could only do so much. Imogen knows how much you love her. That's the main thing.'

William gave her the saddest smile. 'Thank you, Beth. You're a real tower of strength. I'm going to go back in now. They'll only allow family—'

'Of course. I'll go now but, well, I'll keep in touch.'

Beth walked back to the car feeling numb, bereft. It was as if someone had turned off the sound and she was walking through a tunnel alone. 'You are so lovely, but the world isn't.' That is what Kathleen had said, and maybe she was right.

Beth drove to the pharmacy. Sami, seeing her, gestured towards the consulting room and she followed him. Beth felt a huge lump in her throat. It hurt to talk. 'It's serious this time, really serious.' She burst into tears and Sami put his arms around her.

There was a gentle knock at the door. Alex appeared, but started to back away.

'No, come in,' said Sami.

'I do hope I'm not intruding, but I'm concerned about Imogen. How is she?'

Beth wiped her eyes and went through everything.

'William was saying the pills would have been delivered in ordinary brown envelopes like you buy in the post office. He had no reason to suspect anything.' Beth glanced at Alex. She saw nothing but normal concern.

Sami sighed heavily. 'How could they get away with it?'

'I don't think some of the dealers see this as any different to selling, I don't know, clothes or books online,' said Alex. 'It's a commodity that people want, and they are providing it. They claim people have the right to choose.'

Beth was horrified. 'But they haven't got a choice, not once they're addicted. You have no right to say that.'

She felt Sami's hand gently placed on hers.

Alex stood up. 'Of course, I agree with you. I'd better get back to the pharmacy. If you see William, send him my regards. I hope Imogen comes round soon.'

When he'd gone, Sami squeezed her hand. 'I'll come home with you now. Come on.'

Beth found refuge sitting on the floor cuddling Ollie.

'Is this how it is all going to end, Ollie?'

33

It was a relief to cook tea, to talk to the kids about normal things. It wasn't until Beth was loading the dishwasher that her phone rang. Her heart leapt when she saw it was a text from Alex, asking about Imogen.

She replied that she had no more news, then he asked if she still wanted to look at the CCTV as he was free that evening.

Beth thought before she answered. She dreaded looking at the video and seeing Imogen driving the car. However, there was also the matter of Alex. William's suggestions about the affair, the worries about Amy's medication, and now there was the possibility of him being involved in selling drugs illegally online. If Kathleen had suspected Alex of messing with Amy's medication or even providing drugs illegally, it had to be possible that Alex threatened her, even killed Kathleen. She needed to look inside the envelopes, the safe, maybe she would find something.

Beth felt her heart racing, Alex had said to be careful. Had he been warning her? Her hands shook as she put on her coat and she had to steady her voice as she told Sami she was going for a walk.

She walked down to the village and was entering the car park for the pharmacy when she saw William getting into his car.

'I'm surprised to see you here,' said Beth.

'I had to come and check some paperwork. It doesn't stop because I have a personal emergency. I know some patients are waiting for important results. I had to check for them.'

Beth was struck anew by how dedicated William was to his job. 'That is very good of you. How's Imogen?'

'No change. I'm going straight back to the hospital now.'

'I hope things have improved.'

'And what are you doing here at this time?'

'Just coming to see Alex for a chat.'

William gave her a sad, weary smile and left.

Alex let her in. 'Fancy a drink? I've got some white wine from the island vineyard. It's very good.'

'Thanks.'

Alex went into the kitchen, talking as he moved around opening cupboards.

'I've given myself tomorrow off,' he shouted from the kitchen. 'I'll do a bit of work on the online pharmacy work, but then I'm going to have a day cycling around the island. It's a good weather forecast. I have to say, you're lucky with the weather over here.'

As he talked, Beth wandered over to the shelves where the brown envelopes were arranged in two neat piles. In the first pile each was numbered in the left-hand corner. She picked them up and looked inside. They were empty. She ruffled through the next pile and was about to look inside one when she was aware of Alex returning. She quickly tried to put the envelopes back. 'Your glass of wine,' he said, then noticed where she was. 'What are you doing over there?'

Alex gave her the glass of wine but frowned when he saw the untidy pile of envelopes. He moved to tidy them, then looked back at her. The flash in his eyes made her blush. 'Were you looking in these?'

'Why should I? They're just envelopes,' she stammered.

Alex screwed up his eyes. 'I think you were. What did you think you might find?'

'Nothing.'

He picked up one of the empty envelopes.

'Are you thinking this is like the envelopes Imogen's drugs were sent in?'

Beth felt very sick. She half smiled.

He looked at her more closely. 'Seriously. Is that what you're thinking?'

She nodded.

'You suspect I'm doing more than selling coins online?'

Beth eyes widened in fear. 'I don't know.'

He sat down. 'Why would you think that I would have anything to do with selling drugs?'

She swallowed. 'The envelope. You telling Imogen about the dark net, and I saw her come here the night before she took the overdose.'

'I never told Imogen about the dark net. I have no idea how you get on there.'

'I remember when we were talking at the pharmacy after Imogen went in. You said that these people on the dark net saw what they were doing as no worse than selling clothes or something. It sounded like you didn't think it was such a terrible thing to do.'

Alex frowned. 'I was simply trying to explain how some of them might see it. Of course, I don't condone it in any way. It's monstrous. Of course, I would never approve of what they're doing and certainly never have anything to do with it myself. I would no more do such a thing than your Sami would. Look in my safe, the envelopes, the whole flat. There's nothing. You can have sniffer dogs brought here if you want.'

Beth gritted her teeth. 'I'm so sorry, but can you understand why I was suspicious? I saw Imogen come in to see you last night.'

'Yes. She'd found some pills that she'd lost the box to.' Alex glowered at her. 'She didn't come here to be supplied with drugs. I'm fed up of your insinuations. I'm a dedicated pharmacist. I would never, ever, be involved in anything illegal.' He jumped up and rushed over to a drawer. 'And as for Amy, here is the copy of the report from the inquest. Read it.'

Beth took the papers, but her hands were shaking.

'Read it,' he repeated.

Beth tried to concentrate and read, and as far as she could make out from the wordy document, Alex was speaking the truth. There was no mention of the mix-up of drugs, but it was hard to take it in. She handed it back. 'I'm sorry—'

'I've had enough. I'd like you to go.'

Beth got up, feeling humiliated. She left the flat, ran up the road, and up the steps to the graveyard. She collapsed next to Kathleen's grave and sat sobbing. She was so confused: if Alex hadn't done any of these things, no wonder he was insulted.

'Kathleen, I tried to so hard, but it's all falling apart,' she sobbed. 'Everyone hates me. I'm so stupid.'

Beth took out her phone and shone it on the grave. It looked lost here: just a mound of earth. She would be glad when there was a headstone. She noticed another bunch of flowers, like the last time, tied with the pink ribbon. This time there was no message, simply a heart. As she looked at the flowers, she was reminded of something. Of course, it couldn't be a coincidence. She knew who had left those flowers and, looking at the heart, she knew why.

'I'm sorry.' The voice startled her. Through the darkness she could make out Alex. She stood up, wiping the mud off her knees.

'No, you're right. I'm blundering around. I hear one thing, then the opposite. I don't know who to believe.'

'Look, it's all right. Come back, check this CCTV.'

She was about to turn down the offer, but she needed to see that video, so silently she followed Alex back. It was eerie entering the empty pharmacy, white coats hanging on the back of the door watching them, judging her for being there.

Alex turned on the computer, and loaded the file.

'This system we put in at Christmas, it can be downloaded direct on the computer. Saves piles of discs. We record in real time, so the quality is good. Ah, good. We've got as far back as that Sunday night. Don't tell anyone. According to the guidance, we should only be keeping about thirty days, I think. Anyway, let's see what its shows.'

He started it at nine on the night of the house party. They could only see the corner of the pharmacy car, but had a very clear view of the entrance.

'Do we need to go back that far?'

'Just curious. You know, in case, say, someone moved the car the night before. We'll put it on fast forward, though, or we'll be here all night.'

It was all very still, slightly spooky with the night camera. They saw a cat, then a man come in and urinate against the hedge. But no cars, no other movement. It started to get quite tedious, but Beth tried to keep concentrating. At one point Alex went out to fetch his glass of wine, but Beth never took her eyes away from the screen. They reached two, three o'clock. Everything was very quiet.

Eventually, it started to reach the early hours. Alex slowed it down. From six o'clock she was on high alert. At 6.30 she saw William drive in and park his car. Beth sat forward. They slowed down more, watched William take out his briefcase, lock his car and then let himself in through the main door. They carried on watching. No one else arrived until the receptionist at 7.30. They saw William let her in. After that the other doctors arrived in quick succession, and patients soon after. At 8.00 Alex stopped the video.

Beth sat very still. The feelings of anti-climax and humiliation wrapped themselves around her. 'So, that's it. After all that, no one used the pharmacy car. I got it all wrong. You must think I'm so stupid.'

'Of course not.'

She felt her cheeks red, hot. 'Sorry. I should be pleased, shouldn't I? I didn't want Imogen to have come in here.'

'No. It's good news really. So, does that mean you finally can accept no one went over to Kathleen's?'

Beth scratched the palm of her hand. It was too quiet; they were too alone; now wasn't the time. Instead she said, 'Maybe,' and stood up. 'Thank you for helping me despite everything. I'd better go. I told Sami I was going for a walk. He'll have the police out looking for me.'

As Beth walked home, she tried to think through what she'd learned. She was hugely relieved about Imogen, but what was she to make of Alex?

34

The next day, Beth was thinking about Alex as she walked home from the school, when she received a phone call from Patrick. He sounded breathless, panicky.

'Listen. Something has cropped up. Can you come over?'

'Today?'

'Yes. Please, it's urgent.'

'What is it?'

'There's something you need to see.'

'I have to walk Ollie, so I could take him up to the Downs and come to you after. Can you cope with a cocker spaniel as well as me?'

Beth grabbed a packet of crisps and a banana before driving up to the Downs. It was not brilliant sunshine, but instead it was a dull, quiet kind of day. Together she and Ollie walked slowly up the central path. The sea was only just distinguishable from the sky, but it was restful.

She drove on to Patrick's, and rang the doorbell.

'Is it OK to bring Ollie in? I'll keep him on his lead.'

It was a measure of Patrick's distraction that he didn't seem to care.

'Come in,' he said, briskly. 'I finally got up the courage to go through Kathleen's things. It was going well, and then I found something.'

Beth waited, and noticed Patrick glance down at Ollie.

'Wait there and I'll bring them down.'

Beth sat on the sofa; Ollie lay down on the floor beside her.

Patrick returned with some small jewellery gift boxes. 'Sorting through the drawers, and look what I found—'

He laid them on the coffee table in front of her.

'She had some lovely things,' said Beth.

'But I never gave her any of these,' said Patrick. 'They're very expensive pieces. I don't understand. Where have they come from?'

Beth picked up a pearl necklace in a beautiful box, and touched a diamond brooch in a case. 'I've only ever seen jewellery like this at Alex's house,' she said.

'Amy gave her that butterfly necklace. Do you think she gave her these? It seems too much; I don't understand.'

Beth breathed deeply. 'I think you need to ask Alex about them.'

'Is he at the pharmacy?'

'No. He's off today, cycling.'

'I could try his mobile.'

Beth was busy thinking of a way to get away: she couldn't face Alex after last night.

Alex answered Patrick's call surprisingly quickly. Beth heard Patrick explain what he needed to discuss.

Patrick reported, 'Funnily enough, Alex is close by. He said he could be here in ten minutes.'

'Why don't I just leave you to it?' suggested Beth.

'Please stay. I could do with the moral support.'

They went out into the garden. Beth released Ollie and he ran straight to where the chicken coop had been. He ran around sniffing.

'Have the chickens settled in OK with Jilly?'

'I haven't asked. I guess so.'

'How is Conor?'

'We're getting on OK. His dad has a lot to answer for. However, the exciting thing is that Conor likes coming out on shoots with me. He is very eager to learn. Who knows if it's something he'll do seriously, but I enjoy having a protégé: it's given me something to do. And it's given him something else.' Patrick looked out at the sea. 'It's good for me. Although, of course, nothing fills that hole, does it? I see Kathleen, hear her, all the time.'

'Have you thought of counselling?'

'No, not yet. William suggested it the other evening when he came round, but I don't think I'm ready yet.'

'I suggested it to Conor. It can help to talk to someone.'

'I will mention it to him again. He's got a lot to unravel. What I'd love to do is get away. Everything here just reminds me of Kathleen. The trouble is, just when I think I've made a step forward, the pain of it all washes over me and I feel like I'm back to square one.'

'I heard somewhere that grieving the loss of someone so close is like climbing a spiral staircase: you feel like you are going round and round, but slowly you are climbing.'

'I guess that could be right. It's difficult. I don't know that I want to get better. I don't ever want to forget her.'

'Of course not.'

Alex came around the back of the house. Beth could feel her cheeks burning. However, he called out in a friendly way, propped his bike against the hedge and came over.

'Thanks so much for coming,' said Patrick. 'Come and get a cold drink.'

Alex gave Beth a quick reassuring smile, and they went inside.

Alex drank a glass of water, and then asked, 'So, what is the mystery?'

'Come and see this.'

Patrick showed Alex the jewellery on the table. Alex stared at the items and reached out, his hand shaking. He handled the necklace and the brooch. He looked back at them.

'Do you recognise these?' asked Patrick.

'Where did you find them?'

'In Kathleen's drawers. Tell me, Alex, did Amy give any of these to Kathleen?'

Alex sat down on the sofa, shaking his head. 'Amy didn't give them to Kathleen, but they did belong to her.'

Patrick turned pale, slumped down, his mouth open. When he finally spoke, his words stumbled out. 'But how? I don't understand.'

Alex took a deep breath. 'I didn't want to raise it, Patrick. None of it matters any more.'

'I think it does. Please, Alex. Tell me.'

Alex looked at Beth, pleading with his eyes but she said, 'I think Patrick needs to know.'

The patio doors were open. Beth could hear the seagulls and crows in the distance; it was a very still day.

'As you know, Amy became fond of Kathleen very quickly. Well, the second time Kathleen went to stay, that was in October, Amy gave Kathleen the butterfly necklace. I admit I found that hard as I'd given that to Amy when we got married, but it was Amy's choice and I could see Kathleen was delighted with it. But then, after Amy died, it must have been late January, Kathleen told me she'd found the butterfly earrings that match the necklace in her bag. She said she couldn't remember taking them: all she could think of was that she'd picked them up by mistake.'

'That's not likely, is it?'

'No, not at all. I wanted to believe her. She'd been such a good friend, helped me through one of the hardest times of my life. I was desperate to find an excuse. That's why I went to William. It seemed so out of character. But he obviously didn't think there was any medical reason. I had to face the fact that she had stolen them. I guessed it was guilt that made her want to return them. I was so upset, angry. I didn't know how to handle it. Kathleen had been like some angel, coming and looking after Amy occasionally, and then supporting me. I couldn't take them back. I was too hard on her, maybe. Looking at all this makes me wonder if she did have a problem after all.'

'So, you hadn't missed any of this?'

'No. I've hardly been in Amy's room, never looked at her jewellery.'

Patrick's face creased with pain. 'I can't believe it. Kathleen would never have stolen anything. You know her upbringing, strict Catholic. I would have thought fear would have stopped her if nothing else. Didn't the pharmacy fail an inspection because pills had gone missing? Kathleen seemed worried about it; you don't think she stole anything from there, do you?'

'No. I told Beth. I never believed she would do that.'

'But you think she stole these?' Patrick was bent in despair. 'You must take them back.'

'No, I couldn't. I don't want to touch them.'

'But I can't keep them. Kathleen always loved jewellery, but to steal—' Patrick stared at the jewellery as if it was only just starting to sink in. 'My Kathleen did all this? I don't understand. I thought I knew her.'

'The day she died,' he said, his voice trembling, 'they asked me about how she was. Maybe she took her own life: felt so guilty for what she'd done.' He sat down, his shoulders shaking. He moaned quietly like an injured animal, but there were no tears.

Alex sat by him. 'Patrick,' he spoke the name firmly, causing Patrick to still. 'We are all made up of many pieces. Just because we don't like one, it doesn't mean the others are not also part of us. Kathleen may have done this, but she was capable of love, kindness, generosity. I know that whatever she did, she loved you. She told me that you were her world, her everything.'

'Did she really say that?'

'I'm not lying. And you must hold on to that, Patrick. I promise you, any other path will lead to madness.'

Patrick stood up. 'You've been so understanding. Thank you, Alex. That was brave. I still love her with all my heart, but I am so very sorry for what she did.'

Alex gave a heartbreakingly sad smile. 'I've forgiven her. It's in the past now. I think I'd better go. Please, both of you, don't let this go any further: leave Kathleen's memory safe. I don't want any police involvement, nothing. It's finished now.'

Alex left. Patrick found a small bag, and put the boxes into it. Holding it out to Beth, he said, 'Please can you do something with these. Sell them. Give the money to charity. Please, I don't want them in the house.'

'But I don't want them.' Beth could feel herself shaking. Not fear, but anger bubbled away inside her. How dare Kathleen do such a thing? Beth didn't believe Kathleen had been ill: this was greed, and she'd stolen from someone who trusted her. It was despicable.

She saw tears on Patrick's cheeks, 'Please, Beth.'

Beth relented. 'OK. I'll take them. I don't know what to do. What if Alex changes his mind, wants them back?'

'I don't think he will. He doesn't want to think about them any more than I do.'

'I'll take them for now. We'll think in a few weeks' time what we should do with them.'

Beth left Patrick staring at the empty table, lost. How was Alex feeling now? She needed to talk to him: there was something she needed to say. As she drove, she saw Alex ahead of her, cycling into the caravan park. She slowed down and followed him in, up to what she assumed was his caravan. He propped his bike up, and it was only as he was removing his helmet that he saw her.

'Sorry. I hope you don't mind me coming here.'

'Of course not. It was all very upsetting. Do you want to come in?'

'No, it's all right, but there's something I need to ask you.' Beth looked over at the sea, sparkling in the sunshine. 'You were right about your pitch: it's amazing.'

'Thanks. I love it here. Elsa, Imogen's daughter, has been here taking photographs; she's been experimenting with night photography, apparently. I gave Imogen a key, said she could bring Elsa any time she wants.'

Beth sat down on the warm grass. Alex sat next to her. She was aware of the sounds of the sea below, the same sounds of sea washing over the pebbles as she'd heard at Kathleen's. Alex waited patiently.

'I am so sorry for some of the things I've said to you,' began Beth, 'but there's something I'm now pretty sure of, and I need to know if I'm right.'

'And what's that?'

'It's about Kathleen. I think, Alex, that the person she slept with and the father of her baby was you.'

'No, never,' he said, but the words were weak. They carried no conviction. She knew then that she was right.

'It's all right, Alex. I'm not judging you.'

His head dropped low over his knees. 'How did you guess?'

'I didn't know definitely until last night. There had been clues: the way you talked about her, sometimes loving, sometimes so angry. Then there was the coin. A butterfly in a heart: it's quite romantic, isn't it? But then there were the flowers you put on Kathleen's grave, the same pink ribbon with stars on you use for your coin business.'

Alex closed his eyes. 'You're right, of course. I meant the note. I have forgiven her. At the funeral I realised it was time for us to find peace again with each other. I forgave her, and I hope she can forgive me. I was too hard on her. They're only things. Does anyone else know about Kathleen and me?'

'I don't think anyone else knows... well, William suggested it, but he was just speculating.'

'That's something. Living with all this has been a nightmare: the shame of what I'd done. It's like carrying around this enormous boulder of guilt, desperately trying to hide it, but at the same time longing to be rid of it. The person I feel I've let down the most is Amy. I should never have slept with someone else so soon after losing her. It was only a few weeks after.'

Alex put his head in his hands. 'I knew it was a mistake as soon as it happened, but I'd been so lonely. I was talking after work with Kathleen. She was upset. She'd been on this skiing weekend and was very down. I invited her up to the flat for a drink. We were talking, she cried, I comforted her. The next thing, well, we slept together. It was a mistake. We both regretted it, but we thought we could carry on as if it hadn't happened.'

'In January she told me she'd found the butterfly earrings in her bag. I was so confused, and felt so betrayed. As I just told Patrick, it took a while for me to believe she'd taken them, but in the end, I knew it. We made a good fist of working together, but outside that I couldn't bear to look at her. Then, a few weeks later Kathleen found out she was pregnant. I knew she was going to keep the baby. She didn't believe in abortion: it was her choice. I would have financially supported her, but she wanted to talk to Patrick, pretend the baby was his. It seemed ridiculous, but she was convinced that he would accept the story from her, and I agreed. She sent me a text the night she went into hospital. I knew then she'd lost the baby.'

'But what if she'd told Patrick about you?'

'If she had, I'd have lived with it. What we did wasn't a crime: it was a terrible mistake.'

He lifted his head, turned to face Beth. 'If you're thinking I might have killed Kathleen to stop her telling anyone about us, well, you've got it all wrong. My only feeling of shame was towards Amy and her memory. No one else matters. I was upset about the earrings but not that angry. You said she knew something about this other person? Well, I've done nothing. There was nothing amiss with Amy's death. You don't know how carefully I read the report, but it's all there in black and white. I shall give a copy to Sami. He can explain it all. I promise you: I never hurt anyone.'

Beth looked out to sea, saw a ship on the horizon, far, far away, and wished she was out there, away from all this heartache.

She stood up. 'Thank you for being so honest with me, I'd better be getting home.'

At home, Beth thrust the jewellery into a drawer. Like Alex, she didn't want to touch it or think about it. She lay in bed later, slept badly, until, hearing the dawn chorus, she went downstairs. It was cold and quiet in the kitchen. Ollie came running over, delighted to have company so early.

'Layla was right, Ollie, life can be shit.' She filled up his water bowl and made herself some hot milk, more to cuddle the mug than to drink. She heard a creaking in the hallway and Sami came in.

'What are you doing up?' she asked.

He yawned. 'I could ask the same of you.'

Ollie raced over, very excited to have even more company.

'Are you OK?'

She shook her head. 'Not really. I have so many things going round in my head. I feel stupid and angry.'

Beth explained about the CCTV, the jewellery.

'So I thought I was being really clever. I got the car thing all wrong, and now I find the person I've been fighting for was a thief.'

'Kathleen would never have stolen expensive jewellery from someone who had been so sick and had trusted her.'

'Alex is sure she stole the earrings,' she said more gently. 'He didn't say anything because he never wanted to make a fuss. I don't think he'd have ever told anyone if Patrick hadn't found the jewellery in Kathleen's room.'

Sami shook his head. 'It's very kind of Alex. Very sad. Poor Patrick.'

'I feel angry with Kathleen. All this fighting I've been doing for her, confronting friends, trying to find some sort of truth, and I feel she's manipulated me.'

'If she'd done anything like this, it was because she wasn't well.'

'And would you feel the same if she'd been stealing from the pharmacy? She could have been, you know.'

Sami didn't reply. He looked down at the table.

'We don't have to pretend,' said Beth. 'We were both fooled by her.'

Sami spoke sharply. 'Where is the jewellery now?'

'Upstairs in a drawer.'

'We can't just keep it there, you know.'

'I don't want to think about it. I've been forgiving her everything. Even when I thought the affair might have been with you, I didn't get angry with her. I took it all out on you. How much did she lie to me? Maybe the wolf she was so scared of, who was so much bigger than she feared, was not out there but inside herself all the time.'

35

The next day Beth felt numb, exhausted. After work she visited Imogen, who was in a heavy sleep. Beth sat next to her thinking how young and vulnerable she looked. Touching her hand, she said, 'How did we come to this? What's happened to our world, Imogen?'

Imogen's eyelids trembled and her eyes opened.

'Wrong, I was wrong. I never believed her.'

Beth sat close. 'You never believed who?'

'Kathleen.'

Imogen closed her eyes, but a few minutes later they opened again. There was urgency there. She looked directly at Beth.

'Elsa. Look after Elsa.'

'It's all right. You know I will always be here for her.'

After that, Imogen returned to a deep sleep. Beth guessed that she was acknowledging that Kathleen had been right about the number of drugs she was taking. Even Imogen had admitted that Kathleen had been genuinely concerned about her health after the accident.

Beth continued visiting Imogen, who mostly slept. However,

when Beth visited on the Sunday afternoon, she was surprised to find that not only had Imogen been moved to a main ward, but she was sitting up, albeit with drips and various machines attached. Elsa sat to one side of her.

'You look a lot better, thank God.'

Imogen didn't smile, but said, 'I am, thank you.'

'How are you feeling?'

'Awful, but I know I'm lucky to be alive.' It was as if she was choosing each word carefully: she was stepping on a high wire without a safety net. 'I will be charged for possession, but William is hoping I will get off with a non-custodial sentence.'

'I see.'

'I've decided not to rush getting home although, of course, they may need my bed. I want to feel on top of things before I'm discharged.' Imogen looked straight at Beth. 'I hate the fact that everything had got so out of control. To have been doing things I have no recollection of is very frightening. I don't remember going online, or any packets arriving. I know I went on official pharmacy sites to get some prescription medication for my eye infection. It's such a pain getting appointments, but nothing else.'

'I was shocked when Layla was telling me about the dark net: it must be a scary place to go on.'

'As I say, I can't remember anything. I would have sworn I'd never even heard of the dark net.'

'But Alex told you about it—'

Imogen shrugged. 'See: I can't remember that; nothing.'

'Well, it's going to take time to get better this time; you must take the help they offer you.'

'It will be all over the papers. It's the end of my career, isn't it?' Imogen sunk back into her pillow.

Beth placed her hand on Imogen's.

'Your friends will stick by you.'

'I'm not sure I have many of them left now. What if I end up in prison, Beth?' Imogen looked at Elsa. 'Who will look after my girl?'

'That's not likely, is it? And there are a lot of us to look out for Elsa.' Beth shot a smile over to Elsa.

Before Beth could speak again, she heard loud voices coming from the corridor that led to the ward. Imogen's face went deathly white. 'Oh, God. That's my mother. Who told her I was in here?'

Imogen's mother strode on to the ward, her father a few paces behind. Beth stood up quickly to allow Imogen's mother to sit down. 'Imogen, what have you been doing? William has told us all about it. He tried to sweeten the pill, but how could you do this to us?'

'William told you I was here?'

'Of course, thank God.' Her mother looked over at Elsa. 'Now, you are not to worry. We have everything worked out for you.'

'What's going on?' asked Imogen.

'It's obvious you can't look after Elsa. Your father and I have been looking at a private university in the States. Your father has connections in some good ones over there. I am sure we could get Elsa in even at this late date, with an unconditional offer. We'll pay for the best accommodation. It will be her chance to mix with a better class of student.'

'To do photography?'

'God, no. We need something more respectable than that. We were thinking liberal arts.'

'Elsa has an offer from a very good university to do photography. I'm very proud of her. Her work has been outstanding.'

Imogen's mother carried on. 'The point is Elsa needs help. Let's face it: she's not exactly had a great start.'

'She's done very well,' said Imogen, her voice harder. 'I am very proud of her.'

'But it's not the education you had. Poor Elsa. She was telling me she's working in a pub. Honestly, Imogen, of all the places you could have chosen. Still, you don't have to worry now: we are going to take over.'

Imogen grabbed the blanket, her knuckles white. 'No, I don't think so. Elsa wants to do photography. That is what she will do.'

Imogen's mother crossed her arms. 'As always, you are only thinking of yourself. We've heard the rumours, you know, about Elsa and this older man. Despite that, your father and I are offering you a lifeline. This could be the making of Elsa. Let's face it, you don't want her making the same mistakes as you. You have to let us help.'

Imogen glared at her mother. 'I don't know who has been spreading malicious gossip, but Elsa has my 100 per cent support. You are not going to take over my life or Elsa's.'

'And what about William? He is very loyal to you. You're extremely lucky. Don't push him away like you push away everyone else who tries to help you.'

Imogen glared at her mother. Beth took a deep breath. Any child in school would be cowering now.

'I am proud of Elsa, and you don't need to bribe William to stay with me, even though I'm in a lot of trouble now with the police. I have no idea where this could all lead. I will certainly lose my job. As for how the rest will pan out, I have no idea.'

Beth couldn't take her eyes off Imogen's mother. Her mouth hung open, her eyes bulging. Her father stood behind the chair and gripped her shoulders.

'I hope this is a sick joke, Imogen. You can't be in that much trouble for buying some aspirin online.'

'It was far worse than that. These were controlled drugs: illegal for me to have without a prescription.'

Imogen's mother sat down. 'I hadn't realised how bad things were. One thing's for sure: you really do have to let us take Elsa off your hands now. You are clearly unfit to keep her.'

'No, Mum. You and Dad are the last people I would hand my daughter over to.'

Her mother went a strange shade of purple. 'We spent a fortune on you; you were given everything, and you threw it all back at us. Now we come along trying to do something for that poor daughter of yours to stop her making the mess of her life that you did and you throw it back at us.'

'That's it, Mum. Enough, your visit has been long enough.'

'Imogen, you are being most ungrateful, as always, I might add that your daughter will end up just like you. I can see it in her attitude.'

'Mum, you can say what you like to me, but you will not criticise Elsa. She is the thing in my life I am most proud of. I look at her and I'm in awe of the wonderful person she is turning into. I wasn't a perfect mother, but I loved her, sat with her when she was ill. I would do my schoolwork at two in the morning just so that we could have a few hours in the evening, things you never ever did for me.'

Her mother stood up. Her father cowered behind. 'I shall put this tantrum down to your bad reaction to your medication.'

'Mum, I am an addict.'

Her mother sat down with a thump. 'No daughter of mine is an addict. You just need to pull yourself together. We shall make sure you get the best lawyer money can buy, then we can put this ridiculous business behind us and we can all try and act like it never happened.'

'I need help, Mum. Nothing is going to be the same after this.'

'We can pay for one of those rehab places. You know, a decent one. Even stars go to them sometimes.'

Imogen sat up. 'I don't want you to spend any money on me. Nothing was ever good enough for you and I am exhausted. No more, Mum. This is me. I am going to get better, but not for you. This time it'll be for me.'

Her mother stood glaring at her. 'You obviously want us to leave. How you got William I shall never know. You need help keeping him, my girl. He's not going to hang on to a loser: you mark my words.'

After her parents left, Imogen lay back on her pillow, exhausted.

Beth sat back down. 'I'm so sorry, Imogen.'

'It's kind of a relief,' said Imogen, waving her hand at the door. However, she looked at Beth, her eyes steady. 'Do you think what she said about William is true?'

'No, not for a minute.'

Beth stood up to go.

Elsa, who had been silent through the whole of the incident, said, 'I'll come out with you, Beth, if that's OK, Mum?'

'Of course, see you later.'

As they walked out of the hospital together, Beth asked, 'How are you, Elsa? This is very tough on you.'

'I'm worried about Mum. She's going to lose her job, isn't she?'

'She's not in the right state to do it at the moment, is she?'

'But what about me? To have mother who is a drug addict! There's been some nasty stuff online and on Instagram. I tried the "she had an allergic reaction" thing, but it made me look pathetic.'

'If I were you, I'd find those one or two friends you can trust, talk to them in person, not on social media: this is private, your life. Elsa, you are stronger than you think, and you have good friends and family around you. As for your mum, she'll be back up fighting.'

'I don't know how I feel about Grandma now. She wasn't very kind to Mum, was she? I think I understand why Mum kept them at a distance.'

'Would you want to go to the university your grandma was talking about?'

'No. I've got things sorted out and I'm good. That portfolio is all my own work and I can explain exactly the processes I used.'

'I'm sure you can. It sounds to me like you have things well in hand.'

Elsa looked down. 'Some things, not everything. The trouble is, you have no idea what I've done. Hearing Mum say how proud she was of me. But she knows it's rubbish.'

'Can you tell me what has happened?' asked Beth. 'Is it to do with you driving over to Kathleen's the morning she died?'

Elsa bit her lip. She looked like the little girl Beth had asked about spilling her squash on the carpet.

'I've been so stupid. I've made the most awful mistakes. Mum said not to tell anyone but how can I keep this secret?'

'Tell me.'

36

Before Elsa could speak, Beth saw William arriving in the car park.

'Would you be able to tell William as well?'

Elsa nodded. They waited for William to come over.

'We've been to see Imogen. She's looking much better,' said Beth, but she moved on quickly. 'I think there is something Elsa needs to say.'

William put his hand on Elsa's shoulder. 'Whatever's the matter, Elsa?'

'I've done something really bad.'

'Whatever it is, you know me, and your mother, are here for you.'

Elsa burst into tears. William put his arms around her. 'Enough, now.'

Elsa seemed to calm down and started to explain. 'Mum knows. She said not to tell anyone, but I can't hold on to this.'

'It's all right. You can tell us. Mum has been a bit confused lately. Maybe she didn't see how hard it was for you to keep whatever this is to yourself.'

'OK. You see, that morning, the day Kathleen died, you and

Mum had left very early. I decided to go to go and see Kathleen. I thought I was, oh, don't be mad—'

'Was it Patrick?'

'Partly... How did you know?'

'I guessed. So, you thought you'd go and talk to Kathleen?'

'Not speak to her. I thought I'd go and watch to see if anyone visited her. I even filmed the house on my phone, but nobody came. I was sure she was seeing someone. I thought if I caught her —' Elsa burst into tears.

'Patrick would leave Kathleen?'

'That was so stupid. The whole thing was. Oh God, it's awful. I'm so ashamed.'

Beth held her breath, then asked, 'Did you go in to see Kathleen?'

Elsa burst into tears again before she said, 'I promise you, I never even got out of the car.'

William sighed. 'Elsa, I believe you. It will be all right.'

'Mum said we don't need to tell the police.'

'I'm sorry, but she's wrong there. Don't worry. I'll be with you, but we have to tell them. They've been looking everywhere for the owner of the silver car.'

'But they'll think I killed her. I went around telling everyone how much I hated her, and they will know I had this thing for Patrick.'

'I'll go with you, get a solicitor. Have you still got the video on your phone?'

'No. Remember, I got a new phone. I didn't transfer the video. I was too embarrassed, but my phone is in my bedroom somewhere I think.'

'Good. Did you call in anywhere else on your way from Kathleen's? Did anyone see you?'

'I bought some crisps in the garage just after I left there. The man was just opening. I think it was about seven.'

'What time did you leave our house?'

'Just after you went: about twenty-five to seven. I went straight to Kathleen's house, and parked. I think the woman in the house saw me arrive. I looked up as I was backing in and saw the nets upstairs pull back.'

'And then you started filming?'

'Yes, I was recording the whole time I was there.'

'Did you see the woman in the house again?'

'Not really. I was watching Kathleen's house the whole time. I did see her just before I left, though. It's why I left. I thought she was going to come and tell me off, and anyway by then it all felt stupid. You do believe me, don't you?'

'I do, yes, and I'll be coming with you. You don't have to face this on your own. Beth, have you got the number for Sue? I think I'll phone her. She can tell us what to do. Now, don't worry, Elsa. We'll sort all this out.'

'What about Mum?'

'I'll explain that you can't keep this to yourself. She'll understand. It's going to be fine.'

Elsa smiled. 'Thank you so much. I should have told you before, shouldn't I?'

'Yes, but what's done is done. Look, let's go in now and see Mum.' William looked over at Beth. 'She was looking OK when you left her?'

'Actually, her parents had been to visit. That hadn't gone well, and she was pretty upset by it.'

'Oh no, that's difficult. I wish I'd been there to smooth things over. Anyway, now to talk about Elsa, I'll explain everything to Imogen and then I'll sort out telling the police.' He smiled at her. 'Thank you so much for all the support. How are you by the way? I hope someone is looking after you, you look exhausted.'

'I'm fine, thanks, just life is complicated, isn't it?'

'It is, well, you know my door is always open.'

'Thank you.'

Beth watched them walk back into the hospital together, glad that Elsa was being looked after.

She wanted to believe Elsa. She hoped the police would be able to verify the times with the garage and the woman in the house because there was part of her that still needed convincing of Elsa's innocence. The fact that Imogen had been so keen for her to keep it quiet suggested she may have had doubts as well.

* * *

It was the following Tuesday morning. Beth lay in bed watching Sami packing his overnight bag to go to London.

'Imogen is going home today. I said I'd go around and see her this afternoon.'

'What's happened with Elsa?'

'I'm not sure. She's at home. That's all I know.'

'That family are really going through it, aren't they? It's a lot of pressure for William. He's been at the surgery through it all. I told him to take time off, but you know how he is. By the way, if you get a moment, can you pop up to the Hendersons' and water the tomatoes this evening? They're very thirsty at the moment.'

'Of course.'

He paused, blinked nervously. 'Look, you're all right with me going away for the night?'

'Of course, why shouldn't I be?'

'It's just William said he was a bit worried about you, said you seemed very anxious.'

'That's not surprising lately, is it? Don't worry, I'm fine.'

'If you're sure then. Right, see you tomorrow.'

When Beth went into school that morning, she found out that the governors had sent a carefully worded letter to all the parents explaining that Imogen would be on long term sick leave and that in the meantime her deputy would be acting head. There were rumours about this, ranging from terminal illness to misappropriation of school funds, but some of the staff had a much better idea of the truth. However, they were tactful, and the matter was hushed up as much as possible.

In the afternoon when Beth visited Imogen at home, she found her dressed, sitting in her armchair reading.

'Good to be home?' asked Beth.

'Yes. I feel weak, but I will get better this time. The police have been round, going through my things, my laptop, and everything. I've nothing to hide now.'

'And how is Elsa?'

'Coping. We've got a good solicitor. I wish she knew where her phone was, but she has enough evidence without it, I think. I hope all the other things will tie together. Mum, of course, got to hear of it. I told William not to mention it but, well, he had to cope with the hysterics.'

'You're sure that Elsa didn't go over to confront Kathleen?'

'Of course, I am. I'm sure we will be able to prove it as well.' Beth smiled, pleased to see Imogen back fighting.

Imogen sat forward. 'I'm planning now for when all this awful business is over. I've made some decisions for sorting out my life once, hopefully, all this has been put behind me. I know I won't be able to continue in my job. I'll have to find something else. I know I don't want us to sell the house. I had a long chat with William, and he says not to make any quick decisions, but for my mental health I need to distance myself from my parents again. I felt like this late last year but then I gave in. I should have stood my ground. You saw what they're like. They have to take over. Elsa and I don't need that.'

'Sounds wise. It was quite a set-to you had with them in the hospital.'

'I know, but it had been building up. I'd been letting things slide. I have to take back control of my life, for Elsa's sake as well as mine.' She sat forward and lowered her voice. 'And that includes the medication I'm on. I've gone back to keeping a journal, jotting down every time I take my pills, making sure I only take what the hospital told me.'

'When I came to visit you in hospital, when you were just coming round, you said Kathleen was right. Did you mean about your medication? She was worried you were taking too strong a dose, wasn't she?'

Imogen nodded. 'She was.' She paused, then said, 'I think I misjudged her. She said a few things, you know.' Imogen lowered her eyes, seemed to speak more to herself than Beth. 'I keep trying to ignore the things she said to me, but it's like they won't go away. I tell myself she was wrong. It's me... my fault... my mistake... but, maybe—'

Imogen sat wrapped in thought, until she said, 'She told me to trust myself, trust my instincts.'

'I thought you were the kind of person who had always done that.'

'I used to be. Not lately, though. I've always thought of myself as someone who would prefer to know the truth, but I'm finding it a struggle now.'

'You're braver than me—'

'I don't think so. You've shown a lot of courage, Beth. A person is brave when they take on their own personal fear, and you've done that, haven't you? You're a peacemaker; you fear not being liked, but you've fought us all, trying to find out what really happened to Kathleen, because you felt it was the right thing to do. That is brave: you trusted your instincts.'

Beth clenched her fists. The problem was she'd trusted her instincts about Kathleen. She'd chosen to believe her, trust her. A picture of the jewellery in their expensive boxes flashed into her mind: how could the Kathleen she'd known have done that?

When Beth got up to leave, Imogen followed her to the front door. Beth could see William working in his study. 'I'm off, William. I hope all gets sorted out for Elsa soon.'

'We're all hoping that. By the way, Elsa found her old phone, she's charging it up.'

'That's brilliant. I'll take it into the police station later,' said Imogen.

William raised his eyebrows. 'See: she's feeling better already, but we're not going to rush anything, are we?'

Beth looked over at all his trophies. 'I saw them before; they're impressive.'

'Imogen said to put them out. Of course, it's all nonsense.'

'Good to see all your Oxford stuff. I hope Adam is as proud of his one day.'

'He'll have a great time and I'm sure he'll be a very good doctor.'

'Thank you. He's getting cold feet about it. Maybe you could talk to him sometime? He really freaked out when Sami got him a Brasenose scarf.' She looked at the cabinet, smiled. 'His scarf is exactly the same as yours. Not a lot changes there, does it?'

'No, not a lot,' said William, laughing. 'Tell him the scarves are good quality. I wore that every winter. By the way, could you tell Sami I need to speak to him when he gets back. It's nothing urgent but I wanted to ask his advice on some medication one of my patients is taking. He's a fount of knowledge, your husband.'

'Of course, I'll—' Beth suddenly stopped. She stared ahead.

'What's the matter?' Imogen asked.

'Oh, nothing,' said Beth, in confusion. 'Sorry, I must have made a mistake, it's nothing.'

They held each other's gaze and then Imogen spoke. 'I need to have a sit down, sorry. I'll see you soon.' Quietly, she left the room.

Beth licked her dry lips and spoke. 'Imogen looks well. She's come back fighting. You have to admire her. How is she coping with everything with Elsa?'

'Surprisingly well. I know she's cross I told her parents about Elsa, but we need to keep them on board. They care more than Imogen realises. They'll get the best barristers, if we need them, for her, pay for rehab, this private university: which I happen to think is a good idea. We don't have that kind of money to hand. I will release it, of course, but it will take time and we need it now.'

'I see. I spoke to Alex, by the way. He showed me the inquest report. There wasn't any question of a mix-up with Amy's medication. I thought you'd like to know.'

'I don't think I ever suggested there was a problem,' said William, looking confused.

'Oh, sorry. I must have misheard you.'

William smiled. 'That's OK, and thank you so much for all you've done for Imogen; you've been a good friend.'

Beth left, but as she walked to her car her mind was trying to make sense of what she'd just seen. If she was right, then certain things must follow. Suddenly she remembered something Sami had said about a register. She rushed home, opened her laptop and logged on: yes, she was right. Beth wasn't surprised. Something had always felt wrong there and now she thought she understood.

Her mind drifted to the matter of the stolen jewellery; was it possible that the Kathleen she knew had done that? Trust your instinct, that's what Imogen had said. Beth ran upstairs to her bedroom. Taking out the pearl necklace, she held it up, saw the light fall on the creamy pearls, and the beautiful diamond clasp. And then she knew she'd held this before. It shouldn't be possible, but she had. Beth grabbed her phone. Frantically, she scrolled through the photographs. There was the necklace. Her eyes widened.

The jewellery had been at Alex's after Kathleen died. Someone else had stolen them, planted them in Kathleen's room. But why?

The only reason Beth could think of was to incriminate Kathleen, reinforce the notion she was a thief, untrustworthy. Like the earrings... Kathleen had always claimed she'd not stolen them, so had they been planted as well?

So, who could have stolen them? Alex was the obvious person, although according to him he hadn't been home for some time. The only other people from the island who Beth knew had stayed at Alex's house in London were herself and Sami, Imogen, William and Elsa. Logically, it had to be one of them who had stolen the jewellery. But who? The only people she could be sure wouldn't have done it were her and Sami: well, strictly, she could only be sure of herself, but she wouldn't seriously consider Sami. This left Imogen, William, Elsa and possibly Alex, but who was it?

Beth remembered she'd promised to go to the Hendersons' to water the plants and thought the activity might clear her head. She found Ollie and drove up there. As she watered the tomato plants in the greenhouse full of their heavy smell, she kept trying to work things out, but her mind seemed to tie itself into knots.

Eventually, Beth shut up the greenhouse and, as she walked Ollie back to the car, she glanced over at the garage. She remembered the car sitting there and for the first time she realised that here was a means by which someone could have driven over to Kathleen's. It wouldn't be difficult to find the keys and drive off. Of course, Sami had been here. Her stomach twisted, but she pushed the thought away. The trouble was that most of her suspects' own cars had been seen in the village and there wasn't time for one of them to walk out here, drive to Kathleen's, come back, and then walk back home or to work. So how could they have used the car?

Beth realised it was getting late and the dark skies threatened rain, and so she went back to the car, drove home. From the mess in the kitchen she could see the kids had helped themselves to tea and she could hear they were in their bedrooms. Beth wasn't hungry but went up to her bedroom and closed the door. She

needed to concentrate, she still had so much to try and understand. Maybe if she tried to remember what Kathleen had said, not
just to her but to Roisin and Angela as well. Had she missed something there? Kathleen had talked about that awful month last
December. First Amy's fall and then the skiing holiday. Beth
paused. She'd not given that much thought to the skiing weekend.
The one thing everyone seemed to agree on was that it had been a
disaster. Imogen was still living with the consequences, her bad
back, the medication, all from a simple accident. Beth caught her
breath, the accident. Kathleen had told Roisin and Angela that she
was worried about the accident. Everyone had assumed she meant
Amy's fall but what if she'd been talking about something else,
Imogen's fall?

It was like finding the crucial piece of a jigsaw. Other pieces
that had felt random started to fit: the dark net, the untuned piano,
clearing the old lane, the cliff top walk. And, as she fitted the
puzzle together, the full picture of what had happened to Kathleen
started to emerge. But there was more. Beth sat feeling sick. She
clenched her fists: the picture she was creating was terrifying. If
she was right, this wasn't the end. No, there would be more killing;
more people would die.

Beth stood up and started to pace around her room. Should
she go to the police? The problem was that she had so little proof
and superficially it sounded a pretty implausible story. If only she
had found Kathleen's phone: at least she would have something
concrete she could take to them.

As if in answer, at that moment her phone signalled a text.
Glancing down, she saw it was from Elsa.

Please can you come and see me? I can't talk at home or at your
house. I've found a phone. I'm very scared. I don't know what to do.
Please come on your own: don't tell anyone. I'm desperate and very
frightened. I have the key to Alex's caravan, and I'm here alone. I'm so

sorry to ask you to come all this way but I've not got anyone else to turn to. Love Elsa.

Beth reread the text. Poor Elsa. If Beth's calculations were right, she guessed Elsa had found Kathleen's phone at home. Thank God she'd got out of the house. What she needed to do was go to the police, but maybe she was too scared to go on her own. Beth knew she had to go and help her. She replied that she would go out straight away.

Beth opened her bedroom door. The house was eerily quiet. Adam and Layla were in their rooms, watching Netflix, texting, revising, or all three. Downstairs, Ollie would be snoring in his bed. They all assumed they were safe, but they weren't. No one was, and poor Elsa was out there all alone.

Beth told the children she was going out, told Adam to push the bolt across the front door and said she would ring the doorbell when she returned. He looked at her as if she was slightly mad but couldn't be bothered to argue.

Beth locked the back door with the extra Chubb locks. She left the key in the lock, then left by the front door, calling Adam so she knew he had bolted the door after her. She got into her car and drove.

The rain was quite gentle; the windscreen wipers on the slowest pitch were not as alarming as when they were going full pelt. Few people were out, apart from the occasional dog walker.

Beth finally pulled into the caravan site and drove up to Alex's caravan. There were no lights on and no sign of Elsa's car. Had Elsa panicked and gone somewhere else? Beth left her headlights on, took out her phone and started to text Elsa.

It wasn't until she looked up from her phone that she saw an alien-like figure dressed all in white walking towards her. She stared, but then remembered the forensic team at the end of Kathleen's garden. Her heart raced. What were the police doing here?

The figure approached her car but didn't come to her door. Instead she watched as they walked to the passenger door. A growing sense of alarm told her something was very wrong but before she had time to act, the person opened it and climbed into the car. Beth sat paralysed, and then she saw the glint of a knife in the gloved hand. Her heart beat so hard her head felt like it would burst.

'Sorry about the outfit; you'll understand why soon,' William said, holding the knife closer to her.

Beth pushed herself back, could feel the door handle jam into her back. How could she have been so stupid? Why hadn't it even crossed her mind that William could easily send a text from Elsa's phone. Despite all she knew now about William she'd let her guard down, walked blindly into a trap. Now she had a terrible feeling she would pay for that mistake with her life.

Beth slid one hand behind her back, located the door handle and tried to push it down.

'Leave it,' he barked. 'Don't think of getting out. We are going for a ride.' Beth quickly clasped both her hands in front of her.

Rain was now pouring down the windscreen. She could make out lights in a caravan further away. It had to be safer here than on some dark country road. Somehow, she needed to keep him talking, someone might see them, ask if they needed help.

'There is no point in killing me. If I've worked it out, other people will soon,' she stammered.

He grinned. 'I don't think so. I've been watching you, thinking you're so clever, but you're not.'

'Do you have Kathleen's phone?'

He laughed, cold, cruel. 'Of course not. I threw that into the sea the day I got it. Keeping it would have been ridiculous, but I had to take it. I couldn't be sure what was on there, who Kathleen's last call was to.'

'It was to me,' said Beth. 'She told me at the house party on the

Sunday evening, she was going to fight the person threatening her, but you know that, and that is why you felt you needed to kill her. You think you have been so clever, don't you?'

She felt the knife press into her side. 'Everything was very carefully planned, no mistakes, nothing to connect her death to me.'

'I wonder if there was anything in the Hendersons' car, I mean no one has been in it since you drove it to Kathleen's, have they?'

He glared at her. 'No one will think of looking at that car.'

'I did, though. I was trying to figure out how you got to Kathleen's and then I saw the Hendersons' car. But how did you get to it, I wondered. Then I remembered that lane, the old chapel. Of course, you could have parked the car there the night before. I am guessing the next day, you arrived at work about half six, went to your surgery and put up that Do Not Disturb sign. Then you climbed out of the window and drove over to Kathleen's. No one would recognise the car, even if they saw it. You parked, walked along the cliff path and went into her garden. I assume it was then you let the hens out?'

He sat back, scowled at her. 'Bloody hens, I hate them. It's mainly why I wore one of these suits. I arrived, took down a panel, hid by the hen coop. It was all very simple. Once Kathleen was down there, I let the hens out, tried to make them run towards the gap in the fence. Damn things though, not easy to manage and always did make me sneeze. My eyes were still streaming that evening from them. Most of the hens refused to go the way I wanted, but then one scruffy one made its way through and, as I planned, Kathleen chased it. She was within a whisper of the cliff edge. One light push and she was gone. I saw the phone and headphones, picked them up. I checked the cliff path: no one about, so I ran back to the car, removed the suit, bagged it up and drove back.'

'Someone could have seen you driving back into the lane by the surgery, there would have been more people about by then.'

He smirked. 'I'd thought of that. I'd worn that coat hanging up in my surgery. As a precaution, when I got back, I didn't park in the lane. I left the car in a side street, just up the road, walked back... I didn't meet anyone but had plans if I did... I'd thought of everything.'

'So, you climbed back in through the window, disposed of the suit in medical waste, and were there to see your first patient. You even took the further precaution of having the grass cut in the lane, just to cover your tracks, as they say.'

William sneered, 'You think you are so clever, don't you? Well, you walked straight into this tonight, not so smart, are you?' The windows had steamed up now. He wiped his and looked out. 'We need to get out of here.'

Beth went to grab the door handle, but the knife was there at her throat.

'No way.' he said. 'Start the engine. I want you to turn the car round and turn left.'

Beth did as she was told. It felt like he was putting her through some horrific driving test. All the time he held the knife to the side of her throat, but it hardly touched the skin. 'Right, pull in off the road, down here, good, no need to hide it away.' He grinned. 'Now, get out.'

'What do you want?'

'I want you to shut up and do what you are told.' Beth saw in William's eyes the same fire she'd seen that day in the surgery. He had a torch and, keeping the knife close but not touching her, he directed Beth across the field and along the cliff path; the wind buffeting her face.

Beth could hear the sea below: stronger waves this evening; no moon lighting the surface. The path became increasingly narrow. Beth was shaking. She saw stones crumble beneath her feet, could hear them falling helplessly down the cliff side.

'I think this will do,' said William

They were outside the white fence at the end of Patrick and Kathleen's garden.

'Why have you brought me here?' she shouted, making her voice heard over the wind.

'It's obvious, isn't it? It's your turn. Don't worry. I'll explain it all to Sami and your children. Everyone knows how obsessed you've been with Kathleen's death. I'll tell them about when I prescribed antidepressants, the day after you came to see me after the funeral. Yes, it's in your notes now, how worried I was about you. How was I to know you never took the pills? I've prepared the way for a woman who just couldn't cope any more and took her own life in the same spot her close friend had died.'

Beth listened with horror, he'd planned this, he could get away with it.

'You don't need to kill me, you said I've no proof.' Her voice was high, frantic. 'Please—'

At that moment it seemed the wind held its breath and the waves below became a distant murmur. It seemed to calm William.

He spoke again but his voice was steady, quieter. 'Of course I have to kill you. You're just like Kathleen, you won't let it lie, will you. If she'd been sensible, I'd never have killed her, you know.'

'No, I realised that was never part of the plan,' she said.

'You'd figured that out?'

'Yes, I finally realised that, all this time, there was only one person you wanted to kill and that was your wife.'

William almost gave her a look of approval. 'That's exactly it. I'm glad you see I'm not some crazy person who likes going around killing people. I'm a doctor. I heal. I make people better. You did well to work that out eventually.'

'The problem was, I thought Kathleen's death was somehow tied up with her affair, with her pregnancy, but it wasn't, was it? I think Kathleen was threatened and killed because of something she saw.'

'And that was?' William held the knife at his side now, his head was tilted, ready to listen, as if they were carrying on some normal conversation in her living room.

'Imogen's apparent accident on the skiing holiday. Kathleen saw you push Imogen, didn't she, although, of course, at first she didn't really believe it. Then, as she saw the way you were medicating Imogen, again she was confused, didn't take in the implications of it all. Why should she? She trusted you.'

William sighed. 'Kathleen was an irritation, like some fly you hear buzzing around your room—'

'Or a grubby grey pebble on a beach?'

He blinked. 'Exactly. Everything else was going to plan. Imogen hurt her back, I had to keep her on the pills, of course, when we came back, get her hooked. Everything was going so well, apart, of course, from Kathleen.'

Beth nodded. 'I got confused. Kathleen had been telling people she was concerned about an accident. I assumed it was something to do with Amy, Alex's wife.'

William gave a cold grin. 'Poor Alex. You just soaked up all those hints about him messing about with Amy's medication. You were so gullible.'

'But I got there in the end. It was a shame Kathleen hadn't fully realised what you were like before she told you about the pregnancy. She never suspected how cruel you were and how you would use it against her. But you must have known how tempting it would be for her to talk to Patrick and then you'd have had no hold over her.'

'Yes, I needed insurance. Stealing the earrings was a stroke of genius. Kathleen's face when she found them! You know, she was in such a state she couldn't even be sure she hadn't done it. She was pathetic and so easy to manipulate. Shame and guilt: they're brilliant weapons of war. I stole a few pills from the pharmacy as well. I needed, you see, to have as few people as possible on her side. I didn't want to kill her, it's so risky. But then she lost the baby. It changed her. It made her stronger, more determined somehow, and I realised people might believe her. She left me no choice.'

Beth felt anger raising up, smothering her fear. 'You destroyed my friend; you made her last days on earth hell. Don't you tell me you are a good doctor who heals when you can do that to a person and plan to kill your own wife.'

His face darkened. His eyes lit up with a cruel glint. 'I'm not going to kill Imogen. She is going to do that herself. She got herself hooked, and it was so easy. I kept replacing her low dose pills with something much stronger. It's only a matter of time until she kills herself. I've planned it, you see. She needed to have a minor over-dose, get the idea of her being an addict. It's difficult being a doctor. People will look at me. I must be very clever about this. But I think I'm doing it very well. I was rushed into the last one. I didn't expect her to survive that, I have to admit but, well, there's always next time.'

'You know it's not true about her making choices. You under-stand addiction. She trusted you, and you abused that. You're making her ill. You're killing her, slowly, painfully, destroying her piece by piece, because you are a vain, greedy man.'

'Shut it,' he screamed, his eyes burned bright, and he pushed the knife into her neck. She was pinned against the fence. 'You are a stupid interfering bitch, you deserve to die.' His voice had changed. The smooth, public school intonation replaced by a hard-East End voice. He stopped, aware the mask had slipped.

'Yes, that's your real voice isn't it... the real you. You are a fake, William; your whole life is a lie.'

'I am a doctor, a real doctor and a very good one. I was the brightest, most able pupil at school, no one else came close to me. And then I got to medical school.'

'What happened?'

He waved the knife around madly. 'All those rich morons, thick as shit most of them and still they looked down on me. God, I hate them all. Like my ex's family. More rich bastards. She complained to daddy about me, he got the lawyers onto me, I had to give her every penny I'd earned. I wish I'd killed her, she deserved it.' He stopped, held the knife close to her face.

Beth could hear the waves crushing the stones below. She was so close to death she could feel its touch on her face, hear it breathe. Her whole body shook. She grabbed the fence, frightened she would slip at any moment. Her mind flashed to Sami, Layla, Adam. She wanted to live for them, to see them again, but she was running out of time.

'Before I die, tell me. Do you really know my secret?'

He pressed his lips together, and Beth knew. 'You were bluffing. I wondered why you never gave me any clues.'

'It worked. Got you scared.' He pushed the knife gently into her cheek. 'Tell me, then. What is this big secret?'

'No. You don't deserve to know. The truth is wasted on you. If you kill me, you will always know that I knew all your secrets, but you never knew mine.'

Beth could feel the force of the wind gathering again. Her footing was becoming unsteady.

'It's time,' said William. He slid the knife behind her back and used it to push her forward. Beth went to step forward but stopped, instead she stayed clinging onto the fence. She'd remembered what Roisin had shown her.

'You don't want to push me too hard or stab me,' she said, 'Not if you want it to look like suicide.' Beth started to creep backwards, using her hand to search for it... yes, she'd found the notch. As she pushed, the hidden gate slid open.

She turned, ran into the garden. William paused, momentarily stunned, then quickly followed. The house was in darkness: Patrick and Conor weren't there. Beth knew she was trapped.

And then the spotlights came on, lighting her up as if she was on a stage.

'There is no way out, is there?' said William as he walked towards her with the knife. Beth grabbed one of the solar lights from the path and threw it at him. In shock he dropped the knife, his hand went to his head. 'You bitch,' he screamed.

He'd started to run at her when a voice shouted, 'Leave her alone.'

Beth and William turned to see Imogen coming through the side gate. She was holding up a phone.

William's mouth fell open, and the menacing figure melted, leaving a foolish, stunned man behind.

'What the hell—' he stammered.

Imogen held out the phone as she walked towards him. 'You fool, you didn't delete the message on Elsa's phone... she showed it to me, couldn't understand how it got there, but I did. I drove to the caravan, you'd gone, so I came this way, saw Beth's car. I thought, they are having a cliff top walk, I'll go to Patrick's, lucky I have his key—'

'There is no need to get jealous, you're not thinking straight.'

She laughed hard. 'No, for the first time in a long time, I am. Everything Kathleen told me was right. You pushed me down the steps on that holiday, you gave me strong, addictive drugs, made sure I got hooked. I trusted you. I was such a fool.' Imogen stepped forward, her voice shaking with emotion. 'I didn't see it properly until the last time I was in hospital, you went too far. I started keeping track of my pills, you bastard. And then earlier, I saw the way Beth looked at you—'

Beth watched as William's eyes flickered around, he was looking for a way out. He stepped back but in one swift movement Imogen picked up the knife that was lying on the ground, held the point to his chest. 'I was trying to work out what Beth knew about you when I saw the message. Before I left, I looked in your safe... there were packets and packets of pain killers.' Her voice cracked. 'How could you, William? I thought you loved me. I'd have divorced you if you hated me so much.' She started to sob and as she broke down she dropped the knife. In a flash William picked it up, but then Beth heard sirens, cars crunching on the gravel at the front of the house. William waved the knife, looked around frantically.

'I called them when I saw your car at the caravan,' said Imogen through her sobs. 'You always say, better safe—'

Two policemen came into the garden, sprinted over to William who started to run towards the fence, but he was quickly wrestled to the ground and handcuffed. Beth heard the words of arrest and ran over to Imogen, who fell into her arms. 'It's all right, you're safe now,' Beth said.

As the storm settled Imogen stepped back. 'Why Beth, why did he need to kill me?'

Beth spoke as gently as she could. 'It was all for money, status.'

'Money?' Imogen shook her head. 'But he had plenty and my parents were throwing it at us.'

'Actually, he didn't have any of his own money.'

'But—'

'No, he's not the person you thought he was. It was all lies. The rich parents, the public school, Oxford.'

'But... what? Isn't he even a real doctor?'

'Oh, he's that. That is the one real thing about him. I looked on the GMC register, he trained at a London University Hospital. It was everything else that was a lie.'

'How on earth did you work all this out?'

'It started with the scarf, something very small and insignificant, a silly mistake on his part. To build the illusion he went to Oxford he bought a load of bits off the internet. The only problem is, he was careless. He bought a Brasenose college scarf when he was pretending that he went to Christ Church.'

'But why bother when he'd actually trained at such a respectable place?'

'Because it was just one part of the façade he was creating for your parents. He painted a picture of an old money family, public school, a pianist, a reader of Booker Prize novels...'

'And none of it was true, he was a very proficient liar.'

'He was. Kathleen said he had us all fooled.'

'She was right about so much.' Imogen clenched her fists, spoke slowly. 'Did he have anything to do with her death?'

'He did.'

Beth explained what had happened. Imogen stared up into the sky. The moon was creeping out from behind a cloud. 'I can't imagine how a man who was capable of such kindness, who worked so hard for people, could do anything so wicked.'

'Like the moon, he had a dark side none of us saw,' said Beth.

Imogen turned to her. 'Do you know anything about the life of the real William; where he grew up, that kind of thing?'

'William grew up in a run down, high-rise flat in the East End of London.'

Imogen stared. 'Are you sure?'

'He confirmed it earlier. I remembered when he talked to me about his visit to the East End of London, the smells, the sights; it was the real William. The trophies and scarves all felt fake, but when he talked about those high-rise flats, that was real.'

Imogen grabbed her arm. 'I see it now, I thought it was odd when he wanted to go off there when we stayed in London. It was so unlike him, when he came back, he was very emotional. I wondered then—'

Imogen sat quietly; Beth gave her time for things to sink in.

'So, all that talk about money tied up in land was a lie?' said Imogen.

'Yes, the only money he had, he'd made as a doctor and all of that went to his ex on his divorce, a woman I think he married for money but whose parents somehow saw through him.'

Imogen sat, open mouthed. 'And then he did the same to me. It really was all about money, well, I guess my parents' money, pure and simple.' She frowned. 'But hang on, he was getting the money, my parents loved him. So why the need to kill me? Did he hate me so much he couldn't bear to live with me any longer? I could see if he wanted the money, he couldn't divorce me but, to hate me so much he wanted to kill me?' Her hands shook as she covered her eyes.

Beth felt desperately sorry for her. 'To be honest I don't think he exactly hated you, I am pretty sure he was more worried that you were going to alienate your parents. I think the point he decided he needed to kill you was last November when you threatened to cut off your parents after they bought Elsa the car.'

'I was furious.'

'He saw that and he knew it could happen again. it's why he took you skiing, planned the accident, the addiction to the painkillers—'

'I should have worked this out for myself. After the skiing holiday he kept telling me I'd forgotten things like turning off the shower when I was sure I'd done them. I can see now he was just eating away at my self-confidence. I knew the pills were making me a bit muddled but that wasn't like me, so I kept a notebook with lists, ticking off when I did things.'

Beth suddenly remembered seeing the journal in Imogen's drawer.

'I stopped though, it was too scary, and I wanted to be able to trust him. Instead I started to doubt myself, I guess that was the aim.' Imogen scratched at the varnish on her thumbnail. 'It was all so cruel. It did flash through my mind sometimes that he might be messing with my pills, but I was so desperate to think he loved me that I told myself he was doing it for my own good. I wanted the lies, the ones that he loved me, cared about me and Elsa.'

'But you faced the truth in the end, that takes courage.'

Imogen placed her hand on Beth's. 'You are so much braver than me.'

Beth smiled. 'Sometimes.' She took a deep breath. 'But you know, Imogen, I'm not that brave, I've been facing truths about you, William, everyone else who was at the house party but there is still one truth I am hiding and that is my own. I think it's time I face that.'

'And that is?'

Beth shook her head. 'I can't tell you yet, the person who should hear this first is Sami.'

Beth and Imogen were both taken to the police station where, after giving brief statements, both were allowed home. Beth had phoned Adam, avoided telling him too much, but asked him to take care of Layla until she got home.

Both children were up waiting for her when she returned, and she explained as briefly as she could what had happened. When they'd finally gone to bed, Beth sat alone in the dark, quiet kitchen. Ollie looked up from his basket and wagged his tail. She knelt, cuddled him, and cried.

'Oh God, Ollie. What a night. I thought I was going to die; I really did. But now it's finished.' She paused, 'Well, almost: one more thing and then it will be over.'

37

Beth woke early, showered, and was dressing when she heard the front door opening. Panicking, she ran down but, to her relief, it was Sami.

He held out his arms. 'Layla rang me.' Beth rushed into them. After a few moments, he led her to the sofa.

'Tell me everything.'

They ate breakfast together. Beth had to go back to the police station, but Sami went with her this time.

When they were returning home, Beth said, 'I know it's odd, and I know I'm shattered, but I need to do this now. We need to go to Parkhurst Woods.'

'The woods? Whatever for?'

'Please, Sami. I need to take you somewhere. It's time.'

They parked, and Beth led Sami through the woods to the concrete wall: the wall that divided the woods from the prison grounds. At the base were the flowers she'd laid, and a fossil hidden by grass.

Beth held Sami's hand.

'What is it?' he asked, frowning.

And she was there, standing on the edge of the highest board, shaking. Would she, could she finally make the dive?

'I'm sorry. I should have told you about this years ago, when I met you.' Beth hesitated. She wanted to back away, but she knew she couldn't. 'And then I learned more at my aunt's funeral—'

'About what?'

Beth clasped the fossil as if trying to gain strength from it. 'It's about my father—'

'Did you learn more about why he left you and went to America?'

'No. You see, my father never went to America. He wasn't a lecturer. He was nothing like that.'

'I don't understand. You said—'

'I lied. I'm so sorry, Sami.' She pointed to the wall. 'My father died in Parkhurst prison. He was sent there, when I was thirteen, for murder. He stabbed and killed a security guard when he was breaking into a distillery. My father killed an innocent man who was doing his job. He not only took away the man's life but destroyed the life of that man's wife and children.'

Beth paused. There was no going back now.

'Your father killed someone?' Sami spoke the words slowly, utterly dumbfounded.

'Yes. That's the truth.'

'But you never told me. All these years—'

'I kept wanting to tell you, but never had the courage to go through with it.'

'But when we met, you told me then about him being in America. Why did you lie?'

'Because I'd learned that anyone who knew the truth wouldn't want anything to do with me. When my father was arrested, me and Mum became outcasts in our village. We became pariahs, got notes through the door, graffiti on the house. Mum couldn't afford for us to move so she sent me to a high school a long way from the village. She told me to make up this story that Dad had left us, that he was abroad. So I did, and it worked. I think I nearly believed it myself by the end.'

'But you could have told me. We were adults, not kids. You should have trusted me.'

Beth sat down, her back against the concrete wall. She ran her fingers round the rough spiral of the fossil, not daring to look up.

Sami sat next to her. 'Tell me everything,' he said.

'When I was little, Dad never held down a job for long. He would disappear for the weekend sometimes and come back with cash. He said he had worked hard for us. And then one night the police came, lights flashing, bashing on the door, the lot, and they took him away. It was the last time I saw him. Mum told me the day he was sent to prison that he'd been sent up north a long way away; he didn't want to see us, and we were not to speak of him any more.'

'But that wasn't fair.'

'I suppose not, but Mum was all twisted up by it. I was so ashamed of my father: angry, sad, all messed up, I didn't speak about it to anyone.'

Sami wiped his eyes. 'It's so sad.'

'I was so confused. Dad had become the enemy, yet I had some good memories of him. He would take me to the beach looking for fossils. He used to tell me to work hard at school, that I was clever and pretty.'

'So, he tried?'

'I think he did but, of course, I only saw one part of him. He chose to do that robbery and to take a knife.'

'And so, once he went to prison you never saw him again?'

'No. I assumed, because he never got in touch, that Mum was right, that he didn't want to see us. It wasn't until I went to my aunt's funeral six years ago that I found out the truth.'

'And that was?'

'My cousin told me Dad had been sent here, to Parkhurst. She told me—' Beth held the fossil tight, curled her knees up against her chest. 'He killed himself in the third year he was here. I'd have been about fifteen or sixteen. Mum never told me. All that time, I'd thought he was alive, and he was dead.' Beth swallowed hard. 'Apparently, the prison authorities or the council organised a cremation here. There's no plaque at the crematorium, nothing. When I came back from the funeral I didn't know how to cope. Too many emotions all shouting at me: anger with Mum and with Dad, but all this, sadness, and guilt that he'd killed himself.'

'And that is why you were so ill? Oh, Beth. Why on earth didn't you tell me?'

'It felt too late. I was so ill, and I thought you would leave me if I told you. I did tell that doctor. She was lovely. She wanted me to go for therapy, but I couldn't face raking it all up. She did suggest this, though: marking a place, and I'm really glad I did. It's somewhere to come.'

Sami put his arm around her. 'I can't keep saying you should have told me, but I wish you had.'

'But I was so in awe of you; you were so clever and kind. Your life was nothing like mine.' Beth put her head in her hands. 'These are all excuses. I should have told you.'

She felt Sami's cold hands gently take hers away from her face. 'But you didn't. It's all right. You were frightened, and I can see why.'

'I wanted everything to be perfect, for Adam and Layla to have the home I never had.'

'You've been a lovely mother and wife, and still are. You are still my Beth.' He looked down at the stone. 'I hate to think of you coming here on your own. Did you ever tell anyone else?'

'No, no one. Of course not. Apart from the doctor, you were the only person I have ever wanted to tell.'

'We must come here together, me and you. Would you like us

to do more? We could go to the crematorium, ask about some kind of memorial plaque or something?'

'Thank you. I'm not sure yet. I'm still confused about how I feel about Dad and Mum. Maybe one day I'll go and talk to someone about it all, but the main thing is I'd like to not feel ashamed of my past any more.'

'This is your story. You can tell it when and however you want.'

'I'm glad I've told you. It's a start. It's hard to describe how I feel: tired, but lighter.'

Sami held her tight. Beth stood up and put the fossil back in its place. She picked up the dead daffodils, but she didn't wrap the grass around the stone and, as she walked away, she glanced back and saw it leant against the wall, not hidden, not in the dark any more.

38

A month later, they were all sitting in Patrick's garden in the early evening. Patrick had invited Beth, Sami, Layla and Adam, Imogen, Elsa, Alex, and Roisin to come together with him and Conor on what would have been Kathleen's forty-first birthday.

Where the hen coop once stood, Patrick had installed a beautiful bronze sculpture of a young girl with long flowing hair holding a hen, the perfect memorial to Kathleen. When they arrived, it had been covered with a cloth which he removed to unveil the statue. They raised their glasses to Kathleen. On the base of the statue was a plaque, which Patrick read out.

> To my darling Kathleen,
> May the wings of the butterfly kiss the sun,
> And find your shoulder to light upon.

Layla played an Irish folk melody on her flute and they shared memories of Kathleen: stories, photographs, good times, and times they'd cried.

When they had finished, Beth went to sit with Imogen.

'So, how are you and Elsa?'

Imogen smiled. 'We're doing OK. Elsa is gearing up for university in September and it looks like I shall be all set up to return to school for the new school year. I've had meetings with the governors. There are a few things to be ironed out, but I've been cleared of everything as far as the police are concerned. It won't be easy going back, but that's never stopped me before, has it?'

'No, and I'm sure you'll get a lot of support.'

'It will be good to see you there.'

'Actually, you won't see me at school.'

'What do you mean?'

'I'm going to finish my degree, but I don't want to teach. I had a long chat with Sami. I think the reason I was doing the degree and planning to teach was that I felt the pressure to do something academic. But it's not really me. I've decided I want to try something new. I went to see Gemma. I knew they were looking for someone to expand the community room side of things at the Hub. Well, I offered to be the one to take it on. I have talked to the committee. Everyone seems enthusiastic. I have lots of ideas. It should be exciting.'

'I'd never have imagined you doing that kind of thing but, yes, I can see you making a go of it.'

Beth moved closer to Imogen. 'So, any news of William?'

'He's been charged with Kathleen's murder. He confessed it all the first night they questioned him. He seemed almost proud of it. Also, despite that suit, he wasn't as careful as he thought. He'd transferred some dirt and, I think, a feather into the car and onto his shoes. The main thing is, there is no way he'll get out of this.'

'I'm glad.'

'It's hard to believe I got someone so wrong.'

'It was a terrible time for you, but now you and Elsa deserve a fresh start.'

Imogen smiled. 'Thank you.'

Beth walked alone down the garden to the fence. Glancing behind her, and seeing everyone was engrossed, she walked to the end of the fence and slid the panel back. Ahead, she could see the sea: sparkling blue. She could hear it shushing below, just as she had that Sunday evening. She felt something lightly touch her and saw a white butterfly with orange tipped wings had landed on her arm. She didn't touch it, knowing how easily the scales on its wings could be damaged. Instead, she watched its fine wings shiver.

'We won, Kathleen: me and you. We fought together, and we won. You don't need to be frightened now: no more secrets, no more shame. You are free.'

Suddenly, there was a brilliant light. Beth blinked hard and, as she did, she felt the tiniest tingle on her arm. As she looked down, she saw the butterfly take flight towards the sea. She watched it until it flew out of sight.

ACKNOWLEDGMENTS

Thank you to all my family who have been there for me from my first days of writing. In particular I would like to mention my brother in law, Mike Nicholson. He was a lovely, exceptional man, who was always so supportive of everything I did. He was taken from us too soon and is missed every day.

Many close friends have kept me going me with wise words, cups of coffee, and even cake, including Adele Rolf, fellow dog walker, Harriet Robinson, and writer, Lucy Blanchard.

I must thank writer and lecturer, Felicity Fair Thompson, for her inspirational creative writing classes. Also, writers Sue Shepherd and Piers Rowlandson, for helpful feedback in the early days of writing this book. Thank you, Barbara Nathan, for allowing me to use Ollie as the name for the cocker spaniel.

I would like to say an enormous thank you to the wonderful team at Boldwood Books for publishing *The House Party*. Thank you so much to the editing, cover design, and marketing teams. I would like to particularly thank Sarah Ritherdon for her unstinting support, enthusiasm, and insightful comments.

Finally, a huge thank you to everyone who reads my books. To you, the readers, bloggers, and reviewers I am enormously grateful. Every encouraging, generous comment, email, and review has helped far more than you can imagine. Thank you.

MORE FROM MARY GRAND

We hope you enjoyed reading *The House Party*. If you did, please leave a review.

If you'd like to gift a copy, this book is also available as an ebook, digital audio download and audiobook CD.

Sign up to Mary Grand's mailing list for news, competitions and updates on future books.

https://bit.ly/MaryGrandNewsletter

The Island, another heart-stopping psychological thriller from Mary Grand, is available now.

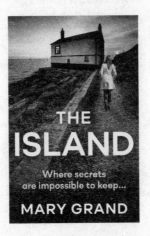

ABOUT THE AUTHOR

Mary Grand writes gripping, page-turning suspense, with a dark and often murderous underside. She grew up in Wales, was for many years a teacher of deaf children and now lives on the Isle of Wight.

Visit Mary's website: https://marygrand.net/

Follow Mary on social media:

twitter.com/authormaryg
instagram.com/maryandpepper
facebook.com/authormarygrand
bookbub.com/profile/mary-grand

ABOUT BOLDWOOD BOOKS

Boldwood Books is a fiction publishing company seeking out the best stories from around the world.

Find out more at www.boldwoodbooks.com

Sign up to the Book and Tonic newsletter for news, offers and competitions from Boldwood Books!

http://www.bit.ly/bookandtonic

We'd love to hear from you, follow us on social media:

facebook.com/BookandTonic

twitter.com/BoldwoodBooks

instagram.com/BookandTonic